"This is a joyful ride of a
and poignant. You'll miss]
book."

—Susie Essman
stand-up comedian, actress, writer, and television producer

"A brilliant rewinding of a life of Hollywood glitz, grit, gluttony and nose jobs and a good, old-fashioned story of rags to riches and hags to bitches and the paparazzi to cause and capture it all. Brava, Dinah!"

—Jamie Lee Curtis
actress, author, producer, director, and activist

"Can this lovely lady write? Oh, my heavens! Oh yes, she can! I loved my experience traveling with her—laughing and crying and remembering and to identify—to be part of the full experience is nothing short of stunning! A brilliant first start on a journey of a literary future to lead us through wherever she is going, I will always follow."

—Brenda Vaccaro, actress

"Manoff's novel is an epic tale that truly lives up to its name. A 360-degree view of Hollywood that only an insider could tell, 'Jackie' is pure gold, a raucous, biting look at the compilations of family, love and fame in an industry that, to paraphrase the author, will gladly eat its young for the price of cheese. The Real True Hollywood Story of Jackie Gold is a delicious story to savor one page at a time."

—Warren Read, author of *One Simple Thing* and *Ash Falls*

"The Real True Hollywood Story of Jackie Gold is pure gold. A fascinating glimpse behind the scenes into a world where people expose themselves as they truly are when they think no one is looking (or able to understand). Dinah Manoff has skillfully woven a fascinating twisting tale of fame, friendship, family, betrayal all set against the juicy veneer of celebrity. Jackie Gold's comatose journey of self-discovery is dazzling and funny from page one and so addictive I couldn't put it down."

—Lynn Brunelle
4-time Emmy Award-winning writer, author of *Mama Gone Geek*

"The Real True Hollywood Story of Jackie Gold is an emotional roller coaster of a debut; at turns tense, funny, and heartbreaking."

—Jonathan Evison, author of
The Revised Fundamentals of Caregiving

"Dinah Manoff has such an original voice in this exceptional debut novel about Jackie Gold, a Hollywood survivor who will win your heart.

Her writing is full of wit, laugh-out-loud humor, and surprising, heartfelt moments. Let's put it this way. She made me laugh, she made me laugh, she made me cry and cry again.

A real page-turner in the best way. I couldn't put it down."

—Melanie Mayron
actress and director of film and television

"Dinah Manoff's first novel is not just a fun romp through the glitzy, decadent, dysfunctional world of glamorous stardom, it is much more. It tells the story of a girl who has suffered terrible maternal neglect only to find herself experiencing adulation and attention that feels unearned and unsatisfying. Through the twists and turns of the story, we get to see Jackie in all her hilarious, indulgent brattiness. The ending is the perfect combination of bad Karma and sweet redemption. I enjoyed it thoroughly.

—Brooke Adams, actress

"High jinx, hilarity, and heartbreak abound in Dinah Manoff's romp through the perilous chase for fame in Hollywood. A comic-tragedy among the glitterati as told by a true insider."

—Mary Guterson, author of *Gone to the Dogs*

"The explosive opening captivates the reader immediately! The story of Jackie Gold is unique, intriguing, and fun-filled! Dinah's creativity never ceases to amaze me. Her descriptions are so vivid that I could feel each location and time period as if I had traveled there. There must be a sequel!"

—Kristy McNichol, actress, comedian, producer, singer

"The very REAL insider look into the ultra-private lives of two hot Hollywood stars. A deep dive into ambition, abandonment, addiction, and sex (lots of it).

Dinah, my old Pink Lady pal, has created a vivid, sexy portrait of the private doings and undoings of a rich and famous movie star who, through a tragic event, finds grace, happiness and her true self."

—Didi Conn, actress

THE REAL TRUE
Hollywood
Story of
Jackie Gold

DINAH MANOFF

Star Alley Press

Dinah Manoff/Star Alley Press
www.StarAlleyPress.com

Publisher's Note: This is a work of fiction. Names, characters, places, and incidents are a product of the author's imagination. Locales and public names are sometimes used for atmospheric purposes, and their stories are entirely fictional.

Book Layout © 2021 Star Alley, LLC
Cover Design © 2021 Star Alley, LLC

The Real True Hollywood Story of Jackie Gold/ Dinah Manoff. -- 1st ed.
ISBN 978-1-946802-76-7
eBook ISBN 978-1-946802-77-4
Audio ISBN 978-1-946802-78-1

To My Mother

Nowhere could you get that happy feeling when you are stealing that extra bow.

—IRVING BERLIN
THERE'S NO BUSINESS LIKE SHOW BUSINESS

Fame
Fame, fame, fame
Fame, fame, fame
Fame, fame, fame, fame
Fame, fame, fame, fame
Fame, fame, fame
Fame

— DAVID BOWIE

THE REAL TRUE

Hollywood Story of

Jackie Gold

EXT. BALCONY - MALIBU SHORES INN
JANUARY 15, 1999
MORNING
SFX: CRASHING WAVES

Finally, it is just as I pictured.

Brett on bended knee, velvet box in hand, his popped question hanging in the salt air. My white silk robe slips ever so slightly off one shoulder as I rise gracefully from my perch on the balcony, my left fingers extended, poised for coronation. I part my freshly glossed lips, preparing to utter that one life-changing word of affirmation when I see the helicopters over Brett's shoulder.

Shit.

They've found us.

The front door explodes open.

"Jackie! Brett!"

They shoot, storming through the suite and onto our third-floor balcony, framing us in proposal position, climbing over each other to get a better angle.

"Jackie! Dollface! Look over here!"

I scream, "Brett!"

Brett is frozen, still on bended knee.

"Get up!" I yell again. "Let's get out of here!"

The sound of the helicopter grows louder.

"Brett!"

His eyes widen, then he blinks, shakes his head, gets on all fours, scurries under the room service table, and covers his face with the jelly-stained tablecloth, sending bits of croissant tumbling down through the iron railings of the balcony. A seagull swings past in time to pluck a fat buttered crumb out of the air.

I will him to come, to carry me through the crowd the way he did in *Space Warriors*. But he's cached behind a hedge of legs and equipment.

Searching for escape, I look to the door and see Nicole battling through the crowd. Nicole, my angel. How did she know I would need her?

"Over here," I cry, but the crashing waves and whirring helicopter blades swallow my voice. I wave my arms hoping she'll see me. The rat-a-tat of a dozen cameras explodes around me capturing my gesture. Nicole swivels this way and that, lost in the melee. Behind her, more paparazzi push forward, cameras cocked.

Brett, now on his belly, crawls stealthily beneath the hordes—a move he learned for the Vietnam sequence in *Month of Heroes*.

His goddamn publicist must've ratted us out.

"Brett, wait!" I try to follow, but the troops surge, swallowing the gap between us and slamming me against the balustrade.

Arms and legs wedge against me; an elbow rams my breast as a fat man struggles to untangle the cameras choking his neck. I squirm away and pull myself onto a sturdy, cast iron chair from where I see the full picture: Panavision. Cameras and sound equipment, photographers shoving. They shoot blindly, our blood scent in their snouts. On my left, the pixie-blonde from *Entertainment Tonight*, on my right the toupee-guy from *Variety*. Towering over all is the Australian from the *Enquirer* in his trademark tan suit.

Another helicopter appears on the horizon.

"Hey, Jackie!"

"Jackie Gold! Hey, is that you?"

"Where's Brett, Jackie?"

Down on the patio, hotel guests are shouting and pointing.

"Jaks!" Nicole sees me now. I wave.

"We want Brett! We want Brett!"

"Nicole help!"

She battles toward me, knocking the pixie-blonde out of the way but gets blocked behind the *ET* crew.

The second helicopter moves closer, stirring up sand. The guests below laugh as they hold on to their hats and beach umbrellas. The blade's wind causes several paparazzi to retreat. My foot slips off the chair and I catch myself on the railing. Three feet over is another balcony. Not far. I could jump and go through the next room, down the back stairs to the parking lot. Brett is probably already waiting in the car. I glance three floors down to where high surf pounds the rocky shore. I've done my own stunts, like the one in *Time Thief,* but there was a trampoline and thirty crew guys under me then. Nothing would cushion me now. Bloody, feathered remains of a seagull lie on the jagged rocks below.

"Come on down, doll!" Stubby fingers tug my sleeve. "You gonna' hurt yourself."

I pull away and step onto the balustrade. Gauging the distance between balconies, I gather up the folds of my white robe and crouch, focusing on my target landing spot with the concentration of a knife thrower. Already I feel free. I present the paparazzi with my middle finger.

"Geronimo!" I jump.

"Jaks! Look over here," Nicole cries simultaneously.

I turn automatically to see my best friend, pointing at me. Smiling.

Her arm is draped over the Australian.

He shoots.

The flash goes off in my eyes. And not until my robe billows over my head like a broken parachute do I realize I have missed the mark.

I wish I could say my life played out before me in slow motion, or that I thought of Brett, or my family, or even about how Nicole had betrayed me. But my last thought before striking the rocks is, *Thank God I'm wearing nice underwear.*

MAIN TITLES
THE REAL TRUE HOLLYWOOD STORY OF JACKIE GOLD

INT. HOSPITAL ROOM
4:52 A.M.
DAY 14

Today is my birthday. I was born right here at Sinai Memorial in the east wing exactly thirty years ago, on January 29, 1969. It was the same day that Mia Farrow, newly separated from Frank Sinatra and in India to meditate with Maharishi Mahesh Yogi, punched out a photographer when he tried to snap her picture at a New Delhi hotel.

My room is shadowed in bluish-gray light. Where the curtains join, a strip of sun laser skims the foot of my bed. I am encased like a mummy up to my neck. The intravenous stands to which I am hooked reflect fragments of my bandaged head and body. Tubes root in and out of my arms and belly; irrigating, hydrating. Blood swishes into plastic bota bags dangling from my sides. An oxygen mask grips the flesh around my mouth and nose like the sucker of a tentacle.

My room is peaceful. Lovely really, with its polished wood floors, marble tiles, and gold fixtures in the bathroom. Other than the ICU where I spent the first two weeks, I haven't seen the rest of the accommodations. But knowing Daddy, this is the presidential suite.

Understand, I can't actually *see*, not in any conventional way. Though my eyes are open, I am technically and by unanimous decision, knocked out. What I witness is more an "experiencing" of my surroundings. Images flash sequentially like a filmstrip running inside my head.

There are no flowers. Thousands of arrangements sent by well-wishers have been donated to other patients or carted away by hospital orderlies and cafeteria workers. On the floor in the corner, a Hefty bag of fan mail sits next to a short stack of week-old issues of *Daily Variety* and the *Hollywood Reporter* featuring headlines of my unfortunate accident: *JACKIE'S JUMP BUMPS PIC SALES WORLDWIDE, JACKIE GOLD: FALLING STAR BRINGS RISING BOX OFFICE*, and my personal favorite from the front page of the *Enquirer, "GERONIMO!" JACKIE'S LAST STAND*. My nurses sneak the copies out of my room, and then carefully put them back as I lie here, enshrined on my Posturepedic. My awareness, this ability to *see*, is not in their medical journals. It's likely those of us who experience it don't live to tell the tale.

The door of my room is thickly painted a soothing, creamy green, the reliable color of government buildings and public schools. Cut into the door's upper half a porthole allows nurses and visitors to peek in as if framing the image before entering will somehow soften the blow. A chair sits by my door, the kind stashed in office closets; black plastic bucket seating, chrome sidearms, light enough for even frail, grieving hands to manipulate. A white wicker loveseat and matching chair with peach cushions from Pier One sit by the window, an ensemble meant to disguise my sterile chamber with an air of hominess. Like the smell of chocolate chip cookies wafting up from the chimney of a crematorium.

Camped in the parking lot below my window are dozens of fans and paparazzi. In the corridors and beyond, the media circus; ABC, CBS, FOX NEWS, CNN, MSNBC, even the BBC have gathered. Some guzzle coffee at nearby Starbucks or in the hospital cafeteria. The more creative hacks station themselves in waiting rooms; armed operatives with listening devices and hidden cameras pretending to be part of a worried or grieving family. Not that they're all scumbags. As a movie star, I just happen to attract the bad guys. Until my accident, newsmen like Rather or Jennings had no cause to mention my name. So maybe

not every reporter is in the rat race but believe me, they'll all eat
their young for a piece of the cheese.

DISSOLVE TO:

INT. HOSPITAL ROOM
AFTERNOON

My visitor hunches over in the black and chrome chair, his hand-some head cradled in his hands. Tears slip between his fingers and drip onto a crumpled copy of the *Los Angeles Times*.

A nurse with a Streisand bob and red-framed reading glasses bustles around him, clucking her sympathy.

"Thank you." Brett sniffles as the nurse offers a fresh Kleenex. It must be strange for the nurses to see *the* Brett Haney crying. On camera, he plays tough guys with steely emotions. When trouble strikes, he juts out his cleft chin, furrows his brow, and squints. In real life, he cries at McDonald's commercials.

She goes to the chart at the end of my bed and makes a nota-tion, then examines the contents of the IV on the stand.

"Course you're upset, dearie," she coos. "Course you are. Surgery went well though, isn't that a blessing?"

Brett sobs and nods into the pile of soggy tissues.

"Poor thing," the nurse says. She pats his shoulder and slips out the door.

Brett blows his nose several times and lobs the Kleenex into the wastebasket. "Jackie honey?" He moves the chair closer to my bed. "Can you hear me darlin'?" He reaches for my hand, examines my chipped nails, strokes each finger, then squeezes sharply. "Please wake up, Jackie. Please."

For one of *People's* sexiest men alive, he looks terrible. Three days unshaven, yellow half-moons of sweat stain the underarms of his rumpled white Polo. He's been sleeping at the hospital all week, putting on a brave face for the Intensive Care staff; the real-life heroes. Now that I've been transferred to a private room, he's fallen apart.

Brett drops my hand and reflexively runs his fingers through his unwashed hair to cover the thinning spot. "Okay, okay, pull it together Haney. You can do this, guy!" He crouches down, springs forward, does ten push-ups, and pops back up to his feet. He circles the room, then retrieves a paper towel from the bathroom to mop his forehead before rushing back over to me as if my condition might have suddenly improved.

"They say they're doing everything, but I don't know." His eyes well up again. "Oh baby, Jackie honey, tell me what to do!" He waits for the possibility of an answer. "I can't sleep. I can't eat a thing, Jackie. I've lost thirteen pounds."

Brett is obsessive about his weight. Worse than me even. He checks it first thing when he wakes up, then again right after he goes to the bathroom. No joke.

"I'm gonna' move into a hotel for a while. It's just…" He takes another Kleenex, wipes his nose, and flops on the wicker couch. "And anyway, I can't stand being home. I can't even work out, I'm so depressed."

Brett reaches for the side table, finds the paper, and shakes it open. "The reviews came in on *Double Barreled*. Two lousy stars. And wait'll you hear what that Jackbutt Abrams wrote about me."

Jackbutt is Brett's way of saying jackass. Brett rarely swears unless he's had a few drinks and even then, he's remorseful.

"He says I 'substitute nervous tics for emotion,' that I act with my eyebrows. Is that true, Jackie? God, I wish you could answer me. You would tell me the truth. Honey, do I act with my eyebrows?"

He sits up. "Come on, please say something. Do something! Wiggle a finger. Open your eyes! Show me a sign!"

It's ironic. All through school, I envied girls who were quiet and mysterious. Boys always preferred girls who were enigmatic and still. Me, I was the pesty one with a big mouth. Not anymore. I have been rendered the perfect listener.

A doe-eyed, red-haired nurse wearing freshly applied lipgloss sidesteps through the door holding a Dixie cup of water. A juicy peach of a girl, she's just bursting with sympathy, her freckles unimpeded by her Cover Girl makeup. The plastic tag over her left breast reads "Dani." A happy face dots the i. Brett wipes his eyes and takes the cup, sipping as she squats before him and waits until he is finished. He hands back the paper cup, mouths a thank you, and puts his hands together in prayer position, the same gesture I watched him practice over and over for a scene in *Eighth Dimension*.

She looks at him pointedly and then stands and smooths the crouch creases from her uniform; one of those matching pants and top numbers that look like Sears catalog pajamas. Hers are orange and covered with pictures of dancing kitty cats wearing stethoscopes.

"I'm so sorry for what you're going through, I…" Her voice trembles. "I just want you to know that we're praying for you. And for Jackie, of course."

"Thank you, Nurse."

"Oh gosh. Please call me Dani." Her voice brightens. "I'm here every day 'cept weekends."

"Okay Dani, much appreciated."

"Anything you need. Anything. I *mean* that." She attempts a look of professional seriousness to mask the smitten look in her eyes. Then she reaches over and gives my boyfriend a not-so-nursely squeeze on his arm. Without remembering to so much as glance at my vital signs, she practically skips out the door.

INT. HOSPITAL ROOM
MORNING
DAY 15

My father is a nice guy, a darling, a mensch. Except in business. In business, Daddy is a killer, a piranha. Physically, he resembles every other Hollywood studio executive, a skinny nebbish with one overdeveloped forearm from a lifetime of tennis. Now he stands over me looking ancient. Anna, through the porthole, occasionally taps her fingernails on the glass to let him know she is there if he needs her.

The nurse with the Streisand hair opens the shades, but the room barely brightens, the sun eclipsed by a knot of storm clouds. Even in this dull light, there is too much clarity, and my father shades his eyes.

"Can I get you something, sweetheart?" Nurse Streisand asks.

My father shakes his head and motions her away.

"All righty," she says kindly. "You just push that button if you need anything."

She leaves the room, crosses past Anna, and shuts the door.

My father pulls the chrome chair to my bed and slowly lowers, hunching over me. He grabs my fingers, a crumpled hanky in his hand. Tears strain at the area around his eyes; so many years of running the studio, of being in control, have rusted his ducts. He speaks into my limp hand, "My fault, baby…done things differently." Dry shards of regret spill into my palm. "Spent more time…sent you to a university…" He struggles for the ways he could have prevented this.

It's utterly inconceivable to my father that events can take place without his authorization like even God is waiting for him to send up a "deal memo," approving His plans. In my father's world, problems are fixable and the people who don't cooperate are moved to a different department.

I want to say, "Daddy, it's okay. I don't feel nearly as bad as I look." But I can't. That's the awful part—watching people suffer without being able to reassure them or even squeeze their hand.

"Sidney?" The door opens and Anna enters. She presses a hand to the back of my father's neck and he quickly straightens up in his chair. "I called the driver. He'll meet us downstairs."

Of course she's doing better than he is. She is Catholic. She lights candles, says prayers. She has the Blessed Mother and the saints to talk to when she's scared. Anna comes to my bedside, brushes phantom hairs off the bandage on my forehead. Underneath the white strips lie my gleaming wounds—the stitched purple tracks, a Frankenstein scar newly minted.

"Dear Mary Mother of Jesus," Anna whispers, her voice a soft wind rustling the leaves of a weeping willow. She seals her prayer with a cross over her chest, bends down, and kisses my cheek. Her lips are cool. I have a memory of being very young with a high temperature; Anna leaning over me, wiping my body with a cold washcloth to bring the fever down, my eyes following the gold crucifix swinging from her neck.

My father points to his watch and signals that it is time to go. In all these years, he has never missed a day at the studio. Regardless of catastrophe—earthquakes, divorce, even death—he maintains a perfect attendance record. Some people cope by drinking, my father copes by coping. He walks to the wicker loveseat, picks up his folded jacket, and looks back at me. I realize that he is not wearing his glasses; diffusing this picture of his comatose, only child through a filter of near legally blind vision. A copy of the *Hollywood Reporter* sticks out of his jacket pocket as it has since the beginning of time.

SLOW DISSOLVE TO:

MALIBU COLONY HOME
DAY
APRIL 1979

When you lose someone early on, your mind bottles the memories and stores them away, airtight. I have recollections of my parents going back to my first years of life. It's possible these are imprints from stories told to me, though who would have done the telling, I don't know. In Sidney Goldstein's house, one didn't speak of the not-so-dearly departed.

My mother was rarely mentioned. Like the word "cancer," her name was mouthed rather than spoken aloud. She lived in Hawaii and kept in touch through long, drunken, hysterical messages left on our answering machine. There were no pictures to remind us of her; Daddy had removed them. Most of the furniture she'd bought had been replaced. In my room, under my new four-poster bed, I kept her old jewelry box. Its contents—abandoned keepsakes—were my only links to our past: a heart locket containing a picture of me at six, a charm bracelet, and (my prized possession) a necklace with violet gemstones. It was part of a set that included dangling, clip-on earrings. While I treasured those pieces, it is important to note that in the two years since she'd been gone, I wasn't exactly pining for her. Life was much calmer and about a million decibels quieter with her gone. Daddy and Anna and I had dinner together at the kitchen table almost every evening. Anna chuckled at my father's jokes. We were like a television sitcom family.

Still, there were times—like on Mother's Day when every single one of my friends was busy making cards or bringing breakfast trays to their moms—that I sort of missed her. Well, maybe I didn't exactly miss *her,* but I missed having a mom. And though I was all too aware of my parent's fights, I wondered what specifically led up to her leaving. Maybe she'd had good reason. Maybe there were events from her past I didn't know about. On

Anna's soap opera, a teenage girl found out her mother was actually her big sister! That probably didn't apply in my case, but still, my mother's life was mostly a mystery.

Several weeks before my tenth birthday, I decided to broach the subject. It was a school day, and I was already dressed in shorts and a blouse, my tennis shoes damp and sandy from having been left outside. Daddy was at the oak breakfast table, drinking coffee and reading *Variety*. Anna was scrambling eggs. News blared from the small television on the counter. Gingerly, I reached over and turned the volume down.

"So, um, Dad," I said keeping my tone casual. "I have some questions about my mother."

My father flinched as if I had poked him in the eye. "Where the hell did that come from?"

"Dad, c'mon. You never talk about her. I don't even know how you met."

Anna placed our eggs on the table and shot me a warning look, which I ignored.

"Dad?"

"Not a good topic." He grumbled.

I pulled the paper away from my father's face. "But every single kid in America knows how their parents met," I persisted.

"Don't bother me with this crapola, Jackie."

"I think I have a right to know some things."

My father wiped the corners of his mouth. "I'll eat at work," he said, then got up from the table, kissed my forehead, and left. There was silence for a minute, then Anna began clearing my father's breakfast plates and silverware.

"Put socks on." She pointed under the table, avoiding my eyes.

"I'm not a baby."

"Jackie."

"None of my friends wear socks. Besides, my shoes are wet."

"It's your father's rules," Anna declared as she scraped food from the plates into the garbage.

"They should never have gotten married, to begin with."

That was the first thing everyone said. With my father stubbornly mute on the topic, I questioned all our friends and neighbors, memo pad and pencil in hand like Harriet the Spy. Tammy, the checkout lady from the Mayfair Market; Mr. Jackson, the gray-haired, black-skinned security guy at the Malibu Colony guard gate who remembered all the comings and goings of the last twenty years; Will, the attendant from the Texaco station. I got an ear load from Brian, the manager at the Colony Coffee Shop where my mother had once worked. I filled up one whole notepad on my mother's history by conducting interviews at the Malibu sheriff's station. The police were especially helpful and surprisingly forthcoming! But the more I learned the more questions I had. Her life was like a giant puzzle with tons of missing pieces.

I scoured our house for clues, looking in forbidden places—in my father's closet and dresser drawers, the file cabinet by his desk—but there was nothing. It was as though she had never existed. Then one day, in the garage while searching for a bicycle pump, I discovered several labeled boxes sticking out from under an old packing blanket. "Documents." "Scripts." "Contracts." I tugged each one out until I came to the smallest carton marked "Photographs." A bundled pile of empty picture frames lay on top, and I put them to the side. Braving a spider web, I stripped off a crisscross of duct tape reached inside and pulled out a photo album. It was heavy, bound in dark-green cracked leather, and coated with a fine layer of beach dust. I turned it around in my hands, the sandy soot sticking to my fingers, and opened it to the first page.

There were dozens of snapshots lodged at careless angles under the plastic. My mother, a drink in her hand, wearing a floppy hat, plopped in a hammock, shielding her face; my mother, a drink in her hand, standing under a tree, pointing at her pregnant belly; my mother in a waitress uniform. I turned the page. Photographs of my parents at different functions. I'd stumbled upon buried treasure!

I rifled further into the album's stiff pages. My mother as a teen, her hair teased into a flip. My father as a boy with his relatives in front of a sign reading "Goldstein's Clothiers." From my sleuthing, I'd partly assembled my parent's history. Now, here were the missing pieces of the puzzle. I could almost picture their story playing out like a movie.

I pushed the cartons back under the blanket and gathered the album in my arms. Several photos spilled out, and as I scooped them up, one caught my eye. A Polaroid of my parents as I could never have imagined them; relaxed smiles, holding hands, squinting against the bright sunlight with a turquoise ocean washing up over their ankles. My mother's tanned, shapely body in an orange and yellow Hawaiian print bikini. Her blond hair flowing over her shoulders as she stands with my father, twenty pounds lighter and fit in navy blue swim trunks. The tip of a green palm frond lashes out of focus in front of them. I turned the photo over. Inscribed on the back in faded blue ink were the words: "Sidney and Merilee, May 9, 1968."

COLONY COFFEE SHOP
MORNING
MARCH 1968

I picture my father, peering through the window of the coffee shop making sure his dream girl was working her shift. Yes! There she was, Merilee Miller, taking orders from a medley of male customers who, like Sidney, came to sit at the salmon-and-gray-speckled Formica counter not for the food but for the service. Merilee was a "stone fox." A for-real California blond kissed by God and the sun and blessed by nature in all ways physical. Unfortunately (as my father would soon discover and as is often true of those blessed with extraordinary physical attributes), foxy Merilee was sorely lacking in other areas.

The Colony Coffee Shop was built in the 1950s in that Googie architectural style. Half the building housed a pharmacy that sold candy and cosmetics. For her twenty-first birthday, Merilee had dropped by the makeup counter that morning and stolen a new shade of Mary Quant "Frosty Moon Glow," which now shone on her moist and luscious lips.

I imagine my father slid onto a stool at the crescent counter and signaled my mother.

"The usual, Sidney?" Her voice had a breathless quality as if she'd been climbing stairs.

"No, uh, just coffee and a bagel," Sidney coughed out. "I have a meeting at Universal in an hour."

Merilee would have flashed him an impressed look, making my father feel taller and more handsome. Was she aware of just how much power he had? Especially for such a young man of only twenty-nine. As she popped his onion bagel into the toaster, I imagine him sighing at the thought of her performing these same duties in his own kitchen, wearing a bathing suit, ponytail swinging.

"Gotta eat!" a voice boomed from behind.

Hank Palmer, clad in shorts and a tank top, swung his strong, long limbs over a stool next to Sidney. Poor Daddy. He became conscious of the V-shaped patch of white skin and black hairs that climbed up his neck in contrast to Hank's smooth-chested, tanned, cocoa-buttered physique. I imagine my father buttoned his top button, rattled his business pages, and focused on my mother, who was busy spooning just the right amount of cream cheese into a little, ridged paper cup.

Hank pulled himself over the counter, biceps bursting, blocking Merilee from Sidney's view. "Hey there, Merry Meri, *never* contrary."

"Hey, Hanky Panky," I imagine my mother said.

"Merilee," my father interrupted, eager to earn back her attention, "you ever thought about acting?"

Merilee and Hank turned to him, startled.

"I mean, I know some people, if you're ever interested," Sidney stammered.

"I don't have any talent," she said, speaking to both of them but keeping her eyes on Hank. "I went on one audition when I was a kid, but I froze up, you know. Choked. I was fine in the waiting room, but when I went in…well!"

I imagine Merilee imitated a deer caught in the headlights.

"Oh, I bet you're talented at something," Hank said. "Whattaya doing later, Merry Meri? Wanna come over and play?"

Merilee laughed nervously and spilled a dollop of cream cheese on the front of her polyester blouse. "Whoops," she giggled and dipped a napkin into a glass of water then dabbed at the stain (Sidney couldn't help noticing) right where the dart of her uniform strained against her right breast.

"I'll write down my address," Hank said, pumping his eyebrows suggestively.

Merilee would have reached into her apron (avoiding the stolen makeup) and removed her pad and pen. She would have placed them in Hank's outstretched hands, whereby after weeks of fooling around in the back of Hank's car they would have surely gone all the way. But fate intervened.

The doors flew open bringing a gust of warm Santa Ana wind along with two policemen and Steve the pharmacist.

"There she is!" cried the pharmacist, pointing.

My mother cowered behind the counter as if she had committed a crime, which she had.

The policemen cornered Merilee. Officer Roy was a tall man, while his partner, Hervé, was shorter than Sidney. According to the police files, each then took a firm hold of one of my mother's delicate arms.

"Let me go." Shaking them off, she ran behind the counter.

"Hey!" said my father. "Just what the hell—"

"Stay out of this please, Mr. Goldstein, sir." In those days, Malibu was a small town, and everyone knew everyone by name.

"Fellas, what's this all about?" Hank asked, rising well above Sidney.

"Where's the lipstick, Merilee?" Steve the Pharmacist demanded. "The Frosty Moon Glow?"

"I-I haven't the foggiest, Steve." Merilee tossed her head and struck what she hoped was a provocative pose meant to throw him off the trail.

Unfortunately for Merilee, Steve was in a ten-year relationship with his housemate, Jim, and couldn't have cared less about Merilee's anatomy. But Sidney, his dream girl in a pickle, was squirming on his seat like a child who knows the answer to a math question but has already raised his hand too many times. He ached to rescue her, sweep her into his arms, and carry her out of harm's way.

"One peek at your apron and we'll get out of your hair," Officer Roy stated firmly.

The customers watched as Merilee backed up to the oven and slowly undid the ties around her waist. Not only was the stolen lipstick in her apron pocket but so was a royal blue mascara taken the day before.

"C'mon babe, just give 'em the apron," Hank said. The customers echoed their agreement. Sidney moved to the edge of his seat.

Merilee's eyes darted around. She looked at the pharmacist in his white lab coat then at the two policemen. With her two prior arrests for shoplifting, she would go to jail for a minimum of two to five. She looked at Hank, who looked back at her, an impatient expression on his normally pleasant face.

Merilee would never have looked at Sidney were it not for the sound of the toaster popping his onion bagel, but fortunately, she did. And in his sympathetic expression, she saw her ticket out. Didn't she know how to make a guy feel *needed*? To make him feel big and hard and strong and *tall*? Merilee's filled her baby blue, Olympic-size swimming pool eyes with helpless tears of desperation, and in response, Sidney drew in his breath and flung himself off the high dive.

"Excuse me, uh…" Sidney stammered. "I am a lawyer and this girl, uh, young woman is my client."

"What?" said Roy and Hervé.

"Yes, and I'm reporting you for police brutality."

"Huh?" Hank said, looking down at Sidney.

The customers gasped and glared at the cops. Police brutality was a term associated with events that happened in far-off places like Watts or New York, certainly not in Malibu, in the morning, on a lovely beach day.

Without warning, Steve the pharmacist lunged for the apron still clutched tightly in Merilee's hands.

"Gimme that, you bitch," he snarled.

Merilee screamed.

The cops sprang into action. With the heat off their own backs, they pulled the pharmacist off my mother (who managed to hang onto her apron and the stolen makeup), cuffed him, and hauled him off to the station.

Amid her customer's cheers, Merilee threw her barely bruised arms around Sidney's neck, and in front of Hank and all her regulars, kissed Sidney in a way that suggested more than gratitude for her freedom.

A week later, the pharmacist and his lover packed up their Malibu apartment to start a new life in West Hollywood while at the same time Merilee Miller took her meager belongings from her mother's in Van Nuys to move into Malibu Colony with Sidney. And only three months later, still pumped up from his conquest, my father proposed to his dream girl after the shocking news of her pregnancy.

INT. MALIBU COLONY HOME
DAY
JUNE 1968

"The honeymoon was over before it started." That's what everyone said.

In the early months of her pregnancy, my previously fun-loving mother suffered from morning sickness that lasted day and night. When she wasn't throwing up, she was desperately trying to make herself over to fit into my father's life. Daddy didn't have friends, he had tennis partners and business associates, and his business associates had wives.

One evening after an arduous day at the studio, my father arrived home to find Merilee had cut off her long, blond hair. Bobbed at her jawline were scissor tracks, fresh as a newly mowed lawn.

"Do you like it?" Merilee asked the moment Sidney walked in the door. "I called your friend Rita Sanderson, and she told me to go to this place in Brentwood. She says everyone goes there. Vidal somebody. I couldn't get in without giving her name. Can you imagine?"

Sidney eyed his new bride sitting on the black leather sofa in front of the television console eating out of a box of Saltines. Crumbs camped out on the front of her T-shirt.

"I didn't hear you, hon. I asked if you like it," Merilee said without taking her eyes from the set.

"What's not to like?" Sidney hated it. Now there would be no lovely ponytail swinging in the kitchen.

Not that Merilee had cooked once since moving in, not even a bagel. She preferred to order his housekeeper, Vi, to "butter me up a toasty one, wouldja, hon?" Vi (who I imagine did not cotton to orders from that same young waitress who used to serve her a tuna melt every Friday evening before she caught the bus) was threatening to quit.

What had happened? Those first weeks together were champagne brunches and sunsets on the shore, like something out of a movie. But from the moment they'd found out she was pregnant and went off to Vegas… Sidney sighed, set his briefcase on the table, and flopped down on the couch next to Merilee. He reached out and stroked her hair, his fingers plunging off the blunt ends.

"How are you feeling?" In consideration of her condition, I imagine Sidney made his voice extra kind.

"Well, I only barfed until noon today, and then I went to the salon. Did you pick up ginger ale?"

Sidney hadn't. He still couldn't get used to the idea that he was going to have a baby. So much had happened so fast. He needed a tennis game. A tough one, but one he could win.

"I'm sorry, Merilee, I didn't. I'll send Vi out. Or no, wait, I'll go in a minute."

She rolled her eyes like a teenager and sprang up. "Geez never mind, I'll go myself."

It seemed to Sidney that whenever he came home, Merilee sought a reason to get out of the house. Maybe she just loved driving the red convertible he'd bought as her wedding gift.

She snatched the saltines, scooped her keys off the front table, and walked out.

Merilee slipped her key into the ignition and backed cautiously out of the garage, a space bigger and nicer than the whole of her mother's apartment. The engine purred under her seat as she shifted into first gear and expertly guided her dream machine over the speed bumps and down the Colony road. The convertible still smelled new. Merilee had never owned a new car, much less a Mercedes. She had grown up so poor that her mother, a waitress at Denny's, had been chosen as a contestant on *Queen for a Day*. Unfortunately, when the date came, Marva was too hungover to get out of bed, thereby blowing her shot at the crown and her chance to own a dishwasher.

Merilee had never brought friends home, fearing Marva might be passed out on the floor. She'd cruised the streets of Van Nuys in souped-up cars with hopped-up guys, aware from an early age of the power and sway of her looks and budding bosom.

After high school, Marva got Merilee a job at the Denny's. Then one afternoon, Merilee and a surfer friend took the bus out to Malibu, and on a whim, she applied at the coffee shop.

As my mother drove to the Mayfair to buy her ginger ale, she considered stopping at a payphone to call one of her old beaus. Wouldn't it be fun just to talk? She missed Earl, the pear-shaped banker from Newport Beach who liked to take her dancing. And that sweet Bob Katz, the married doctor she slept with on and off. She thought wistfully of Hank, with whom Merilee had fooled around, letting him finger her in the back of his Mustang. As the payphone on the corner loomed closer, Merilee hesitated, then planted her foot firmly on the gas pedal. No, she was determined to remain faithful to Sidney. And though she hadn't exactly broken things off with her suitors, she'd clearly informed them she'd moved and was presently unreachable.

INT. BANQUET HALL
BEVERLY HILTON HOTEL
NIGHT
OCTOBER
1968

"So, um, Rita," Merilee chirped, "Sid tells me you bought a brand-new house?"

They were clustered with several of Sidney's set—the Sandersons, the Calloways, and the Boshowitzes—attending another charity event at the Beverly Hilton Hotel, the third this month.

Merilee was flushed and brimming with the manic energy that often arrives in one's second trimester. She'd had a morning swim, and she and Sidney hadn't fought all day. In the car on the way, he'd let her turn on KRLA and hadn't complained or shushed her when she sang "Daydream Believer." Now surveying the wealthy patrons who occupied the marble-floored, velvet-draped hall with its tall ceilings and ornate fixtures, she felt confident progress had been made. No one could accuse her of not blending in. Her hair was cut and blown dry in the most current style. She had on a new cocktail gown, the most expensive she could find that covered most of her chest, which, like the rest of her body, was getting larger by the day. She'd memorized every one of the wives' names, their rank and file, plus who did their nails, cut their hair, and what their husbands did at the studio. She also knew from Sidney a few other things about the husbands that their wives didn't know. But Merilee was not about to tattle. Besides, men needed recreation. Merilee understood all about that. She herself had once been the recreational type.

"Um, Rita? I was just saying—"

"Were you speaking to me?" Rita Sanderson blinked as if she had only just realized Merilee was there. She lay a slice of Brie on a cracker and slipped it neatly past her red lips, then shot a glance at her best friend, Marge Calloway, an athletic woman with cropped salt and pepper hair and large shoulders made larger by the unfortunate cut of her gown.

"Yes." Merilee took a deep breath and reminded herself to stay steady. After all, Rita was old and probably hard of hearing. She leaned in closer. "I said I heard you bought a brand-new house."

Rita shuffled back a step. "Yes, dear, we sold Roxbury and moved to the hills."

A frosty woman on the eve of her second facelift, Rita Sanderson sat on the board of a dozen charities, and had neither time nor interest in befriending a young, naturally blonde, former *waitress* for God's sake, even if she was married to Sidney Goldstein! The Sandersons were old money Republicans, along the lines of the Rockefellers or the Bloomingdales. It was alleged that Rita and Nancy Reagan were third cousins by marriage.

"I'd hardly call the house 'brand new' however," Rita chortled.

"It was built by Chaplin," Marge added.

"Is he the architect?" Merilee asked, munching rapidly on a carrot stick. The smell of the pâte was making her nauseous.

"*Charlie* Chaplin. You have heard of Charlie Chaplin, haven't you?" Marge honked a laugh, gave her drink a swizzle, and made disbelieving eyes at Rita. Then she motioned across the room at her husband Gerald and mouthed, "More foie gras."

Sidney, standing a foot away, was alternating stories of his latest tennis and business coups while trying to appear unaware that Merilee was being devoured by sharks. It never ceased to amaze him how oblivious she was, or how determined. Like an amateur boxer staggering around the ring refusing to take the count.

"The actor? He built houses?"

"Oh my." Rita sighed and tossed her stiff highlights over one shoulder. She knocked back the last of her champagne and scouted the room distractedly.

"I know who Charlie Chaplin is," Merilee said, emphatic. It was crucial she salvage the conversation. "He's dead now, though, right?"

Rita snapped open her evening bag and took out a pack of Benson & Hedges. With a flick of her lighter, she lit her cigarette and inhaled. "Where is that damn champagne?" she muttered gazing past Merilee.

Sidney couldn't stand it any longer. He felt as if this night would never end. He stood on tiptoes and craned his neck for a waiter with a drink tray. Finally spotting one, Sidney reached over the guests and signaled, causing his neck to go into a spasm. "Christ," he grimaced, slapping the side of his collar as if he'd been bitten by a mosquito.

"Whatsa matter, hon?" Merilee asked absentmindedly. She was trying to work out where she had gone wrong on the Chaplin thing.

"Nothing is the matter." Sidney replaced Rita Sanderson's champagne glass with a fresh one from the tray. He wouldn't be able to play tennis for days. He picked off a salmon croquette from another tray and tried to ignore the pain.

"So, um, Rita…"

Sidney's jaw clenched tighter as he watched his wife climb back in the ring.

"I hear you're pouring a new foundation for the tennis court," Merilee said brightly.

"Blue," Dave Sanderson interjected.

"What?"

"The color is blue."

"Well, good for you. Sidney says it costs a shit wad."

"Shush," whispered Sidney through gritted teeth.

"Oh, shush yourself!" Merilee retorted. "Geez. Is it getting warm in here or is it just me?" She drew up her hair and fanned the flush blooming on her neck.

A rally of sharp looks ricocheted between Marge and Rita.

"We can't have a tennis court at our house," Merilee continued, taking several steps to the table to retrieve another bunch of carrot sticks. "Everyone in the Colony has to share courts because of the small lot sizes. But we have the beach. I guess that makes up for it. Gosh, I wish I could have another glass of champagne, but the doctor says it's not good for the baby."

Sidney stepped closer and put his arm around Merilee, hoping to squeeze her into silence. But Merilee, misunderstanding, snuggled into Sidney and squeezed back.

"Ellen. That is your name, hon, right? Ellen?" Merilee asked.

Ellen Boshwitz, cutting a square figure in a mauve cocktail dress, nodded, her mouth full of crackers.

"You have a little fish egg on your chin." Merilee reached forward with a long pink nail and flicked at Ellen's face. "Got it."

Rita and Marge's giggles snapped Merilee's head around.

"Caviar," Sidney whispered.

"What?" Merilee felt queasy. Something wasn't sitting right. Maybe it was those skewers or the mushrooms with the stuffing.

"It's called caviar."

"Well, sorreee. It's still fish eggs," Merilee snapped, defensive. "I used to use them as bait. I don't know how you people can even think of eating the stuff. I get nauseous just thinking about it."

"Merilee's pregnant," Sidney said weakly.

"You certainly can't tell," Dave Sanderson marveled until he felt the spike of Rita's heel drill through his shoe.

"I think I'm gonna' barf," Merilee announced. Dropping her carrots, she ran for the bathroom.

INT. MALIBU COLONY HOUSE, EVENING
NOVEMBER 1968

Sidney removed his shoes at the front door and tiptoed through the living room, praying his wife was asleep and he could dine in peace. Instead, he found her at the kitchen table, bare legs stretched out, wearing one of his pajama tops that scarcely buttoned over her expanding belly.

"How was your day?" she asked, patting the chair next to her.

There was a seductive slur to Merilee's voice that he might have found attractive if he hadn't also noticed the half-empty wine bottle on the kitchen table. Stomach grumbling, he eyed the covered casserole on top of the oven. Thank God Vi hadn't quit.

"Can I make you some tea?" Sidney asked, trying inconspicuously to move the bottle of wine from her reach.

"Aren't you going to ask about my day?" Merilee leaned back in her chair precariously. "Or maybe you don't care what I do."

"Hey, stop that." My father jumped up and righted the chair.

Merilee laughed and stuck her tongue out at him.

"Not funny," Sidney muttered. He went to the dish drain, picked out a fork and knife, and took a deep breath. "So, what did you do today, Merilee?"

"Sid, how come we never use the dining room? Huh? It's so fancy, and we can cozy up at one end of the table and watch the waves."

"It's just easier in here. Besides, didn't you eat already?" Sidney asked hopefully.

"Nuh-uh. Couldn't stomach it. C'mon," she whined, "let's move into the dining room." She reached for the bottle, but Sidney pushed it farther away.

"Give that back," Merilee growled.

"Okay, sounds like bedtime for you," Sidney spoke as equably as possible. He couldn't wait to see what Vi had cooked. It smelled like meatloaf and potatoes.

"Geez, sorry. Okay? I waited up for you and while I was waiting, I had one extra little glass of wine. It's not my fault you're always late. C'mon, I'll have a Pepsi if that'll make you happy. I just want to talk, Sid," Merilee pleaded, gently covering his hand with her own. "Just talk to me."

For a split second, his fingers found hers and the contact caught him off guard. It reminded him why he'd been crazy about her, so crazy that he would not even consider her having an abortion, and instead (when she weepily told him of her condition) shyly suggested that she marry him. If he had only...but he couldn't let himself think that.

"C'mon Sid," Merilee implored, tugging at the cuff of his sleeve. "I never see you."

He felt guilty for working late. Here he was, newly married with a baby on the way. He should be rushing home to his bride, but for Chris'sake, he couldn't even get her to read the newspaper.

"I hate anything in black and white, especially those stupid old movies you're so wild about," Merilee snapped when he'd suggested she might at least enjoy the entertainment section.

And the one area he'd counted on to sustain him, their sex life, had ended the moment Merilee found out she was pregnant.

Sidney glanced around helplessly and rubbed at his forehead. He was hungry and exhausted. All he wanted to do was watch Carson and go to sleep. He got up and went to the stove.

Merilee rose unsteadily. "Sidney. Goddamnit. I'm talking to you."

There were better choices he could make. Would make, maybe next time, but not tonight. Without a word, he removed the casserole, grabbed a plate and silverware, and fled past his wife to his study.

"Prick!" Merilee shrieked at his back. She grabbed the wine bottle and threw it after him. It landed with an unsatisfying thump on the carpeting by the stairs.

Shit. She shouldn't have been drinking. She'd only meant to have one, maybe two glasses. For a moment Merilee considered apologizing, but why should she say sorry when he was the one turning her life into a prison?

And it's not like she wasn't trying. Just that morning she had gone through Sidney's phone book, determined to stay occupied.

"Hello, you've reached the Sandersons."

"Hi, is Rita there?" Merilee sat at the bottom of the stairs twirling the phone cord around her fingers.

"The Sandersons are not in. May I ask who's calling?"

"This is Merilee Goldstein, please tell Rita I'm on the phone. I've called three times and I don't think she is getting my messages."

"We're just the answering service ma'am, we aren't in the residence."

Merilee sighed. "Okay, give Mrs. Sanderson another message then. Tell her Mrs. Goldstein says let me know if you need any help with that charity deal she was talking about last Wednesday night. And tell her I'm home. All goddamn day!"

Merilee reached for her empty wine glass and shook the last drops into her mouth. Then, hit with a wave of nausea stronger than she'd had for weeks, rushed over to the kitchen sink, and threw up.

As she moved into her third trimester, my mother sank deeper into herself. She especially resented the weight piling onto her body; her one dependable asset and the only one she held in her own name. After a breakfast of Pop-Tarts and a Pepsi, she would throw a T-shirt over her bikini and escape to the beach walking the shore, pushing through water calf-deep, her shapely legs vouching for the rest of her.

While I rocked along safe and warm in the sweet water of my cocoon, she strode through the soft current, bending occasionally to pick up a shell or piece of tumbled glass and throwing it back to sea.

After countless humiliations, she'd given up trying to belong in Sidney's world. Now, when accompanying my father to charity balls or functions, she packed a fashion magazine in her purse. The moment Sidney was caught up in conversation, she'd retreat to the car and flip through the pages by the glove compartment light until it was time to go home.

DISSOLVE TO:

INT. HOSPITAL ROOM
DAWN
DAY 16

Pierre, the night nurse, is rummaging through my things. There isn't much to look at. A framed picture of Brett inscribed to me, a Bible left by Anna, a boom box, and an Enya CD with a Post-it Note reading "Thought she might enjoy this!" from good ol' Nurse Dani.

With his rich dark skin, contrasting blond, curly hair and green eyes, I imagine Pierre is often quizzed on his ethnicity. From his name, I'm guessing Haitian, but he could be Jamaican or even Cajun. A fair amount of his time has clearly been spent at the gym; his thick, muscled arms pop out where the end of his sleeves. After changing my urine bag, he fiddles with Brett's photo, tapping his finger along the frame, perhaps debating whether to take it. It would be worth a lot of money.

The door pushes open. Pierre jerks back and makes like he's straightening the picture.

"Whoa, hey there, Flo. You're early. It's not even light yet."

"Buses are running funny, don't want to be late." Flo, a stout African American woman enters with a square, black pocketbook squeezed under one arm. She leans over me, her breathing labored. Perspiration shines on her forehead and the fuzzy black hairs of her upper lip.

"You mean because of the 'special assignment.'"

Flo shoots him a look and flips back my top sheet. Then she turns my body with one hand while whisking the bottom sheet out from under me like a magician pulling a tablecloth.

"Here." Pierre offers Flo my chart.

"Just leave it please."

"Right. Goodnight then," Pierre says over his shoulder as the door swings shut behind him.

Flo B. (as her name tag reads) unbuttons her red wool coat and goes into the bathroom. She reenters with two pans of water that she clanks down next to my bed. Tossing back spidery hair extensions, she throws her coat over the chair, revealing her pink-heart nurse's uniform. Humming, she begins my bath, washing my face, swabbing each of my ears, and moving slowly down my neck and shoulders, patting me dry along the way. Purposefully but gently, Flo hoists my body on its side, careful not to disturb my IVs, then pulls down the top portion of my gown. Avoiding the tape around my ribs, she washes in circles where my breasts are free of bandages. As the soapy spirals near my areolas, my nipples stiffen reflexively.

Flo stops, shakes her head, and steps back, perhaps waiting to see if my other body parts will spring to life. Then she reaches the cloth between my legs and gives a prudent one, two, swipe. With a grunt of satisfaction, she swaddles me in fresh sheets, empties the wash pans, retrieves her coat and pocketbook, and hurries out the door.

SLOW DISSOLVE TO:

INT. MALIBU COLONY HOME
1969 – 1974

The day of my arrival marked the departure of Vi, who was even less keen on caring for me than for my mother. And if Merilee had any notions of being a full-time mom, they were put to rest within several days of nursing and changing diapers.

I was just three weeks old when Anna came to live with us. Newly emigrated from Guatemala, she was young and innocent with smooth, creamy skin like the inside of an almond. Like me, she was a recent arrival and spoke no English. We had everything in common.

The only thing I shared with my mother was that we both drank from a bottle.

As I lay in my bassinet, shrouded in pink lace and sucking on my pacifier, my mother and father scrutinized me, their brows knit and furrowed.

"She's got your nose, Sidney," Merilee blamed, shaking her head at my father.

"And your personality," my father shot back. "All she does is lie there. Shouldn't she be doing more by now? Maybe we should have her tested?"

But when Anna looked at me, all I saw in her black eyes was the glow of love and pride. All day long, she coddled and cuddled and cooed at me, kissing my belly, my cheeks and toes. Anna had no friends, no family in Los Angeles. I was the center of her universe and she was mine.

"An-na," I said one day when I was nine months old. I was sitting on the terracotta-tiled kitchen floor, watching her clean the dinner dishes, swatting at her dangling apron strings like a kitten with a ball of yarn.

My mother and father were in the living room watching television (the one activity they could share without fighting), perched on separate orange and yellow squares. In the weeks before my birth, my mother had banished all of my father's casual beach-bachelor furniture to the Salvation Army. With modular the latest in-home fashion, she had purchased a living room set of orange and yellow cubes, which when strung together, created an L-shaped sofa. Whenever anyone stretched out, the cushions would roll apart. Daddy had twice fallen to the floor.

"An-na," I said again, bouncing on the cool tiles.

"Senor, senora, es Jackie!" Anna called out excitedly. My mother jolted up from her orange perch and ran into the kitchen.

"Whatsa matter, hon?" Her voice was already slurred from martinis.

"Anna!" I repeated proudly for my mother's benefit, as my father raced up behind her.

"Did she say Anna?" My father crouched down and examined me with keen interest.

"Si, senor." Anna smiled proudly and lifted me into her arms.

My father tickled me under the chin, and I giggled, drool spilling over my bottom lip onto his shirt cuff.

"You're crazy." My mother yanked me from Anna's arms. "She said 'Mama.' I heard it." She kissed my cheek with chilled lips and bounced me up and down. "C'mon say it. Mama!"

I started to fidget, then cry.

"There is something wrong with this child," my mother accused as she handed me back to Anna, who calmly rocked me while I howled and sputtered my outrage. My father was already on his way back to the television.

"She said 'Mama'!" Merilee screamed in his direction. "I heard it clear as a bell." She marched back into the living room and poured herself a fresh drink from the pinkish mirrored bar cart she'd recently installed.

According to Anna, I didn't speak again until I was two.

DISSOLVE TO:

INT. HOSPITAL ROOM
MORNING
DAY 17

"She fails to respond to Babinski, which we saw as a positive sign, but the patient lacks a gag reflex and is being fed intravenously."

Daddy is standing along with five residents, listening to Dr. Foreman review my case. With his chin buried in his collar and red-rimmed eyes, my father looks like a lost child. His grief and powerlessness over my condition have no place among these notebook-bearing observers.

While Dr. Foreman continues his assessment, a rotund, bespectacled resident tagged "Dr. Tishman" sidles over to the window and gives a fast wave to the ever-present crowd of fans gathered below, eliciting a chorus of muffled cheers.

Dr. Foreman clears his throat. "Besides head trauma, the patient broke several ribs, fractured her jaw…" He walks past Tishman to the window, yanks closed the blinds, and continues, "…and sustained extensive internal injuries. She had one operation upon arrival to repair her spleen."

Tishman buries his reddening cheeks in his notebook. Dr. Foreman turns back to the group. "Posturing occurred only on day one. The patient has had no seizures since. There has been no clotting, the fluid in her ventricles have receded, and brain swelling has reduced considerably."

"Pupil reflex? Response to stimuli?" a female resident asks.

"None. Pupils are fixed. The patient does not respond to light or pain."

The students scribble furiously.

A basketball star throughout his years at UCLA, Dr. Foreman is my father's age and about two feet his senior. A physician at the tippy top of L.A. Magazine's "Best Of" list, he's a neurosurgeon with incontrovertible capabilities and experience. To question anything Dr. Forman says or does is out of the question.

He is the only person I have ever seen my father defer to about anything.

"That's good, right?" Daddy asks when the lesson concludes.

Dr. Foreman shuffles through the papers on his clipboard as the residents file past him and out the door. Their relief is evident in the bursts of muffled laughter as their steps fade down the hall.

He looks up. "Sorry?"

"What you said about the reflexes and the swelling going down?"

"It's not bad, Mr. Goldstein," he states. "At this point, 'good' is not on the menu. As I've mentioned, the longer your daughter remains unconscious, the lower her odds are for recovery. I'm sorry," he says, his tone softening, "I wish I could be more encouraging."

"I-I…Christ…excuse me." Daddy takes his glasses off and presses his knuckles into his eyes.

Dr. Foreman turns and makes a note on my chart, allowing my father time to compose himself. Daddy takes out his hand-kerchief, blows his nose with two short honks, and repositions his glasses.

"Look, Dr. Foreman—"

"Call me Jim, if you prefer."

"I'll stick with Doctor."

Dr. Foreman nods.

"I-If there is anything that can help," Daddy says, shifting his weight, struggling to find familiar footing, "anything, some piece of equipment you might need—money is not an issue." My father is back in business, trying to suss out the negotiation strategy for my survival.

Foreman's long face droops. He gently places his large hand on my father's back. "Mr. Goldstein, thank you, but we have everything we need."

Daddy coughs his comprehension into his hanky then concentrates on folding it into his pocket.

"Oh, I forgot to mention, your ex-wife called my office," Dr. Foreman says.

My father's head shoots up. "Merilee?"

"She left a message but no phone number. I'd like to get back to her."

"No. No, don't do that."

"It might be helpful for Jackie."

"No. Trust me. You don't know her mother," my father says bitterly.

Dr. Foreman moves to my bedside and lightly presses his fingers around my head. "I know it's not much to go on, but we have been lucky that there haven't been any complications."

"Meaning?"

"In coma patients, there is always the danger of a secondary infection, most commonly pneumonia."

My father pulls himself up into his full height, far below Dr. Forman's shoulders. He inhales, then expels his words in a rush, "If Jackie comes out of the coma, could she…is it possible she could lead a normal life?"

Someone had to ask it. I wish it didn't have to be my father. He squints as if to ward off the bad news.

"Well, that all depends on your definition of normal." The doctor pauses to give my father a chance to weigh this. "Are you a religious man, Mr. Goldstein?"

"No. Anna, she goes to church, but I…" he trails off, then crumples into the chrome chair, burying his face.

"I'll get you some water," Dr. Foreman pours from the pitcher on my bed stand, places the cup on the floor by my father's feet, and lightly touches his shoulder. "You know you can call me any time, night or day."

My father nods.

He waits until Dr. Forman leaves the room then folds into the solace of his own arms.

SLOW DISSOLVE TO:

INT. MALIBU COLONY HOME
1974

Our house was not typical of the other Colony houses of that time. My father was the first person to have entirely knocked down one of the old cottages and put in its place a five-thousand-square foot "Contemporary," completely engulfing the tiny beach lot. A concrete behemoth, it stuck out like Gulliver's sore thumb. Three thick steel arches swept over the roof with no practical purpose other than to intimidate neighboring houses. The effect was an assault and challenge to the quaint old beach shacks that surrounded it. Offended though our neighbors were—letters of protest poured into the *Malibu Times*—in the following few years, barely half of the Colony cottages remained in their original form.

In an attempt to distract my restless, unhappy mother (and keep her off the booze), my father handed her a stack of credit cards and free rein to decorate. With pent-up frustration and unlimited resources, she hurled together paint, fabrics, and furniture like a child clumping colors of Play-Doh into one muddy ball. Every day, boxes or crates arrived at our doorstep: tables, dressers, art, a birdbath. Most items resided only days or weeks before being re-crated and returned. Besides the pink mirrored bar, the modular sofa was the only piece that survived my mother's whims, it being the original inspiration and centerpiece around which she constructed her decorative vision. Often, awakened by footsteps in the hours past midnight, I would go downstairs and find my mother walking through the house, carrying fabric samples from room to room, drinking and fretting.

By the time I was six years old, my father came home late every night and slept in his study (the one room my mother was not allowed to mangle). My mother, who slept most of the day, went out at night to Alice's Bar and drank until last call. Were it not for their misery, the machinations of their comings and goings would have been farcical; my mother listening for my father to close his study door before leaving the house; my father at his desk, waiting to hear the bedroom door click shut before racing into the kitchen for a snack. Weekends were trickier with my father at home, and their system often malfunctioned. An unexpected change in weather would cancel a tennis game, and the whole operation would fall apart.

"I want a divorce!" was my mother's refrain as she stormed through the house with gin (or wine or vodka) sloshing over the rim of her glass.

"You're not getting one fucking penny!" was my father's response in their well-worn duet. "You don't do anything! Get a job for Chris'sake!"

They'd continue up the stairs while I hid under my bed, their voices reverberating off newly sponge-painted, orange walls.

"You're giving me a migraine!" My mother would yell as they stomped past my room, my mother slamming the door in my father's face.

In the silence that followed, Anna would come to my rescue and carry me off to her little nest over the garage. There, with my head safely resting in her lap, I fiddled with the cross around her neck, swinging and tangling it in my fingers as she watched her soap operas.

The room was spare: a single bed, wooden nightstand, and dresser. She had decorated the walls with colorful pictures of Jesus, Mary, and various saints. My favorites shimmered in 3-D, shifting as I walked slowly around them, stepping back and forth to make Jesus' eyes open and shut. At six years old, I already harbored guilt for liking the Jesus pictures, one, because according to my father they weren't "artistic," and two, because even though we weren't religious, Daddy had told me that "Jews don't believe in Jesus." But most of all, I felt guilty because from the very start, I loved Anna more than I loved either of my parents.

I came home from kindergarten one day, surprised to find Anna in my mother's room, sitting on the red velvet pouf in front of the art deco reproduction vanity, my mother crouched over her.

"What are you doing?" I asked.

"Hold still," my mother commanded as Anna turned to look at me. Her hair had been combed loose and swept to one side, spilling shiny and black over her shoulder. Her lips were red, full, and pouty. Her eyes were outlined in black and tilted up at the ends, framed by thick, long, black lashes. Her cheekbones had been sharply accented with blush.

"Look, Jacqueline!" my mother exclaimed. "Isn't Anna pretty?"

I nodded, awed by the sight of her. She was more beautiful than anybody I had ever seen, a Spanish princess in a fairy tale.

Anna, embarrassed by our attention, shook her head and got up, wiping the pouf as if she had left a dirty mark by sitting there. "Thank you, okay, Missus Merilee. I go fix dinner." She bowed her head and walked quickly out of the room. Automatically I turned to follow, but my mother grabbed my hand.

"Would *you* like a makeover, Jacqueline?"

She took a zebra-patterned pillow from her floral bed, put it on the red pouf, and motioned for me to climb aboard. Warily I sat in front of the makeup table. She turned me toward her then took a puffy paintbrush and softly caressed my cheeks, releasing particles of powder that floated up in the air, catching the light. She took one of her lipsticks and dabbed it on my lips, then swept something feathery above my eyes. Excitement bubbled within me. Now I would look just like Anna—Anna with swirls of black hair and cheeks dark and rosy like the cherry wood of a Spanish guitar.

"There!" my mother said with a flourish of her hand. She smiled approvingly, then knelt beside me and turned us to face the mirror. Except for my dark curls, I was the spitting image of my mother. Plastic pink barrettes flanked the sides of my head, pink on the apples of my cheeks, frosty blue eyelids, lips a glossy tangerine. My reflection was airy and pastel as if I'd been dipped headfirst into a container of rainbow sherbet. I burst into tears.

"I hate it!" I screamed and ran out of the room.

Later that night, perched in Anna's window, I watched my mother peel out of the garage in her little red Mercedes, flying over the speed bumps and down Malibu Colony Road.

DISSOLVE TO:

INT. HOSPITAL ROOM
EVENING
DAY 18

ET is broadcasting a feature on my life. Mica, a petite nurse-in-training with long hair and a boyish body and Amanda, her broader superior, wiggle together, backs to my door, bouncing with the excitement of kids in a toy store.

"Man, this is weird," Mica whispers. "I never once seen a couch and shit in a hospital room—never."

"You don't need to whisper. She can't hear you."

"I know but…" Mica glances over at me.

"Trust me, girl!" Amanda, pushing forty, has short, muscular legs and spiky yellow hair, the roots of which betray her Filipino ancestry. She pulls Mica away from the door. "All the big stars get this room," Amanda says with authority then she flops down on my couch yanking Mica with her and corkscrews her rear end into the cushion. "Governors too probably. Hey, I bet our butts are sitting right where Brett Haney's butt's been sitting."

"Look!" Mica points at the mounted TV.

They are showing a clip from *Circle of Life*. My first acting job.

"Aww, she's so young." Mica rests her head on Amanda's shoulder. "That was my Nana's favorite soap opera."

"That was right before she had her boobs done."

"How do you know?" asked Mica. "They seem the same to me."

Not quite. After *Circle,* I'd gone from a B (minus) cup size to a C. I thought the implants wouldn't be that obvious but then *The Enquirer* ran before-and-after photos of me in a bathing suit.

Pierre comes in from the bathroom, checks my IV line, and makes a note on my chart. "You guys need to leave," he admonishes.

"Hey, um, Pierre," Amanda says nonchalantly. "You seen Brett Haney yet?"

"No. I heard he only comes in the morning." Pierre steps to the door and anxiously peers out the porthole.

"Yeah, straight from the gym and all sweaty!" Amanda high-fives Mica.

"Hey, check this," Amanda points back to *ET,* now playing a clip from *First Degree.* She looks over at me and sighs. "That was her last film."

Mica takes a rubber band from her skinny wrist and pulls her stringy blonde hair back into a ponytail. "Yeah. I tried to rent it. All out at Blockbuster."

The *ET* host swivels to face a monitor where a matronly woman appears. A microphone pinned like a brooch, tugs down her turquoise knit sweater. The screen flashes: "Dr. Jan Brenner, Psychiatrist."

The host glances at the notes in his lap. "Dr. Brenner. In your professional opinion, was Jackie Gold's recent behavior consistent with someone harboring suicidal feelings?"

Suicide? There were a few people I wanted to kill, but none of them were me.

Dr. Brenner clears her throat. "Well, we would have to consider Jackie Gold's *entire* history. The stay at Betty Ford, her battles with depression…"

What the? Sure, I'd gotten depressed, but not enough to make me jump off a building. And I'd only gone to Betty once for a fundraiser! Was this to be my legacy?

Amanda picks up the remote and lowers the volume. "You think she was as screwed up as everyone says?"

Pierre shakes his finger at her. "*Is.* She's still alive, remember."

"I wouldn't want her odds," Mica says, as the three of them surround me, gazing down like they're at my viewing.

A public service announcement and a number for a suicide hotline flash on the screen.

"Should we peek at her boobs?" Mica whispers.

"Girrrl!" Amanda punches her arm.

"You know what you could get for a picture of her?"

"One of the orderlies was offered ten grand," Amanda says.

"Come on you two. Time to go," Pierre insists.

"Relax dude," Amanda straightens a corner of my blanket—a gesture I might find touching were her presence less disingenuous.

"I love you, Jackie," and, "We're praying for ya, honey," come muffled shouts from the fans below my window.

Mica snorts "Damn don't those people ever go home?"

The host returns with a preview of the following evening's show then swivels back to the monitor. Suddenly, shockingly, Nicole's face fills the screen.

She looks haggard. Dark circles under her eyes, hair dull and lank.

"Who's that?" Mica points.

The nurses look up at the TV.

"We're here with Nicole Abrams, Jackie Gold's publicist and lifelong best friend."

"Aww, like us," Mica puts her arm around Amanda.

Hell no. *Former* best friend. Brutus to me now! Am I really the only one who hears me yelling?

"Miss Abrams, maybe you can set the record straight."

Yes, *Miss* Abrams. Start with how you ratted me out to the paparazzi.

Nicole squirms in her seat. "All I know is this. The last time I spoke to Jackie she was extremely upset."

But not suicidal. Tell them!

"Suicidal?" The host leans forward.

"Um, maybe."

What? No! What was she saying? My heart pounds as if my chest will explode.

"Jackie had…I mean *has* issues."

My blood pressure monitor starts beeping. Pierre rushes over.

"Holy shit," he frowns at numbers. "Her pressure is at one-eighty. Get the hell out of here. I'm paging Dr. Foreman."

SLOW DISSOLVE TO:

EXT. MALIBU COLONY BEACH
MIDDAY
AUGUST 1977

Our mothers met first, sidling toward each other in straw sun hats. Merilee wore her gold bikini while Steffi was stuffed into a green crocheted number, her breasts like fruit swinging in a woven bag. They both held tumblers, and as they puffed on menthol cigarettes, they extolled the virtues of cold vodka on a hot sunny day.

It was the weekend, Anna's time off. "Don't forget to put on your Sea & Ski," she had reminded me before my father drove her to the bus stop. Anna spoke often in brand names. Like, "Do you want Heinz on that?" She called all soups "Campbells."

Now in my mother's care, I sat down by the shore in my yellow playsuit, building sandcastles, my arms streaked white with sunscreen.

"Lookie, Jacqueleeene," my mother drew my name out. I hated my name, to begin with. I didn't need her making it sound any longer than it already was.

"This is Steffi's little girl. She's going to be in second grade with you this fall." Nicole had choppy blonde hair and bangs like Hayley Mills, and she was wearing the exact purple two-piece I had recently begged for and which my father had rejected as "too mature."

We nodded at one another with the weary look of fellow travelers.

"Don't just stand there like you've got sunstroke, say hello, Nicole." Her mother nudged her forward. Nicole stubbornly took a step back and reclaimed her original stance.

Merilee brought out lounge chairs and our mothers reclined their shiny, buttered bodies on the woven plastic, conversing, ice clattering in their glasses. Nicole and I sat in the sand and began wordlessly digging tunnels. Soon, we competed, each of us digging faster and harder until our fingers unexpectedly met underground. We kept our hands there for a while where no one could see, thumb wrestling and giggling.

On that narrow strip of priceless sand, Steffi and my mother gossiped and commiserated as the tide crept closer to their chairs.

"At least you've got a husband," Nicole's mother said too loudly, slathering another handful of oil onto her long legs.

My mother laughed and shushed her. "Lemme freshen that drink, hon," she said, rising.

"You're getting a burn." Steffi pointed to where my mother's chest and belly had reddened significantly.

"Not you, lucky ducky!" Merilee said, referring to Steffi's mahogany-toned skin.

"I got Portuguese in me," Steffi called out.

Merilee came back out with freshly poured glasses of vodka mixed with grapefruit juice.

Between sips and puffs, Steffi recounted how Nicole's father had left four years earlier right in the middle of a tennis game— a doubles tournament.

"We were ahead three games to two when suddenly Leonard-the-bastard excused himself to get a drink of water and never came back." Steffi stubbed out her cigarette in the sand. "Can you beat that? Never came back. I was so embarrassed I thought I would die." She sounded choked up.

Steffi told Merilee how her ex sent alimony checks with a P.O. box return address. The money just covered her rent on the condominium she shared with Nicole on the other side of Pacific Coast Highway; a two-bedroom with laundry facilities and a partial ocean view. Steffi lowered her voice, which made me know she must be talking about Nicole. I strained my ears to hear.

"…driving me crazy…sent her to my sister's…"

Nicole seemed not to hear a word her mother said. A little tune buzzed at her lips as we dug in the sand.

Then Steffi's voice returned to normal. She went on to say she and Nicole had parked just outside the Malibu Colony gates and pretended to the guard they were scheduled to look at a house for sale. Steffi told Merilee she was "on the prowl."

"I know of a coupla cute ones." My mother winked. "None in the six-figure range, though." She reached into her beach bag and took out a prescription pill bottle. "Migraines," she explained, popping two in her mouth. "They run in the family."

"Divorce runs in mine," Steffi's voice slurred. "You gotta pill for that?"

By sunset, Nicole's and my tunnels crisscrossed the beach in front of my house. The temperature had dropped, and we huddled together, wrapped in my towel to keep each other warm. Our feet stuck out, our toes still digging involuntarily like sand crabs. Our mothers, in their vodka-and sun-soaked state, stared blearily off into the distance, oblivious to us and the cold. Their chatter had slowed to an occasional mumble and as the sun disappeared over the horizon, Steffi held up her empty tumbler signaling *time to go.*

"It was nice sharing the afternoon with you." Steffi handed the glass to Merilee and perched on all fours, steadying herself before pushing up from the lounger. She pulled her stretched-out bikini bottom back in place. Reluctantly, Nicole rose out of our shared mantle and walked shivering to her mother's side.

Steffi took Nicole by the hand and pulled her down the beach. I ran after them holding out the towel.

"Thanks." Nicole reached, but Steffi spanked her hand away.

"Nicole Ann, you do not take what does not belong to you," Steffi snapped, continuing down the beach unsteadily.

Nicole shrugged her shoulders in a *what can you do?* gesture.

"See you when school starts," I called after her.

"Come back again sometime," my mother said drowsily, her eyes almost shut. I'd need help getting her to the house. I hoped my father was home.

INT. MALIBU COLONY HOME
MORNING
FEBRUARY 1976

We spent several hours getting ready. Merilee painted our nails
Peach Passion and set our hair with Dippity Do and hot rollers.
Because it was a "special circumstance," I was even allowed to
wear lipstick.

"Just this once. But don't you dare tell your father."

That morning after Daddy had left for work, my mother told
me she would be keeping me home from school. I glanced over
to where Anna was doing dishes, but she didn't turn around.

"What for?" I asked suspiciously.

"We're going on a short trip."

"Where?"

"Well, Jacqueline, I am taking you to meet your
grandmother."

"On an airplane?"

"No, dum-dum, she lives in Van Nuys," my mother said.

This was news to me and a relief. Van Nuys was only about
ten miles away.

"Then why haven't I ever met her before?"

"Ask *her*."

Now it was almost noon and we hadn't left the house. I had
never seen my anxious mother this anxious. She was even more
nervous than the time Daddy called to say Paul Newman would
be coming for a drink after tennis. That day, my mother went
nuts rearranging the furniture and yelling at poor Anna to make
some kind of crab "ho-re de-vors" she found in a magazine. Then
with all that, Paul Newman didn't even show.

After smoking a pack of Marlboros and trying on twenty
different clothing combinations, Merilee finally settled on a flowered tube top and white capris. I was already dressed in my

newest, most favorite outfit; a purple pantsuit that Nicole had owned and outgrown.

"Oh hon, you're going to fry in that," my mother fretted, looking over at me while she sprayed her hair for the third time. She threw a bunch of makeup into her purse and grabbed a sweater from the pile. "Let's go, Jacqueline," she admonished like I hadn't been waiting for her all morning. Then, she rushed past me, hollering, "I'll be in the car!"

I stepped into my sandals and checked my reflection in the mirror. Not bad, except my mother had sprayed so much Aqua Net that my hair appeared lacquered on like doll hair. She had forgotten to turn off the rollers. I pulled the plug so the house wouldn't burn down and crowned myself with a purple plastic headband.

Now, strapped into the red convertible, my hands gripping the side of the car, we flew over the speed bumps of Malibu Colony Road, and off to grandmother's house we went. With KHJ blaring on the radio, we blew past the security gate, my mother—her face half-hidden behind large black sunglasses, her stiff curls slapping and twisting under a pink silky kerchief—was unfazed by Jackson the guard, who shook his fist and yelled for her to slow down.

"What should I call her?"

We wound through Malibu Canyon, approaching the tunnel. We passed Our Lady of Malibu, the church where Steffi and Nicole sometimes went. Tumbleweeds bounced along the side of the road and disappeared over the cliffs. It was unseasonably hot for winter. Santa Anas were gusting, and the wind swallowed my words as soon as I spoke them.

"Mom? Should I call her Granny or Grandma or what?"

My mother shrugged and licked a bead of sweat off her glossy upper lip. "Someone once painted a picture of Lady Godiva up there." She pointed to the worn rock above the tunnel's entrance. "You can still make out the place where they covered her up."

"Why did they cover her up?"

"She was naked, dum-dum."

I put my arms up and let out a long "hoooooooooot" until the tunnel filled with my echoes. We plowed back into the bright sun, my voice still bellowing behind. On the valley side of the tunnel, the canyon flattened with miles of parched, grassy meadows and rocky hills with horses and cattle pastured in the distance. As the temperature rose, the inside of my pantsuit heated up. I wouldn't give my mother the satisfaction of predicting my discomfort, so I pretended to brush a speck from my chest as I pulled the burning metal of the zipper away from my skin and unzipped the top down as far as I could without her noticing. I caught my reflection in the side mirror; the wind had completely and mercifully unraveled my coif.

As we neared the freeway, my mother swerved around a long train of trucks and motorhomes lined up on the road, their rear ends sticking out.

"Goddamn it," she muttered. "Think they own the world."

"Who?" I asked, and when she didn't answer, I repeated, "WHO?"

"TV people. That's where they shoot *Bonanza*."

"Really?"

"Mmm-hmm. You know little Joe?"

"Yeah?"

"He was one of my regulars at the coffee shop."

"Wow. Was he on horseback?" It wasn't a stupid question. Lots of people rode their horses on the beach and in the fields next to the Colony.

"Well, he drove a Mustang. Close enough, I guess." My mother laughed at her own cleverness.

My grandmother lived off Van Nuys Boulevard in the same eraser pink, stucco condo complex my mother had grown up in. though she'd downsized to a studio apartment.

"Welcome to paradise," my mother smirked, pulling into a vacant parking space. The temperature had shot up to over a hundred and the smog and humidity blanketed the valley air. We entered through an iron gate that led to a kidney-shaped pool. Several young mothers stood in the shallow end, smoking and chatting, holding their beers and cigarettes out of the way every time one of their screaming children splashed too close. I ached to strip off my sticky pantsuit and dive in.

Merilee hustled me past several vending machines and a broken ping pong table and into a three-story building. We walked down a narrow corridor, our feet soundless on the red and black carpet, patterned with clubs and hearts, diamonds and spades like in a casino. The smell of grease clung to walls the color of wet clay. Merilee abruptly stopped in front of a door marked "Number Seventeen" and began fumbling around in her purse.

I reached for the buzzer. She slapped my hand away. "Wouldja' keep your shirt on?" She pulled out her compact and scrutinized herself.

I took off my headband and shook out my tangled hair.

"Listen to me Jacqueline, no matter what she says, don't let her fool you."

"Is she mean?"

"Well, she's a witch is all I can say."

"I want to go home."

"Oh, go on," Merilee said, twisting her fingers through her blonde locks. "You can ring the bell now, she's not going to hurt you."

"What's her name?" I whispered.

"Marva, I told you."

"No, you didn't."

She gave me a little push. "Go on."

I pressed the buzzer and we waited. A minute or so went by, and I put my ear to the door. "I don't hear anything." I knocked.

"Hello?" I called into the keyhole before turning hopefully. "Maybe she forgot."

"Probably passed out." Merilee used her compact to give the door a series of hard raps. From inside, I heard a chair being pushed back and seconds later, the door swung open.

She sure didn't look like any grandmother I'd ever seen, nor did she appear witch-like. In kitten heels, she was close to six feet tall with wavy, platinum hair that slanted over one eye. Blazing red lipstick seeped into the deep smoker's lines that ringed her mouth. She wore her gauzy, animal print blouse unbuttoned, revealing sun-whipped cleavage and the top of a lacy brassiere. Under beige culottes hung a pair of shapely legs that, except for the extra pouches of skin at the knees, matched my mother's. In her hand was a giant plastic cup from 7-Eleven.

"You're forty-five minutes late," Marva said, looking down at her bony wrist. She was not wearing a watch.

"We've been ringing forever," Merilee snapped.

"Buzzer's broke."

Nervously, I reached for my mother, but her fingers turned to mercury, slipping through my hand as she sauntered past Marva into the dark apartment. My grandmother frowned. Then, turning to me, she smiled. Sharp lines shot out from the corners of her pale blue eyes.

"So, you're Jackie." She pressed something moist and crumpled into my hand.

"Please call her Jacqueline," my mother sang from across the room.

"Well, okay, Miss Fancy Pants," Marva croaked brightly. "I gave you five dollars, now pucker up."

Though her face was crumbly and old, I could see the blueprint from which my mother had inherited her good looks. She swooped down for a kiss and I swerved, giving her a quick peck on the cheek.

"Don't let your mom make you buy something *practical*," she said, flattening the word into a dry pancake. She laughed and lurched into a raspy cough that seemed to go on forever. I glanced over to see whether my mother had heard this remark, but she was looking off in another direction. Marva pulled a tissue from under the cuff of her blouse and gave one last hack into it.

I stuffed the bill into my pocket. "Thanks, um?"

She took my hand. "You call me Nana. That's what I called my grandmother."

She led me into her apartment. A large, noisy air conditioner blew full force against the curtains, making the room uncomfortably cold. A chemical smell singed the air, like chlorine or cleaning fluid. My mother sat erect on a nubby gold sofa, goosebumps covering her arms. Pieces of sheets and blankets stuck out from under the cushions. I wondered whether it would be rude or helpful of me to tuck them in, then decided to pretend I hadn't seen it. The sofa's arms were worn as if they'd been used as a scratching post. I checked for a cat but didn't see one.

Marva picked up a pair of pink bedroom slippers and tossed them into a narrow closet by the front door. Then she crossed back to where I stood. "Want some free advice?" She swayed above me like one of those tall, skinny palm trees that appear incapable of supporting themselves. A cluster of keys swung from a pink and white lanyard clipped to her belt. "Always put on fresh underwear and makeup before bed."

"Mother!" Merilee pounded the sofa next to her and motioned me to sit. I ignored her.

"Why?"

"In case there's a fire." Marva winked a few times and raised one eyebrow.

"I don't get it."

My mother pulled me down on the sofa. "What she means is, in case there's a fire*man*."

"I still don't get it."

"Good!" My mother glared a warning at Marva.

There wasn't much furniture to speak of; a glass and chrome coffee table pushed against the wall leaving room for the sofa bed when extended. In the kitchenette, two folding chairs with fussy gingham cushions sat parked at a card table covered by a cherry-patterned tablecloth. A worn, rust-colored carpet covered the floor except for a rectangle of dull, white linoleum in front of the refrigerator, sink, and two-burner stove. No pictures or paintings, not even a poster. Instead, a hodgepodge of wallpaper covered the apartment: a puppy and kitten jamboree next to a pattern of pumpkins and fall leaves; in the breakfast area, cheerful teapots romped across the wall. Clearly, Merilee had inherited more than just good looks from her mother. I prayed their taste in décor would not pass down to me.

My grandmother kicked open a television tray and set down a plate of Ritz crackers top-heavy with Cheese Whiz.

"What are you drinking?"

I waited for my mother to answer, then realized Marva was talking to me.

"Um..."

"How's fruit punch?"

"Great," I said.

Marva walked to the fridge. From the back, her large, angular frame appeared crooked. She reminded me of Rosalind Russell, the head nun in *The Trouble with Angels*. Except, of course, for the outfit.

"I'll have whatever *you're* having, Mother," Merilee called after her.

"I'm serving fruit punch. That's what's on the menu."

My mother slumped down on the couch and rolled her eyes to the ceiling like an exasperated teenager.

There was no reading material visible. A bookcase overflowed with miniature glass figurines: bunnies, ducks, chickens, cats with big eyes and plastic whiskers. I was dying to examine them, to weigh the tiny creatures in my hands but was afraid my mother would see this as a sign that I was consorting with the enemy.

Marva returned carrying a bottle of Hi-C and two tumbler glasses filled with ice. She set them on the floor. "Sweet stuff. You got a sweet tooth?" She kneeled in front of us, pouring the punch.

"I guess."

"You like cookies?"

"Uh-huh."

"What's your favorite?"

"Um, Mallomars?"

"Well, I don't have those."

"That's okay," I said.

"I have Nilla wafers."

"Those are great too."

With a grunt, Marva hoisted herself back on her feet, went to the kitchen, and retrieved a box of cookies from one of the cupboards. I was so thirsty I drank down half the glass of punch before she came back.

"If your mom had told me you liked Mallomars, I would've bought 'em," she said pointedly, looking over at my mother who stuck her tongue out in return.

"Really, whatever you have is fine, um, Nana," I said, testing the word. It felt good to say.

She handed me the whole box then sat on the arm next to me. "Now, how's your dad?"

"He's um, fine?" I glanced at my mother, then took out a cookie, bit into it, and nodded to show my grandmother how much I liked it.

"You musta gotten those dark curls from his side of the family." She patted my head.

"I guess." From the corner of my eye, I saw my mother stiffen.

"You know, I only met him that one time at the wedding, but he seemed nice enough. Short, though. You small for your age?"

"Don't be stupid, Mother! Do not answer that question, Jacqueline." My mother threw daggers at me with her eyes.

"As I was saying," Marva continued, her voice slightly rising, "I only met him the one time. I wanted to come when you were born, but I was not invited. I just don't want you to have the impression that your Nana didn't want to meet you." From my place on the couch between Marva and my mother, I could feel the air beginning to pulse, hot and electric. I had to pee. The bathroom door was covered in daisy wallpaper, the portal toward a brighter, friendlier room.

"I need to—" I started.

"I guess I'm just not up to her standards," Marva continued. "Your mama didn't use to have such high standards."

"Shut up, Mother."

"Oh, I'm just making *small* talk is all." Marva put finger quotes around the word small. "That's a joke." My grandmother winked at me. Reflexively, I winked back.

My mother yanked away the box of cookies I was holding.

"Why?"

"You've had plenty."

"But—"

"Gather your things, Jacqueline."

Her voice had taken on an all too familiar tone, low and vibrating like thunder. I counted the seconds, waiting for the lightning strike.

"Did I say something bad? Did I, Sugar Pop?" My grandmother's eyes were wide.

"I-I don't…"

"She doesn't like Jewish people, Jacqueline." My mother cut me off. "But she won't come right out and say it."

"What on earth? I never said—"

"No, Mom," I jumped to my grandmother's defense before remembering it would infuriate my mother, "all she said was—"

"Shut up, Jacqueline." Merilee stood now, her body shaking. "You don't know who you are dealing with. I could tell you tales that would curdle your milk." She took a step toward Marva.

"Merilee," Marva said, standing her ground. "That is enough now. Do you hear me? Enough."

Merilee raised her arm, and for a split second, I thought she was actually going to strike her mother. But then she swiveled toward me. "C'mon!" She grabbed my hand and pulled me up sharply. I barely managed to set the Hi-C on the coffee table without spilling before she yanked me out the door. Back down the heart and spade carpeted hallway we went, my mother pulling me by the wrist, past the ping pong table and vending machines, the screaming splashing kids and their mothers, and out the pool's iron gates.

Merilee collapsed, sobbing into the driver's seat of the Mercedes, mascara leaking between her fingers. "Fucking drunk!" She emitted a low scream and threw herself against the steering wheel, honking the horn which made her pop back up.

I climbed into my side. My heart raced, the seat was burning, and I still had to pee. "Let's just go." I prodded her arm to start the car.

My mother stared at me as if she were struggling to interpret what I had said. Then she pulled herself up to the rearview mirror. "I look like shit!" She yanked open her purse and began angrily reapplying her makeup. She dipped one finger in a pot of gingery gloss and hammered her lips. "Now do you understand why we don't visit?"

I didn't. I was mad. I thought Marva was nice and kind of interesting. She had seemed interested in me which I found very appealing. And she hadn't seemed drunk. At least not the way I'd seen my mother. But I didn't want to fight and my bladder was killing me and I was dying from the heat. "I understand, okay? Let's go."

Merilee wound her kerchief around her head and turned the key in the ignition. As the car lurched backward, I heard a gate clang shut.

"Wait!" Marva ran alongside the car, waving her long arms.

"Mom stop!" I yelled.

Merilee screeched the car to a halt. "Christ!"

Panting, Marva held on to the door of the Mercedes and motioned with one hand for us to wait while she caught her breath.

"Merry Christmas, Sugar Pop," she wheezed, handing me a small package wrapped in holiday paper. She tossed another one onto the seat next to my mother, who stared straight ahead.

"Okay then." With a shoo-fly gesture, Marva waved us off.

Back on the highway, my mother sobbed and smoked while I considered the gift in my lap. It was lumpy, wrapped in gold and red paper illustrated with angels and baby Jesuses. My fingers crumpled along the outlines of the package trying to get a clue as to its contents. I definitely hadn't expected a Christmas present in February. I felt lopsided. We should have brought flowers. I could have made a Valentine card.

I hunched low in my seat and picked at one of the pieces of Scotch tape. Given my mother's mood, I knew I was taking a chance opening Marva's present, but I didn't have the patience to wait until I was alone. Carefully, I pulled apart the wrapping and discovered a bundle of Kleenex. Inside the Kleenex was a miniature glass duck, translucent yellow with a red beak. Attached by a chain through her tail were three glass ducklings.

"Oh. It's so cute." I held it up to the sunlight, careful not to let the wind carry it away; traffic was moving fast, and my mother drove well above the speed limit.

"It's cheap," she said, glancing at me. Her kerchief had slipped. Hair danced furiously around her face. "And it's not new, she's had that one for years."

I wanted to smack her, but instead, I reached over and pulled a strand of hair from where it was stuck in the corner of her mouth. I folded away the Jesus paper to bring later to Anna, then I placed the delicate duck family back in their tissue nest and pressed them deep into my front pocket. "Can we please go to a gas station? I really have to pee."

Merilee stabbed out her cigarette. Sooty tears spilled out from under her dark glasses.

"Mom?"

I picked up her present. It was larger than mine and heavy; wrapped in some kind of anniversary paper, shiny silver and blue. I held it up to my ear and gently shook it.

"What do you think it is?" I asked, hoping to change her mood. She kept staring ahead, so I opened it. Three rocks plopped onto my lap. I picked them up and rattled them in my hand looking for the meaning in them, willing them to be kittens or sheep; something I could show to my mother to say, "See! You got a present too." But there was no denying it. They were just rocks picked out of the dirt somewhere.

Before my mother could see, I threw them out the window then took my present from my pocket and threw it out too. I watched the little ducks fly from their tissue, skip off the tire of a pickup truck, and disappear.

DISSOLVE TO:

INT. HOSPITAL ROOM
MORNING
DAY 20

Brett steps through my door sporting a big grin like a suitor about to whisk a dozen roses from behind his back. For a second I'd almost forgotten how dazzling his smile is with those perfect white teeth and dimpled chin. I'd go weak in my knees if I could feel them.

He wears a Dodgers cap, not because he likes baseball but to cover his bald spot. With so many photographers camped around the hospital, Brett isn't taking chances. On his last film, he used a small round hair piece pinned on top of his head like a yarmulke.

He shrugs off his jacket and hauls the chrome chair over to face me "I've got news," he whispers in my ear.

I've got news too. Dr. Foreman came in this morning and removed the wiring from around my jaw. I wonder how long it will take Brett to notice. Like most actors, he has a kind of built-in narcissism that narrows the aperture of his attention.

Instead of roses he pulls a script from his back pocket and waves it in front of my face. "I've been offered the Reiner film. Isn't that incredible? They're replacing Eddie Jenks. The studio couldn't get insurance on him. I heard he's back in rehab. Penny is ecstatic."

The Reiner film. I'd been offered the female lead right before the accident. Brett had been jealous, said he hated Reiner's pictures. Apparently, he's changed his mind. The irony is breathtaking. Of course he had to take it, it's the breakout role he's been longing for. And of course they want him. With the publicity surrounding my "suicide attempt," Brett Haney is sizzling hot property.

"We start next week, babe. But don't worry, I'll come just as often. There's one week on location in New York, but that's not for a while. The only thing is, why would Reiner want me? I'm not very funny."

It's true, he's not funny. At least not in a comedic way. Brett, however, is charismatic and beautiful. He emerged from the womb destined to be a movie star. Not me. God may have created me in His/Her image, but not up to Hollywood's standards. I paid big bucks to be recreated.

"Oh, hey." Brett looks at my face as if I have suddenly sprung into focus. He runs his fingers along my jaw. His touch is soft and gentle, his nails manicured. In his teens, he was a down-to-the-bloody-quick, compulsive nail-biter, but now when he has the urge to chew, he pulls out an Emory board. He touches my lips with one finger, opens my mouth. My front teeth are missing.

"God. Goddammit!" He takes a deep breath and pounds his fists against his stomach, pulls the chair closer to my bedside, and inhales several times, catching his breath.

Poor Brett. He's not cut out for tragedy. He still has both sets of grandparents and sends them cards for every holiday. Even with his acting fears and insecurities, he's an optimist at heart.

"It's okay, sweetheart. D-Don't worry, they can do stuff for that, you know. They can just implant you a whole new tooth…teeth. Can you hear me, honey? Honey? If you can hear me just give me a sign. Blink your eyes or—"

"Knock, knock?" Nurse Dani sticks her head in the door.

Brett draws himself up and adjusts his cap. "Mornin', Dani. Come on in."

"Well hello, you two," Dani says in a voice matching her polka-dotted uniform. "Hey, Brett, she looks super today!"

"Oh yes, hey." Brett tries to mirror her tone.

"And thanks, YOU," Dani says playfully, miming a flirty swish of an invisible skirt.

Brett looks confused. "Thanks?"

"For the signed photo. To a special gal, your fan Brett Haney?"

Somehow, I'd missed that little exchange. Little did she know Brett's assistant forged all his autographs.

"Oh right, glad you got it."

"It was the talk of the fourth-floor nurses' station!" She shimmies her shoulders then comes to my bedside and adopts a concerned tone. "How's our patient?"

Dead yet? is what she wants to say. She runs her fingers down the IV tubing and replaces one of the empty bags.

Get away from me, you conniving bitch. I picture Amber, my soap opera character from *Circle of Life* grabbing Dani by the collar of her dotted pajamas and shoving her out the door.

Brett sulks over and slumps down on the couch. "They took that wire off her jaw. Other than that…" He drops his face in his hands.

Dani makes a note on my chart then lays it on the foot of my bed. *On my actual foot.*

"I know how hard this can be. I've watched many families go through this."

Brett nods.

"I've seen miracles," Dani says softly.

"Really?" Brett asks from behind his fingers.

"Mmm-hmm. Just this morning a patient, a little black girl, twelve, went home, almost as good as new."

"What happened to her?" Brett takes a Kleenex from a box on the coffee table and swipes at his nose.

"Car accident, poor baby. We lost her mom."

"Wow," Brett exhales. "I'm sure glad I don't have your job."

Dani marches over, aligns the magazines on the coffee table, then moves to the window and fiddles with the blinds.

"Don't want the sun in her eyes," she trills.

"Oh thanks, sorry I-I should've done that."

"Nonsense, just part of my job. Besides, I like to keep busy." As if to prove her point she traverses the room, plucking up several used tissues and depositing them in the trash.

"Don't you ever take a break?" Brett asks.

"Not in this part of the hospital." Dani puts my chart back in the holder, gives my tubes and IVs another once-over, then leans back against my bed facing my boyfriend. Her long, stocking-covered legs are stretched out in front of her. One toe of her Stride Rites traces circles on the floor. "If you'd like to talk about anything, y'know, or need a friendly shoulder, there's always a fresh pot of coffee in the staff room."

I have never felt so outmaneuvered. Here I am, lying face-up like an abandoned lab experiment, greasy patches of hair sprouting out from my shaved and bandaged head, cracked lips half-open, semi-toothless, tubes rooting in and out of my arms, belly, and between my legs, all while Dani offers solace to my boyfriend. Almost my fiancé! Fortunately, it seems Brett is too stricken and preoccupied to notice Dani's advances.

"Hey, that would be real nice. But right now, I've gotta get to rehearsal." He comes to the other side of my bed, leans down, and brushes his lips against my cheek. It is the first time he's kissed me since the accident, and I can't help feeling smug in front of Dani. Like I've nabbed the crown off the Homecoming Queen.

"Jackie, honey, I love you, sweetheart." His eyes well and he shakes his head.

"I'm sure she can hear you," Nurse Dani says. "Coma patients are aware of a lot more than we give them credit for."

She has that right.

SLOW DISSOLVE TO:

INT. MALIBU COLONY HOME
LATE AFTERNOON
1977

It was a Friday afternoon, the week before I turned nine. I'd come home from school to find my father and Anna, somber-faced, sitting on the yellow cubes of the modular couch with an orange square empty between them. Right off, I knew that seat was meant for me. My father was rarely home before dark, and Anna always greeted me with a smile. I must have done something terrible, but what? I tried to remember as I lay down my books. Had Daddy found the planter where I stashed my bobby socks on the way to school? Or had Anna found the candy Nicole and I had stolen from the pharmacy?

"Sit down, Jackie," my father said in the gravest tone I had ever heard him use and patted the vacant seat. This was serious. I lowered slowly, knowing I was about to be given a shock. I wished I were bigger so my feet could reach the ground.

"Your mother is gone," my father said simply.

"Gone," I repeated.

Anna had tears in her eyes. I had only ever seen Anna cry during soap operas when something tragic happened to one of her characters.

"Did she die?" I asked my father.

"No, of course not, honey." Daddy appeared confused and began waving his hands around like a frustrated toddler.

"She's alive?"

Anna attempted to rescue him. "Jackie, what he is TRYING to say—" She had, by now, learned to speak English primarily from watching the soaps. As a result, her phrasing was dramatic and intense regardless of the subject. "Your mother has chosen to GO. And live in another place. She still loves you very VERY much, and I'm sure that she will LOVE to visit you soon."

"Where is she?" I asked my father.

"We aren't sure." He turned to Anna, who nodded.

"Didn't she leave a message or something?"

My father shook his head.

"Did you check with the answering service?"

"Jackie—"

"Well then, how do you know she's not dead?"

"She wrote me a letter," my father said.

"What did it say?" I demanded. "I want to read it."

"No, Jackie."

"Did she write one to me?"

Anna and my father exchanged worried looks. My father regarded me sorrowfully and shook his head.

We sat in silence. I could hear myself breathing. My heart beat fast and hard at the spot where I touched my chest during the morning pledge of allegiance. What would my friends say? A couple kids had parents who were divorced, but that was different. Their parents had left each other. My mother had left *me*. I suddenly felt nauseous. A sunburned feeling poured down my face and shoulders. I stood up from the couch then became dizzy, sat down, and started to cry. Anna pulled me to her. My father moved over a crack in the modular to sit closer.

How could she be gone? Her scent was still in the room; menthol cigarettes, Dentyne gum. I couldn't remember when I had last seen her. That morning? Or the night before? What had she been wearing? What had we said to one another?

Until then, I hadn't given my mother's presence or absences much thought. She was like those neighbor characters on TV who made appearances but didn't alter the lives of the main people. On the occasions that we spent time together, I was mostly irritated or plotting my escape. It had never occurred to me that she might feel the same way about me. This was terrible. A real "shit storm" as my father would say. What if I never saw her again? What if I never had the chance to tell her what an awful mother she was and that I would never forgive her? I wished she *had* died so I wouldn't have to think about her anymore, then I hated myself for wishing such a terrible thing.

A few nights earlier, she had come to my room dressed in a tight pink pantsuit with the top buttons open and her boobs pushed up. Those undone buttons embarrassed me. I pretended to be asleep when she whispered "G'night" and she "wuvved" me, her whiskey breath steaming my ear.

Did she take all her belongings? Like the glittery earrings that fell almost to her shoulders, or her silk scarves? Or the rows of high heels I secretly dressed up in? Had she left anything for me?

Next week was my birthday! She was supposed to drive Nicole and me to the Santa Monica Pier. She was ruining my birthday! I hated her. I began to sob again. My father grasped one of my hands and Anna held my forehead steady the way she did whenever I was sick and needed to vomit. I wanted to tell them what I was thinking and feeling, but I was afraid if they knew about my mean, selfish thoughts they wouldn't feel as sorry for me, so I just stayed there, crying, wedged between them.

The doorbell rang, a formal sound at the beach. Normally our guests walked right in, preceded only by the sound of our garden hose washing sand off their feet. Anna raised her brows at my father, who shrugged and shook his head. Had my mother returned? Why would she ring the bell? Anna released me to my father and went to open the door. Through my tangle of hair and tears, I made out the freckled face of Caroline Richards, a girl who lived a few doors away, and her nanny, Cappie, who was related to Vi. Caroline and I weren't friends. We went to the same school but were in different classes. Everyone referred to Caroline's father as "Richie Richards." Nicole thought Caroline was stuck-up, but Nicole thought everyone who lived in the Colony was stuck-up except for me. I couldn't imagine why she was here.

"Caroline and Cappie, PLEASED to see you!" Anna spoke so brightly it made my eyes squint.

"Mrs. Goldstein set up a playdate for the girls," Cappie said, scanning the room and stepping her imposing frame into the doorway. "Caroline had the chance to go to a party, but she turned down the invitation because she had made a com-*mit*-ment," Cappie said pointedly.

Caroline stared at her patent leather shoes, a sour expression on her face. She wore a sparkly red party dress, her strawberry-blonde hair pulled back with a velvet ribbon. She was clearly hoping not to find me home.

Anna swiveled to us with a silent plea for help.

"Um, hello." My father waved, squirming.

Cappie fixed her eyes on me. "You sick?"

My reputation hung on how I handled this moment. It would be one thing if my mother *had* died, but no way was Caroline Espers going to school on Monday, telling everyone how I was crying because my crappy mother left. I wiped the snot off my nose with my shirtsleeve. Then, I wadded up all my rotten thoughts, my anger, sadness and hurt, and crammed them down so deep inside myself I would spend a lifetime stumbling accidentally upon them, like land mines.

I stood. "Hi, Caroline." I whipped my mouth into a smile.

"Hi," she said unenthusiastically.

I ran up and hugged her stiff frame. "Oh, Caroline," I exclaimed. "We are going to have so much fun!" Then I grabbed her hand and dragged her off to my room.

DISSOLVE TO:

INT. HOSPITAL ROOM
MORNING
DAY 21

"Right below the knee, that's the reflex point," Anna instructs as the sounds of Enya waft from the boom box.

Brett's hands search nervously along my legs. "Here?"

Though I can't feel a thing, I like that he's touching me. He looks great; the weight he lost is back on, and from the contours under his polo shirt, he's back at the gym. In prep for the film, his hair's been lightened and he's acquired a tan. Funny story: Once when we were making love, I'd accidentally given him a hand job with my tanning lotion turning his entire groin area orange. Needless to say, there'd been a lot of carrot jokes. Good times.

"Let me show you." Anna takes his hands, guiding them to the spot.

"Maybe if we put on different music," my father offers, pressing the player's eject button. Thank God. That dreary Enya has been on ever since Dani's shift. I'm positive she plays it to torture me.

Daddy parses through the bag of cassettes and CDs. "How about Mahler?"

"Too slow," Anna replies. "She needs excitement."

"Aerosmith was her favorite…*is* her favorite," Brett corrects, pointing.

My father slips the disc out of its sleeve, clacks it into place and presses play. "Walk this Way" blares from the speakers.

"Good, Sidney." Anna nods approvingly.

I wish I could save them the effort. In my condition, Steven Tyler naked in my bed couldn't get a rise out of me.

Earlier in the week, Brett, Anna, and Daddy had met with a "coma-stimulation specialist" who had recommended a series of exercises and protocols. Now, after a mix of music and prodding and poking, the only thing I feel is the gas pain I woke up with.

"I don't know what else to do." Brett sniffles. "I feel like if Jackie were here, she would tell us all, 'Quit bugging me.'"

"Jackie is here," Anna says kindly, patting Brett's arm.

"Oh God, I-I'm sorry, that's not what I meant." He turns away and goes to the window. "Don't these folks have jobs?" he says, peeking through the blinds at the crowd in the parking lot. "It's not even nine o'clock and there's fifty of 'em already."

"Good morning, everyone." Nurse Dani saunters in holding two Styrofoam cups. "Coffee anyone?" She's wearing a crisp, pink uniform with short sleeves that stand stiffly out from her arms. "I have sugar packets in my pocket if anyone needs."

"Oh, hello, Dani," Anna says wearily, easing back to give Dani room to check my vitals and IVs.

"Coma-stim?" Dani sets down the cups, straightens out a kink in my feeding tube, and squeezes the hanging sac until it flows smoothly.

"We are trying," Anna says.

"Foreman says it's a bunch of crapola," my father says.

"Not 'crapola.' He said it wasn't scientific," Anna counters.

"Same thing."

"We agreed to try everything, right?" Anna asks, looking around for confirmation.

Dani nods enthusiastically. Her long curls bob up and down her back like copper Slinkys as she bounces to the rhythm of the music. "Did they tell you about the stim-puppy?"

"Puppies!" My father shakes his head, incredulous.

Anna holds up her hand. "Sidney."

"Seriously? They allow dogs in the hospital?" Brett asks.

"Only therapeutically. Well, besides the research lab." She winks.

"Should we get a puppy?" Brett asks my father and Anna.

"How the hell is a puppy gonna help?" Daddy demands, throwing up his arms.

I'm with Daddy. Not even Lassie could save me. Besides, I'm not really a dog person. Would love a stim-cat though.

"Sidney, please. Who knows what can help?" Anna nods to Dani. "We want the puppy."

Dani takes out a pen from her shirt pocket. "I'll put on her chart that you've requested it."

Knowing Dani, she's requesting a pit bull.

"Anna." Daddy motions to her. "Come on, it's time."

"One minute, Sidney." Anna turns to Dani. "You don't think all of this is crazy?"

Dani shakes her head. "It's not crazy at all."

Says the nurse angling for my boyfriend.

Brett leans over my body and places his fingers tentatively under my knee.

Dani moves swiftly to his aid. "There are two kinds of reflexes; voluntary and involuntary. The trouble is figuring out which is which," she says, taking Brett's hands into her own with the earnestness of Annie Sullivan teaching Helen to sign. She molds Brett's hand into a fist. I'm thinking any moment she'll take him to the sink and teach him to say "Waaaater." Instead, she raps his knuckles sharply below my knee.

"Nothing's happening," Brett says.

Anna joins Brett at my side. "Let me try."

Daddy shakes his head and stands by the window. The gas pains are getting worse. I hope someone presses on my stomach. Maybe I'll fart and get some relief.

"C'mon, Jackie baby," Brett whispers.

"Like this?" Anna asks.

"Yeah, um, you're doing it right, she's just not responding. Oh look, see, there, her foot. Do it again."

Sure enough, my foot twitches. Dani has probably attached an invisible string to my toe.

"Sidney, look!"

"You heard what she said. These are involuntary reflexes." My father goes into the bathroom and closes the door.

"Well, there's a way to find out," Dani says. She moves to the base of my bed, carefully frees my foot from under the covers, then fishes a set of keys from her pocket and digs one into the nail bed of my big toe.

"What are you doing?" Anna asks, alarmed.

"Pain reflex. It's one of the techniques the doctors use." Dani continues grinding the key.

Though I can't feel anything other than my worsening stomachache, I'm pretty pissed off at Brett for passively watching Dani gouge my flesh. If I ever do wake up, I will be bringing this issue to marriage counseling.

"Stop, please." Anna puts her hand on Dani's arm. "Enough."

"I'm so sorry," Dani says, startled. "I didn't mean to upset you." She drops the keys back into her pocket with a jangle.

"It's not you, dear." Anna takes Kleenex from her purse and presses it to her eyes.

Brett takes a breath and shakes his whole body like a dog after a bath. He checks his watch then retrieves his script. Pink plastic tabs stick out where he's marked his scenes. "Time to skedaddle," He kisses my cheek then picks up the framed photo of himself and examines it critically before replacing it on the nightstand.

Daddy enters from the bathroom as Anna retrieves his sport coat from the chair.

"Okay, Sidney. Let's get you back to work." She hands Daddy his Jacket, collects her purse and sweater, and turns to Dani. "I want you to know how much we appreciate what you and the staff have been doing for Jackie."

"Of course, Mrs. Goldstein. If you have any questions, please feel free to call me anytime, here or at home." She hands a card to Anna.

"That is generous of you." Anna leans down and kisses my forehead.

"Call us if anything changes," my father says, shrugging his jacket up over his shoulders.

"Of course, Mr. Goldstein," she says with a little curtsy. "By the way," she lowers her voice, "there are a few reporters outside the main lobby. Take the service elevator and go out through the cafeteria."

Brett pulls his cap lower. "Thanks for the warning."

As Anna and Daddy walk out the door, Dani taps Brett's shoulder and holds out her card.

"Here's one for you," she says like it was an afterthought.

She slides it into Brett's jacket pocket and gives it a pat pat.

"Oh, I don't think…okay well, thanks," Brett says in the polite way he reserves for women who've shoved not just phone numbers in his pockets but panties.

Dani shuts the door behind Brett and heaves the sigh of an adolescent who has accidentally brushed up against the cutest boy in class. I am grateful Brett hasn't responded to her overtures, but how long can that last? Especially when one's girlfriend is so un-sexily rotting away in a coma.

Dani ejects Arrowsmith and puts the Enya CD back on and waltzes about my room straightening up, throwing away tissues and paper cups as if she's had a party. What I wouldn't give for a nanny-cam.

The pain in my stomach sharpens and my belly swells tighter like a balloon. Is this jealousy? A stim-reaction? A delay of my pain reflex? Has Dani poisoned my breakfast? My stomach feels like a volcano erupting and my heart beats faster and faster.

Beepbeepbeepbeep.

Ringringringring.

Dani turns to the monitors and gasps. "Oh my God." The blinking red lights flash in her eyes.

She hesitates, then dashes into the hall.

INT. HOSPITAL ROOM
4:15 A.M
DAY 22

Rain pounds my window. A piece of tin, loose from a corner of the frame, pings with a fast drip-dripping rhythm that counters the slow, steady drops of blood going into my arm. The transfusion is replacing the buckets of blood I lost when the stitches in my spleen ruptured, causing me to go into hypovolemic shock. According to the attending surgeon, were it not for the "swift" actions taken by Nurse Dani, I would have been a goner. My pal Dani. I am uncomfortable with this new twist in our relationship and suspicious of Dani's dash out the door when it would have been far "swifter" to reach over and press the call button.

Half an hour earlier, Pierre stopped by to empty my bag of stomach fluid, check on the progress of my transfusion, and make several notes on my chart.

Pierre's no saint, but I trust him more than the others. He pays close attention to my vitals and is always professional with my care. I've decided to give him the picture of Brett as a present if I make it out alive. That is, providing he doesn't steal it first.

Now, Nurse Florence rushes in, panting, a plastic scarf tied under her multiple chins. Her orange raincoat is snapped neck to knees over her pink-hearted uniform, her white shoes squeak from the water lodged in rubber soles. She circles my bed, zeroing in on the inside of my elbow, and stops to examine the adhesive strip that covers the needle of my newest IV.

"What happened to you, girl?" Flo clucks, intoning her displeasure as if I am her wayward child who's gone and done that thing she's warned me about a dozen times. Her tongue is stained yellow with tobacco and late shift coffee and her breath smells sour as she mouths the words to a song playing in her head. She hacks into her sleeve then pours herself a glass of water from my nightstand, drinks it in a shot, reaches over me, and pulls a strip of antiseptic wipes from a drawer.

I'm reminded of another rainy night when I was maybe five or six. My mother had stumbled into my room crying (as she often did) dragging an old afghan of Daddy's that she kept throwing away and that he kept saving. It was wet from where he'd retrieved it that evening from the trashcan outside. She was mumbling parts of a lullaby she insisted I knew but that I had no recollection of ever hearing. "The north wind did blow and what does the poor robin do then. Remember baby?"

I pretended to fall asleep as she hummed and sobbed and tucked the smelly blanket hard up under my chin.

Wheezing, Flo B. squints down at my face as if reading a menu without the benefit of glasses. Still in her raincoat and without stopping to don the customary sterile gloves, she hurriedly unwinds the bandage on my forehead, tears open one of the packets, and swabs the coarse stitches of my Frankenstein scar. The smell of antiseptic is perfume compared to Flo's breath and the sting of the alcohol reassuringly familiar, like Bactine on a skinned knee. With uncharacteristically shaky hands Flo B. winds a fresh layer of gauze around my skull then tucks the frayed end under, wipes the sweat from her own forehead, and slides her palms down the front of her thighs. Puffing and huffing, she lumbers to the window, cracks it open, and leans into the fresh air. I hear the drone of traffic and faint sounds of the crowd, reduced now in the rain. I imagine the media hauling tarps, covering their cameras. I wonder if Nicole is among them and if she'll ever work up the guts to see me.

Flo lowers the blinds and returns to my bed. She brings her face close and peers down into my half-open eyes as though looking for keys dropped down a subway grate.

"Anybody home?" she whispers, snapping her thick fingers in front of my eyes. Glancing at the door, she pinches open the clasp of her pocketbook and pulls out a disposable camera.

She aims, shoots—nothing happens.

"Oh Lord, please Jesus," she pants. Sweat drips from her forehead and the odor of her fear fills the room. Again, she checks the door, then fiddles for a few seconds, winds the camera until it clicks, and rapidly fires off all twenty-four shots of my supine body from twenty-four different angles. Then she shoves the camera into her purse and moves out as fast as her bulk will allow.

Someone was going to do it. It might as well be Flo.

SLOW DISSOLVE TO:

INT. MALIBU COLONY HOME
AFTERNOON
JUNE 1980

In June, Malibu is socked in with fog. It can be sunny everywhere else, even five minutes inland. But on the Pacific Coast Highway, cars drive with their headlights on.

With only a week remaining in sixth grade, class had been dismissed for a half day. The school bus dropped me at the guard gate, and after a few pleasantries with Mr. Jackson, I skipped home through the mist, anticipating whatever afternoon snack of freshly baked cookies or cake Anna would have waiting on the counter.

I turned the knob of the front door and found it, curiously, locked. Detouring around the walkway, I came in through the beach entrance, laid my books on the cluttered dining table (a place reserved for items in limbo), and fished my hidden bobby socks from my bag.

"Hello?" I called out.

The house was oddly quiet. Normally, Anna would be puttering around the kitchen, watching soap operas and practicing her English. Today, there were no sweet smells of her baking. No snacks waited on the counter, save for the usual bowl of fruit. Disappointed, I popped a couple of grapes in my mouth, walked into the living room, sat down on the modular couch, and put my feet up on the coffee table. Blisters had formed where my tennis shoes rubbed against the back of my bare ankles. I bent down to put on my socks when I heard a man's voice upstairs. Had someone left the television on? And where was Anna? My heart jumped and blood rushed in my ears. Just the week before, Daddy had let me watch *The Desperate Hours*, the movie where Humphrey Bogart holds a family prisoner. It had given me nightmares.

I crept up the stairs, my breath held, reassuring myself it was probably nothing. Then halfway up, I heard a loud banging. I froze. Something was definitely wrong. Then I heard Anna scream.

I flew downstairs, picked up the kitchen phone, and dialed 911.

"You've reached 911."

"I'm at 46 Malibu Colony Road. Please hurry. Send someone!"

"What is the emergency?"

"Murder maybe. I don't know. HURRY!"

I ran outside. The sun burned behind the clouds, heat shimmered off the asphalt creating a liquid mirage. I squinted into the haze, but no one was on the road. I was afraid I would miss the police if I ran to the neighbors. So I waited, shaking and breathless. For the first time in my life, I prayed. I didn't know what to pray to, so I searched in my head and came up with the 3-D picture of baby Jesus that hung on Anna's bathroom wall.

"Please, God or Jesus, please make Anna okay, please. I'll do anything you ask, I'll be good, just please don't take Anna from me." I got on my knees and clasped my hands together. It felt good. Right. Like Hayley Mills in *The Trouble with Angels*.

My prayers became more confident. "Jesus and God, if you save Anna, I'll go to church. Maybe I'll even become a nun, yes, I *will* become a nun, just please make Anna, okay?"

Sirens!

I jumped up and began waving. A police car raced toward me, sailed over the speed bumps, then screeched to a halt.

"This-a-way!" I yelled. Tall Roy and Little Hervé flew out of the car. I recognized them immediately from the time I'd questioned them about my mother.

I led them inside, shushing them with a finger on my lips. Motioning them into the living room, I pointed upstairs in the direction of the bedroom. Now the house was deathly quiet, except for the sound of the shore breakers; those harmless-seeming waves that smash you down and rough you up as you scrape the sandy bottom.

The policemen mounted the stairs carefully, guns drawn. I couldn't believe this was happening in my home. I couldn't believe that kidnappers or murderers had been able to get past Mr. Jackson and the gates of Malibu Colony Road.

The tall cop eased his way down the hall until he was flattened against one side of the bedroom door. Hervé took a crouched position at the top of the stairs. I watched from behind a yellow cube in the living room, holding my breath. Then, without warning, Roy kicked open the door. Anna screamed again.

"Police! Put your hands up," Roy shouted. The cops disappeared inside the room. I gripped the upholstery to keep from fainting.

"Are you fucking crazy?"

My father emerged from the bedroom, pulling a black silk robe around him. Behind him, Anna followed, wrapped to her armpits in Laura Ashley.

"Sid, sir, Mr. Goldstein, we're sorry. We got a call."

Roy kept his face down—his shoulders were slumped. The gun was back in its holster and dangled loosely as if it too were hanging its head.

"For Chris'sake, who called you?" my father said, descending the stairs.

"The kid," Hervé yelped.

"A kid?" my father said.

"Me," I admitted, crawling out from behind the couch. "I called them. I thought someone was hurting Anna. What are you doing home?" I said accusingly.

"Taking a nap," he snapped. "What are *you* doing home?"

"Half day," I shot back. "Are you okay, Anna?"

"Of course she's okay," my father yelled.

"Anna?" I waited for an explanation, but she just shook her head and smiled. It was a coy smile, and I didn't like it one bit.

"Okay. Fun's over!" Daddy barked, motioning the cops out of the house.

They scurried down the stairs. Roy pretended to check something on his walkie-talkie and Little Hervé narrowed his eyes at me as they walked out the door.

My father sat down on the top stair and began to shake. I thought he was going to have a heart attack or explode in anger. But when he looked up, he was laughing. He laughed and laughed and laughed, and then Anna sat beside him and started laughing too. The two of them bowled into each other, their faces contorted. They clutched their bellies and each other, laughing so hard that tears rolled down their cheeks.

I steamed with fury. What was wrong with them? I glared, waiting for their hysteria to subside and for someone to come comfort me and tell me how brave I had been, to *thank* me for being worried and protective of Anna. But every time one of them tried to stop laughing, the other would start again. They were acting like annoying kids on a school bus, or like when Nicole and I stayed up too late. I stood there, hands on my hips until their laughing fit wound down into bursts, like the last kernels of popcorn popping. Anna wiped her eyes as my father helped her stand.

"Well, well," my father chuckled, holding his side.

"There is a pie in the fridge," Anna said to me. She pointed to the kitchen.

Then they disappeared back into the bedroom and closed the door.

A few weeks later they announced their engagement. At first, I thought they were kidding. In my mind, they hardly knew each other except as employer and employee. Anna's whole reason for being in our house was to take care of me. What did that have to do with my father? I couldn't imagine them marrying. I mean, when exactly had they started dating? Except for that "nap day," they slept apart. Daddy still played tennis on the weekends and went to screenings alone.

Then, invitations went out announcing the October 15th wedding.

And that summer, for the first time, I was sent to sleepaway camp.

INT. DEPARTMENT STORE, BEVERLY HILLS
DAY

I sat cross-legged on the cold marble floor of the Bridal Department at Sax Fifth Avenue, holding a box of straight pins while Magda, the seamstress, tucked and pulled at the white satin and lace of Anna's wedding gown. Anna, erect as a ballerina, pivoted mechanically like a music box figurine around the raised platform.

"Your turn soon, Jackie," Anna said. "She is going to be the flower girl!"

"Important job, young lady," Magda muttered.

"Uh-huh." I stared at the floor.

"Why the long face?" Several Annas looked at me in the three-way mirror. I glanced up and counted nine of us altogether, including Magda.

"I just don't feel well."

Magda grunted in my direction. I handed her another pin.

"You want some Coca-Cola? Magda, do you keep soft drinks here?" Anna's English was getting better and better. She still had an accent, but now when she spoke, her voice sounded smooth like a foreign diplomat.

The seamstress hoisted herself up. Her knees were red and aggravated from spending so much time on the floor.

"Coca-Cola in refrigerrrator, ma*daam*," Magda replied in her own distinctly unpolished accent.

It was strange hearing Anna addressed as a "mad*aam*." I wondered if when she was my age and living in her village in Guatemala, could she have ever pictured herself here in Beverly Hills? At Sax Fifth Avenue? Being treated like royalty by a Russian lady with chapped knees? Had this been her aim all along? I felt cold. And scared. I didn't know who she was anymore. It was as if Anna had vanished and this other person had come to take her place. Or maybe there were two Anna's, like in the *Parent Trap,* where one twin was upscale and the other was just a normal girl.

Magda handed me a chilled Coke. I needed a bottle opener, but I didn't have the will to ask. Anna concentrated on her reflection, rearranging a seam along her hip. Magda disappeared into a back room and moments later reappeared carrying a white veil, its length revealing itself only when another woman even more hunched and chapped than Magda emerged from the same room, lightly holding the sheer ends in her fingertips.

Magda stepped up to Anna and waited. Her helper approached the platform and tripped, but managed to keep the veil afloat.

"Be careful, Dodo!" Magda warned.

Dodo, it turned out, was actually the helper's name.

"Almost your turn, Jackie!" Anna exclaimed again. "Your dress! Aren't you excited?"

"Mmm-hmm," I answered, pinching my mouth shut lest I speak my true feelings.

Magda went behind Anna, stood on tiptoes, strained precariously forward, and managed to gently and with ceremony, place the veil on Anna's head. Then the seamstress stepped to one side, allowing Anna a full view of herself in the mirror. Tears spilled from Anna's eyes and her shoulders trembled, but she was smiling. Magda and Dodo nodded their frowny faces at one another with what I guessed were expressions meant to convey satisfaction. Dodo reached into an apron pocket and handed Anna a packet of tissues.

"Gracias," Anna said. "Usted es tan amable. You are so very kind."

It had been a long time since I'd heard Anna speak her own language. It made me miss her even more. She dabbed at her eyes like the soap opera actresses and turned her gaze from the mirror to where I still sat, pins in hand. She was even more beautiful than the time my mother had given her the makeover. She glimmered like one of the saints in the 3-D postcards, her long neck arched and graceful. She was a swan, an angel.

Just not my angel. Not anymore.

I turned away, my cheeks burning, my throat swelling, about to burst into tears of my own.

"So, Jackie? Do you approve?" she asked.

I squeezed my eyes together and covered them with my hands.

"What's wrong?" Anna bent down, her veil draping over me.

"It's a migraine," I said. "It runs in my family. On my mother's side."

On the morning of the wedding, I crawled out of bed, crept from my room, and peered over the stair railing. Staff dressed in starched white shirts and pressed black slacks scurried back and forth carrying trays. A multi-tiered white wedding cake—a caterer's bowed legs sticking out from under its base—marched out of the kitchen and into the dining room. Two giant white tents had been staked on the beach.

From my window, I watched the guests arrive to the strains of Bach played by a string quartet of four UCLA music majors struggling to sit upright while the legs of their folding chairs sank unevenly in the sand.

Though I had never met anyone in Anna's family, I spotted her relatives right off the bat; the women in narrow high heels, flouncy festive dresses and matching hats; the men shorter, in somber suits but with shoes so shiny as to reflect the sun. They stood out in striking contrast to the other guests in their beach-chic beige linens and pastel chiffons. Not only was Anna marrying Daddy she already belonged to a whole family that did not and would never include me. I fit into this picture exactly nowhere.

For all its pomp, the ceremony was brief and business-like. Judge Merrick pronounced Sidney and Anna Goldstein man and wife, and while I stood off to the side holding Anna's wilting bouquet and trying not to scratch at the stiff underpinnings of my flower girl dress, I saw for the first time my father and Anna kiss.

Initially, things didn't seem terrible. I got to stay with Nicole and Steffi for a whole week while Daddy and Anna flew off for their honeymoon at the Venice Film Festival, a plan allowing my father to conduct business. Staying with Steffi was always a good time, she lit incense and blasted rock and roll music, and taught Nicole and me the latest dance moves. We stayed up even on the school nights whispering about boys, gossiping about the girls at school, and comparing our breast sizes; Nicole was, at twelve, already breaching a B cup while I was still flat as a board, though encouragingly, one nipple was plumping up. When Daddy and Anna came home, however, my father announced that we were in for some "big changes." Anna had stepped into her new job as Mrs. Goldstein, and it was time to find her replacement.

The first one came and went in a week; a tall Scandinavian with patience neither for an angry twelve-year-old nor for vacuuming sand from every crease and corner of the house.

The second lasted less than a day.

"Jackie, why did you speak to Ylena so rudely?" Anna admonished.

"*Hell*-ena you mean?"

"Jackie!"

"She kept telling me what to do."

"But calling names—"

"She smelled bad!"

"Now, when you meet Jordana—"

"*Whore-dana?*"

It was one thing for Anna to marry my father. I had no control over what they did. But no stranger was going to take Anna's place in either my home or my heart.

Ellen Boshwitz had taken a shine to Anna and had joined forces with Rita Sanderson and Marge Calloway in teaching Anna the ropes. They plied her with tips and advice during long lunches followed by shopping binges on Rodeo Drive. She, in turn, flattered them with her gratitude for their benevolence and proudly demonstrated the fruits of their labor. Anna was a quick study. Her wardrobe filled with Chanel suits, Hermes scarves, Gucci shoes and purses. The clothes in which my mother was haplessly out of place, Anna wore with style and grace. Jose Eber cut and streaked her rich, dark hair, she never missed her weekly facial and manicure. And those tender hands that had washed my bottom, those hands I had clutched as I crossed the street or jumped on the bed, those beautiful hands so common and good and pure, now sported a huge diamond ring and a set of long, acrylic, maroon scratchers.

This new Anna reveled in her position as Mrs. Goldstein. Twenty carats spilled from her wrist and neck, accessorizing the designer tennis clothes she often wore. Though she'd never played the sport, Anna loved the starchy skirts and stretchy blouses. Or sometimes, when the weather was chilly, she would shed her skirt for the comfort of a velour warm-up suit. Several days a week, she'd limo down the Pacific Coast Highway to lunch with Rita and other grand dames of Hollywood society; all wives of powerful and influential husbands.

"I yam telling ju girrrrls—" Anna spoke softly but her accent—which had once all but disappeared—was now cunningly and charmingly back in full employ. Rather than hiding from her past, she had cleverly chosen to use it to her advantage, weaving her history into provocative entertainment. "Leetle Yackie called dee cops, and dey busted down dee door of dee bedroom before dey saw eet was Seednee end me, bof of us nekked wid hees ju know what jez hanging dere in dee breeze."

She'd always had a knack for storytelling. When I was younger, Anna told me Bible stories that sounded more like plotlines from the soaps we watched. The luncheon ladies screamed with laughter, dabbed at their eyes, and squeezed Anna's bejeweled hands with their own. By the time the meal was over, Anna was on the board of another committee or function, and the ladies would pat each other's backs and return to their respective mansions, proud of themselves for having treated "a Hispanic" ("Was she a Mexican, or Salvadoran?" they would ask each other later) as nicely as if she were one of their own.

Between her commitments and my father's need for companionship, Anna rarely had time for me. Now when I came home from school, a brown, beige, or pink-skinned stranger wearing a white apron would meet me at the door with an Entenmann's donut and a note from Anna outlining my itinerary for the day.

INT. MALIBU COLONY HOME
EVENING
1982

"Jackie, Anna, I need to see you in my study." My father called from downstairs. It was nine-thirty at night, and I was lying on my bed, still in my bathing suit, doing my math homework and listening to Nicole on the phone complaining about her mom's latest boyfriend, some sleaze bag she'd picked up at Alice's Bar the weekend before.

"Jackie." Anna peeked her head inside my room and waved urgently.

I hung up the phone, pulled on a T-shirt, and clomped downstairs to Daddy's study, hopping over the vacuum cleaner lying on its side in the living room. That morning, our latest housekeeper had quit when I once again tracked sand all over the freshly cleaned carpet.

Something was definitely up. It was unusual to see my father home this early. Recently promoted to Head of Production, he'd been working around the clock bringing several runaway film shoots back on time and within budget. According to Daddy, Hollywood was on a cocaine binge. The studio's directors had fallen weeks behind, turning in dailies with scenes missing or out of focus and sync. Daddy was a numbers man and a square. He had never so much as taken a hit off a joint, and though he enjoyed his nightly martini, he never got drunk. He even turned down invitations to party at the Playboy mansion. My father's drug was power and with this promotion, he had a "crapload."

Daddy gestured for me to sit next to Anna, who was already seated in one of two conference chairs.

"Ladies," he said, thrumming his fingers on his desk. "It takes me an hour on a good day with no traffic, not to mention fires or mudslides, to get to my office. By moving to the city, I can cut that figure by two-thirds. That gives me an extra hour and a half of work each day, which could double the payoff in productivity. I can get ten times what I paid for this house and build a goddamn mansion in Beverly Hills for a fifth of what it costs to live here."

He lifted slightly from his seat, pulling his silk robe out from where it had become stuck up under his backside.

"Besides," he pointed his martini at me, "you're almost thirteen. I don't want you growing up in a place where people smoke pot, surf all day, and get skin cancer. Anna, you'll be closer to your friends and the shops, and the real estate agent I've been talking to said there's a Gelson's with a produce department that beats the crap out of the Mayfair."

Anna raised her professionally arched eyebrows but stayed silent. Daddy swiveled his chair toward his desk. When he swiveled back, the martini was gone, and he was twirling a pencil.

"It should take us a month to find a place, a month to pack—ample time, ample time. I'm sure you will both agree that ultimately, this arrangement is of benefit to us all." He rose from his chair. I thought we all might shake hands, but Daddy closed the deal with a courtesy smile. Suppressing a burp, he pulled his robe tight around the fleshy part of his belly and went upstairs. A moment later, the beginning of Johnny Carson's monologue filtered down to where Anna and I still sat.

"Well. That's that," Anna said, shrugging her shoulders. She got up and took my father's empty martini glass into the kitchen. I stayed a while longer, staring at my father's chair. There was nothing to say. Daddy had done the numbers, and in our house, the numbers were the equivalent to God's hand pointing the way.

It felt like the end of the world.

Nicole and I stood on the beach sobbing, arms around each other, our candy necklaces entwined. We had stolen them from the Colony Pharmacy the day before, hearts racing as we'd casually strolled past the cash register, practiced looks of innocence on our faces, the fruit-flavored trinkets stuffed deep into our pockets.

The Santa Ana's were blowing hard, and I shielded my face from the flying sand as we crunched off the chalky circles one by one, reassuring each other with promises to get together every weekend and every holiday.

"Ladies, it's almost time!" My father's voice called from inside.

I scrambled into my tennis shoes and we hurried around to the front of the house where the last of the moving vans drove away, slowly, carefully over the speed bumps. Daddy had threatened them with a lawsuit if even one cup was broken.

"Well, this is it." I sniffled.

"Wait." Nicole pulled back the long strands of hair whipping around her face and reached into her pocket. She took out an old "Carter for President" button and held it out for me to see. "I have a plan."

"I thought your mom voted for Reagan."

"There's a pin on the back." Nicole turned the button over. "If we prick our fingers and rub them together, we'll be blood sisters."

I took the button from her and examined it.

"It's clean if that's what you're thinking," Nicole said. "I boiled it."

"C'mon, quick." I pulled her back through our gate and checked around for a spot where nobody would see us. There were cleaning people everywhere, and Anna was going in and out making sure nothing had been forgotten.

"Up here," I whispered.

I pulled her up the stairs over the garage and inside the room where Anna had lived when she still belonged to me. The single bed and nightstand were long gone and wires hung out of the ceiling where the light fixture had been. We latched the door against the wind and sat down on the sand-dusted floor facing each other.

"I'll go first," I said, pushing the pin against my thumb. It took a couple of tries before I was brave enough to pierce the skin, but I managed to squeeze out a little dot of blood.

"Now me." Nicole took the Carter button and jabbed the pin into her thumb so hard I thought she would need stitches, though only a small bead of blood appeared. She pinched until the drop spread to an impressive size and I did the same.

"We should say something," I said.

"Like what?"

"Y'know, do some kind of vows." I contorted my palm outward so the blood wouldn't spill.

"Okay," Nicole said, "say them and I'll repeat after you."

I took Nicole's other hand, the one without the blood, and moved so that our knees touched. The only vows I knew were the ones I'd heard Judge Merrick perform at Daddy and Anna's wedding.

"I, Jackie, take you, Nicole, to be my blood sister."

"I, Nicole, take you, Jackie, to be my blood sister."

"For richer or poorer."

"For richer or poorer."

"In sickness and in health."

"In sickness and in health."

"Till death us do part."

"Till death us do part."

Nicole motioned to me, crooking her bloody thumb. I raised my thumb in response. Carefully and ritualistically, we aimed our thumbs at each other's until they met.

"Amen," I said.

Nicole nodded.

We pressed our thumbs tightly together. Now we'd be sisters, there for each other forever, no matter what happened. I imagined my blood seeping out of my veins and into hers; my cells becoming part of Nicole's body and hers becoming part of mine. I didn't know where to put my eyes. I was afraid if I met her gaze, I would blush or giggle and break the spell. I focused on the wall where Anna's pictures and 3-D Jesuses and saints had hung. All that remained were squares of bright flower print trumpeting out from the surrounding faded wallpaper.

"Jackie!" Anna's voice rang out and we both sprung apart as if we'd been caught doing something naughty.

I wiped my thumb against the leg of my jeans. "Call you tonight," I said and ran down the stairs to where Anna was waiting, tennis skirt blowing around her legs. With a frantic gyration of her hands, she nudged me into the backseat of the limousine where Daddy sat, his face burrowed into a folder of papers.

"You want to give us the heart attack?" she chided. "I thought you ran away!"

I turned around in my seat and craned my neck to find the garage window where Nicole still sat, one cheek pressed up against the glass, waving. I waved back and made the finger-swirling gesture of dialing a telephone. Then, as our limo rolled over the speed bumps, past Mr. Jackson and the guardhouse, and out the Colony gates, I bid farewell to the beach, the ocean and Malibu, the souls of my feet still sandy in my shoes.

INT. BEVERLY HILLS HOME
1981 – 1983

We rented a twenty-room Traditional in the flats of Beverly Hills while my father and Anna searched for the perfect property on which to build their "dream house." Our new home was the opposite of the cement and steel beach house. Built in the 1930s, it still had the original maple floors and warm wood paneling in the living rooms. Plaster molding decorated the high ceilings and there was an actual, working brick fireplace in the oversized kitchen. The upstairs had dormer windows and my bedroom had a window seat, where I would curl up with headphones, blasting Blondie on my Walkman while looking out over the wood-shingled roof.

Nicole and I remained true to our vows. Every weekend she came to my house or I went to hers, and during the week, we spoke every night by phone. I had made a few friends at my new school, but with my casual approach to fashion (shorts, T-shirt, and puka shell accessories), I never felt like I fit in with the Beverly Hills girls in their cashmere cardigans and diamond tennis bracelets. I envied their identical, tiny, upturned noses.

I lived for weekends with Nicole. When she arrived, it was as if she was bringing my true self back to me. How had I taken for granted the simple luxury of walking barefoot along the shore or going body surfing with friends after school? I longed to hear the ocean's tumble, the calm waves lulling me to sleep. In Beverly Hills, I lay awake, listening to the sound of police helicopters, and I often woke to the rumble of tour buses rolling through our neighborhood. Our house had once belonged to James Cagney and sat between Judy Garland and Clark Gable's former homes, so we were on the "Map to the Hollywood Stars" itinerary.

When the busses went by, I'd run to the street and strike a pose or put on dark glasses and pretend to be a movie star. But I soon wearied of the tourists and their flashing cameras. After all, I was just a stand-in for a bunch of dead celebrities.

When my father worked late, and Anna didn't have a committee meeting, she and I had dinner together in the kitchen, but our conversations felt forced, effortful.

"How was school today?"

"Fine."

"Sidney and I found such beautiful property for the new house." Her accent was practically non-existent when it was just me or Daddy.

"Uh-huh."

"You want to see it tomorrow?"

"No thanks. Nicole's coming over."

After a few more exchanges, we'd turn on *Wheel of Fortune,* a show we were both good at, followed by Jeopardy, a show at which we both stank.

Late one afternoon, I came home after painting scenery for a school production of *A Midsummer Night's Dream.* The boy playing Puck was a cute eighth grader I'd been flirty with, so I'd signed up for stage crew to be near him. I was in my bathroom, changing clothes for dinner when I noticed wet paint on the seat of my overalls. I took them off to discover the source of the red stain came from my underwear. My period. Yes! I couldn't wait to tell Nicole, who hadn't gotten hers yet. We were both sure she would be first because she already had boobs and pubic hair and I barely fit in a training bra. I changed my clothes, wadded a bunch of toilet paper into fresh underwear, and went downstairs. Trini, our housekeeper was in the kitchen washing lettuce and Lupe, our other housekeeper, was behind her in the laundry room.

"Anna? Donde esta?"

They pointed upstairs.

I found Anna in their bedroom pressing a pair of my father's slacks on an ironing board. She never let anyone else iron

Daddy's clothing, saying she was the only one who "knew how Sidney likes his creases."

"Um, I need to talk to you."

She spritzed the pant leg and a cloud of steam rose around her. "Please sit." She nodded to an upholstered bench at the foot of the bed. "Is everything okay?"

"Yeah, except I think I just got my period."

She turned off the iron and sat next to me.

"You're not going to slap me, are you?"

Anna's eyebrows shot up. "Why I do such a thing?"

"I dunno. I read that it's an old custom like in the Bible or someplace."

"Really? I never read that."

"A Jewish custom," I explained. "Old Testament."

"In my culture, is a good thing when a girl starts her menses. You are a woman. Are you having stomach paining?"

"Cramps, you mean? No. I just feel, I don't know, kind of weird."

"I had terrible pains. When I first get my period, my mother make me sopa de pollo—chicken soup. That a Jewish custom too, no?"

I laughed. "Only for colds or the flu."

"Then my mother, she tell me, 'Stay away from boys or I'll keel you.' And I was a behaved girl. I did stay away from boys. Until your Daddy."

We locked eyes. I think we were both surprised by the intimacy of the moment, and for a moment, neither of us said anything. So, Anna had been a virgin before my father. I let the news register.

"Anyway, I just thought you should know." I stood up, awkward now, wanting to ask her advice like what products to use, but I was afraid to embarrass her or myself more than I already had.

She must have sensed my discomfort because she took my hand and led me into the bathroom, rummaged under the sink, then handed me two unopened boxes; Kotex and Tampons. I had the feeling she'd been saving them for me. Maybe it was my new woman hormones, but the thought made me weepy.

"Okay," she said. "There are instructions here." She opened each and gave me the inserts pointing out the directions and diagrams. "Give Lupe your soiled clothes to soak. Make sure you tell her to use extra Spray 'n Wash."

"Okay. Thanks, Anna."

Anna leaned over and kissed me on the forehead. It had been a long time since she'd been tender with me that way.

"You want some chicken soup?" she asked.

"Wow, really?" I sniffled. "That would be nice."

Anna walked to the door and pressed a button on the intercom.

"Trini! Campbell's, por favor, calienta la sopa de pollo para Miss Jackie!" Then she walked back to the ironing board and turned on the iron. Steam blew out the top. "I need to finish pants for your daddy. We have dinner with the Sandersons at Mr. Chow's."

She bent over the dark slacks and resumed ironing. I gathered my new supplies and crossed to the door feeling as though I had stayed too long at a party.

"Oh, and Jackie!"

I turned.

"Stay away from dee boys or I'll keel you!"

She was still chuckling to herself as I shut the door.

That very night, my mother called.

Daddy and Anna were still out with the Sugarmens when the phone rang. I figured it was Nicole, so I picked it up right away, anxious to share my big news.

"Guess what?"

"Hello? Jacqueline? Baby, can you hear me?" My mother's words were slurry. "Do I have the goddamn number right? Hello? Jacqueline?"

We had a rule in our house, or I should say Daddy had a rule: No one talks to Merilee without his permission. But hearing from her out of the blue confused and worried me. She usually only called on my birthday and Christmas.

"Mom?" I ventured.

"Jacqueline, oh my God! Oh, baby girl, is that you?"

"It's me. Did something happen?"

She started crying and talking crazy. I kept interrupting, trying to talk to her, but I couldn't understand most of what she was saying. Then she began screaming stuff about Daddy and Anna. I remembered why Daddy screened her calls.

"That little bitch, I told that cocksucker, I told him if he was going to marry that spic, I'd—"

I slammed the phone down. I was shaking. It was all too much. Becoming a woman and hearing from my mother on the same day. I burst into tears and ran up to my room.

Later that night, when Daddy and Anna came home, I didn't tell my father about my period, and I didn't say anything about the phone call.

My mother called again the next night, and the next night and the next, each time leaving terrible messages on our answering machine until my father changed our phone number. I was relieved, but I also felt unmoored. What if something happened to her? How would we know? Or what if one day she got better? How would she ever find me?

INT. BEVERLY HILLS HOTEL
OCTOBER – DECEMBER
1983

Who didn't recognize that iconic green sign with bold, white cursive lettering perched high above Sunset Boulevard? The Beverly Hills Hotel was as famous as its famous guests; from John Kennedy to John Lennon to the Queen of England. According to Daddy, our own spacious suites had once housed Howard Hughes and his staff for an entire year!

The lease in the flats had ended but completion of our new home was delayed because the builders had ordered the wrong marble for the floors. So, with most of our belongings in storage, we settled into two of the hotel's coveted bungalows while we waited for the replacement stone to be blasted out of a quarry in Italy.

On Saturdays, Nicole and I would lie at the famed pool, sipping Cokes, and spying on celebrities from behind our sunglasses. Once, we saw Sally Field, Liza Minelli, Dudley Moore, and Richard Gere all in one afternoon! At fourteen, we were too cool to pull out our autograph books, a hobby we'd had back in the Malibu Colony days.

While working on our tans, we drooled over the latest heart-throbs in Tiger Beat Magazine, and poured over articles in Cosmopolitan like "Tips to Please Your Man."

All we thought about were boys. All we talked about were boys and sex; how sex would feel and when it would happen. Nicole said she wanted to just get it over with. I'd only made out with a few boys, but Nicole had gotten pretty far. She'd grown to five foot eight inches and with her long blonde hair and amazing figure, she could easily pass for eighteen.

"Steffi says you don't start enjoying intercourse until the third or fourth time," Nicole said. Her mom was our expert in all things men-related.

I planned to wait until I was seventeen or until I had a serious boyfriend. Whichever came first. Both of us had a list of our ideal matches.

#1 - Cute.

#2 - Good kisser.

#3 - Nice person.

#4 - Preferably actor and/or singer.

I loved everything about the hotel; its flamingo-colored exterior and landscape of palms and emerald lawns mowed to ridiculous perfection; the infamous Polo Lounge where after sunbathing Nicole and I would giggle our lunch order to stoic waiters while trying to act sophisticated. I loved the bungalows and their boxy, motel-like informality that masked the opulence within its stucco walls. I especially loved the hustle and bustle.

As an only child, the company of hotel staff was like finding a giant family, and I wanted desperately to belong. I folded sheets with the women in the laundry room, asked the concierge and bellmen to see pictures of their families, and made self-deprecating jokes about mine. I tried anything to set myself apart from the other guests, plenty of whom treated the staff terribly. I routinely left the housekeepers half my weekly allowance in a tip envelope so they would know how much I appreciated them. I was also, admittedly, buying their silence. I didn't want anyone reporting to Daddy about my various adventures, like my makeout session in the parking garage with Russ, an eighteen-year-old valet who, as it turned out, was severely tongue-tied, leaving me with a negative first impression of French kissing.

Daddy and Anna went out weekend nights, either to a screening at the Guild or to one of Anna's charity events. As soon as they left, Nicole and I would put on our most grown-up clothes, apply scads of makeup, and roam the hotel, looking for boys to flirt with, smoking cigarettes, and pilfering wine from glasses left in the banquet rooms or on the patio. Now, even on weeknights, I barely registered Anna and Daddy's absences. I felt lucky to have the freedom and new companions. The only worry I had was that their dream house would soon be finished and that would spell the end of the good life for me.

In December with only weeks 'til the big move, Anna and Daddy decided I should have "input" into the décor of my room. While their last-minute effort to include me in this detail of their project was appreciated, it felt like being asked to climb aboard their bicycle built for two.

Gerard Piccard, the interior designer was a dapper fellow sporting faded jeans, a graying ponytail, and round rimless glasses. He wore black cotton Japanese shoes that went between his big toes. I found his hip style and brusque manner intimidating.

"Purple and silver?" He gazed down his long nose at me.

"Yeah. I mean, not bright purple or anything," I qualified, already reading his disapproval.

"Mmmmm…hmm," he said.

We sat in the lobby facing one another on a plush velvet sofa. Alphonse, one of the bellboys, brought us drinks; a greyhound for Gerard Piccard and a Coke for me. Nicole and I both had crushes on Al. He was sweet and funny and looked a lot like Scott Baio. Once before my escapade with Russ in the parking garage, Al and I had hung out behind the kitchen, smoking cigarettes and talking over the voices of the dishwashers and the clanking pots and pans. He'd grown up in the valley, not far from my grand-mother's condo. Now I was too embarrassed to look at him. Chances were he'd heard all about my make-out session with Russ. In the hotel, news traveled fast.

"Thanks, Alphonse." I avoided his eyes. "Um, just charge it to our room."

Gerard took a sip of his drink, then reached into his khaki canvas shoulder bag and pulled out several pieces of paper with swatches attached. "This is more what *I* had in mind."

"This?" I held up the fabric; peach and yellow Swiss dot. Doll-house fabric.

"For the bed and curtains. And this," he said, holding up another swatch of peach and yellow stripes, "for the pillows and love seat."

I couldn't keep my eyes from rolling. "You know I'm fourteen, right?"

"Your stepmother thought you would love it." He pursed his lips and wiped his mouth with a cocktail napkin, sighed, and filed the swatches back in his bag.

"I do, it's just that, I mean, are there any other choices?" I squirmed in my seat. Both of us knew this whole input thing was a waste of time.

Gerard checked his watch.

"Never mind," I said, not wanting to offend him any further. Also, I feared I might have inherited my mother and grand-mother's lousy decorating genes. "Use those. It will look great."

"Good. Well then, it's been pleasant meeting you." Gerard put the renderings back into his bag and left.

When he was out the door, I slid the remains of his greyhound to my side of the table, checked if anyone was looking, and drank it down.

"You want another?" Al had come up from behind, startling me.

"What?"

He pointed at the empty cocktail glass in my hand.

"Um, sure, but—"

Al dashed away and minutes later deposited what I thought was a Shirley Temple in front of me.

"Hey, no fair! This is a—"

"Vodka and cranberry," Al whispered. "I put the cherry on top so no one would know."

"Ohhhh."

I'd never been brought my own drink. I took a sip. It was delicious. Cold and tart. I could hardly even taste the alcohol.

"Thanks, Alphonse." Even his name was sexy.

He smiled down at me and my heart skipped a beat. I was crazy about his dimples and the way his shiny black hair fell over one eye.

"What are you doing tonight?" he asked.

"Um. Tonight?" My cheeks went hot, and my heart began to race. Daddy and Anna were out for the evening. Still, it was out of the question. My father would never approve. That is if I asked for permission.

"What do you have in mind?" I asked with a flirtatious side-glance, a look Nicole and I had practiced in the mirror.

"I know where there's a party," Al whispered. "I get off at six. Meet me on level-two parking."

In a sea of Mercedes and BMWs, one didn't have to look hard for Al's car metallic purple van with orange and red swirly decals on both sides. White shag carpeted the dashboard and a plastic Jesus hung on a pink ribbon suspended from the rearview mirror. Behind our seats, a curtain of wooden beads shook and rattled with every bump. It was nearly six-thirty when we pulled into the westbound lane on Santa Monica Boulevard and commuter traffic was thick. The sun was low and shining in our eyes. Al lowered the visors. "Better?"

"Oh yeah." I smiled, to cover my nerves. "Thanks."

I had dressed in casual party attire—a jean skirt and a cute cotton T-shirt that was low cut enough that you could see a peek of bra.

He slipped a tape into the cassette player. Van Halen blared from the speakers.

"Where are we going?" I shouted. I crossed my legs and leaned back as if I was relaxed. As if I were someone who'd been in lots of vans with lots of older guys.

He turned the volume down and pushed in the cigarette lighter. "To the beach."

"I have to be back by ten. You know my dad and all."

"Oh yes, ma'am we all know Mr. Goldstein. Home by ten. You bet Miss Jackie."

"Hey!" I punched his arm.

"Just messin' with around. You like weed?"

My heart lurched. I felt disoriented and out of my depth. I'd smelled pot at the hotel, but no one had ever offered it. I considered pretending, but I knew I wasn't cool enough to pull it off.

"I've never tried it."

"You're kiddin' me?" He laughed. "Reach in here," he instructed, signaling to his shirt pocket.

I put my hand inside, and as I reached down for the joint, my fingers brushed against his hard chest. A current zapped through me. Al must have felt it too because he glanced at me and grinned. I tried to act casual as I pulled out the thin cigarette, slightly bent and wrapped in brown paper. Al opened his mouth and nodded for me to put the joint between his lips. Suddenly it struck me I was on an actual date—something that Al, being older, surely had assumed all along. What had I expected? That we were going for ice cream? We'd been flirting for weeks. Anna's words echoed in my head; "Stay away from dee boys or I'll keel you!" I pushed Anna's warning out of my mind and focused on the swingy beat of the music.

He lit the joint, inhaling deeply. The smoke furled around his full lips and up his nose. I was nervous. Nicole had smoked with one of Steffi's boyfriends and said it mostly just made her laugh and act stupid and I didn't want Al to think I was silly or immature. Al tapped an ember into the ashtray and handed me the joint. Our fingers touched and again, that *feeling*! Like electricity surging through me. I put the joint between my lips, inhaled, and began coughing uncontrollably.

"Shit! Shit!" I wheezed.

My eyes teared up and my throat smarted. I handed back the joint and pressed my hands into the carpeted dash while I fought to stop coughing. Embarrassment flushed my already red cheeks. I hated not being good at things.

"Pull slowly, baby," Al laughed. "You'll get the hang of it." He waited for me to catch my breath. "You okay?"

I nodded and he handed back the joint. This time I inhaled a tiny bit.

"Now, hold it in your lungs," he instructed.

The smoke tasted sweet, much better than cigarettes. I exhaled and coughed but just a little.

"Good job." Al patted my knee and rested his hand on my thigh. Heat rose in parts of my body only I had ever explored. It was terrifying and wonderful.

Al wore a thick gold ring with a dark purple stone on his middle finger that reminded me of my mother's earrings; the ones I had never worn but still kept in my jewelry box.

"Purple's my favorite color," I said, touching the ring.

The sun had set, and the sky was ablaze as we pulled into the Venice Beach parking lot off Rose and Ocean Boulevard. Cars scattered here and there with couples and families milling around. On the boardwalk, skaters and bicyclists whizzed by while the last of the vendors closed up shop, pulling down metal awnings to protect their wares from the junkies and crack addicts who rose after dark like vampires.

Al pulled the van into a spot along the beach and turned off the engine. "My lady, we have arrived," he announced.

"Is the party going to be here?"

Al smiled and his whole face seemed to glow, or maybe it was the pink hue of the sky. "Yeah, some of my friends usually show up sooner or later." He leaned over and unlatched my seatbelt. "It depends. C'mon, let's take a walk."

Al jumped out, opened my door, and helped me down. Then, he hoisted an ice chest and a blanket under his arm. The blanket caught my attention, but I wasn't about to say anything. Beach-goers still dotted the sand and besides, we were meeting his friends.

We both removed our shoes and Al took my hand. I felt light-headed and dreamy as we floated through the rosy light toward the ocean, the sand under our feet still warm from the afternoon sun. Al chose a spot within sight of but some distance away from other picnickers. He put the ice chest down and cast the blanket out a few times until it settled evenly.

The cool evening breeze ruffled the corners of our blanket and chilled my bare arms. Neither of us wore sweaters. Al put his arm around me, and my heart revved in my chest. We nestled together facing the water, watching the waves tumble and the frisbee players and the joggers and the dogs chasing sticks or balls into the whitewater. The sky swirled like spin art in shades of orange, magenta, and purple. Every sense seemed heightened, every color more saturated. I could feel the brine of the ocean's mist on my skin. I let the sand sift through my fingers and each grain seemed to contain a universe. I was acutely aware of Al's arm, his soft hairs brushing against my neck, the moisture in the crook of his elbow, the warmth of his skin against mine. He hummed softly; a tune we'd been listening to on the drive, and as we swayed back and forth, our feet reached out and met in the sand.

"Your toes are funny." I giggled.

"If you say so, Princess."

"I do say so," I stated.

Al combed my hair with his fingers, and I leaned my head into his hands and swished back and forth like I was getting a shampoo.

"I really like pot," I said.

"I really like you, Miss Jackie," Al whispered in my ear. Goose-flesh sprang up on my neck.

He stretched over me to the cooler, pulled out two beers, and popped the tabs. The golden liquid foamed over the sides and Al shook off the excess onto the sand. I took a long sip. It was ice-cold and felt wonderful as it went down my throat.

"That was refreshing," I exclaimed when I had finished the last drop.

"Glad you enjoyed it," Al said, laughing. "Want another?"

"Sure." I felt great. Relaxed to the max. Free as a bee. This was how I should feel all the time. Al opened another beer for me, then he took my face in his hands and kissed me. His lips were soft and his breath sweet with the taste of beer and marijuana. His tongue gently probed past my lips, exploring my mouth, brushing against my teeth and gums; so different, a million times better than with Russ the parking guy. He pulled me closer so that I was sitting across his lap. Between swallows of beer, we kissed and kissed until all the beer was gone and we were lying on the blanket with me on top of him, both of us breathing hard and looking into each other's eyes. I had wanted to make out with Al forever.

"Jackie," Al murmured then kissed me deeply and pressed his hips against mine. His erection against my leg startled me and I pulled back.

"Feel how much I like you?" he asked. Then he reached under my shirt and cupped my breasts into his heated hands.

The sensation aroused me, and my breath became shallow. Nicole had already gone to second base and once even third. She'd described it as "no big deal." It seemed a pretty big deal to me. Nicole's large breasts were a hot topic among the staff at the hotel. I hoped Al thought mine were okay.

"Al?" I checked to see if anyone was watching.

"Let's find some privacy," he whispered.

The skies were graying as I stumbled across the sand toward the parking lot. "Whoops," I giggled, realizing my shoes were on the wrong feet.

"Watch your head," Al cautioned, holding my arm as I climbed unsteadily into the front of the van. He guided me past the seats and through the beaded curtain. It took my eyes a moment to adjust to the dark. There was a mattress covered in glossy bedding; satin or polyester. Several mismatched pillows cozied up to an oversized, pink Teddy bear with outstretched arms, the kind of stuffed prize you'd see in a booth at an amusement park that nobody ever wins. Overhead, a gauzy fabric had been stretched out and billowed across like a canopy.

"You like it?" Al seemed proud like he'd decorated it especially for me. I answered that yes it was *very* nice.

But the shiny sheets troubled me, or maybe it was the sound of the car alarm nearby.

"What if your friends come?" I asked, pulling my knees up to my chest. "How will they find us?"

"Shh." He put a finger on my lips. "Lie down with me." He gently untangled my limbs and laid me down. Two Als swayed above me and overlapped in my vision. I blinked and concentrated on his nose to bring his face into focus.

"Jackie, Princess," he murmured, rubbing my shoulders. "You are my princess."

Al rubbed his fingers into my back and my tension receded like the tides. I reached for him and we kissed.

It felt natural when Al pulled my shirt over my head. But when he unhooked and removed my bra, I crossed my arms instinctively. Al laughed and crossed his arms too which made me laugh. I allowed them to drift back to my sides.

I laid still, trying to relax and enjoy the sensations of Al playing with my breasts, but I was still seeing double and my body had gone on alert.

"What time is it?" I asked, my voice sounded funny in my ears.

"Don't worry, baby," Al rolled on top of me and pulled up my skirt.

I bit my lip, embarrassed because the place between my legs had become wet and sticky and I didn't know if that was normal. I wanted to slow things down, go back to the beach, maybe swim in the ocean. I wanted to swim.

"Hey," I raised on my elbows. "Let's go for a swim."

"Shhh." His fingers tugged at the elastic on my underwear, and then one of his fingers went inside of me. He moved it in and out, his purple ring rubbing uncomfortably against the side of my vagina. Then he took my hand and placed it inside his pants until I was touching his penis. It felt bigger than I'd imagined, and I didn't know what I was supposed to do with it. I tried to hold on as Al thrust up and down, but my head was spinning. I let go and squeezed my eyes shut to make everything stay still.

Al rolled to one side. "Are you okay?" he asked, concern in his voice.

"Just…dizzy."

"You drink too fast. You have to learn to slow down."

I nodded woozily. "Mmm-hmm." I struggled to sit up. I took some deep breaths and held on to Al's shoulder to ground myself.

"You are so beautiful," he said softly.

No one had ever told me I was beautiful. Not even my father. The thought made me weepy, and I buried my face in my hands.

"Oh Jackie, what's wrong, Princess?" Al kissed me on my cheeks and forehead and began stroking my hair. I leaned against him and let myself be soothed.

"S'okay," I murmured.

"Better?" he whispered.

I nodded and opened my eyes. Al came into focus. His grin, his dimples. That lock of hair over one eye.

I thought of the list Nicole and I had made.

"Hah." I said, "You are cute and a good kisser."

Al propped up on one elbow and tilted my chin in his hand. "Jackie, I need to make love to you."

I stared back blankly, trying to process through the fog in my head.

"Make love?" I managed.

"Don't you like me, Jackie?"

"Yes, I—"

"You don't want to be a cocktease do you?"

"No. What do you mean?" It sounded bad.

"I mean don't leave a guy hanging," he said in a tight voice. Then he chuckled, tapped me on the nose with his finger, and reached back with his other hand.

"What's that?" I squinted at the packet he was now tearing open.

He passed the rubber back and forth in front of my face like a hypnotist's pendant. "It's what boys use to make love to girls to keep them from having babies, dummy."

"Oh." I wanted to explain that I wasn't dumb, I'd just never seen a condom in person. But Al had already lowered his pants and unrolled the rubber over his penis. I'd also never seen an erection in person. His was swollen with a vein on one side. It was ugly. But wasn't that wrong? Weren't women supposed to think penises were wonderful?

"Don't you want me to feel good?"

"Yes, but—"

"You see how hard you made me?"

"I—"

"Or could a rich girl like you never have a boyfriend like me?"

That pierced through my stupor. A knife to my Achilles heel.

"Huh? Am I not good enough for you?" Al turned away with a hurt and angry expression.

"Oh, Al…Alphonse, you're good enough," I searched for words to reassure him. "Way more than good enough, you're great, it's just–"

"I'll be so gentle." He swiveled back and took my shoulders. "Please? I need you, my Princess. Let me make love to you."

I was woozy and confused. Heavy with the responsibility of Al's wellbeing. I knew that there was something else I should say or do but I was too wasted to figure it out. Behind him, the giant teddy gazed down at me.

"Jackie?" He whispered in my ear, "Pretty please? It'll be good, honey, you'll see." Al said. When I didn't reply, he climbed on top of me still wearing his shirt.

Al pulled down my underwear and slowly guided himself inside me. I shut my eyes. I thought about Nicole. We'd always assumed she'd lose her virginity first. What would she say when I told her about Al? Would she be jealous? Would she approve?

"Owww, I—" I was jarred back to the moment by the chafing friction of Al's thrusting.

Steffi had said sex wasn't great the first time, but I hadn't understood it would be painful. I gritted my teeth. Then suddenly Al pushed hard, and I felt a sharp tear.

"It really hurts!" I gasped. "Al, please. Stop, or just please—"

"Shhh," he said over and over while he thrust himself in and out, my head bumping against the bear.

I dug my nails into my palms to not scream until finally Al moaned and collapsed on top of me sweaty and spent. When he drew away, hot liquid poured from between my legs. I was mortified to discover a viscous pool of blood soaking into Al's sheets. I sat up quickly and crossed my legs, squeezing them together.

"What's wrong?" he asked.

"I'm—"

"You okay?"

"Yeah, but..." I gestured with my eyes.

"Oh, here, use this."

He pulled off his T-shirt and handed it to me. The middle of his chest was a valley of curly black hair which shocked me because I had thought he'd be smooth like a boy.

"I'm sorry for staining your sheets," I said.

I wiped between my legs with the white shirt, and when Al wasn't looking, I stuffed it under the bear.

It was dark on the drive home. Al smoked cigarettes and sang along to the music. I opened the window and focused on the tail-lights streaming by. I was spinning again, and my stomach churned. I leaned my head out and took big deep breaths to keep from throwing up. Finally, we pulled up to the service entrance to the hotel. Al stayed in his seat, eyes straight ahead, the motor running. I waited for him to say something.

"Okay then, so..." I prompted.

He turned. "Okay, Princess. Thanks for a great evening." He leaned over and gave me a peck on the cheek. The kind a boy gives to his aunt or his sister.

"So, will I see you in the morning?" I asked, trying to sound casual.

"Nah, I'm off tomorrow."

"Oh, I thought..."

His fingers tapped on the steering wheel.

"Okay, well..." My throat swelled, and tears pressed behind my eyes. He hadn't even hugged me goodbye or given me a real kiss. I got out of the car, looking right and left to make sure I wasn't spotted.

"You okay though, right?" he called after me.

I swallowed hard and slung my purse over my shoulder.

"Sure. I'm fine."

I wasn't. I didn't know what I was, but it definitely wasn't fine.

Still, that was all the permission he needed. Al slapped the side of the purple van twice like a jockey whipping a horse, then gunned the engine and was gone.

DISSOLVE TO:

INT. HOSPITAL ROOM
NIGHT
DAY 30

Brett sits on the loveseat, tapping a rolled-up script against his thigh while going on and on about the shoot; the compliments Reiner gave him after screening his scenes, the *crisis* he had with the hair department over dying his hairpiece to match his new highlights, the makeup woman who was from *guess where?* His hometown! And while I'd normally enjoy the shop talk, I'm not thrilled about him having a dandy time doing the same movie he'd encouraged me to turn down. Apparently, what was bad for the goose is now good for the gander, and he is a lucky little ducky while I lie here all comatose and pissed off seeing as my almost-fiancée has not so much as glanced at me once since arriving.

Except for my hair growing in weird tufts, a new drip, and another bag-o-fluid, I don't look any worse since spleen surgery, though I don't look any better. So, who can blame him? Still, pardon me if in my present state I am feeling sorry for myself. To top it all off, he is *right now* doing this thing I hate: picking out chocolates from the heart-shaped box Nurse Dani left on the coffee table FOR HIM this morning. He cracks open the bottom of each piece then reseals it like nobody's watching. If I weren't in a coma right now, I'd still be giving him the silent treatment.

"It's going super, though, Jackie. And New York! What a great location. There's so much to do…" he trails off. "But anyway, the crew laughs at all my stuff. Honestly, I think that's a pretty good sign."

He looks out the window to the parking lot where a crowd of our most devoted fans sit on camp chairs. He is spotted immediately.

"We're praying for Jackie!"

"Tell Jackie we love her!"

"I love you, Brett Haney!"

Brett waves, lowers the blinds, takes a few deep breaths, then looks back at me and cringes. It's a gut punch every time. I decide to forgive his blathering about the film and to applaud his efforts at communication. How hard it must be to keep a one-sided conversation going. I can't blame him for wishing he was back on the set. Or anywhere other than here. How long will it take before he lets himself off the hook and moves on? Weeks? Months? Years? He's devoted now, but will poor Brett stick with me until the hair under my bandages turns gray?

He comes to my bedside, kneels, and bows his head.

"Dear God, if you can hear me, please help Jackie to get better."

My poor guy. His bald spot is spreading. The trauma must be speeding up his hair loss. *I'd* find him hot even with a combover, but for Brett, it's a sensitive subject.

"Honey?" he whispers, "I have to know… *were* you trying to commit suicide? The press, they're asking. I'm confused, I don't know what to believe anymore." Tears spill from his eyes. "Koppel's people called, Barbara Walters' agent left messages, what do I tell them?"

I can't believe this crapola. Nicole might be letting herself off the hook by pushing the suicide spin, but I could have sworn my boyfriend, of all people for Chris'sake, knew me better. My blood pressure monitor beeps sharply but Brett doesn't react. Everyone has gotten inured to these "anomalies," as the doctors refer to my sudden spikes and dips.

"Arggh." He pinches his eyes and pounds his fists into his head. "C'mon now, fella," he admonishes himself. Taking a deep breath, he reaches up to my bedside table, pulls a Kleenex from the box, and blows his nose.

"Honey, I have a confession to make."

Wait, what? Is he seeing someone? Has he already moved on? I steel myself.

"I-I'm thinking about seeing a shrink."

If my jaw could drop it would be on the floor.

Brett Haney was raised by conservative Texans whose every other sentence contained the word "bootstraps."

"Yep, that's right. Me. Buck Haney. I mean, not forever but just to get…til you're, you know, back on your feet." He shakes his head and walks in circles around the room. "I keep going over and over it, Jackie. I swear I thought you were right behind me when I ran downstairs. I've replayed it a thousand times." Brett rises, bends over me, and searches my open, vacant eyes.

He slides back to his knees and grips the sheets in his fists. "This is a nightmare."

A shrink. Wow. Brett might have his insecurities, but he is by far the more stable one in our relationship. In the past, if he was upset, I was the only person he went to for comfort and then, rarely. It's hard to picture my cowboy "processing feelings" with a therapist, but I hope he finds comfort there. Anywhere. Just as long as it's not with Dani. Anyone but Nurse Dani.

"God, please help me to get through this," he whispers. "Please help Jackie, God. She doesn't deserve this."

The jury is still out on that one. I wasn't always the comatose angel I am today.

When I first met Brett, he was fresh off the farm, and I was a neurotic, chain-smoking, diet-pill-infused mess with three years on a soap and a few minor films under my belt, plus one big tabloid scandal. I'd just been cast in my first major studio picture playing a prostitute opposite Alex Harvey, a mediocre but popular and bankable actor. The casting breakdown had described my character as a "young Debra Winger type." Ironically, Debra Winger was at least ten years younger than Alex Harvey. Still, she was over thirty, and in this town, you have to look like a virgin to play a whore. Out of my six scenes, I was to be semi-naked in five of them, and I was terrified.

The film was titled *Restless,* and that was how I felt that day—restless, edgy and tense, sitting in the makeup trailer with rollers in my hair, naked under a loose, terry cloth robe.

I had barely slept the night before, panicked that Alex wouldn't find my body sexy, or worse, that the studio wouldn't find me sexy and I'd never work again.

I tried to calm my nerves as I sat in the makeup chair, a strategically placed fan gusting hot air between my spread legs to quick-dry the makeup on my lower regions. Katie, my makeup woman with whom I had worked since the soaps, was camouflaging my face with foundation and dotting concealer over the smattering of stress-induced acne on my forehead, after which she set about applying mascara.

Occupying the other three chairs were actresses in various stages of readiness. They had minor roles but I couldn't help but compare myself, especially to the gorgeous, auburn-maned long-legged lioness to my right. She looked cool as cucumbers, joking around with the others, all of them relaxed and enjoying their coffee. None of *them* were worried about whether or not to ice their nipples to make their breasts appear firm on screen or had the studio insist they wax their "furry" lower back after seeing their screen test.

"Sweet Emotion" blared from a boombox as the makeup department raced to meet the 8:00 a.m. set call. We had just sent a production assistant off with our breakfast order when footsteps sounded on the aluminum stairs. The wagon lurched and Katie's hand slipped, poking the mascara wand into my eye.

"Shit," I spat. "Probably that stupid P.A."

"Careful! We're working here!" Katie called out as the door opened and the morning sun flooded the trailer.

Backlit in the doorway stood a tall, broad-shouldered man in a cowboy hat wearing Levi's, a leather belt with a turquoise buckle, and a checkered flannel shirt. He closed the door and his features emerged. With blue eyes, a deep cleft in his chin, thick brows, and a Roman nose, he could have been Tom Selleck's even handsomer younger brother. He removed his hat revealing clipped, dark hair.

"Mornin', folks," he greeted politely.

Out of the corner of my good eye, I saw the lioness sit up.

"Well, howdy there," I quipped, eliciting titters down the row of chairs. "Lost your horse, cowboy?"

He flushed red from his neck to the roots of his buzz cut. It was disarming to see a guy that good-looking blush. Katie dunked a Q-tip in water and began dabbing at the mascara splotch.

"You're Jackie Gold," he declared.

While I wasn't thrilled to be recognized with a fan blowing up my crotch, I was pleased to be the one commanding his attention.

"Yep," I said. "Can we help you?"

"I was looking for my trailer. I'm kind of confused. This is my first day." His Southern drawl only added to his appeal.

"It's my first day too," the lioness chimed in. She swiveled her chair and wrapped one of her shapely legs around the other like a climbing vine.

"Yeah well, it's everyone's first day," I retorted more sharply than I'd intended.

The makeup lights were making me sweaty and needed a smoke. Or maybe it was this cowboy. This ridiculously attractive cowboy. I was flattered he'd recognized me, even for the wrong reasons. Living on the cover of the tabloids in every supermarket in the country for a year had made me easy to pick out.

Katie patted my cheeks a little too firmly with a powder puff and gave me a raised eyebrow in the mirror. I reached for my Evian.

"Got a ciggy?" I asked him, trying for a more pleasant tone.

"Sorry, no. I don't smoke. You shouldn't either, you know." He winked and shook a finger at me.

Even with that corny wink, he was sexy.

"Oh, really? Are you trying to save me?" I flirted, momentarily forgetting the curlers in my hair and the fan between my knees.

He laughed and his face relaxed. His incredible smile twisted to one side creating half-inch dimples low on his cheeks.

His blue eyes met mine in the mirror. "Are you a woman who needs saving?" His look was direct. It caught me off guard and made my stomach flip-flop.

"Katie, gimme a Camel?" I detoured.

There was, of course, a non-smoking policy in the trailer, but I was the star, and no one was about to stop me. Katie sighed, took a non-filtered cigarette from her pocket, and lit it for me.

"What role do you have?" the lioness purred.

"Oh, I'm not acting, not yet. I'm Alex Harvey's stand-in," Brett replied, waving my smoke out of his face. He pointed to his hair as if to explain the buzz cut. "I'm supposed to look like Alex, well, like his character that is. They picked me because we have the same build."

I was thinking what everyone else in the trailer had to be thinking. Alex Harvey's body hadn't looked like this in, well, never.

"Anyway," he continued unaware, "Mary Gaul, the producer, said she'd look around for a couple of lines for me. She's going to help me get my SAG card."

"I just bet she is," I smirked.

"What part are *you* playing?" Brett asked the lioness, ignoring the giggles that followed my remark.

"Oh me? Nothing much. The ex-wife. Two scenes. A phone call and a flashback," she answered.

"Wow." He smiled that smile again. "Sounds great to me. I haven't actually seen the script. But anyway, congratulations!"

Was it his naiveté or his sincerity that grated on me? Jealousy over the lioness? All I know is I felt a rise in my throat, that tight flush of energy I get when I'm about to do or say something I will end up regretting. At another time, I might have censored myself, but three weeks on prescription diet pills had made me jagged and impolite. Mix that with a heaping tablespoon of insecurity, and I was a Molotov cocktail.

He put his cowboy hat back on and inclined it with a tilt. "It was nice meeting y'all. I guess I'll go back to looking for my dressing room."

I took a sip of coffee, now annoyingly cold. "Hey! Wait, cowboy. What's your name?"

He turned. "Barney."

"*Barney?*" I searched the trailer hoping to muster support for my incredulity. But the faces were impassive, except for Katie's whose brow was furrowed with concern. She knew me all too well.

"Yes, Barney Macahaney, ma'am, but my friends call me Buck."

In retrospect, it was probably the "ma'am" that lit the fuse.

"Oh well, Buck, that's a lot better," I snorted. "Listen, Barney, I hate to break it to you, but you don't have a trailer. Stand-ins are herded with the rest of the cattle. And take it from me, you might want to think about changing your name."

A crimson flush started at his collar and burned up his handsome face, scorching the tops of his ears. He blinked as if to clear his vision and opened his mouth, but no words formed.

"Bitch," the lioness muttered under her breath. She got up from her chair and without a glance in my direction, took the clearly shaken Barney by the arm. "Come on sugar, I'll show you where to go."

As the door latched behind them, everyone in the trailer glared at me.

I should have apologized that moment, or at least that day. But my worry concerning the size of my rear end at certain camera angles took up all the space in my head.

"Excuse me, knock knock?" Nurse Pierre's voice interrupts my reflections. He sticks his curly head in the door as Brett scrambles to his feet.

"Oh, hey." Brett hurriedly places the cap back on his head and motions for him to enter.

Pierre's eyes grow wide at the sight of my boyfriend. He clears his throat. "Hi! Sorry for intruding, I just need to…" His shoulders hunch as he wheels in, gesturing to the fresh IV bags he's bringing. "I'm, uh, usually on a different shift," his voice is steady, but his shaking hands are betrayed by the instruments rattling on the cart. "I'm starting some classes, so they let me switch some of my…not that it matters."

Brett sits on the wicker couch and pretends to be interested in the chocolates. I can tell by the clench of his jaw he's struggling to hold it together.

"Sorry, this will just take a minute." Pierre snaps on a pair of plastic gloves, pulls back my sheets, reaches under my gown and between my legs. His hands tremble as he adjusts my catheter.

Brett quickly averts his eyes.

"She's doing much better today," Pierre says as he checks the flow in both of my IV bags.

Brett turns to him with a confused expression on his sad face. "What does that even mean?" he blurts.

Yeah, what *does* that mean? Enquiring minds want to know. I'm sure as hell not feeling better.

"Well," Pierre takes a deep breath, "her vitals are stable, oxygen saturation is excellent, and her lungs are clear." Reciting stats seems to relax him and his shoulders drop from his ears. Pierre strips off his gloves, puts them into the wastebasket and picks up my chart. "Also, she has a terrific urine output." This last fact he delivers like it's the cherry on top. He makes a note on the checklist and repositions my chart. "Honestly, for a coma patient with severe head trauma, half a dozen broken bones, and a ruptured spleen, things are pretty darn good."

And I'd have to argue that things couldn't be shittier unless, well, you know.

"That's all for now," Pierre says. "I'll give you and your…Miss Gold some privacy."

Brett rises to his full six feet three inches and extends his hand. "Jackie here sure would appreciate all you've done." The Texas gentleman back in his boots and minding his manners.

Pierre grasps Brett's hand. "Oh, um, one thing, Mr. Haney."

Brett squares his shoulders, steeling himself for the gushing, the autograph request. It's always the same.

"I just want to say," Pierre's voice is somber, "I'm so *very* sorry for your pain." He releases Brett's hand and unlocks the cart's wheels. "Take care now," he calls over his shoulder as he pushes toward the door.

Huh. Not what we were expecting.

Brett slumps and his eyes fill. "Uh, hold on a minute there fella'."

Pierre turns.

"Are you…"

"Oh, Haitian," Pierre says. "Everyone asks. And probably some Swedish on my mom's side."

Brett shakes his head and clears the lump in his throat. "I was going to ask if you're married?"

"Oh," Pierre chuckles, "I wish. Haven't found the right guy."

"I see." Brett attempts a grin. "Jackie and I…" the muscles of his face crumple and he moans. "Sorry, fella." He claps his hands over his mouth to stifle the sobs.

Pierre stands at the cart for a moment, uncertain, then relocks the wheels, goes over and puts a muscled arm around Brett's shoulder. "It's okay. It's okay, buddy."

"Oh God, oh God, oh God." Brett turns into Pierre's chest weeping. "It's not okay. I'm sorry, Jackie. I'm so sorry."

"Shh, you got this, yeah? You'll be fine," Pierre whispers in Brett's ear. He pats his back and rocks him gently from side to side.

I am gobsmacked! One, that my cowboy is crying in another man's arms, and two, at Pierre's professionalism in containing his pleasure at having Brett Haney in his embrace. Another nurse (one who, let's say left Valentine chocolates for my boyfriend) might not have the willpower to restrain herself from enjoying such a moment.

There is a knock at the door. Brett jumps out of Pierre's arms and swipes at his eyes.

"Who is it?" Pierre calls out.

"Stim-puppy," a deep male voice answers.

Several sharp yips echo in the hallway.

Pierre looks at Brett who shakes his head furiously. Pierre opens the door a crack. "Sorry, we're in the middle of a procedure, would you mind rescheduling? 'Preciate it."

Pierre closes the door.

Brett clears his throat, does his chin jut thing; an attempt to reconstitute some semblance of his tough-guy self. "Thanks, man. I-I'm okay now."

"You sure? I can stick around?"

"No, no, but I appreciate your um, and if you wouldn't mention…"

Pierre brushes him off with a wave. "Already forgotten." He rolls the cart to the door.

Brett dashes to his aid. "Here lemme get that." He opens the door and stands back to let Pierre through.

"Hey, Pee-yayer is it? I say that right?"

Pierre laughs. "Pierre," he pronounces adding the accent. "It's French for Peter."

"Mind if I call you Pete?"

"Not at all."

"Well, thanks again." Brett shuffles and looks at his feet. "I just gotta' ask…Goddamnit Pete…what do you press? About two-fifty?"

Pierre grins. "Three hundred, actually. You?"

"Not quite that," Brett manages a chuckle. "But I bet I'd beat you at arm wrestling."

That's the man I wanted to marry. That's my guy.

SLOW DISSOLVE TO:

INT. BEL AIR MANSION
DAY
NOVEMBER

If our beach home had been contemporary, the "dream house" was positively futuristic. Eleven thousand square feet of concrete and glass set at various angles on seven gated and terraced acres in Coldwater Canyon. Every piece of furniture and art had been purchased new by Gerard Piccard to fit his overall design. I hated every inch of the place with its cold Italian marble floors, travertine tables, and *objets d'art.* Our living room was about as cozy as a museum lobby. It was like residing in a mausoleum.

There were four levels and an elevator. The first level was devoted to the tennis and pool facilities; indoor and outdoor cabanas, a game room, and a massage, spa, and workout accommodations. The second floor housed the living room, kitchen, dining room, and maids' wing. My room was on the third level, along with five unoccupied guest bedrooms, while the entire fourth level had offices for Daddy and Anna and an enormous master suite.

I would have been more depressed about the new digs, but in a miraculous turn of events, Nicole had moved to Beverly Hills just in time for our sophomore year. All Steffi's hard work had finally paid off.

"This time, she caught a big one!" Nicole said the day she'd given me the news.

"How big?"

"A fucking whale. The guy's name is Stan Kemper. He owns like half of Camden Drive. And guess what else."

"What?"

"We're moving in with him. And Jax, are you sitting? Guess where I'm going to school?"

That was three months ago.

"Hello!" My voice echoed in the foyer. "Anyone home?"

I threw my backpack down on the marble floor, then quickly checked inside to make sure nothing was broken. At school, I drank from mini airplane bottles which were easier to hide and cheaper to buy. The house was quiet. Daddy and Anna were at a film festival in London, Lupe was on vacation, Trini had quit when we'd moved up the canyon, and I couldn't remember the new maid's name. I was pretty sure it started with a C. Camilla? Conchella? What the hell was it? I walked into the kitchen and heaved open the door of the sub-zero. It was empty except for a few condiments and last week's takeout from Spago.

"Jesus," I muttered. I opened a cabinet, found some Ritz crackers and jelly, and climbed the two flights to my room. I refused to take the elevator no matter how tired or wasted.

I was almost at my landing when I heard the phone ring.

"Con...what the hell's her...Concetta! Can you get that?" I called out. The phone continued to ring. Trying to keep the crackers from spilling, I ran back down the stairs and into the den on the second floor.

"H-Hello?" I panted.

"Hello, Jacqueline."

I froze.

"Are you there? It's your mom."

Blood rushed to my head and my chest pounded. I hadn't heard her voice in...how long had it been? Two years? Three?

"How did you get the new number?" I asked, more harshly than I'd intended.

"My lawyer."

"Oh." I put my crackers on the coffee table but didn't sit. I wasn't about to get comfortable.

"I thought I would get the machine," she confessed.

"Yeah, well, I was waiting for a friend of mine to call."

"How have you been?"

The part of me that hated her wanted to fire off a zinger. Aim for the heart, shoot-to-kill. But another part in me, a part I had no explanation for, wanted to keep her on the phone. Especially since she sounded sober.

"I've been okay," I ventured.

"Just okay?"

"I'm fine, all right? Everything's fine. Jesus!"

"Well good, honey, I'm glad to hear it." Her voice was huskier than I remembered.

I didn't say anything.

"Jacqueline? Don't you want to know how I am?"

"You're not going to tell me you've got cancer or something, are you?"

"No! Of course not. I'm just making conversation, for goodness sake."

"Okay, then 'for goodness sake,' how are you?"

"Actually, I'm great. I just got back from three weeks of windsurfing in Maui. A friend of mine, a great windsurfer, is teaching me."

"While he's at it, maybe he could teach you to get a job," I said in my father's tone.

She didn't respond.

"Hello? Merilee?"

"I'm still here, you can't get rid of me that easily. How's school?"

"Crappy."

"I hated school too. I hope you didn't catch that from me." She laughed softly.

So far, she hadn't said one terrible thing.

"You sound different, Merilee."

"Well, I haven't been drinking, if that's what you're hinting at. *Is* that what you're hinting at?"

"No, I'm—" Suddenly I got nervous. *Quit now before things turned bad,* I told myself. Plus, if Daddy found out… "Look, I should get off the phone."

"Jacqueline—"

"Jackie!"

"Jackie."

"What? What is it? What do you want?"

"I was wondering if you would like to come to Hawaii," she paused, "for your birthday."

Now, I sat down.

"Is this a joke, Merilee?"

"I thought it might be nice."

"Nice?"

"I thought it might be time."

"Time?"

"Well, obviously I'm not saying it right."

"You know Daddy'll never let me."

"You're probably right. I thought I'd ask anyway. I'm sorry I upset you."

"I'm not… I mean, I didn't…"

There was silence. I thought she might have hung up.

"Mom?"

"I'm still here."

"Are you serious about this?"

"I'll buy the ticket right now if you say yes."

"Since when can you afford to buy a plane ticket?" I asked.

"You sound just like… Oh gosh. Give me a chance, huh?"

I still hated her. But that silly "gosh" softened me. Besides, everyone, even Merilee deserved a chance.

"I'll consider it," I said. "But don't hold your breath."

EXT. BEVERLY HIGH
NOON

Nicole and I sat in the quad outside the cafeteria, passing a plastic Ronald McDonald's to-go cup filled with tequila between us. She was working away at the tear in the knee of her jeans, the lunchtime activity reflected in her Ray-Bans. She looked particularly pretty that day, her skin almost clear now after a bout with acne. She'd cut bangs and her blonde hair hung loose to her waist. I straightened mine with a blow dryer, but it still only reached the middle of my back, and if it rained it curled back up to my shoulders. Nicole had gotten even taller that year. I felt almost invisible beside her. Not to mention her amazingly big boobs I would have killed for, but which in my opinion, she accentuated too much.

Most kids were in the cafeteria eating. We were on "yellow alert," which meant the smog was so bad no one should be outside breathing.

"Are your eyes stinging?" I asked. "Mine sting like crazy."

"Yes, and my chest hurts when I breathe. But maybe that's from smoking," Nicole said.

"God, I miss the beach."

"Me too." Nicole sighed. "The city sucks."

She'd been down in the dumps all week because of what had happened with Andy Webb, this senior she was into, with gorgeous green eyes and a killer bod. He appeared way older than eighteen and had already been in a commercial for shaving cream. Nicole had gone all the way with him, and he hadn't called her since. I knew exactly how she felt. What was it with guys? No wonder women in the olden days kept a lock on it 'til marriage.

"Don't worry, Nic, you'll get over it." I passed her the McDonald's cup. "Andy Webb isn't worth your time."

She took the plastic straw out of the cup and drank from the edge. "Yeah, well, he's now on my shit list, and that my dear is that."

"And that my dear is that" was Nicole's favorite expression.

She handed back the empty cup, and I reached in my backpack for a refill.

"So, what's this big news you couldn't say on the phone?"

"We need drinks first. What's your pleasure, vodka or gin?" I asked, showing her the mini choices.

"Both," she said.

I checked that no teachers were around, then unscrewed the caps on the tiny bottles, dumped the contents into the plastic cup, and took a big swig. "Okay. Guess who called yesterday?"

Nicole shrugged.

"The WPE."

WPE stood for Worst Parent Ever.

"No shit!"

I took another swig. "Here's the kicker, she wants me to visit her."

"What?"

I nodded. "In Hawaii."

Nicole's eyes widened. "Are you serious? Go!"

"Are you crazy? Daddy would never let me. Besides what am I going to do, go and tell her what a rotten mother she is?"

Nicole cocked an eyebrow. "Maybe she wants to apologize."

"As if I'd even accept her apology in this lifetime."

"If it were my dad, and he wanted to see me, I'd do it. And he's been gone longer than your mom. Yeah, even though he's a double WPE and a bastard and doesn't deserve the time of day, I would still go."

"Yeah, but—"

"Jackie, what if this is the only chance you'll ever have? I mean, think about it. What if something happens to her? Or to you? How would you feel then?"

"Listen to you, Miss Mature," I smirked. "Hey." I elbowed her and pointed across the quad to where Andy Webb approached. "Don't look now." I pretended not to see him, hoping he'd veer off, but Nicole waved him over.

"Hello there, Andrew," she said brightly.

"What happened to your shit list?" I hissed in her ear, but she nudged me away.

"Got any weed?" Andy asked. I shook my head and handed him the McDonald's cup.

He took the lid off and gulped the rest of the booze. I grabbed the cup away from him as he let out a big, asshole guy-belch.

"You're such a pig, Webb," I said.

Nicole reached into her purse and held out a joint.

"Hey, Andy?" she singsonged, waving it like a temptress.

"You didn't tell me you had any dope," I said.

Andy reached for the joint, but Nicole pulled it away, giggling. He grabbed her around the waist and tackled her. They tumbled on the grass, Andy wrestling her to the ground until he snatched the joint.

"C'mon, let's go smoke," Nicole said, straightening out her blouse.

Andy jumped to his feet and stuck the joint behind his ear. "No can do. Got an audition after school. Thanks for the buzz though ladies."

He sauntered off down the path to the cafeteria, laughing.

Nicole's face turned red and frozen like she'd been slapped by snowballs.

"I'm gonna kill him," she said.

"Yeah okay, kill him," I said. "Let's ditch Algebra and buy some ciggies, okay?"

Nicole didn't answer. She kept staring at the spot that had been Andy.

INT. BELAIR MANSION
MORNING

I waited weeks before bringing up the phone call. My birthday was a month and a half away, but I, for several reasons, had been stalling. On the one hand, I was curious whether my mother had actually quit the booze, and if she and I could have some sort of relationship. But on the other, I was petrified of seeing her. What if she said or did something stupid that made me angry, or worse, made me cry? I couldn't let her get to me that way. Also, I was scared of my father's reaction. Just the mention of her name usually sent him into a tizzy. For two weeks, I'd hidden behind the convenience of our conflicting schedules. But then came a morning where our breakfasts overlapped, and I decided the time had come.

"I'm failing math." I poured myself some orange juice and took a few pieces of bacon off the plate Concetta had laid out.

"What happened to that tutor you had?" Daddy asked from behind the paper.

"He was a schmuck. I told him not to come back."

"Jackie, mind your language, pleeeese." Anna winked and shook her fork at me. After four years in Beverly Hills, Anna had settled into speaking as if she were a dignitary; like the ambassador to Spain, her thick accent returning only when she was excited or upset.

"I don't know why I have to learn geometry anyway. Am I going to be a carpenter when I grow up?"

I was vamping, working up the guts to start the real conversation.

"Hey, Dad, guess what. There's a teacher at our school who everyone thinks is a lesbian. Her name is Agnes, isn't that perfect?"

Anna tapped my father's arm.

"Yes, okay, I'll tell Grace to call the school for a new tutor." Grace was my father's secretary. I pushed around the eggs on my plate.

"Concetta!" Anna signaled the housekeeper to clear the dishes.

"Um, there's a musical at school everyone is trying out for," I said.

"A musical?" Anna asked. "Is it *Bye Bye Birdie*? I love that one."

"I thought it was *West Side Story* you loved," Daddy said.

"No," I interrupted. "This musical is about Hawaii. Oh, Dad, that reminds me, speaking of Hawaii—"

My father was half out of his chair still reading the paper as he fished for his jacket.

"*South Pacific*?" Anna asked. "With that song 'Bali Hai?'"

"Daddy! Wait! Wait!"

"What is it, Jackie?" he asked impatiently.

"Um, oh, just that… I need someone to sign a consent form for a field trip on Friday."

"Fax it to your father's office and Grace will fax the school," Anna said, rising, her purse in hand.

It was now or never. My window of opportunity was closing, and I couldn't afford to chicken out. "Oh, one more thing. Mom called."

That did it. Everyone froze. I could almost see my words suspended in the air. Finally, Daddy turned around.

"How did she get the number?" he asked, measured.

"She said her lawyer got it."

Anna raised her eyebrows at my father.

"Oh, for Chris'sake." He shook his head.

"And here is the thing, she wants me to come and visit."

"What?" he said, alarmed. "No! No. No. No. Bad idea, Jackie. Very bad idea."

Whether it was my rebellious nature, my talk with Nicole, or my curiosity which currently outweighed my fear, in that instant I made up my mind.

"I want to go."

"Out of the question." Daddy set his lips in a line.

"Fine, then I'll get a tattoo," I parried.

"You are not getting a tattoo."

"She even said she'll pay for the ticket."

"How? With Green Stamps?" he snorted.

"What are Green Stamps?"

"Never mind."

"I want to go for my birthday."

"Oy, Jackie!"

"Dad! I'm going to be sixteen," I said, putting on a reasonable voice. "Dad, Daddy, I can handle it."

"Sid." Anna pointed at her watch. My father nodded. "Jackie, we can discuss this later."

"When later?"

"Tonight."

"Dinner?" I asked hopefully.

"No, wait, I can't. I have a meeting." He scratched his chin.

"Daddy, please." Suddenly, I was on my feet championing my cause. "I know you hate her, and you have every reason to feel that way and to want to protect me, but she *is* my mother. What if something happens to her and I never see her again?" I said, using Nicole's argument. "Think of how you would feel if that happened and you were the one who had prevented me from at least having that chance."

Daddy and Anna looked at one another.

"Sidney?" Anna said. "Perhaps take it under consideration?"

This surprised me. Anna seldom intervened between my father and me.

"All right," my father grumbled on his way out the door, "I'll consider it. But don't hold your breath."

LIHUE, HAWAII AIRPORT
AFTERNOON
JANUARY 29
1985

Naturally, she was late. I sat on my duffle bag scrutinizing every forty-year-old woman with blonde hair. The airport was tiny with only one baggage area, so there was no place else she could be. I was beginning to think she had forgotten about me (a plausible theory) when I spotted her. She was at least thirty pounds heavier, wearing red nylon swim trunks and a plaid bathing suit top two sizes too small. Her once-shiny hair was sun-fried, her skin mottled. She paused for a second to talk with a skycap in a Hawaiian shirt, then as she started in my direction, I suddenly wished I could jump on the next plane home.

Heart pounding, I rose to greet her, but she hurried right past me toward the baggage carousel.

It hadn't occurred to me that my mother might not recognize me, even though it had been eight years and I had purposely not sent her one picture. I approached from behind, a lit cigarette twisting in my hand, and tapped her shoulder. She turned around and stared at me for a second before shrieking.

"Jacqueleeeeeeeene!" she cried, hugging me to her. I smelled marijuana. "You're all grown up!" She squeezed and patted at various parts of my stiff body as if to reshape me.

I pulled away.

"What?" she asked.

I shook my head. "Nothing."

She yanked the duffle out of my hands and swung it over her broad shoulders. She was more muscular than I remembered. "How was your trip?" she asked, walking two steps ahead of me.

"Dandy," I said sarcastically, catching up to her. "Except for the last hour when I was waiting for you to show up."

150 · DINAH MANOFF

"Oh, honey, I'm so sorry. I was, well *we* were getting things ready at our place. You'll see."

We? Our place? Two big red flags. She'd never once mentioned living with anyone. What was I thinking? Why hadn't my father locked me in a closet? Well, it was too late now. I had chosen to come and I would deal with whatever and whomever. It was only for a week, I reminded myself.

Outside the terminal, the humid air enveloped me, making my thighs stick together and my cigarette soggy. I pulled my hair back into a ponytail, hoping to keep it from curling. I removed my leather jacket, but the heat plastered itself on my back, igniting the black spandex shirt I had worn. I knew I shouldn't have brought the jacket, but Daddy had given it to me that morning for my birthday. It was a real motorcycle jacket with a Harley-Davidson logo on the back. It had made me feel tough earlier, bulletproof. Now, I just felt hot and stupid.

When we arrived at the car, I was taken aback to discover a Mercedes coupe exactly like the one my mother used to drive. Only this one was corroded with rust, the convertible top patched with duct tape.

"That's not…?" I gestured.

"Yes indeedy. I had her shipped."

She opened the compact trunk and shoved my duffle on top of a bunch of garbage bags full of stuff. Then, she sat her rear end on the trunk and bounced up and down until the latch clicked.

"There!" she said triumphantly. Merilee opened my door and, like a little girl, skipped around to the other side. She ground her key into the ignition, and we drove away from the airport and out to the open road.

"Oh honey, there is just sooo much I have to tell you," she sang out. "Wait'll you see your birthday surprise!"

All this and a surprise too. Great.

One of the wettest spots in the world, Kauai is known as the "Garden Island." From the main road, waterfalls can be observed. Sugarcane fields traverse the base of the majestic mountains. I picked up a travel brochure at the airport, and now as we drove, I buried my head in it for lack of knowing what to say. Merilee turned on the radio and sang along to what sounded like a local garage band. Her voice, like her car, was rustier now.

Reading made me carsick, so I folded the brochure, leaned back into the cracked upholstery, and focused out the window.

Along the road, plantation shacks squatted in a palette of weathered primary colors. Roadside stands advertised papayas and bananas. Rain fell intermittently causing Merilee to constantly fiddle with the wipers. Out of the wet red earth grew impossible bright pink and orange flowers. We drove past a grove of tall palm trees, their hairy tops swaying in the ocean breeze like hula skirts. The greenest fields I had ever seen stretched down to white sand that then melted into emerald-colored water. No wonder Merilee had chosen to live here.

My mother reached past me and popped open the glove box. It was stuffed full of junk: maps, candy wrappers, hair elastics. From inside the jumble, she pulled out a baggie half-filled with pot and a couple of rolled joints and handed it to me.

"Really?" I arched my brows. I checked around as if God, or worse, my *father* was somewhere in the car.

"Only if you want to," she said.

I took out one of the joints and my mother pressed in the cigarette lighter. Neither of us said a word as I lit the joint, inhaled like the pro I'd become, and passed it to her. She gave me a curious half-smile then shrugged. I was relieved. I had wondered how I would get through the whole week without it but had been too afraid of getting caught with a stash on the plane. And at least my mother wasn't drinking.

"Good stuff," I croaked, taking another hit.

I handed the joint to my mother. As she smoked, I observed the deep lines around her thin lips. Mine were fuller, but our faces were the same shape, both ovals with high cheekbones, and the contour of our brows were alike. But the resemblance stopped there. The rest of me was pure Goldstein.

"The best on the island," said my mother proudly. "We grow it in one of our friend's backyards."

We? Our? What was I in for? I had so many questions.

"How much farther?" I asked.

"Don't children ever outgrow that question?" my mother joked.

Her saying that scratched at something vicious inside me. I started formulating a retort like "You didn't stick around long enough to find out" when my mother shouted.

"Hey! Look up to your left!"

A waterfall splashed down giant rocks and into the pool of a wide cave. As we passed, a cool mist sprayed my face and I noticed that the lush foliage had grown larger, expanded into cartoon-sized leaves—or was it the pot?

Merilee smiled and passed me the roach. It burned my fingers and I dropped it onto the floor.

"Shit! Sorry," I said, stamping the ember with my Doc Martens.

My mother laughed and gave my arm a little pinch.

We drove for a while in silence. I gazed out the window, mesmerized. The mountains were vibrant green, plump, and fertile looking. Their tops disappeared into rain clouds, waterfalls streamed down their crevices. In the valley below were flat fields.

"What is that? Rice?" I ventured.

"No, dum-dum," my mother laughed. "Taro fields."

I didn't like her laughing at me.

A few minutes later, my mother pulled off the main road. We drove past a mermaid fountain spitting streams next to a sign announcing "Welcome to Princeville."

"Home sweet home!" she declared as we drove the rim of a golf course. Tract homes and condominiums rested on subdivided green lawns. It resembled a retirement resort. I had pictured my mother in some funky island community of aging hippies who ate organic vegetables and washed their clothes with rocks in a river. She pulled into a driveway past a sign that said Sea Star II and parked in the carport next to a small, blue Toyota pickup with a license plate that read, 2MCHFUN. She killed the ignition, but the engine continued coughing and sputtering a while longer before shutting down.

She opened the trunk and took out my duffle. "This-a-way!" she caroled.

Tentatively, I followed her down a cement pathway lined with spiky plants. We stopped at a door with a rainbow sticker arched over the number four and a green Astro-turf welcome mat with a mud-covered, yellow happy face in the middle. Merilee kicked off her sandals. A lizard scurried past my head and up the wall, disappearing into a crack in the stucco. Children's laughter echoed from somewhere. I felt disoriented. It was a mistake to have gotten stoned. Merilee swung open the unlocked door and disappeared, leaving me on the happy face mat. Then she came back, took my hand, and led me inside.

The living room was dark, the sun outside too high in the sky to reach under the condo's low eaves. A cottage cheese ceiling flecked with glitter hung not far from our heads. Across the room, a long window framed the golf course and part of a public restroom with the word "Wahini" stenciled on the wall. In the corner of the living room hung a rattan chair swing, and in it sat a little girl.

She was seven or eight years old with long, blonde hair. Skinny legs dangled from the hem of her flowered dress. She resembled those pictures I'd seen of my mother as a child—pretty. So much prettier than I had been.

The little girl swiveled back and forth as Merilee stood between us watching with a stupid grin. In the silence, I became aware of the far-off sound of breaking waves. I felt nauseous, dizzy, way too stoned. From the door of another room, a tall woman appeared wrapped in a rust-colored, tie-dyed sarong. She pulled apart the dark strands of her wet hair with a wide pink comb. My first thought was, *Oh good, I made a mistake, and this is that little girl's mother.* But I knew she wasn't.

The woman smiled at me. "How's everybody doin'?" she said, overfriendly.

My mother nodded to the little girl who walked over to me and from behind her brought a lei made from white flowers. "These are for you," she said in a rehearsed tone.

I froze.

"Bend down, Jacqueline," my mother coaxed.

The little girl lifted on bare tiptoes, put the flowers around my neck, and kissed me on the cheek. My mother floated over and put an arm around my shoulders. I knew what she was about to say, and I didn't want to hear it.

"Jacqueline, meet your sister, Mirabelle."

Mirabelle. Another rotten name.

Moments went by while I stood, sweat pouring down my back, just staring at the three of them. They wore matching grins and seemed to be waiting for me to do something, but I was paralyzed. The lei itched my neck and it smelled so perfumey I thought I might throw up, but I didn't dare remove it for fear of hurting the girl's…that is to say, my *sister's* feelings. So, this was my birthday surprise.

"And this is my friend, Bea," my mother proclaimed of the woman with the wet hair.

Bea leaped forward and extended a hand, but my arms stayed glued to my sides. Undeterred she looped her arm around my shoulder declaring, "I think Jackie needs to sit down."

I filed away points for her calling me Jackie and let her guide me to the futon. My legs trembled as I bent to sit. Bea brought me a glass of water and I drank it fast, trying to push through the cloud of pot in my head. Food would bring me down.

"I need something to eat," I said.

"Munchies, honey?" my mother said.

Oh, shut up, Merilee, I said to myself, pinching my lips together so the words couldn't escape. *Just fucking shut up and die.*

"Bea, do we have any food prepared?" my mother trilled.

"We have Jackie's birthday cake," said little Mirabelle.

Oh, goody, my birthday cake. I was reeling.

"On second thought, I'll just have a cigarette." I reached into my jacket pocket for my Marlboros.

"Outside," my mother pointed. "No smoking in the house. And no shoes! Take off your shoes, Jacqueline." She pointed at the Doc Martens. They appeared huge sticking out on the end of my feet. Clown shoes.

"Nobody in Hawaii wears shoes in the house," Bea offered.

Outside, the ritual of lighting my cigarette helped steady me. I leaned against the nubby outer wall of the condo and inhaled. Okay. I had a sister. Not such a big deal, really. Hadn't I always wanted a sister? No. A sister would steal my makeup and wear my best clothes. What was I saying? She was a little girl, seven or eight, just about the age I had been when my mother left. The realization nearly doubled me over. She hadn't wasted much time between dumping one daughter and having another.

I took another drag off my cigarette. And where was the kid's father? I knew Merilee hadn't married again because Daddy still sent her alimony. Who took care of her when Merilee was on a bender? And what would poor Mirabelle do if Merilee ran off looking for her freedom again; who would she live with? None of my business, I told myself. This is not even really my family. I stubbed my cigarette out on the wall and stuffed the butt into my pocket.

I unlaced my Doc Martens and lined them up with the other shoes by the dirt-caked welcome mat. I was still stoned, but I had come down a notch.

Inside, a small, round cake dripping with white icing and over-adorned in pink and yellow florets had been set out on the coffee table, sixteen red-and-white-striped candles crowded on top. Merilee, Bea, and Mirabelle sat on stools at the kitchen counter, their expressions hopeful like three pups waiting for me to throw a ball. I walked to where Merilee had dropped my duffle bag, unzipped it, and fished around for my Walkman. How was I going to survive a whole week here?

"Mommy, can we light the candles now?" Mirabelle whispered loudly.

Had I once asked the same thing of that same person? It seemed impossible.

"Jacqueline?" Merilee poked me with her voice.

"Yeah. Whatever," I muttered.

Bea lit the candles, and they all sang *Happy Birthday*, first in English, then Hawaiian.

"Make a wish," my little sister said, bouncing on her stool.

I blew out the candles and wished for no more surprises.

At dinner, Bea and Merilee did most of the talking while I managed to choke down a bowl of tofu and tasteless brown noodles.

"If the wind holds, otherwise we'll go to Mahalapoo," Bea was saying.

"Or Maui?" Mirabelle asked. "Mama, can we go to Maui?"

"Have you ever windsurfed Jackie?" Bea asked.

I shook my head.

"It's hard," Merilee said. "It took me weeks just to stand."

"She's doing great now though." Bea smiled at Merilee.

"Bea could give you a lesson," Mirabelle offered, looking at me.

"No, thank you. I don't think I'd be any good at it," I replied in the politest voice I could muster.

"You know they filmed *South Pacific* not far from here. Bali Hai? That's the beach at the end of the road," my mother said.

"Mom loves that movie," Mirabelle said.

"Bali Hai!" Bea and Merilee sang together.

My little sister shook her head. "It's so embarrassing."

"You have to see the sunset there," Merilee said. "If I could live anywhere in the world it would have a view of Bali Hai."

After dinner, Merilee cleared the table while Bea and Mirabelle washed dishes and swayed their hips like hula dancers to an Island band on the radio. I had never cared for the slide guitar and warbled harmonies of Hawaiian music, but with the warm breeze blowing through the open doors, the distant waves, and the floral-scented air, it almost sounded beautiful.

Merilee put a practically empty bottle of mango-papaya juice in the fridge, wiped the counter, and handed me a dishtowel. "Bea is our roomie. The rents are so high here it's the only way we can afford a nice place."

"You can sleep in my room," Mirabelle said shyly, handing me a wet coffee cup.

"We borrowed a foldaway." Merilee took the cup from me and put it back in the sink in front of Bea. "You missed a spot."

"Sorreee," Bea said rolling her eyes. She whipped a towel at my mother who scooted away playfully.

"Unless you'd rather sleep with me, Jaqueline?" My mother offered.

"Huh?" The question set off an eruption of feelings. I'd slept with my mother only once that I could remember when I was four or five. Anna was off and Daddy was away somewhere on location. I'd woken with a nightmare, gone to my parent's room, and snuggled up next to her. She got up, went to the bathroom, vomited, then stumbled back to bed. I doubt she knew I was there.

"Would you like to sleep with me?" My mother pressed. "I have a king-size mattress."

If I answered, I would say something terrible, something none of us would recover from.

"I'll be outside." I grabbed the cigarettes out of my jacket. "I can sleep in her room," I said, pointing to Mirabelle on my way out the door.

"Yay!" Mirabelle clapped her hands together as if she'd won the prize.

The next morning when I woke up, Merilee and Bea were gone. I got my cigarettes and went outside in my pajamas. I'd survived the first day. All I had to do was make it through six more.

When I came back, Mirabelle was sitting at the kitchen counter eating papaya and some kind of sticky-looking cereal.

"Where is everyone?" I asked.

"Mom and Bea went to work. Usually, I go to my friend's house, but today I get to stay with you!"

"Oh. Work?"

"Yeah."

I hadn't pictured my mother with a job, and she hadn't mentioned one. Merilee was chock full of surprises.

"Want some?" Mirabelle held out half a papaya with the seeds removed.

"Oh, no thanks, I don't usually eat this early."

"We have Pop-Tarts if you prefer."

"Maybe later, I'll just make some coffee or something."

"We don't have coffee, but there's tea bags in the cupboard. After, can I show you the beach?"

I shrugged and rummaged through the kitchen. From the looks of things, Bea and Merilee were on some kind of a health kick. Everything in the fridge and cabinets was natural this, or organic that. There was no alcohol—none that I could find anyway. Maybe Merilee had turned herself around. I found a couple of old bags of Lipton, put some water in a pot on the stove, and waited for it to boil.

We put on bathing suits and shorts. A light rain fell on our shoulders as I followed Mirabelle to the end of the street, then down a trail beside a complex of white, luxury condominiums. The narrow path led to a river lined with wooden, one-story homes; boxes atop concrete stilts in washed-out shades of green, pink, yellow, and orange. Several small fishing boats were docked along the verdant banks while white egrets perched on tips of grass blades as comfortably as if they had been sitting atop a cow's back. At the mouth where the river met the ocean, the sea was glassy and calm. Children ran in and out of small waves that lapped the shore. Further down the beach, families, most of whom appeared to be locals, gathered at an open pavilion, barbecuing around picnic tables.

As we neared the pavilion, Mirabelle suddenly plopped down and began furiously digging in the sand like a dog who had picked up the scent of a bone. I stretched out beside her and sifted the hot silt through my fingers. It was different from the sand in California; finer, whiter, and more reflective like ground glass.

"I used to live at the beach," I said.

"I know, Mom told me." Mirabelle scooped a pile of wet sand from where she'd been digging.

What else had "Mom" told her about me, about us, about our life before she left?

"So, how old are you?" I asked, picking what I thought was a safe question.

"Seven."

I did the calculations. Merilee had gotten pregnant the very same year she'd left us. Anger rose in my chest. I reached for my cigarettes before remembering I'd left them at the condo.

"Christ," I muttered.

"What?"

"Nothing. Just, you're pretty tall for your age."

"I'm the tallest in my class, except for Noah."

"Noah is a boy in your school?"

"No, dum-dum," Mirabelle laughed. "Noah is the teacher. You're sixteen."

"Yup."

"That makes you nine years older than me."

"Right."

"I'm good at math. Mom says I get that from my Dad."

This was the first I had heard about Mirabelle's father. I couldn't help but be curious. I propped up on one arm. "So, what does he do? Your dad?"

"He's a counter," she said. "He counts stuff."

"A counter? Oh, you mean an accountant," I offered.

"Yes. What does your dad do, Jacqueline?" Mirabelle asked politely.

"He, um, helps people make movies, and if you don't mind, I prefer to be called Jackie."

"That's your nickname," Mirabelle said with a knowing nod. "Nicknames are supposed to come from other people. My friend Elisabeth's nickname is Tootie because her brother couldn't say Elizabeth when he was little. If you couldn't say Mirabelle, what would you call me?"

The conversation had veered off the safe path into territory I hadn't even known existed much less planned to explore. Mirabelle was guileless and unguarded, while I walked through life like Chicken Little waiting for the sky to fall.

"I don't know, I guess maybe Belle? Bella?"

"No, too princessy."

"Um, well, can I have time to think about it?"

"Okay."

The clouds gave way and the sun streamed down lighting up Mirabelle's long, silky, yellow hair. I had an urge to braid it or tie it back with ribbons. She was so pretty. A mini version of our mother. I couldn't help thinking I'd been traded in for a better model.

I took off my sunglasses and cleaned them with the bottom edge of my shorts. I wanted to ask Mirabelle more about her dad but worried the topic might cause her distress.

"Can you make a sand angel?" Mirabelle asked. She rolled onto her back and flapped her arms up and down in the sand.

"I'm an expert at sand angels," I said. "I used to make these with my friend, Nicole."

"Was she your best friend?"

"Yup. Still is."

"Did she give you your nickname?"

"No, I gave it to myself."

Mirabelle narrowed her eyes like she was scrutinizing me.

"Jackie!"

"What?"

"Your hair! It's getting all curly."

"Yeah, the rain."

"When I curl my hair, it just falls straight in five minutes. You are so lucky!"

"Right," I laughed.

I turned over on my back and for a few seconds, we flapped our arms together. The sun burned hot on my skin and it felt good to push my arms and legs into the cool wet substrata.

"You and I have the same mother but different fathers, Jackie. That makes us half-sisters and not stepsisters. Stepsisters aren't as good. That's what Cinderella had, wicked, ugly stepsisters."

Every time the sister thing came up, my stomach lurched, and my thoughts became muddled with worry. After all, this could be the only time we ever saw each other, what was the point in building a relationship. Just the subject of our family was tricky. Like playing that game where you go for the thighbone, but one wrong move makes that horrible buzzer go off. I had a store of resentments I might let out by accident or in anger. Stuff that Mirabelle didn't need to know, at least not now.

I got up and brushed the sand off my body. "Aren't you hot? I'm hot." Mirabelle followed me down to the water, and we waded in up to our thighs. The water was warm, silky, and clear. I walked until it grazed the frayed bottoms of my shorts.

"What work does Merilee, I mean your mom and Bea do?" I asked, changing the subject.

"They sell stuff."

"Oh yeah? What kind of stuff?"

"Bea likes to knit, so she sells hats and baby booties sometimes, and she makes these air-brushed sarongs that the tourists buy, but mostly she and my mom sell Turkish tobacco."

"Turkish tobacco?"

"But you can't tell anyone! It's a secret, Mom says. Only for family, so that means I'm allowed to tell you."

I tried to hide my shock. Turkish tobacco my ass. Merilee and Bea were dope dealers! If Merilee got caught, she would go to prison and then Mirabelle would wind up without a mom, just like me. Suddenly the whole situation felt a lot more familiar and, in a way, made me feel better. It gave me authority and validated my anger toward my mother. The wild card in all of this was Mirabelle. I had to be careful. If I threw any punches, it was a good bet that several would land on my sister.

"It's illegal! What if you get caught?"

"Don't be so judgmental, Jacqueline," Merilee said when I confronted her that evening. Mirabelle was already asleep, Bea was taking a shower, and Merilee sat at the kitchen counter loading a crusty old bong that she had retrieved from under the sink. Apparently, the no-smoking-in-house rule only applied to cigarettes. She carried her paraphernalia into the living room.

"Nobody cares here. Everyone smokes. The cops, even the judges. By the way, I am happy to see those curly curls again. I'd forgotten how cute they are!"

"One square cop and you'd be in jail, probably for years."

"Well, I can't live on just what your father sends me. Besides, it provides a way to give Mirabelle extra things like hula lessons."

I gaped at her incredulously. A dozen comebacks rose like prisoners banging their cups against the bars demanding to be set free. I gritted my teeth and sealed my lips against them.

"Hurry up, Bea!" Merilee yelled toward the bathroom door. "I have to use the toilet." She picked up a pile of clothing and stuffed it into a closet. Bea slept on the lumpy futon in the living room. Her clothes were scattered throughout the apartment and she was constantly pulling out a wrinkled sarong or shorts or underwear from different closets.

"She is such a flippin' mess," Merilee said irritably. Her mood seemed to have darkened since I'd brought up the possibility of her being arrested. Maybe she was remembering her police record from her younger days. She snapped on the radio and fiddled with the tuner until she came to some kind of oldies station.

"La la la la la la la hey hey hey Bobby Mageeee yeah!" My mother sang along, her voice as raspy as Joplin's, though nowhere close in key. She readied the bong once again, lit the bowl, and inhaled slowly, forcing the heavy smoke to rise. Microscopic pieces of resin danced in bubbling amber water.

"Turkish tobacco," I muttered. What genius came up with that for a cover? And how long before Mirabelle figured it out?

Merilee pointed the bong in my direction.

I shook my head. "No thanks."

I wasn't making that mistake again. Getting high with my mother was as much fun as entering a house of horrors. I needed my wits about me. From now on, I was staying straight as an arrow. At least until I got home.

From the bathroom, Bea turned off the shower and turned on a blow dryer. She opened the door a crack and stuck out her wet head. "Two minutes, I promise!"

My mother waved backward at Bea and exhaled all the smoke from her lungs, then covered the top of the tube with her hand, trapping the swirling smoke. "Oh Jacqueline, you know what I've missed the most about the old days?" she asked, her voice wistful.

I stayed silent. I was not having this conversation.

"Really?" my mother said. "You can't guess?"

It was a Catch 22; anything I answered would bite me in the ass. If the answer was that she'd missed *me*, then too bad so sad. I hated her way too much to miss her. I didn't want to hear about whatever pain or thoughts she might have experienced on the day she decided to take off. I envisioned my heart turning into a steel shield protecting me from the emotional trap she had set me.

Merilee sighed. "I miss having more than one bathroom."

We had been hiking for what seemed like miles, lugging sandwiches and ratty beach towels in our backpacks. My Doc Martens had turned the color of brick from the wet, red earth of the steep path. I was breathless and regretting my morning cigarette, which had been met with a disapproving (and unsuitably parental) glare from Merilee. I ignored my short-windedness and trudged forward.

Thankfully, the path leveled out and sidled by a stream fenced with tall, pale grass that sprouted white, tropical flowers. We had climbed high enough that we were looking down at an arc of beaches, the water clear and blue, sparkling like a meadow of diamonds. In the distance, hundreds of white gulls circled a lighthouse and roosted on the cliffs of the rocky shore. I had never seen a sight so beautiful. I felt as if this must be heaven's prototype.

It couldn't be the real heaven because my mother was here.

After about twenty minutes, the path descended. The stream split off in another direction, and dark, leafy shrubs replaced the tall grass. We headed away from the beaches toward the mountains. The sun was directly overhead, so I pulled a baseball cap out from my pack and pulled it on. My mother took a few quick steps to catch up to me and offered a lit joint.

"Thank you, no," I said, miming the glare my smoking had received.

"Suit yourself," she croaked, holding the toke deep in her lungs.

The path narrowed and a breeze cut through the trees. A cloud passed before the sun and cast a dark, purple shadow. Earlier, I had asked about the possibility of a storm, but Merilee assured me that good weather was in the forecast.

"I hear the falls, Mom," Mirabelle called out.

"I'm getting bitten up. Did anyone think to bring bug spray?" I asked accusingly.

"You won't need it once you jump in," my mother reassured me.

"How big is this waterfall, anyway?" I asked. "I hope it's worth it." I knew my mother wanted me to be impressed but I wasn't about to give her the satisfaction.

"You just wait and see," she said.

"Oh, they're a good size," Bea chimed in from behind. She was always "chiming in," like she was my mother's backup singer or something.

"Not as big as Niagara Falls, though," Mirabelle said.

I could have sworn she was defending me. I smiled at her and she smiled back.

"Have you been there, Jackie?" she asked.

"Nope. Have you?"

Mirabelle sighed. "I've never even been to the mainland."

"But you've been to lots of other places," Merilee said.

I wanted to tell her not to butt in on our private conversation, but I kept quiet.

"Yeah, but they were all in Hawaii. I want to go to California. Can we go and visit Jackie?" Mirabelle was treading on hazardous territory. My mother and Bea turned to me expectantly like I should say something. I didn't.

Finally, my mother spoke. "Maybe when you're older."

"You mean when I'm sixteen?" Mirabelle asked.

"Maybe you can go see Jackie like she came to see you," Bea added.

"Can I, Jackie?" Mirabelle asked, her wide green eyes gazing up at me, a picture of innocence. I wondered how she'd possibly been spared the complexities I had experienced at her age.

"Yeah, I think so." I tried to remain positive but noncommittal. I didn't want her to count on some future plan that probably would never happen.

There still hadn't been mention of where Mirabelle's father fit in. Today was Saturday. Wouldn't he have visitation or something? Asking would open a dangerous line of questioning and I didn't want to risk harm to Mirabelle, but I had a few theories, mostly involving Merilee running out on the poor schlub. Only why, this time, had she taken her child with her? Maybe he didn't want poor Mirabelle. At least my father had wanted me.

My sister hiked along, happily glued by my side, an Instamatic swinging from a strap on her wrist. She hummed a tune, walking to a private rhythm in her head. A step, a step, a skip and hop, a step, a step, a step and skip.

The night before she had asked me to choose a story to read. I poked through her bookcase. Most of her books were Hawaiian-themed: *The Legend of Queen Lilikulani*; *The Story of The Three Geckos*. Happily, I came upon *The Cat in the Hat*, her only Dr. Seuss.

"This is one of my favorites," I told her.

We propped up pillows on Mirabelle's bed. She wore a thin, pink nightie with a faded seahorse on its front. I was in my boxer pajamas and a tank top.

I had no memory ever of Merilee reading at all, much less to me. "Does your mom ever read to you?" I couldn't resist asking.

"Hmm. Maybe," Mirabelle furrowed her brow. "She sings to me sometimes. Mostly Bea though. Bea *loves* to read," Mirabelle said with a dramatic accent on *loves*. I couldn't tell if that meant Mirabelle enjoyed it or if it was too much.

We took turns reading aloud. I confessed how anxious the part of the book used to make me when the parents were coming home and Thing One and Thing Two had left the pink stuff all over the house, and how relieved I felt when the Cat in the Hat managed to clean things up just in the nick of time.

Mirabelle nodded as if she understood and then, laying her head on my arm, cuddled close and held me. Her neediness, for reasons I couldn't explain, repelled me. Reflexively, I pulled my body away then covered the move by pretending to itch my back.

"What's wrong?" she asked.

"Nothing," I answered. "Mosquitoes."

"They never bite me. Want me to scratch for you?"

"No, no thanks." I moved over to the fold-out bed. "I'm just going to lie over here." I found my Walkman and untangled my headset. I had Joan Jett cued and ready.

"I can read to you while you fall asleep," she offered.

"Um," I hedged. I didn't want her to feel rejected. "Okay, one story but that's all."

"Yay," she clapped. "I'll make one up. Do you want a happy story or a scary one?"

"A scary one. Short though."

"Okay. Shut your eyes, Jackie."

That night, I lay awake on the cot for hours, hard-hearted, and uncomfortable, ashamed that I couldn't be the sister Mirabelle needed me to be. I was desperate to talk to Nicole, but I'd have to go to the market to get to a phone booth for privacy, and I wasn't about to walk the two miles in the dark. I had hoped to go this morning, but then Merilee announced the hike.

The bushes were growing thicker, the path only a couple feet wide. Suddenly nervous, I imagined what might slither out at me from the underbrush. "Are the snakes here poisonous?" I tried to sound matter of fact, like, "Oh, by the way."

"Mirabelle," my mother sang out, "Jacqueline wants to know about snakes."

"There are no snakes in Hawaii," Mirabelle said. "They're not allowed."

"Seriously?" I asked my mother. "No snakes?"

"That's right," Merilee said.

"Don't worry, Jackie," Mirabelle said, taking my hand.

Her fingers wiggled around mine, her palm was moist. Again, the physical contact made me uncomfortable. I didn't want to hold hands with my sister. She was asking for a promise I couldn't keep. How could I have a relationship with her if I chose not to see my mother again? When the path forced us to walk single file, I was able to pull my hand away naturally.

The sound of the waterfall was unmistakable now. Branches nicked at my limbs as foliage encircled and pressed against us, like we were being squeezed through a thorny funnel. A ceiling of sharp twigs and leaves brushed the tops of our heads and we stooped to avoid having our hair snagged. Just when it seemed as though we couldn't possibly push through another inch, the copse miraculously gave way to a clearing, revealing Angel Falls.

Water spilled from a cliff over a hundred feet high then plummeted, crashing into a shaded pool of water encircled by banana and mango trees. Bea smiled at Merilee, who winked back.

"So, Jacqueline, what do you think of our swimming hole?" My mother had to shout to be heard over the thundering falls.

It was amazing, incredible, nirvana.

I shrugged and glanced around coolly; a once-over gesture stolen from my father when he walked into a new place. I shouted back. "It's all right."

"We're on private property." She giggled mischievously.

My indifference didn't seem to bother her, which irked me.

Merilee and Bea set their backpacks under the shade of a banana tree. I followed with Mirabelle as a sweet but malodorous scent inched up my nostrils.

"What stinks?" I shouted.

Mirabelle pointed to where dozens of mangoes had fallen, dotting the ground, split open, overripe, and half-eaten by birds and insects. She walked to the edge of the water. The middle was dark like an eggplant, deep and foreboding. As the pool fanned out to the shore, the color turned violet, then lavender, dissolving to a light, glassy green. Mirabelle took off her shoes and waded in up to her ankles.

"It's refreshing," she called out. "C'mon, Jackie. Take off your shoes."

I walked over dipped in my fingers. "Yikes." I shuddered at the ice-cold water. "I thought all water in Hawaii was set at bathtub temperature," I said wiping my hands on my shorts.

My mother laughed and Bea thumped me on the back as though I were her good buddy. They gave each other a thumbs up and untied their sarongs, revealing bare naked bodies. They weren't even wearing bathing suit bottoms. I turned away, pretending to be busy with my backpack, embarrassed. Then, I wondered if the word "embarrassed" was derived from "bare assed," and filed that thought away for when I talked to Nicole. Boy was she in for an earful.

As Merilee and Bea spread towels under the banana trees, I sneaked a peek at my naked mother. Her big boobs had gotten saggy, and her butt was a lot bigger than I remembered, but her legs were still great. Most of her fat sat around her middle, probably from drinking, though she swore up and down that she hadn't touched alcohol in a year. "Marijuana maintenance," she called it.

Bea was the opposite body type with little tube-shaped boobs that protruded and then kind of drooped at the end, a skinny torso, and a flat stomach that stretched into wide hips and a pan- cake ass. They both needed a bikini wax, or preferably, a bikini bottom. Even their armpits were unshaved. Merilee wouldn't be caught dead with hairy pits in her Malibu days. Now she'd turned feral. They kicked off their flip-flops and waded out into the water, clutching one another and shrieking as each descending body part was exposed to the chill.

"C'mon in!" they waved to me. I shook my head and fished in my pockets for my cigarettes. As I shrank back against the soft, putty-colored trunk of the tree, I felt as I had for the last three days, torn between anger toward my mother and the richness of my surroundings. My biggest fear was that I could weaken· and be pulled over the line into enjoying myself. *What would be so terri-ble?* I had asked myself a dozen times. What if I just let myself have a good time with Mirabelle and my mother and even Bea? *Bad idea, Jackie,* I kept reminding myself. *Your mother is not a person you can suddenly become girlfriends with.* I shut my eyes and beckoned my wall of defense to rise and protect me from the beauty of Angel Falls. I concentrated on the smell of rotting mangoes and inhaled deeply.

A hand tapped my shoulder. Mirabelle stood before me in a red, white, and blue one-piece bathing suit a size too small for her long torso.

"I got it last Fourth of July," she said proudly.

"Nice." I closed my eyes again.

"Aren't you coming in?"

I opened my eyes.

"I'll go in first and show you it's not so bad," she offered. "You just have to get used to it."

Go away, I wanted to say. *Leave me alone.*

I shook my head. "Sorry, kid. Too cold for me."

"Suit yourself," Mirabelle sighed and with a running start, dove straight under the water. I peered at her from behind my dark glasses. She swam like a seal pup, wriggling just below the ceiling of glassy water then surfacing and launching into a smooth crawl, her long, skinny legs fluttering like a propeller. I caught myself smiling. How could I help but admire her ease? She scrambled up onto a flat, moss-covered rock and stretched out her slick body, inviting the sun to bake her bare back. Had Merilee thought to put sunscreen on her? I got up and walked to the water's edge.

"Are you wearing sunscreen?" I yelled.

Her head popped up, long blonde hair falling in drippy ropes in front of her eyes.

"Can't hear you," she mouthed, pointing to the falls.

I waved and retreated under the security of my tree.

Pulling out my Walkman, I flipped over my well-worn Blondie cassette and watched as my mother and Bea swam at the base of the falls, splashing each other, screaming and acting stupid, chasing each other underwater like kids pretending to be sharks. It was revolting. My mother had no inhibitions, which was fine I guess if you were living in your own made-up civilization. Bea was nice enough. But she was one of those infuriating people who always talked about living "in the moment," whatever the hell that meant. The sun was directly overhead, stealing its way through spaces amid the tree's wide leaves. Sweat trickled down my neck and I wanted to eat. I stood up. Both my mother and Bea were underwater, probably having a hold-your-breath contest or something. I waited until they surfaced and waved my arms.

"Let's do the goddamn picnic!" I yelled.

Either they couldn't hear or were pretending not to see me. They put their arms around each other and bounced up and down. "One, two, threeeee." I read their lips before they disappeared again underwater.

I slouched over to my backpack and fished out the avocado and scary sprout sandwich that Bea had prepared. No one seemed to care if I was having lunch by myself. Mirabelle still lounged on her rock, eyes shut, looking as relaxed and comfortable as if she were on a chaise. Bea and my mother had swum to the far side of the pool and were climbing the large boulders, their naked bodies colliding, arms and legs splayed in unsightly angles as they scrambled for footing. I hadn't realized it was possible to do that. From where I sat, the rocks appeared jagged and too far apart. They struggled, slipping, hanging on to one another's bare skin until they came to rest on the largest of the boulders. Then their bodies vanished through the rushing water, emerging seconds later as ghosts behind the dense waterfall.

I was struck with envy. I wanted to go behind that waterfall, if only just to tell Nicole. Maybe Mirabelle could snap a picture of me. Not that I wanted to record one second of this stupid trip, but the waterfall was different, separate—a landmark like the Grand Canyon. As I considered stripping down to my bathing suit and going for it, fear clobbered me like a cartoon character stepping on the end of a rake. What if I couldn't make it across the pool? I could body surf, but I wasn't a strong swimmer and the icy water made me nervous, not to mention what awaited in the murky depths. Poisonous or not, there just had to be disgusting species of tropical amphibians. What if I got out halfway across and had to turn around? I'd make a fool out of myself.

I watched the silhouettes of Bea and Merilee float behind the watery curtain. Their naked bodies seemed natural now, lovely almost, airy like sea maidens dancing gracefully together, apart, then together again as though embracing. The rush of tumbling water played tricks on my eyes, and I imagined they were kissing. I took my sunglasses off and squinted. Jesus. They were kissing, *really* kissing, on the lips. Totally making out!

Mirabelle continued dozing, unaware. Did she know? Was this just happening now or had it been going on for a long time?

Roommates my ass. I sat back down and tried not to watch, tried to concentrate on anything else. I took a bite of my sandwich, but my appetite was zilch. The sea *cows* were going at it now, knotted together, twisting behind their glass curtain, then suddenly they flew apart. *Oh God, they caught me watching.* I dropped my head and pretended to eat, but they were already scrambling back down those rocks, slipping into the water, swimming back toward shore toward me. Now what?

I grabbed my Walkman, put on my headphones, and scrunched myself as small as I could as the sea *monsters* lumbered onto shore, water dripping off their bodies.

My heart pounded as they came nearer, toweling off and wrapping themselves in those ugly sarongs. Merilee whispered; Bea nodded. I glanced around furtively for an escape as they plodded in my direction, clump-clump, holding hands, wet heads hanging bashfully, staring at me with bad-puppy eyes as if they'd dug up the flowers and were about to get punished. I prayed something terrible would happen before they reached me—an earthquake or volcanic eruption. Behind them, Mirabelle climbed onto shore. She hopped up and down on one foot, tapping her head to clear water from her ears.

They stood before me, naughty girls. My mother tried explaining something, "…wanted to wait…" "…really love her…" "…should have told you…" "…right honey?"

I let the Walkman fall from my hand as I ducked past them. Their words skidded off my back. I stripped down to my black, shiny bathing suit; a superhero revealing her true identity. I took a deep breath and charged into the water. Cold, but not as cold as me. I was no longer afraid. If an electric eel had swum up to me, I'd have grasped it in my hands and twisted its neck—lights out for good.

From shore, the falls had appeared a lot closer. I swam as hard as I could, pushing forward and trying not to swallow water. My superpowers were fading, and I remembered that in my other identity, I was a weak swimmer. I bore down and gulped at the air, pulling myself toward the falls. Gasping for air, I arrived at the base and gripped the rocks, heaving myself up.

My body vibrated from the intensity of the tumbling water. Stretching out, I grabbed hold of a pointy rock and managed to pull both feet across to stand. Believing I could splash right through, I leaped forward. But the pounding water rammed me back and I slipped halfway down the rocks. My chest hurt. I'd cut my hand. Grunting, I wedged my shoulders between two of the boulders and rested my shaking arms and legs while I fought to catch my breath. Blood ran down one arm, but I wasn't about to give up. With renewed resolve, I managed to pull myself up and climb, scraping hands and knees against the slick rock until, at last, I heaved atop the highest boulder. With a final push, I slithered under the falls, the water clapping my back in congratulations.

I stood carefully, testing my knees. The cavern curved back like the curl of a giant wave and water puddled in the ruts of the floor. I skimmed my fingers along the wall and was surprised at how dry it felt, like touching a snakeskin.

"Hoot! Hoot! Hoot!" I called out to make an echo, but my voice was absorbed and smothered by the fall's heavy drape.

"Fuck youuuuu!" I yelled as loud as I could, the waterfall a force field protecting me from the world.

Across the pool, Mirabelle, my mother, and Bea arranged towels and unwrapping sandwiches. Through my bleary filter, the scene dripped like a watercolor held upright before it had had time to dry. They were just going about their normal day as if nothing had happened. Okay fine, they were in love or whatever, but couldn't my mother have prepared me?

"Let's give her some space," I imagined her saying. There was also the possibility that she had just forgotten about me altogether. Always that possibility.

And here I was, inside an actual waterfall, and had anyone even thought to take my picture? Isn't that what families *did* on vacation?

Looking back, the evidence was there. No wonder Bea's clothes were all over the living room. My mother was just a jack-in-the-box of surprises.

I wished I could kidnap Mirabelle, take her home with me to California and be the loving sister she wanted. But then what? She seemed happy and adjusted. Maybe growing up in paradise with a couple of middle-aged pot dealers wasn't a terrible thing. And anyway, I doubted Daddy would jump at the chance to raise Merilee's love child.

I walked up and down behind the falls, sticking out a hand, an arm, a leg, feeling the water's power on different parts of me. I still had to get back to shore to deal with this whole fucking *thing*.

I shivered, sat down, and hugged my arms around my body. The numbness from the icy water was wearing off and I rubbed my thawing arms and legs as I tried to bring the picnic blur into focus. Mirabelle was standing at the edge of the shore. Then Bea and my mother got up and started dancing, fuzzy people jumping up and down. No, not dancing, they were waving their arms. I lay down on the rocks where I could see them but they couldn't see me. Let them worry. Let them think I was dead. I watched my mother run back and forth, her hands cupped together in front of her mouth.

"Fuck you!" I cupped my own hands together. "Bitch. Motherfucker. Asshole! I Hate You!" Christ, it felt so good to get it off my chest.

A flash of light cracked the sky. Bea pulled Mirabelle under the tree. Then another burst—lightning. Goddamn Merilee. She led us right in the middle of a lightning storm! Another flash broke in the distance and the skies turned dark as rain began to pour. Merilee ran to the edge of the pool, threw off her sarong, and dove into the water. Was I to be rescued by my naked mother? I'd rather wait out the storm here for however long it took—an hour, a *week*. After all she'd put me through, I was not about to let her off the hook by saving me.

I stood now, pressed against the back of the cave. I could make out her anxious face as she swam to the rocks at the base and climbed effortlessly up and over the boulders.

"Jacqueline!" I read her lips as she searched for me.

I got down on my hand and knees, pushed myself forward through the waterfall, and crawled to the edge of the boulder.

My mother reached out her hand to me. "Oh, honey."

"Geronimo!" I gave her the finger and jumped, wrapping my arms around my knees like a cannonball just as a bolt of lightning flashed across the sky. I hit the frigid water with a huge splash, the blow knocking the wind out of me, suspending me in shock. I fought toward the surface in broken strokes and gasped when I finally reached the air.

"Take it easy." Merilee bobbed beside me. I couldn't speak. I tried to swim but my limbs weren't working right. I flailed in a circle like a plastic windup toy waiting to be set off in the right direction.

My mother drew me into the crook of her arm. I tried swatting her away.

"Lemme go," I managed to sputter, but I was too tired to resist.

She swam like a lifeguard, one-armed, pulling two of us toward shore. The rain poured down in sheets, the air crackling with electricity. My feet touched the silt-covered bottom as my mother pulled me along, hurrying us under the tree. Bea tried to wrap me in a towel, but I yanked away, went straight to my back-pack, and tore into a pack of cigarettes.

I paced back and forth under the banana tree, fighting tears, puffing furiously. I had too many feelings to process. What did they want from me? How was I supposed to act after all these years? Was I supposed to be grateful now? Every angry moment

I'd ever felt in my life combined could not compare to how I felt at that moment. I sure as hell wasn't about to give my mother a medal for heroism. For doing what mothers are *supposed* to do.

While I literally fumed, Bea cooed over Merilee and Mirabelle sat cross-legged on her towel eating an orange and arranging the peels in patterns on the ground. She kept looking over at me, but I pretended not to notice. By the time I'd smoked three cigarettes, the sun was back out and without anyone needing a signal, we all packed up and trudged home.

By morning, the storm system had moved in, blanketing the island. Merilee had planned to take me to "Bali Hai," but the weather kept us housebound. Mirabelle stayed busy, making art projects out of seashells, glue, and glitter or running around the condo in her hula skirt and my Doc Martens, which were allowed inside "for costume purposes only." My sister invented what seemed like a hundred "rainy day games," all of which required my participation. I did my best to go along, frequently pleading for a break to read a magazine or listen to my Walkman.

I wrote postcards to Nicole, venting my tsunami of anger and all the shitty thoughts I kept inside. I reassured myself only three more days left, just three more! I'd probably beat the mail.

With all pretenses gone, Bea and my mother snuggled together in front of the television and bickered over who'd used up the hot water in the shower. As Bea lovingly baked a batch of pot brownies, they fussed over each other in tones normally reserved for pets. The living room was tidier with Bea's clothes back in the bedroom, and Bea herself seemed relaxed and happy to be back in the king-size bed with Merilee. Not to say there wasn't still tension, only that what tension remained was all mine.

Despite the rain, my mother and Bea donned ponchos and went to "work," returning in the afternoon drenched and sleepy. Mostly I avoided them, much the same way my parents had avoided each other, waiting to emerge from the room I shared with my sister until after they had left for the day. At dinnertime, their attempts to engage me in conversation went unrewarded. For me, every topic had a trap door to the past, and I was just trying to make it home without falling in.

In my miserable state, I was forced to admit that I'd come with the fantasy of reconnecting with my mother. She'd done her best to bring us back together, but the reality was, we'd never been whole in the first place. Reconciling would mean starting fresh, trusting that my mother would never again pull the rug from under my feet and take off on another magic carpet ride. And I knew better. So, for the rest of the trip, I wore my disdain like my baseball cap, the visor pulled low over my eyes, and counted the minutes until I could go back home.

Tuesday afternoon, the sun returned. I set my packed bags by the door even though I wasn't leaving until the next morning. Earlier, Merilee and Bea had danced out the condo in their shorts and bathing suit tops singing that stupid Bali Hai song. Mirabelle had school and then a playdate with someone named Kahlua. I had assured everyone I would take advantage of the good weather and walk to the beach, but the minute they were gone, I made myself a bowl of stale granola, drew the shades, and turned on the television.

I was sitting on the futon watching (ironically) a rerun of *Hawaii Five-O* when the doorbell rang. Still in pajamas, I threw on my leather jacket and went to the door.

"Yes?" I called out suspiciously.

"It's me, Elliot," a man's voice answered. "Is that you, Merilee? Let me in."

"It's not Merilee. It's Jackie," I said.

"Jackie who?"

"Jackie, her daughter?"

Silence, then shuffling then, "Uh, Jackie, um, this is Elliot, Mirabelle's dad. Can you let me in?"

Now I was the silent one.

"Jackie? Uh, hello?"

I opened the door. Elliot was maybe thirty-five and short; even shorter than my father at five-five tops, with wavy blond hair and a neat mustache. He was dressed conservatively by island standards in tan slacks, a Hawaiian shirt, and shoes, which he slipped off, revealing the only pair of socks other than my own I had seen on Kauai. He seemed fairly confident as I gave him the old once-over: freckled skin and bluish-greenish eyes, the kind that adapted to whatever color might be nearest to them. He had a habit of licking his lips, which were chapped with fresh blisters on top of healed blisters. He probably surfed or owned a boat. In a sort of contagious response, like catching a yawn, I licked my own lips and motioned for him to have a seat.

"Mirabelle's not here, she's playing at Kahlua's house," I said, turning down the TV.

"Oh. Right on."

He licked his lips again and pulled out one of those mini tubes of Vaseline. He wore a wedding band.

"I guess Merilee forgot I was coming," Elliot sighed. "Again."

We let a moment of awkward silence pass between us, then we fumbled for our voices at the same time.

"So…"

"So how long are you here for, Jackie?" asked Elliot, beating me to the punch.

"I go home tomorrow."

"Oh. Cool, cool…"

Another silence.

Elliot crossed and uncrossed his legs. "I don't know what she told you about me."

"Not much," I answered. He didn't say anything. I was pretty sure she hadn't told him much about me either.

He noticed me looking at his ring. "I wasn't married at the time."

I nodded. Cleared my throat.

He licked his lips again.

"Would you like a glass of water?" I asked, breaking the silence.

I didn't know how long he was planning to stay, and it felt rude not to offer.

He shook his head. "She worked for me for a short while. I keep the books for the time-share office over at the Hilton. Merilee was the receptionist."

"Ahhh," I said as if that explained everything. Suddenly I felt nervous like I might get more information than I bargained for. "I bet that job didn't last long," I quipped. "For her."

Ignoring the remark, he continued. "Then she, well, we got pregnant and well, for a while there…" He whistled low. "But now," his tone brightened, "y'know, she's doing awesome so looks like everything's worked out." He tried smiling at me then seemed to think better of it and gazed down at his socks.

Another silence spread between us, this one too wide to traverse. Elliot pushed up from the chair and walked to the door. "Well, I guess I'm off to Kahlua's then to pick up Mirabelle. It was nice meeting you, Jackie."

"Yeah," I said. "I'll tell Merilee you were here." I held the door open for him as he passed through.

"Thanks," he said, heading for a tan, mid-size Chevrolet sedan with traces of rust creeping up the fenders.

"By the way," I called after him. "Mirabelle is a great kid."

He turned around then nodded at me; three quick pops of his head. "I know. And thank God she looks like her mother." He winked.

I hoped he meant it conspiratorially. Not in the sense of "Too bad that *you* don't look more like your mother." As I watched him drive away, I decided it must have been the former. After all, he seemed harmless. A time-share accountant; a job as beige as the socks he wore and the car he drove. At least Merilee provided some color in Mirabelle's life, and maybe Elliot gave her stability. Maybe he had a nice wife and other kids for her to play with. I thought of all the questions I would ask if I saw him again, but that time never came.

That evening, Merilee drove us all several miles away up a winding road lined with coconut and banana trees and tall clusters of birds of paradise. We parked at the top on a wide, grassy promontory overlooking the ocean where the air was sweet with the scent of plumeria and gardenia. I had wanted to stay in the apartment, but Merilee insisted I could not leave without seeing the sunset.

Mirabelle pulled me to where a low brick wall stood, barely the suggestion of a barrier between us and the cliffs. "Look down there." She pointed to where hundreds of seagulls circled a white lighthouse, the same one I'd seen on our hike but from a different angle.

"That's the Kilauea lighthouse, Jackie," Mirabelle chirped.

She had on my leather jacket. It came to her knees and the sleeves were a mile too long. I'd decided to leave it for her even though I loved it. I felt like it was the least I could do.

"We'll take you next time you visit."

"Uh-huh." I nodded. The chance of that happening was exactly zilch.

"Stand right here and I'll take your picture." She pushed up a sleeve and fished out her Instamatic. "I just got a new roll of film and I'm gonna' use it all up on you." Mirabelle declared.

I waved her off. "Oh no, that's not—"

"Say cheese!"

"—necessary." I sighed as she snapped my picture.

It was warm and clear. Three days of rain had left the air fresh and moist. Bea pulled a few old folding chairs from the trunk of the car and Merilee brought out a picnic basket of fruit and cheese. Mirabelle ran around us, her camera clicking.

In the distance, north of the lighthouse, the sun hovered over the horizon right at the spot where the sea met the jagged cliffs of the Napali coast, now silhouetted against an increasingly colorful sky. I pushed my sunglasses onto my head to fully appreciate the view.

Merilee came up beside me and pointed to the farthest tip of the shore. "That is Bali Hai," she whispered reverently.

For the next half-hour, cars arrived, parking haphazardly along the side of the road. Families poured out of rusted trucks and vans toting blankets and beach chairs. They spread out picnic fare and opened bottles of wine. A guy in a straw hat brought out a steel guitar and serenaded his friends. Children chased one another. Mirabelle pocketed her camera and scampered off with some girls from school.

The sky continued painting itself with streaks of orange and pink and magnificent purples. Everyone rearranged their positions to watch the sun's descent, its flame spreading across the ocean, turning the blue seas magenta. On cue, the music stopped, the children stilled, and everyone went silent as the sun slowly melted into the horizon. Finally, when the last molten drop disappeared, a collective exhale washed over us, and the crowd broke into spontaneous applause.

Immediately, activities resumed; guitar strumming, families eating and chatting, Mirabelle scampered back to her friends. I couldn't help but be swept up in the moment, casting a quick smile at Bea and Merilee. We stared out at the Napali for a while longer, but soon the sky began to darken. The magic was over, and we were just us again.

Merilee picked up the remains of our picnic and Bea loaded the chairs back into the trunk of the car and went off in search of Mirabelle.

My mother turned to me, her eyebrows furrowed and lips pursed in a way that suggested she had something of importance to say. I pulled my sunglasses over my eyes and felt my back pocket for the security of my cigarettes.

"Well, there you go Jacqueline," she said. "If nothing else, you have seen the sunset over Bali Hai."

DISSOLVE TO:

INT. HOSPITAL ROOM
NIGHT
DAY 36

There is a new nurse. She's quite overweight and moves cautiously around my bed so as not to jostle the machinery. Her uniform is a solid hospital green, no hearts or kittens. She has longish, mousy-brown hair pulled back with the kind of child's ponytail holder that has two plastic balls. She would blend in with the walls if it weren't for her unusually pretty face. Almond-shaped green eyes, dark brows, full bow lips, and high cheekbones visible under a chubby layer of skin. Looking at her, you know she has spent a lifetime hearing how she would be so pretty if she only lost weight. For two days, she has been coming to my room at various times. She came early this morning and then again tonight. She seems not to have been given a regular shift, or maybe she's filling in.

Her visits are always the same: she hangs up her cardigan, checks my chart and vitals, stands at my bedside, and rubs lotion on my hands and feet. She doesn't do stim-work; her touch is the right blend of personal and professional. Not once has she pried into my things or spent even a second mooning over my famous features. She just pumps lotion into her palms and rubs and rubs until my hospital-dry hands and feet have drunk up as much moisture as they can hold.

Her name tag says "Emme," which suits her. Emme sounds gentle and kind—the name of a person who has a calico cat, jars their own jam, or makes patchwork quilts.

This morning when she was rubbing my feet, the dreaded Nurse Dani popped her red head through my door. By her sour expression, it was clear she was disappointed not to find Brett.

"Trying to get a commendation?" Dani asked Emme with a little laugh.

"No, just doing my job," Emme said, pumping more lotion into her palm. It was the first time I had heard her speak. Her voice had a cute, husky quality. The kind of sound you try to make last when you get laryngitis and not at all what I'd have expected. I waited for her to say something else or make a joke, but that was it.

Dani charged in and set about the requisite tour and squeeze of my IVs and bota bags. She checked my monitors then picked up my chart and scribbled a few notes. Emme had done this already, but Dani seemed to find it necessary to prove she had a reason for being there, and Emme was too polite to say anything. Or maybe she just didn't want a confrontation.

"*Circle of Life* fan?" Dani asked, fussing perfunctorily with my bed linens.

"Pardon me?" Emme asked.

"Amber on *Circle*, remember? Was she the first Amber or the second? I'm not sure now."

"I don't know. I don't watch much TV." Emme continued working my feet, mindful to rub away the excess lotion between my toes.

Dani swooped down in front of her so that they were eye-to-eye. "I don't know how you managed to worm your way into this shift, but I want to warn you that if you do anything improper, I'll have you moved to another floor. Understand?"

Emme nodded and pressed her fingers into my arch a bit. Her cheeks had flushed pink. I longed to make my toes twitch back my support.

"Well, ring if you need anything," Dani said ultra-pleasantly on her way out the door.

"Will do," Emme called after her.

"I don't like her one bit," Emme whispered after she had gone. Then she pulled the covers over my feet, pumped fresh lotion into her palms, and took my cold hand into her plump, warm ones.

SLOW DISSOLVE TO:

INT. PEYSER AGENCY
DAY
1987

To Daddy's disappointment, I decided against pursuing higher education. Not that I had a choice having flunked every class except P.E. my senior year.

So what if I didn't know capitals or continents? If I couldn't tell the proper usage of a comma over a colon? I had all the pre-requisites for a career in show business—connections and an unquenchable thirst for attention.

Penny Peyser was a former child actress and gymnast who had opened her own agency. Though not hugely successful, like William Morris or ICM, she had forged a nice reputation for delivering fresh young faces with talent.

Her office was located in the Nine Thousand Building on Sunset. For my appointment, I'd chosen a summery dress that I hoped made me look fresh and ingénue-like. My hair was being extremely uncooperative. Though I'd blow-dried it straight that morning, frizz shot out and sprang sideways. Still, I felt fairly confident, at least from the neck down, and as I rode the elevator to the sixth floor, I felt like I was ascending into adulthood.

Penny met me at the door with a firm handshake. She was barely five feet tall, with blonde hair cut in a Dorothy Hamill wedge, a style likely leftover from her gymnast days. She motioned me to sit.

"So, you're Sid's kid," she sighed, shaking her head. "Oy, Jackie Jackie."

This was not the greeting I was hoping for. "What's wrong?"

Penny pulled up a chair next to me. She picked up a roll of peppermint Lifesavers and popped one in her mouth. She held it between her front teeth and exhaled.

"Jackie, dear," she said through the O, "no offense, you are a very attractive young lady and it would be one thing if you could sing like Streisand. But if you want to be an actress, you're gonna have to go for rhinoplasty."

"Rhinoplasty? You mean…?"

"A nose job." She crunched down on the Lifesaver then twisted open a bottle of Perrier and chugged half of it down. "I hope your feelings aren't hurt."

Hurt? I couldn't have been happier. I'd wanted a nose job ever since Beth Lowenstein had shown up in eighth grade transformed into Christie Brinkley, but my father was dead set against it.

"You're perfect the way you are," he'd say.

Clearly, he'd been wrong. Now, I was old enough to decide for myself, but financially, I'd still need his approval.

"If I get the bob, will you get me a job?" I joked.

Penny popped another Lifesaver into her mouth. "Oh, little doll," she spoke warmly, "Don't you know? You were signed the day you were born."

"Daddy, I need a nose job."

"Me too."

"I'm serious, Daddy."

"Jackie, forget it."

"Daddy, you don't understand! My agent thinks I need it. To get hired. For *work*."

"Work?" Now I was speaking his language. "Why didn't you say so."

With a check from Daddy and a referral from Rita Sanderson, off I went. Two weeks later, with my nasal cavities packed with cotton and pharmaceutical cocaine, Dr. Bergoff broke my nose, shaved away the Goldstein bump, and refined what he termed my "bulbous" tip so that it sloped, ever so slightly, toward heaven. After the swelling had gone down, I went to a photographer for headshots.

Penny examined them and shook her head.

"What's wrong now?" I asked her. "Cheekbones? Chin?"

"I can't put my finger on it," she muttered, tilting my pictures this way and that.

"My hair?"

"It's too—"

"Curly?"

"Ethnic," she proclaimed.

I jumped into my Rabbit convertible and drove to my father's office. "Penny wants me blonde."

Another signed check and off I drove to Jose Eber. All I needed now was a bigger pair of boobs.

Those would come later.

EXT. FRANKLIN APTS
HOLLYWOOD HILLS
DAY
1988

"Jackie baby, don't bogart!" Nicole poked me in the leg.

She had taken to calling me "Jackie baby" ever since I'd gotten an agent.

"Quit calling me that." I handed her the joint.

At nine o'clock in the morning, it was sizzling poolside, the hottest day of the summer. Nicole and draped ourselves on deck chairs, drinking pina coladas and smoking pot, celebrating. I'd gone to my first ever audition and landed a job on the daytime soap, *Circle of Life*. I had never had a job. Not even babysitting. Since high school, I had been living off an allowance from Daddy with the proviso that I attend acting classes.

"Do you even own an alarm clock?" Nicole smirked. She kept running her fingernails back and forth across the plastic weaving on the lounge and the sound was driving me crazy.

We shared a cramped, two-bedroom apartment in Hollywood above Franklin Boulevard, adjacent to the Magic Castle and with views of two freeways. It was one of those bubble gum pink, stucco, one-story complexes, built in the 1960s. The apartments horseshoed, motel-style around a kidney-shaped swimming pool, the patio of which was adorned with bronzed, mostly male, mostly homosexual, mostly unemployed actors and models, sipping protein shakes and scouring *Dramalogue*.

Since becoming roommates, Nicole and I weren't getting along. Just because *she* had a job, she ordered me to wash the dishes and sweep the floors. Okay so I wasn't the tidiest person, but I *was* paying the lion's share of our bills. It didn't seem fair.

"Hey, knock it off," Nicole shouted as water splashed over us.

"Sorry," a voice called from the pool where several young men were wrestling and playing Marco Polo. They reminded me of my mother and Bea.

After returning from Hawaii, I stayed in bed for two weeks. I said it was the flu, but it was obvious I had a bad case of Merilee. Fortunately, both Daddy and Anna had been respectful enough not to say, "I told you so." And in the months following, my mother left messages but I didn't respond. Then, on the last message, she was drunk. Now three years later, I had mostly wiped her from my mind. I hoped poor Mirabelle was living with her father. I hoped she'd forgotten me by now. She'd written me half a dozen letters, but I'd answered only the first one and I felt guilty for ignoring the rest. But I didn't want Merilee reading my letters. I didn't want her to know the slightest thing about me, and there was no way to have a relationship with my sister without involving my mother.

I took a last hit of the joint then stubbed it out in a drop of water on the cement.

"I need a boyfriend," I said. "Isn't anyone at the Cafe cute?" Nicole waitressed at Café Figaro on Melrose Avenue. Her third restaurant job in a year.

"Oh, sure," said Nicole. "They're all cute. And they're all gay."

I groaned. "I'm hitting the clubs tonight to try to meet someone."

"Like where?"

"Helena's, maybe? Some friends are going later."

"Don't you have an acting class?"

"I'll blow it off."

"Jackie." She admonished me with a wagging finger.

"Oh, c'mon. All we do in class is sit around pretending to peel oranges and acting like we're hot or cold. It's bullshit."

"I thought you were working on a scene." Nicole pushed herself upright on the deck chair. The bottoms of her thighs sank through the plastic weave; making individual squares like packaged biscuit dough. She had gained at least twenty pounds since high school. She and Steffi could be mistaken for sisters now.

"It's dumb. It's from *Cat on a Hot Tin Roof.*"

"Why is it dumb?"

"I don't know, it just is, okay?" I was getting irritated at her persistence. I loathed acting class. My teacher was John Cavallos, supposedly the best. Supposedly he had trained Kevin Kline and Susan Sarandon. Supposedly a framed love letter from Kathleen Turner hung in his office. The students treated him like he was God.

"Nic, drop it. Besides, I'm supposed to be celebrating, right?" I leaned my whole body over until my forehead pressed against hers. "Right?"

"Hey blondie, your roots are showing." Nicole pointed at my scalp. I pushed her away.

"You should come too," I said. I didn't really want her to come. She'd taken to monitoring my drinks and acted like my chaperone, but I had a motive.

"Oh, wow, I'm invited?" She widened her eyes in mock surprise. "Okay. But I have to work until ten."

"No one gets to Helena's until midnight."

"Fine. But have a salad waiting when I get home." Nicole commanded. "Oh, and Jackie, one more thing—no drugs tonight. That's the deal."

"Little late for that doncha think?" I snapped.

"You know what I mean—no coke, Jackie. Last time you were gone for three days."

"But what an amazing three days it was," I joked.

Nicole held out her hand to pinky-swear.

"Fine." I hooked her little finger with mine and gave it a hard twist. Nicole twisted back until I let go.

"All right. You win. Now, will you make the call?" I asked, batting my eyelashes.

This was the deal. Nicole had a special gift. She could get us in anywhere—clubs, premieres. She would call up the person in charge pretending to be my publicist and somehow make them believe that even though they had never heard of me they *should* know who I was and that if they didn't it was because *they* were not doing *their* job. She demanded VIP treatment, wielding the Goldstein name like she was the *cappo di tutti cappi*. I could never make a call like that on my own behalf.

"You should do this stuff for a living," I said. "Seriously, Nic, this town is full of people getting paid to make scary phone calls for other people so that they won't have to risk getting rejected themselves."

"Yeah, yeah, go back to your fantasy world, Jackie baby."

"Marco?" a deep voice from the pool called out.

"Polo!" several other voices called in return.

I lit another joint then turned onto my stomach so my tan would even.

Nicole turned over too. "Just wait 'til you're on the soap," she said. "You'll meet plenty of guys."

"I'll bet they're all gay too." I took another hit and exhaled, tasting the sweet smoke pass through my lips, watching it drift away over the pool.

"Not the actors, the grips."

"Yeah, grips are hot." I sat up. "Whoa, I'm a little dizzy." I spritzed water on my face with the spray bottle.

"I'm going in the pool," Nicole announced, rising heavily from her chair.

I squinted down at the water. A thick layer of dirt, eucalyptus leaves, and dead bees floated in a wide ring around the edges. I shook my head. "Not me."

She jumped in, splashing water and onto the burning cement. It evaporated with a snaky *hissssssss* that seemed to go on forever. I lay back down and let myself drift off to the sounds of the men flirting with each other and the whoosh of cars and trucks barreling down the 101.

I startled awake. *What? Had someone said something?* Steam rose off Nicole's wet footprint where she stood before me blocking my sun and wrapping a towel around her waist and thighs.

"I think I fell asleep," I mumbled, reaching for my drink. The ice had melted. It was warm and syrupy.

Nicole sat on the edge of the deck chair and peered at me over her sunglasses.

"Why are you looking at me like that?"

"It's just... Why don't you try a different acting class?" She reached over me for the sunscreen and her breasts sloshed over the tiny triangles that made up her bathing suit top.

"I don't know," I said. "I mean, I'll be working now most of the time, and I'm going to need my nights to study lines and stuff."

Nicole snorted and took a sip of her drink.

"What?"

"You don't want to hear it, so I won't say it."

"Oh God, Nicole, just say it. Say it and get it over with."

Nicole moved her sunglasses onto her head and gave me a stern look. "I'm not trying to be mean, Jax. I'm not. I just think you should take your career seriously."

I sat up. "Goddamnit, I am taking it seriously," I proclaimed.

She was purposely poking at my insecurities. I'd often confided how frightened I was of being seen as a fraud. I'd gotten an agent because of my father and now with no previous acting experience, I'd been hired for a job.

"Don't get hysterical Jax, I'm just saying."

"What do you want, Nicole?" My heart beat fast, my cheeks turned hot.

She leaned forward, placing her hands on my knees. "Look, I just don't want to see you get fired. You've been partying a lot lately and—"

"Oh my god, what does partying have to do with anything?" I threw back defensively. "So, I miss one boring acting class."

"More than one." Nicole said "See? Now you're lying to yourself."

"How dare you!" I sputtered, shoving my feet into my flip-flops. "Go fix your own rotten life and leave mine alone."

Nicole started to say something then stopped. Her eyes filled, and for a second, I thought maybe I should back down. But then a rush of adrenaline lifted me from my chair. "You know what? Fuck you, Nicole." I gathered up my towel and sunscreen, slammed back the rest of my drink, and strode off.

"Jackie, wait!" she called after me.

I lifted my middle finger and kept walking.

"Watch it, baby." In the pool, an overly muscled blonde pushed his lover's head under the water and giggled. Was he talking to me or his boyfriend? Several of the men on deck chairs sat up as I passed and leaned together to whisper. I glared at them, daring anyone to say anything. One glanced at me briefly then went back to squeezing lemons in his lover's hair.

INT. SUNSET GOWER STUDIOS
CIRCLE OF LIFE SOUNDSTAGE
MORNING
1988

Lyle Tracy slid into the mock airplane seat next to me and buckled his seat belt. He then reached over and brushed peanut salt off my chin.

"Check your teeth," he said and opened his newspaper to a crossword he was working on.

Lyle had been on *Circle of Life* since its inception twenty-five years ago as the character of Ben Strong, the suave, irresistibly handsome president of Strong Industries.

When Anna was my nanny, we were madly in love with him; swooning over his every word as we sat in the kitchen—Anna drying dishes and practicing her English, repeating everything he said with her heavy accent, me with my homework and snack. We couldn't have imagined then that I would one day be on *Circle of Life* as Ben Strong's stepdaughter.

I shoved a few cocktail peanuts into my mouth while we waited for the crew to finish lighting. It was my first day of work and I was trying to appear cool and confident despite my pounding head and the sweat pooling under my arms. I held them out to avoid staining my wardrobe.

The night before, I'd gone to a party and despite my best intentions ended up doing coke and drinking too much. I'd staggered home at five a.m. and managed to take a shower before calling a cab to drive me down Sunset to the studio. Now I was hungover and guilty and terrified about remembering my lines. Well just one line, but I was nervous. *I'm scared, can you hold me, please?*

I examined the compartment where the oxygen masks were set to drop and checked that my seat belt was fastened. There was a tremendous amount of work involved in shooting the plane crash; props and pieces set to break apart, windows designed to shatter. We had been warned several times that there could be no mistakes; to reset from the top would take hours.

"I'm scared, can you hold me please?" I repeated it over and over in my head. Penny, my agent, had told me that if all went well, meaning if I did a good job—meaning if they *liked* me—my character would stay in the story. That's how it worked in the soaps. If not…well, it was a plane crash. I'd die a day player.

As the makeup and hair departments made their final touches, the director, Mike Hannigan, came over to inspect the mock plane.

"Remember, I need this in one take, sweet cakes," Mike said. The corners of his mouth furled up at the edges, like paper burning as he attempted to smile at me. On his hulking frame, he wore a rumpled denim shirt over loose khakis. Somewhere in the spread of his shoulders were the remains of a high school football player who had smiled easily and genuinely and had made more than a few cheerleaders slide around in their panties. Now, he was tired and grouchy, and from what I heard, in the middle of a nasty divorce.

Mike leaned down and whispered something in Lyle's ear. They laughed conspiratorially. Was it about me? Could they tell I was hungover? Lyle shifted toward the makeup man who was waiting to powder him down.

Doug, the young stage manager, slight and prematurely bald, adjusted his headset and called for a bell, the signal to lock down the stage. The hair and makeup department scurried off the set, and Mike walked up the stairs, positioning himself in the glass-walled director's booth above the soundstage. I crossed my fingers. "I'm scared, can you hold me please?" I said the line under my breath.

"This is it, everybody!" Doug announced. "Ready? And in five, four, three, two…"

"Action!" Mike's voice boomed over the P.A.

198 · DINAH MANOFF

A dozen grips shook and rattled the shell of the mock plane. The script supervisor shouted out the F.X. cues, while Lyle and I reacted to the thunder and lightning.

"It's okay, Amber," Ben/Lyle yelled. "It's just a bit of turbulence."

The crew gave the shell a violent rock to the side. The peanuts I'd been holding flew into the air and a plastic glass filled with mock Chablis spilled onto my lap. Lyle looked expectantly at me. Was I supposed to speak already? Oh, God! The crew rocked the plane again sharply. I grabbed the armrests.

"Amber, sweetie, it's just *turbulence!*" Lyle was vamping. What the fuck was that line? A piece of shrimp flew past me as the crew jerked the plane. A cup of cocktail sauce tipped over. I tried to reach for the script under my seat, but it was too far back. I fumbled with the clasp on my seatbelt, but a sharp jolt rocked me back. I screamed. I wasn't acting.

"Amber! Honey!" Lyle was desperately trying to save the scene. "Do you want me to *hold you?*" he coached.

I shook my head. I couldn't breathe. I grabbed the airsick bag in the seat pocket. Lyle leaned over and began shaking my shoulders.

"Amber, Amber, get a hold of yourself," he improvised.

I was dizzy, nauseous. The room was spinning. I opened my mouth to say something and threw up into the bag.

"Oh, God." Lyle flung me away like a hot frying pan. "Cut, cut! For Chris'sake." He yanked free of his seat belt and stuck his head around the side of the rocking plane. Doug began speaking rapidly through his headset.

"Michael! Cut the goddamn scene!" Lyle held on to the edges of the mock-up and screamed at the booth. "Mike!" He freed one hand and mimed a knife across his throat.

"She's kind of freaking out," Doug whispered into his mouth-piece. "I think she barfed."

"Cut!" The words thundered over the P.A. system. Immediately, the plane stopped rocking.

"Jesus Christ! We've got eighteen fucking pages left today." Mike Hannigan's voice was loud enough to be heard in the stage manager's earphones. He threw down his headset and stormed from the booth.

Katie, the makeup woman, rushed over to me. She had chestnut hair, freckles, and a no-nonsense attitude born out of the Midwest.

"What can I do?" she asked, rapid-fire but kind. She tore open a packet of hand wipes and gave them to me.

"I think I'm having... I need something...a...a Valium," I said between breaths. I was trying not to hyperventilate. I had no choice but to call Nicole "Please, phone my roommate. We live nearby."

Katie rushed off with my number scrawled on a cocktail napkin with an eyebrow pencil. Hands shaking, I unfolded the wipe and cleaned the vomit from around my mouth.

"Coffee?" Doug stood over me, eyes bright, his pate shining with perspiration. He strained to mask his impatience.

"No, thank you." I didn't want to cry. Over his shoulder, I could see Hannigan speaking angrily into the stage phone. "I swear this has never happened to me before," I said weakly. What *was* happening to me? I was having some kind of panic attack; stage fright mixed with mock airsickness. Across the room, Mike signaled to Doug.

"Take five, everyone," Doug called out. "A long five!"

The bell sounded and the stage lights shut down, leaving everything dark except for the plane's interior where I sat, alone, holding my vomit-filled bag, professionally lit from all sides by thousands of megawatts and an eye light that was positioned to catch my "sparkle." Doug herded the extras toward the holding area while the crew ran outside to smoke.

"I'm okay," I announced as they walked by. "I'll be fine in a minute." I prayed Nicole would be home, that she would come. I felt terrible about our fight now. She'd been right; if I'd partied less, listened more in acting class, not faked my way through those boring sensory exercises—felt the cold, tasted the orange—I was a failure, a fraud. I should have never gone into acting. I burst into tears and tried to tell myself that I was not going to be fired and that I was not going insane. After what felt like days, I saw her familiar shape emerge from the darkness of the soundstage.

"Jackie, Jackie," Nicole clucked. "What have you done?" She held up the vial of pills.

"Hurry," I muttered and grabbed the Valium, took two, and choked them down. I was still feeling nauseous and prayed the pills wouldn't come back up.

"My dear, you look like shit." Nicole moved Lyle's crossword out of the way and sat down in the seat next to me.

"What do you expect?" I snapped. "I'm sick and I'm having an anxiety attack." I had meant to be sweet and apologetic, but her patronizing tone made me defensive.

"I meant your hair. Are you playing a country-western singer?" She leaned toward me with a chuckle. "And excuse me but are you wearing blue contacts?"

The groan of the heavy stage door sliding open kept me from answering. Sun poured through the entrance. A cluster of producers and writers were headed my way, stiff smiles on their faces, scripts in their hands.

I turned and waved at them. "It's nothing. I'm fine, really. Listen, you'd better go." I turned back to Nicole, but the seat was already empty.

The producing and writing staff engulfed me, making cooing, concerned noises. I tried to rise to greet them, but I was still belted in.

"Now, now, now, what have we here?" Ingrid, one of the writers and a former soap actress herself, bent to rub my shoulders while Josh, a sandy-haired preppie producer tweaked my chin, a move that at any other time I would have hated. Now, I wiggled my head toward him like a needy pup.

"Nerves, cutie," Josh said.

I smiled up at them through my tears. "I swear this has never happened to me before."

He nodded sympathetically. "Happens to everybody."

Suddenly, a shadow descended. The mighty figure of Moira Parent stood, backlit by my eye light. Moira was the creator of *Circle*, an imposing house of a woman. Square faced, with a salt-and-pepper mane that flowed floors above the rest of her, she kept her massive structure cloaked under loose-woven, fiesta-colored caftans from Putamayo. Silver hoops hung from her ears—dozens more climbed both her arms. I had met her only once at my audition.

"Clear out!" she commanded the crowd surrounding the plane. Her staff and assistants scurried off in various directions.

She sat her ample figure down on the floor of the mock-up causing it to list to one side. I clutched my hands together so that she wouldn't see them shaking and braced myself for the worst.

"Are you okay?" she whispered.

Her voice was so kind. It threw me completely off guard causing my eyes to fill with fresh tears.

"Are you on anything?" she asked matter-of-factly, without accusation.

"No." I shook my head. Technically it was true, I hadn't drunk or used anything since midnight except for the Valium, which was of course medicinal.

"You know what I think?" she asked.

I shook my head again.

"I bet you're afraid of flying like I am." Behind her, I could see Mike Hannigan stamping his feet and fidgeting like a kid waiting to use the bathroom.

"Yes," I lied. "Terribly afraid." If she wanted to be sympathetic, I wanted her sympathy.

"And I can imagine having Sid Goldstein for a dad can't be easy."

"No. It's not."

"A lot of pressure, right?"

"So much." I nodded in agreement. I took a deep breath. My hands were no longer shaking, and my heart was slowing.

Moira waved for an assistant, who then presented me with a glass of water. Several of the staff drifted over, subtly checking their watches.

"Moira, dear," Mike called out. "We're losing the day."

"How long to reset?" she called back.

Doug's head popped up beside her. "Well, the windows haven't shattered yet, we didn't even drop the oxygen masks."

Half an hour later, in fresh wardrobe, makeup, and with hair re-teased and styled, I again buckled myself into my seat. The Valium was taking effect and I felt just fine. Mike was back in the booth, Doug and the prop master made final adjustments. Lyle slid into his seat and buckled up while leaning a safe distance away from me.

Suddenly I remembered Nicole. Christ, I hadn't even thanked her. Where had she gone?

"Ready!" Mike's voice rang out from the P.A.

Moira rushed over, leaned down, and spoke into my ear, "Don't fuck up."

"I won't, I promise."

"If you fuck up, I'll eat your firstborn. I'm not kidding, Jackie."

I nodded. I believed her.

"And…action!" Mike called from the booth.

"Thank you, everyone. Thank *you*, Miss Gold," Mike's voice boomed over the loudspeaker.

"Oh, dearie me, I'm afraid you might have a future after all," Lyle joked before moving over to the makeup table.

A female production assistant shoved a manila envelope at me, the contents of which were still warm from the copy machine. "Tomorrow's script." Did this mean I'd survived the plane crash? I was desperate to know what was written on those pages. As I tore open the envelope, there was a tap on my shoulder.

"Hi, um, Jackie, is it?"

It was Peter Hamlet. Ben Strong's TV son. I'd seen him on the show, but he was even more handsome in person, tall and lanky with dark silky hair and intense emerald eyes. He had a thin scar above his lip which gave just a hint of character to his otherwise flawless face. I tried not to be aware of the cocktail sauce that covered the front of my dress as I peered up at him through false eyelashes.

"Hey, I saw that last take." His voice had a fuller more mature quality than his boyish looks suggested. You captured Amber's inner struggle and her feelings of conflict toward her stepfather."

I didn't tell him that I'd been merely struggling to keep from throwing up again. I gazed into his eyes and tried to project my own intensity through the blue contact lenses I was wearing. Then I realized he had stopped talking and was waiting for me to say something.

"Oh! Thank you. For what you said before, I mean." My voice sounded squeaky.

"Who do you study with?"

"Huh?"

"Acting. Who's your teacher?"

"Oh. John Cavallos, but—"

"Wow. He's like so amazing."

"Yes. Yes, he is…sorry, my throat's a little dry. Too many airplane peanuts," I attempted to laugh but it came out a cough.

"Wow, of course, well you're still in character. Please don't let me interrupt you." He touched my arm. "Bye then. See you tomorrow." He waved over his shoulder and walked to his chair on the other side of the stage.

Wait! I wanted to say. *I'm not in character, I don't know anything about my character!* But I liked that he thought I was as serious about my work as he obviously was. As he began going over his lines, I remembered the script I was holding. Was I in it? Would there be a tomorrow for Peter to see me in? I opened to the first page. I was listed among the cast. Amber survived! I took a full breath for the first time that day. A tattooed grip in bicycle shorts walked over to me carrying a canvas folding chair under his arm.

"Here you go." He popped it open.

I sat and caught my reflection in the makeup mirror. My new, blonde, blue-eyed reflection.

And on the back of my seat printed in big bold letters was my new name, "Jackie Gold," shortened and refined. Just like my nose.

I was in love. Madly, desperately, hopelessly in love. I couldn't eat, barely slept, and yet I felt pumped with energy. Ten pounds melted from my body. My jeans hung loose, my arms were twiggy, my cheekbones angular. Penny hired a publicist to field the interview requests that were coming in for me, mostly teen magazines and soap journals. They asked the same question: "What is your beauty regimen?" What could I tell them? I was having sex day and night with the most adorable, incredible guy in the world.

Our conversations were endless and fascinating. We wrote poems for each other about each other, we made cassettes of songs we had loved as individuals that had to be shared. I could no longer imagine a time or a world without Peter and knew with all certainty that we were destined to spend our lives together.

Peter Hamlet had grown up on television. He had begun his run on *Circle* when he was only eight years old, already a veteran of two other soaps. He'd had his first kiss ever in front of millions when he was fourteen, and a few weeks later, in the privacy of his dressing room, lost his virginity to the actress who played his mother.

We had started dating my second week on the show. In the storyline, Amber and her stepfather, Ben Strong, survived the plane crash but were marooned on a deserted island. Just when it seemed like they wouldn't last another day, a rescue boat pulled ashore carrying Storm Strong (Peter), Ben's adopted son from several marriages prior. And though they are technically half-brother and sister, Storm and Amber fall in love.

"Christ, you two—get a room," Lyle would grumble whenever Peter and I were together. Now after three months, we still couldn't keep our hands off each other. We kissed during makeup, during lunch, between takes. More importantly for the show, our chemistry paid off in big numbers. Ratings for *Circle* had gone up ten percent in the months since Storm and Amber's romance began. Moira was giddy.

"My discovery," was how she introduced me. And my work was getting better; I started to feel comfortable in front of the camera. I had quit partying and was down to a daily half-a-Valium, more for security than necessity. Daddy was thrilled that I was supporting myself. Anna was ecstatic because I was on her favorite soap. And I was deliriously floating through it all.

There was just one problem. Nicole hated Peter.

"He's not up to your standards, Jax."

I couldn't imagine what standards she meant. Until now, I'd only dated dope-fiends and losers. No one came close to being as talented or handsome or successful as Peter.

"It's not that I don't *like* him," Nicole would protest. "I'm just protective of you."

I wanted to believe her, but whenever Peter came over, she stomped around the apartment like she was raising dust out of a rug, trudging past us to the kitchen, making a big show of opening and closing cabinets and whining about how "I can't find my fucking Wheat Thins."

"Peter might have eaten some."

"Do I bring people home who eat your food? Huh? Do I?"

She barely left our apartment now except to go to her job at the restaurant. "You need to get out more," I encouraged her. "Take some classes, get a job you enjoy."

But every suggestion I made was met with the same response. "Go live in your fantasy world, Jackie baby."

We began leaving each other angry notes on the refrigerator, full of accusations and blame along with itemized receipts for our expenses. I was hurt and furious that Nicole wasn't happy for me. If the shoe were on the other foot, I'd be throwing her a party. As the weeks rolled by, the tension between us thickened, neither of us daring to say what we were thinking—that the bonds of our childhood had been broken.

But I couldn't worry about us anymore. I had a job and a boyfriend and new, fun friends who didn't make demands on me, and a newfound devotion to acting class—Peter and I went to Cavallo's together now—and interviews with *E.T.* and *Soap Opera Digest.*

I wound up doing the cowardly thing. Little by little, one sleepover at a time, I took my clothes and books and stuff to Peter's house until finally, there was nothing of me left for Nicole to come home to.I wound up doing the cowardly thing. Little by little, one sleepover at a time, I took my clothes and books and stuff to Peter's house until finally, there was nothing of me left for Nicole to come home to.

DISSOLVE TO:

```
INT. HOSPITAL ROOM
MORNING
DAY 40
```

Rupert Greenwald, aka the Australian, is the most ruthless of paparazzi. When not in disguise, he wears tan slacks and a safari jacket. He tracks his victims relentlessly, paying big bucks to whoever can furnish him with a good lead. He is particularly skilled at hunting down forgotten first spouses and babies given up for adoption. Family secrets are his specialty, his marksmanship evident in the number of divorces and lawsuits in which he is called to testify. He started at the *London Mirror* and now works freelance, a gun for hire. I first saw him when I moved in with Peter. I opened the back door and found him rummaging through our trash. He greeted me with a friendly "G'day, Jackie" as if it were the most normal thing in the world.

"What the fuck do you think you're doing?" I'd yelled.

"Care to comment on the engagement rumors?" he asked.

"I'm calling the cops!" I slammed the door.

This morning, he snuck into my hospital room. At first, I didn't recognize him, wearing glasses, dressed as an orderly, bent over, and pushing a cart piled with towels and linens. When the door shut behind him, he took a camera out from under his shirt and began shooting.

There was a time not long ago when I had photo approval in all my contracts. I controlled how I wanted my body seen. And while candid photos of me have graced many a tabloid cover, none compares to those that will soon be featured at the check stand of your local supermarket courtesy of Nurse Flo's disposable camera and The Australian's Nikon 90.

I hate them; the Australian and his brethren; who ply otherwise competent nurses with offers they can't refuse.

And though I am certainly guilty of courting fame. The punishment far outweighs the crime.

SLOW DISSOLVE TO:

INT. SUNSET GOWER STUDIO
DAY
1990

Peter and I had been together for a year and our on-screen passion continued to boost the show's ratings. Off-screen, the tabloids followed our romance as closely as if we were members of the royal family.

I couldn't keep up with my fan mail, so I hired one of the extras to send out my 8x10s. Scotty was a bookish gay man with codependency issues; perfect qualifications to be my assistant. He loved reading my mail and responding to the fans. Special letters he set aside from the pile and marked to my attention.

I came into my dressing room one morning to find that Scotty had left out a pink envelope addressed to Jackie Goldstein. But the "stein" had been crossed out.

Dear Jackie, (The handwriting was shaky.) *I don't want to disturb you, I only want to tell you that you are the best thing on the goddamn show and even though I don't believe personally in abortion, I don't hold yours against you.* (She was referring to my character, of course.) *Would you be so kind as to send me a picture from the show and sign it to Marva?*
All the best,
Your Nana

I sat on the couch and reread the letter several times. It took my breath away, and honestly, I was surprised that she was still alive. It had been fifteen years since I'd seen her, and she hadn't seemed in particularly good health then. I picked up a pen and a piece of stationery and wrote "Dear Nana," but then I stopped. What was there to say? She'd never tried to get in touch with me before. Not in fifteen years, not even after my mother left us. Never. She hadn't asked me anything personal about my life. She wanted a signed picture. Of my character. There was nothing

special about this letter. Not one goddamn thing. I put it back in
the envelope and tossed it on the pile for Scotty.

INT. HUGO'S RESTAURANT
MORNING
1991

I ordered my usual pasta scramble. Peter had asked for Eggs Benedict, a serious departure from his usual egg white omelet. He was normally fastidious about his weight.

"Wow, what's the occasion?" I asked after the waiter left.

"I just feel like it, okay?" He picked up his script. He had been very moody in the last couple of weeks. The night before, he'd been exceptionally passionate in bed, and then this morning, he'd snapped at me for leaving the cap off the toothpaste.

We were sitting at our regular window table, both of us wearing dark glasses. We'd managed to lose the paparazzi coming out of Laurel Canyon. But it was only a matter of time before they caught up with us. They followed us everywhere now. And the fans! We couldn't go anywhere without someone wanting an autograph or a handshake or a hug.

"Let's run lines before our food comes," Peter said, opening his script.

"No, let's wait 'til we get home," I pleaded.

"I have a shitload tomorrow."

"So, use cue cards," I teased.

Peter shook his head and ran his fingers back through his hair. He was so beautiful. Pretty almost. I loved the color of his eyes, like shoots of spring leaves. And his physique; natural, not overly muscled but sinewy and strong. At night after lovemaking, I would lie in the crook of his arm, basking in the glow and caressing his chest, his ribs, his belly, following the contours of his arms, and then later as he slept, I'd run a finger along the scar over his lip and trace the arc of his eyebrows.

In my tote bag, I had several designers' books filled with sketches and swatches. I'd been waiting for the right moment to reveal them. After a year and a half in Peter's house, I was yearning to nest. With its 1970s' wood paneling and his parents' hand-me-down living room set, the house cried out for a woman's touch, just not mine, specifically. I had consulted several decorators on the probability that Merilee and Marva's design gene had been passed down and was lying dormant inside me.

Peter leaned back in his chair concentrating hard on his script, mouthing his lines.

"Peter," I said. I repeated his name several times, but he didn't acknowledge me. "Honey?" I reached my foot under the table and gave his chair a little shove.

"Hey! Jackie. What?"

"C'mere, I have something to show you." I put one of the books on the table and opened it.

"What is it?" he asked, leaning forward.

"Our living room."

He took the book and turned it around to face him. He moved it back and forth, seemingly studying it from all angles. "Wow. I love it," he said. "It's fantastic."

"Moira recommended the designer. She can start right away."

Peter handed me back the book.

"Wait, I have more to show you." I started to get another out of my bag, but Peter leaned over and took my hands. I noticed several of the patrons looking at us and giggling. I smiled at them and they lit up.

"I need to say something, and it can't wait any longer," He took a deep breath and slowly exhaled, like when he was about to start a scene, "I love you, Jackie."

"I love you too." My heartbeat sped to half measures. Was he going to propose? Here? Now?

"Sweetheart?" He took my face in his hands and pressed his forehead to mine.

"What?"

"I can't do this anymore."

214 · DINAH MANOFF

I took his hands off my face. "What are you talking about?"

"This. Us. I just don't think I can be in a committed relationship."

"Ohhh. This is in the script."

He shook his head. "No, Jackie, I mean it. It's over."

The room spun out from under me. "Petey, you're joking right?"

"No. I'm sorry. No."

I fought for breath. "Oh, Christ. Have you met someone?"

"Not really."

"Not really? What the fuck is that supposed to mean?" I got up, nearly knocking over the table.

"Rehearsing," Peter called out to the concerned patrons.

He threw a couple of bills on the table, grabbed our scripts, and herded me out the door and away from the eyes still watching through the window.

"You just said you loved me," I hissed, stumbling past several groups waiting outside to be seated.

"Shhh!" Peter checked to make sure there were no cameras in sight, then guided me down an alleyway and around the back of the building.

"I do love you Jackie, but—"

I opened my mouth to protest, but a sob caught in my throat. I collapsed against the wall.

"Please, Jackie. Don't cry. I do love you, honey, but I'm not ready to settle down."

"But I thought…" I waved my hands around helplessly.

Peter put both his arms around me and pulled me to him. "Sweetheart, look." His voice shook with emotion. "If someone were to hold a gun to my head and tell me I had to be in a serious relationship, I swear, Jackie, it would be with you."

"A *gun*?"

"You don't have to move out right away. I've taken a place at the beach for a month. That should give you some time."

While on *Circle of Life*, Amber and Storm fell ever more deeply in love. In real life, Peter and I fought bitterly. Miraculously, the press had not yet gotten wind of our breakup. I managed to be polite and professional on the set, but at night after work, I'd get drunk, call Peter, and scream "Ass fuck!" into the answering machine at his beach house and then beg him to come home. One month became two. I couldn't bring myself to move out of Peter's house. I kept hoping he'd come to his senses. Any minute, he'd burst through the door, flowers in hand, begging my forgiveness.

Then, in March, as the show was due to go on hiatus, I came home to a police car in my driveway.

"What's going on?" I asked the officer.

He handed me an official-looking document.

"What's this?

"Sorry, Miss Gold. You've been evicted."

That night, I got so drunk I called Peter over and over until I passed out with the phone still in my hand.

My immediate options were limited. I couldn't go back to living with Nicole. We hadn't spoken since I'd moved out, and last I heard she was living somewhere with Steffi. In desperation, I took a studio at the Oakwood Apartments in Burbank, a temporary living compound comprised of transient actors, corporate workers, and fucked up people like me who were just trying to figure out their next chess move.

With the show on hiatus, I had nothing to do. Each day I drove to Laurel Canyon and cruised by Peter's house. I longed just for the sight of him. At night I went to my dealers in Van Nuys where I would buy a few grams of coke and hang out until the morning hours while his customers came and went. Roger was a nice Jewish boy dealing as a way to "pay for law school."

After snorting a few lines, he became interesting and I was desperate for company.

Usually, when I arrived several people were already crowded around a mirror on the coffee table in his small dark living room. His apartment was on the first floor of a complex two blocks off Ventura Boulevard. The ceiling was low and there was one street-level window with heavy floor-to-ceiling drapes, drawn against the neighbor's prying eyes. Leaving Roger's perpetually nocturnal apartment in the daytime was like walking out of a movie matinee.

One of his regulars, Debby Davies, was an actress on *Welcome to Mary'sville,* a popular sitcom. She was petite with brown hair and eyes, small features, and tiny hands; cute in a chipmunky way. Roger's longtime crush on Deb was of the hopeless romantic variety and he'd grown comfortable in his misery as if it were an old favorite recliner.

"Have you asked her out yet?" I lit a cigarette and opened my second origami-folded gram. It was past midnight and the rest of Roger's customers had departed. We sat next to each other, cross-legged on the floor where our noses could reach the surface of the coffee table.

"I tried," he said with a hangdog expression on his face.

I offered Roger a smoke, but he waved the pack away. "So? What did you say?"

"I said, 'Debby you wanna grab dinner sometime?'"

"Way too vague." I hit Roger on the arm.

Roger shrugged. "It doesn't matter, she's never going out with a schlub like me."

"Stop that!" I admonished. It was true—Roger was kind of a schlub. But that was mostly because of the way he carried himself with poor posture due to low self-esteem. Objectively, he was almost handsome with thick, dark hair, and a decent body. His complexion was pale for a Southern Californian, but that was because he slept days and worked nights. If he stood up straight and lost the glasses, maybe hit the beach once a week, he'd do all right.

"Hey, I'm almost down to the last gram. Have any more?" I started to feel panicky whenever my stash got low.

"Nope. Sold the rest to Kristi and my supplier's not back 'til tomorrow."

"Wait who?" I leaned back and uncrossed my legs. I had on sweatpants and a *Circle of Life* T-shirt. Lately, I couldn't seem to make an effort. I wasn't sure when I'd last had a shower.

The couch was covered in plaid fabric, not unlike my rented furniture at the Oakwood. Under the coffee table lay a homey-looking green and blue braided rug I guessed to have come from Roger's mother who lived nearby and dropped by once a week with groceries.

"Gretchen, my supplier? She's the man."

"No. Who's Kristi?"

"The blonde who was here earlier? Short, shorts, pink halter top."

"The chick hanging all over you?" I tapped out some of my coke on the mirror, put out my cigarette, and lit another. "Why don't you ask her out?"

"I'm not attracted to her," Roger said.

"Seriously? She's like a *Baywatch* babe. I think she was the stand-in for Pamela Anderson."

"Not my type, what can I say?"

"What is your type?" I snorted, coughed, and held the straw out to Roger.

"Sexy *and* smart." Roger scraped some coke out of his envelope onto the mirror. He chopped up a few lines and snorted them before motioning to me.

"Why are you hanging out with me then? I barely graduated high school." I laughed and took the straw.

"Well, for one thing, you pay upfront." He chuckled.

"Very funny."

"And you're savvy."

"Savvy. Huh. Like clever? Never thought of myself that way. I like it though. Good word. You have an excellent vocabulary, Roger."

"Yes. Also, I find you very 'eyesome,' Jackie. How's that for a word?"

"I hope it's a compliment."

"It means pleasing to look at."

I snorted up the lines and immediately fixed another one. I tapped out another cigarette. Roger leaned over and lit it for me.

A Jim Morrison song came on the radio and suddenly, we were caught up in reciting his lyrics, which I had never thought of as being poetry. Tonight, they felt profound.

Roger went into his bedroom and emerged with a large coffee table-sized book with Morrison on the cover. "Every single lyric Jim Morrison ever wrote!" He swooped down and sat on the couch. I bounced up next to him.

"Oh my God, this is sooo amazing!" I exclaimed, turning the pages. "How have I never seen this before?" I was suddenly filled with admiration for Roger and Jim Morrison. They seemed like the same person, and I had the privilege to know them both.

"A funeral pyre…"

"Like a bonfire"

"Right, but it could also be…"

Peter was a distant memory. I melted into *this* moment, connecting with Roger as we analyzed the meanings behind "Light my Fire," which was *way* much more interesting than it appeared on the surface. Oh, man! I took a huge drag from my Marlboro. And smoking was so great! I loved smoking!

"You should smoke, Roger. It is so amazing."

"I can't. I have asthma."

"Really? How could I not have known that about you?"

That began a long conversation about Roger's early years, leading to his Bar Mitzvah—fascinating stuff to my coke-fueled brain.

I took a long drag off my cigarette and exhaled. "I worry about you getting busted, Roger." Then I picked the razor blade from the mirror and scraped a couple of lines off the pile. Chop, chop, chop.

"Hey, don't give it a thought." He leaned into me. We were shoulder to shoulder now on the couch, our knees touching.

I kicked off my sandals and raked my toes over the ridges in the braided rug. "I mean you're, what, a semester away from getting a degree?" I took another drag of my cigarette then pour, scrape, chop, chop, chop, snort.

"Two semesters. Nah, I don't think about it. I mean I only deal to my close friends." Scrape, chop. Chop, chop. "Besides, I'm in it for another six months. No, seven months 'cause of spring break, and then I have to fly to Jersey for my cousin's wedding." Scrape, scrape. "My dad's got a few friends he's gonna introduce me to so…" Snort, snort… "I might intern at Druckman, Kotler, and Stein next summer if it pans out."

SCRAPE. Roger drew out two lines the length of the table, using the entire pile. "One for each of us." He handed me the straw.

SNORT. Cough. Cough. Whoa, whoa. Yes! Yes! I was flying now! The song "Touch Me Babe" played. I licked my fingers, wiped up the rest of the coke, smeared it on Roger's lips, and kissed him, using my tongue to swipe the numbing coke all over our gums. Then I unbuttoned Roger's shirt. His chest was so smooth and hairless and he was pulling down my pants and okay, he was going down on me, but I couldn't feel anything and mostly I just wanted to talk and smoke, but I was out of coke and I was starting to feel scared about how I was going to get up in the morning. I had two auditions before noon and fuck, I had done it again. I'd sworn I wouldn't stay up this late and I knew I would never come down and I had left the Valium at home. Wait, no I had one in my purse, but Roger was still going down on me and I calculated how long it would take to have sex and then take the Valium and I pushed Roger's head away and pulled him up, on top and inside me so we could have sex and get it over with, but the coke had made us too numb to feel our organs and we just kept pushing at each other.

Roger paused and squinted at me, unfocused. Seeing him now without glasses, I decided he looked better with them on.

"Um, I don't think I can come," he said matter of fact.

"Me neither," I said relieved.

He pulled out of me and reached down for his pants, his underwear bunched up inside one leg. I turned away and pretended not to notice while he hopped around sorting himself out.

"You have any Valium?" he asked while I lit a cigarette.

"Sorry no," I lied. I couldn't afford to split my Valium with him. I needed to come down enough to sleep. I had to be up in four hours for an audition. "I'm out of smokes," I said. "Fuck." I put on my clothes, picked up my purse, and found my car keys.

"You leaving?" he asked.

"No, um, yeah. I'm just going to use the bathroom." I was sinking now, plummeting into that familiar place of remorse. I wouldn't sleep. I'd feel crazy. I'd have to cancel the auditions and Penny would be pissed. I missed Peter.

In the bathroom, I took the Valium out of my purse, shoved it into my dry mouth, and gagged it down. After peeing and cleaning myself up, I stumbled off into Roger's kitchen and dialed Peter. The answering machine picked up. "Hey," I whispered, "it's me. If you can hear me, please pick up. Please Petey. I'm loaded and freaked out, I just need to hear your voice. Peter, please? Peter, I need you! I don't even care if someone's there, please just talk to me." I started crying. "I miss you Pete, just pick up the phone." I sobbed. "I'm going crazy. Peter? Can you come and get me? Please pick up!"

"Hey."

Roger stood in the doorway, now wearing his glasses and a look of pity. If Roger felt sorry for me, I was bad off. I hung up the phone.

"You okay?" he asked softly.

I shook my head. I felt desperate and alone. Why had I gotten so high? Why couldn't I have stopped at ten o'clock, eleven—left with everyone else? Why was I always the last one at the party?

"You want to just crash here?" he asked.

I nodded.

Roger went to his room and found me a T-shirt to sleep in. While I changed my clothes, he transformed the couch. Sheets, top and bottom, fresh pillowcase, a wool blanket. I didn't deserve his kindness. I doubted I'd have done the same if the roles were reversed.

He handed me a glass of water. "If you need anything else just wake me up, okay? There's beer in the fridge if you want." He turned and went to his room.

I lay on top of the comforter, my heart slamming my chest. The Valium hadn't made a dent. I had more at home, but I was too wasted to drive. I needed to sleep but felt like I was going to have a heart attack. I tried meditating to slow the rhythm but kept thinking about Peter. Fuck! Why had I left that message? What was I thinking? What was wrong with me? I checked the time: 5:00 a.m. I started bargaining with God:

Let me fall asleep and I'll do better. I'll start over. I won't do coke. I'll get my shit together.

Nicole had been right. I was a fuck up, a mess. At that moment I wished with all my being that I could talk to her. How long had it been? A year? No, closer to two. We'd had one awkward encounter at Greenblatt's Deli when I was still with

Peter. She'd said she was moving to Flagstaff, Arizona to be with Steffi, who was living in her last ex-husband's guesthouse.

Light peeked around the edges of the curtains, followed by the unwelcome sound of birds chirping and early morning traffic.

I made one last promise to God. *If I could just fall asleep, I'd find Nicole and apologize.*

I sped down Ventura Boulevard on my way to the gym, chewing an energy bar and humming to Wilson Philips. Since the night with Roger, I'd sworn off coke and hard alcohol, largely due to the reaming Penny gave me for missing my auditions. Now, after almost a month of good sleep, diet, and exercise, I was feeling more like my old self again. Most importantly, I hadn't called Peter once. Though that was the hardest of my withdrawals.

It was noon and I turned the dial to Dr. Dave, the radio shrink. He usually gave sage relationship advice. I'd even thought about calling in myself.

"This is Dr. Dave, who am I speaking with?"

"Margaret in Bakersfield."

"Hello Margaret, what can I do you for?"

"My boyfriend broke up with me and I haven't been able to get over him."

"You and me both," I commiserated.

"How long were you together?"

"Two years," the caller said.

"How long since the breakup?"

"I'm ashamed to say it's been a year. I just can't stop thinking about him."

"Have you talked to him about why you broke up?" the Doctor asked.

"He won't see me. But I honestly feel like I just need some answers before I can move on."

A car honked behind me. I'd been listening so intently I had slowed under the speed limit. I waved him past and pulled over to the side of the road. This woman was telling my story.

"Well Margaret, it sounds like you need closure. You can get closure on your own, but it often takes therapy. Does that sound like an option?"

"Mmm. I don't know."

"Perhaps you could ask the gentleman if he wouldn't mind having one more conversation with you, to help you move on."

One more conversation! That was exactly what I needed. Our hiatus would end in August and *Circle of Life* would soon be back in production. I had been anxious about what it would be like once we returned but Dr. Dave had nailed it. I needed to seek closure before we were back on set. I pulled back on the road, made a U-turn, and headed for Laurel Canyon. Twenty minutes later, I parked in Peter's driveway.

As I approached the front door, I felt supremely calm, composed, and sure of my motives.

Velma, our housekeeper, the housekeeper *I* had hired, answered the door.

"Hi, Velma. Is Pete here?" I kept my voice steady and unemotional. Aware that the last time she'd seen me, I screamed while hurling dishes at the floor.

"Well now, Miss Gold! It's so nice to see you." Velma's blue eyes darted around nervously. "Mr. Hamlet's not at home."

"His car is here," I said, holding the door open.

Velma shook her gray head. "I'm not supposed to let you in, I'm sorry," she whispered.

So, he'd seen me drive up. This was going to be harder than I thought.

"Is he with someone?" I tried to peek inside, but Velma blocked me.

"Peter?" I called out. "It's okay, I'm not mad or anything. Come on, I know you're there. This is silly. I just want to talk to you." I stepped inside.

"Now, now." Velma patted me on the shoulder and attempted to escort me backward. "Go home, dear."

"No, I... Peter!" I surged past her into the living room. "Peter!"

"Sorry, Mr. Hamlet." Vilma followed wringing her hands.

He sat alone at the kitchen table, hair tousled from sleep, wearing the bathrobe I had bought him. A script lay open next to his coffee mug. God, I had forgotten just how beautiful he was. Especially in the morning before he shaved. I wished I were wearing something alluring, or at least changed out of gym clothes.

"Hi Petey," I said, in the sweetest, least threatening voice I could muster.

"What do you want, Jackie?" His voice was monotone.

"I need to talk to you, it's important." I could feel a flush coming into my face and my heart raced.

Peter nodded at Velma, who scurried out of the room. He remained seated, waiting for me to continue, his face impassive.

I took a deep breath. "I-I wanted you to know that I might not have tried as hard as I could to be understanding, and I want to say I'm sorry."

These were not exactly the words I'd planned.

Peter kept his eyes on me but didn't respond. I cleared my throat.

"I wanted to ask, I mean..."

The questions I'd rehearsed in the car to help me find closure vanished from my mind, and instead what came out was, "I mean, maybe we could just date? Or, I don't know..." I was way off track, but I couldn't stop, "maybe you could see other people and I wouldn't have to live here, but..." I was crying now.

Peter got up from the table. He moved toward me, and for a moment, I thought he was coming over to hold me. But he walked past me into the living room, opened the front door, and turned to me with dead eyes.

"Get out of my house, Jackie."

"Petey, Pete! Don't you have feelings for me anymore?" I grabbed his sleeve.

God, what was I doing?

He shook himself loose. "Yeah, Jackie, I have feelings." His lips curled, his face was red. "I'm feeling fucking angry and sick and tired of seeing you drive by my house spying on me. I am sick of your crazy phone calls." His voice rose, "Do not come here again or I will get a restraining order and have you arrested for stalking. Do you understand? Do you?"

"Prick!" I screamed in his face and launched my fists at him.

He grabbed my arms, pushed me outside, and slammed the door.

I collapsed on the porch, hysterical, sobbing and screaming, banging my fists on his door over and over. I cried so hard I didn't even see the man in a safari suit jump out from behind the bushes until the flashes went off in my eyes.

Two days later, the picture hit the tabloids: *DUMPED* ran the headline. It was on the cover of every magazine at every check stand in every supermarket in every town in America.

INT. SUNSET GOWER STUDIO
CIRCLE OF LIFE SOUNDSTAGE
DAY

AMBER: I want you so much, Storm.
STORM: I want you, Amber. It's driving me crazy.
AMBER: I can't go on like this.
THEY EMBRACE.

"And cut! Take five everyone, we'll reset from the top."

"I really *can't* go on like this," I hissed to Peter, as we retreated to the makeup trailer.

"What are you talking about?" Peter said.

"This. You and me!" I said exasperated. "I know you're feeling this, Pete. You get a hard-on every time we kiss."

"No, Jackie," Peter said wearily. "Storm gets a hard-on for Amber. Peter feels nothing for Jackie. It's called acting."

We were back in production, and I still wasn't over him. It was excruciating. Amber and Storm's kisses felt as real to me as Peter's and mine had, and every love scene rekindled my hope and desire. When the scene ended, I fled to my trailer and cried my eyes out. Peter, on the other hand, quickly untangled himself and walked off to where his latest squeeze was waiting.

Several weeks earlier, I'd left the Oakwood and moved into a historic two-bedroom on Rossmore Avenue with a fireplace, crown moldings, and the musty smell of a glamorous past. At another time, it would have been my dream apartment, but now all I could see were the earthquake cracks in the walls and the uneven floors where the foundation had settled. Still, I was trying to move on. I'd been sleeping with Greg Pallucci, a producer in his forties. The physical opposite of Peter, he was streetwise, short, and rough around the edges. Every morning, I arrived on set exhausted from a night with Pallucci, who couldn't get enough of me and went straight into the arms of the man I loved but who couldn't stand me.

Pallucci was into kinky stuff. He kept an arsenal of paraphernalia under his bed: vibrators, massage oils, silk cords with Velcro ties. He bought a Pilates machine "strictly for sex." We spent hours in his apartment contorting into different, often ridiculous positions, in pursuit of bigger, better orgasms. His attention was validating. Plus, it kept me from going to my dealer.

Since the night I laid awake at Roger's, I'd kept at least one of my promises to God: I'd been trying to find Nicole. Steffi's number was disconnected and Café Figaro's, the last place Nicole worked, said they hadn't seen her in years. I hired a private investigator, who turned up a P.O. box in New Mexico for Nicole's father, her WPE. I wrote to him but never heard back. I was clueless about where to look next. One thing was for sure, if she wanted to see me, I was easy to find.

INT. WINNEBAGO
SUNSET GOWER STUDIO
DAY
1992

BELLS ARE RINGING FOR AMBER and STORM!
After two years of straining the limits of daytime television permitted foreplay, Amber and Storm were getting married and the network predicted record-breaking ratings. Peter and I were on the cover of *Soap Digest. TV Guide* and *People* were arriving to cover the ceremony. Further fueling the excitement was the tabloid scandal that dogged us ever since I'd been thrown out of Peter's house. Paparazzi followed me everywhere. For a time, they'd camped out at Pallucci's, but once we exhausted the Pilates and paraphernalia, the relationship ground to a halt like old batteries in a vibrator.

On Amber's nuptial day, I was holed up and pacing in my Winnebago anxiously awaiting the outcome of Penny Peyser's negotiation with the network. My contract was due to expire and according to Penny, with the wedding hoopla and high ratings, it was the optimum time to go to the table. When I'd started on *Circle,* I'd been making scale, fifteen hundred dollars a week minus the ten percent that went to my agent.

Now, Penny was asking for what I considered an exorbitant twenty thousand an episode which, she argued was commiserate with my popularity and "celebrity status."

I was corseted in a wedding gown so sheer and low-cut my nipples had to be covered with Band-Aids and so tight I couldn't sit, much less breathe. A veil was pinned onto my head, and I tried not to trip on the train as I teetered around my trailer on four-inch pumps that already gave me blisters.

The cast, crew, and all the producers, waited for me on stage, not to mention news and entertainment media. Holding up production was contrary to every instinct I had and everything I had ever been taught. Daddy raised me since birth on the cautionary tale about the bad little actress who cost the studio money. This gamble of Penny's could cost me my career.

The trailer steps shook. I peeked nervously out the window before opening the door. A new production assistant with spiky maroon hair and a wrist full of studded leather bracelets stood holding a sheaf of pink pages. Revisions.

"Leave them on the chair," I told him.

"If you say so." He had a pierced tongue and his tone was cocky. I would speak to someone about him later.

I took the pages and waved him away before calling Penny's office for the third time in an hour.

"Penny Peyser's office."

"Yeah Marissa, it's me again. What the hell is going on?"

"She's still on the phone with Business Affairs, I'm sure it will just be a few more minutes. Hang on Jackie." Marissa's voice was so pleasant and reassuring.

I took a deep breath. "Okay, but please tell her to hurry up and close this deal!"

"Will do, sweetie."

I peered outside, hoping someone from Wardrobe might walk by and loosen my bodice, but they were all on set. The set call had been for nine a.m. and it was almost noon! What was taking so long? I was a wreck. I couldn't even begin to think what Daddy was going to say. Even if I didn't tell him, it would be in the trades by tomorrow.

And what was going through Peter's mind? Probably nothing. He was probably in his trailer fucking one of my bridesmaids. I wanted the raise if only because I'd be making more money than Peter and that would piss him off.

The phone rang. I picked it up immediately. "Penny? What the hell is—"

"No, this is Moira Parent."

"Oh, oh, shit," I said, flustered. "Hi, Moira, um, sorry about all of this. It's not personal."

"Nothing to be sorry about, dear. Business is business. Did you get the revisions?"

"Oh, yes, they were just dropped off."

"Have you had a chance to read them yet?"

"I was just about to do that now."

"Great. Hope to see you on the set soon."

"I'm sure you will. Um, Moira, this is awkward, but could you send someone from wardrobe over to loosen this dress?"

"Of course, dear."

I hung up, relieved that Moira wasn't angry with me. If she were confident that this would work out, then Penny was right. If only I could breathe! I tried again in vain to reach back where dozens of hooks held me captive. I gave up, picked up the revisions, and began to read.

SCENE A. CHURCH EXT: *Amber hurries out of the limousine and rushes toward the church. A SHOT is heard. Amber falls to the ground, shot in the brain by a SNIPER'S BULLET.*

I read it over once more and then I called Penny's office and told Marissa to put me through.

"Whaddaya want?" Penny barked. "I'm in the middle of the Cuban Missile crisis."

"Hang up," I told her. "We've been nuked."

INT. BEVERLY HILLS MANSION
EVENING

Moira and the network had decided to make an example out of me. Not only were they not giving me a raise, they weren't renewing my contract.

"Too bad, dear," Moira said dismissively when I finally appeared on set. "Nothing personal." Even worse, until the contract expired, I was to lie motionless in a hospital bed, my face visible in every scene so there would be no possibility of a body double.

That evening, after fifteen takes of getting shot in the head, I ripped off my bloodied wedding dress and fled, black streaks of mascara running down my face to Daddy and Anna's, hoping for sympathy. In the vast living room beneath the wall-eyed gaze of an original Picasso, I threw myself, sobbing, onto the burgundy velvet divan and poured out the details.

My father listened, his face reddening with every word. He paced right under the giant Swarvoski chandelier, a place I avoided in case of an earthquake.

I couldn't wait to hear him blow up at the injustice of my treatment. But to my shock, turned his anger toward *me*. "What were you thinking? No one is going to hire you again!"

"What? But Penny said—"

"I don't give two shits what Penny said. Of course they're punishing you. I'd have done the same thing. Otherwise, they'd have every actor on the show making demands. You acted like a spoiled brat."

That did it. I buried my head in the pillows and wailed. Anna ran to the powder room and returned with some Kleenex and a spray bottle of spot remover.

"Sidney." Anna approached my father and took his arm. "Jackie's a good girl. It's this agent's fault. She should sign with CAA."

I blew my nose. "A person's got a right to ask for more money," I muttered. "If I were a man, they would've given it to me."

"If you were a man, they would've shot you in the balls instead of the head," my father retorted.

The doorbell rang.

"That's the limo," Anna said to my father. "Concetta!"

Concetta darted out from the kitchen and walked quickly across the living room. Anna handed off the stain remover and gestured to the pillows under my head.

"We will be right there," Anna called out, heels click-clacking along the marble floor as she retrieved coats from the foyer closet. She donned a cashmere wrap then handed Daddy his tuxedo jacket and straightened his tie. They were off to the premiere of Daddy's latest picture. Anna was dressed in a rose satin evening gown, her complexion flattered by the hue. In the last several years she had put on weight, and her features were softer but still beautiful. I wished they weren't leaving. Even if Daddy was furious, I didn't want to be alone.

"Well, I'm not going back." I groused, as he slipped into his jacket. "They can all go fuck themselves. I'm quitting."

Daddy spun around, his face turning purple. He came at me, finger pointed.

"Listen to me, Ja-ckie Gold-stein." He stabbed each syllable. "You will show up at work tomorrow and honor your contract. Do you understand me, young lady? You will not walk away from your responsibilities like—" He stopped short, turned away. "Let's go," he snapped at Anna.

"Wait," I said, rising. "Like who? Who Dad?" I knew I was baiting him. I wanted him to stay and fight.

"You know very well who."

"Daddy!" I sobbed and collapsed back on the divan. "It's not fair. Everyone's against me," I wailed, "even you."

"Oy vey, enough with the drama," my father said sternly. "You show up for work until that contract expires. You hear me?" He turned, walked out the front door, and climbed into the back of the stretch Limo idling in the driveway.

Anna bent down and pressed her cheek to mine. One of her dangly diamond earrings caught in my hair. "Take his advice, it will all work out, you'll see," she whispered, untangling herself. She kissed me lightly on the forehead and followed my father out the door.

Often art imitates life, but then sometimes life imitates…well, daytime television.

For the next two months, I lay "comatose" in a mock hospital bed, my eyes open, unblinking while Peter, Lyle, and Gloria—the actress who played my mother, vied for Emmys, dripping tears and sweat onto my face. During the long hours when I wasn't on set, I served out my sentence in new cramped quarters, my Winnebago having been hauled away and replaced with a Honeywagon dressing room the size of a closet.

Surprisingly, Penny was thrilled with the outcome. "Now I can submit you for real parts. No more of this daytime dreck," she'd cajoled. Like this had been her strategy from the start.

I, on the other hand, held out the secret hope that Moira's plan would backfire, that fans would paper the network with letters on my behalf or better, that the ratings would plummet now that Amber and Storm were no longer heating the airwaves. But the ratings held strong.

There was one fortuitous side effect of my stuporous state. With zero possibility of physical contact—save for his snot dripping over me—I finally lost my desire for Peter. Apparently, my "addiction" to him was triggered by my "chemical response to his body." At least that's how Dr. Dave explained it when I called in anonymously with a made-up story about my "co-

234 · DINAH MANOFF

worker." He also said that the "anticipation of contact" kept me hooked. Now, in hindsight, I saw how naïve I'd been. Peter was years off from being able to commit to a mature relationship. He'd gone through a dozen girls since our breakup, all of them pining in his wake. Still, I wasn't exactly pleased when Peter received a Daytime Emmy nomination for the fraught emotional performance he'd given over my comatose body.

Finally, my contract ended, and after three years of work at the only job I'd ever known, I was let go without so much as a fruit basket. Only Scotty and Katie, my sweet and loyal makeup person, joined me in the commissary for a farewell spinach salad.

And as often happens in the world of daytime television, the very next day, Amber miraculously woke up from her coma with another actress playing the role.

DISSOLVE TO:

INT. HOSPITAL ROOM
MORNING
SFX: CODE BLUE ALARM
DAY 45

And…action!

Bells and whistles, Jackie baby. Code red, white, and blue.

"Paging Dr. Foreman. We have a code blue on the sixth floor. Paging Dr. Foreman."

"Oh my God," says Pierre. "Her temperature's rising."

"Flatline!" says Dani.

Bag her, baby. She's going down.

Take one. Jackie Gold in memoriam. Take two. I'm cold. Cannot breathe. I scream for a blanket. It's not my voice. I am drowning. Passing out or coming to. I release myself and open my arms.

Let go let go let go…

And…CUT.

EXT. THE GATES OF HEAVEN
DAWN ETERNAL

I hover, weightless, expansive. Below, on the operating table, a body—smelly, ugly, a fleshly container far too small for my being—lies surrounded by doctors and nurses.

"We're losing her," someone says.

A blade slices the chest.

"Sponge!"

"Did you reach the father?"

"The boyfriend is in New York."

"Jesus!"

"I can't hold onto her."

"Her heart rate is dropping."

"Blood pressure?"

"Sixty over thirty."

"Jesus."

Vibration. Buzzing. Like hornets in my head. I am sucked down a tunnel, blasting through a dark tube. I move fast, faster than anything, faster than Space Mountain or a speeding bullet.

Slow. Stop. Hang. Suspended before a beam of light. It grows brighter and hot, inviting me forward. I laugh because it's such a cliché. But then it rolls toward me, a burning white ball. Static electricity shoots up my arms and in my hair. Out from the light steps...Jesus?

He walks toward me, hands outstretched, dressed in red robes and wearing a crown of thorns. I am relieved to see his head and hands are not bleeding and he doesn't even have scars. I can see all around him. He is the 4-D Jesus. *Holy Christ,* I whisper.

You were expecting Buddha, maybe? Our words blend as we talk with our minds. *But I'm Jewish.*

So, who isn't? He laughs and the sound resonates all through me.

I'm not religious.

Neither am I, he says. *If you like, you can call me Great Spirit.*

That's nice, I say.

Or you can call me Joe, he says.

Okay, Joe, I say.

He opens his arms and I walk into the folds of his red robe. It's as if we've always known and deeply loved each other, like in dreams where I am best friends with the president or Mick Jagger—we understand each other as no one else can. And I am happier than I have ever imagined happiness to be.

I tell him my life story but it only takes a fraction of time because he already knows me, and then Joe looks over my shoulder to where Mother is walking toward us: Mother Earth, Mary, Theresa, they are all The One Mother, and Mother is saying it's my turn now, and I am passed to Mother's arms. Mother rocks me, and I cry from the time I am born to the time of my death and I say, *Is this the end, Mother? Please don't let me go,* and Mother holds me in her arms.

Don't you worry, Sugar Pop, she says, and I look up into the face of Marva, my grandmother, and I scream.

"Heart rate is rising."

"Blood pressure?"

"Ninety over sixty."

"And rising."

"Clamp."

"What?"

"Clamp!"

"Sorry."

"Ninety over seventy."

"Heart rated stable."

"Okay. Let's sew her up."

"That was close."

"I'll tell the family."

SLOW DISSOLVE TO:

EXT. PARAMOUNT STUDIOS
SOUND STAGE
MORNING
1995

"A nonfat latte with a triple shot of espresso," I barked.

Scotty lopped off toward the coffee cart. For reasons I attributed to his masochistic tendencies, he had remained in my employ after the soap debacle.

I hunted around for a patch of shade to stand in. The sun relentlessly beat down as I fought through a residual hangover. I pulled the beak of my baseball hat lower over my eyes and tried to soften the glare.

"Ms. Gold? Hi, I'm Janis. The second A.D.? Do you know where your trailer is?"

She wore a vintage *Star Wars* T-shirt, brown corduroys, and a headset. I knew her type: the kind of passive-aggressive, thin-skinned subservient, who brought out my abusive nature. I hugged my arms across my chest to prevent my black heart from escaping.

"Hi, Janis. Yes, Janis, I've got everything I need, thank you. Just waiting for coffee."

Scotty was taking way too long. Probably flirting with the cappuccino guy. He was a sucker for men in food service. Unfortunately, the Adonises he sought were seeking other Adonises and not bespectacled, concave-chested, fanboys like my Scotty.

Janice cocked her head sideways and pushed on her earpiece. "Yeah, I've got her right here?" Janis reported in a quavering voice. "She says she's waiting for coffee?"

"Uh, Janis, has Brett Haney made an appearance?" I had yet to meet this "up and comer" who'd been cast at the last minute when, to everyone's disappointment, Bruce Willis dropped out.

"I-I think he's getting ready for his makeup test? Third trailer down?"

It was my first big studio film, a sixty-million-dollar futuristic action-adventure movie about space warriors who fall in love while battling for Earth's survival. I was so nervous I'd taken a Valium before even getting out of bed. I wasn't worried about the acting; my dialogue was limited to phrases like, "Hurry! Inside the pod transporter!" But Penny said the studio had "concerns." First, I was too short. Second, I didn't have enough "star power" to carry the picture now that Willis was out. Three, that I had a reputation for being "difficult"—a deadly label for an actress, especially a difficult one.

I'd shot six films in the three years since *Circle of Life* and had affairs in cities from Stockton to Stockholm, but none lasted. And while I managed to stay relatively sober when filming, I leaped off the wagon between jobs. On my last publicity junket, I had stolen the keys to my limousine and hit a parked motorcycle. That was in Portland. In Denver, I missed my morning TV appearance, having awoken in a hotel suite blocks from my own. I was well behaved in Dallas, but Tampa saw me ejected from two bars before the police escorted me to my hotel.

Penny had warned me to clean up my act. The director, Vilmar Boyson, was a consummate professional, and my co-star, this Brett Haney fella, was some down-home type who didn't smoke or drink or pepper his conversations with words like "cocksucker." I had promised Penny that as of today, I would turn over a new leaf.

Scotty came rushing over with my cappuccino, his short legs stuffed into tight chinos flooding above loafers.

"About fucking time," I growled. "Where are your socks?" I demanded sounding exactly like my father. "And where's my Sweet'N Low?"

"I put it in already," he said patiently as if I were a badly behaved child in need of a nap. "Y'know," he whispered, "if you're trying to change your reputation, you're not getting off to a great start."

That was the problem with assistants, they were always around when you felt like confiding things.

"Sorry." I forced a smile. I had to keep on his good side. There was always a temptation with assistants, even loyal ones, to sell you out to a tabloid. One juicy tidbit could garner a small fortune. Many confidentiality agreements had gone through the shredder for a price. "I'll try to do better," I told him.

He heaved his narrow shoulders and with a martyr's sigh, his eyes drifted back to the cappuccino man. Poor Scotty. He didn't stand a chance.

"Okay, okay," I said, benevolently "Go get 'em, tiger. I'll be in makeup if you need me."

He flashed his recently whitened teeth and trotted off in the direction of the coffee cart.

With the cappuccino kicking in, my mood began to lighten. I strolled over to the makeup trailer, climbed the rattling metal stairs, and knocked.

"Easy!" a woman's voice yelled from inside. "You're rocking the boat!"

"Sorreee," I called out, opening the door.

He sat shirtless facing the mirror, eyes closed, while the makeup lady applied foundation. I checked him over: killer body, thick, curly black hair, thick eyebrows, an earthy skin tone.

"Is that Jackie?" he drawled, catching me off guard. His eyes were still shut. His hairdresser moved in with a comb and spritzer bottle.

"Uh, yeah. Hi, there." I stepped forward and the trailer lurched. The hair lady gave me a stern look.

"Whoops, sorry."

My leading man opened his eyes and swiveled to face me.

"Hi, Jackie Gold."

His eyes were the color of the sea, aquamarine, ringed with a band of green. I could swear I had seen those eyes before. And those lips, full but masculine, supple and chiseled. He smiled and suddenly I felt incredibly nervous, adolescent, and fearful that he could see the level of attraction I felt for him, positive he couldn't possibly feel the same. He reached out and as we shook hands, chills slithered down the back of my neck, my knees went soft, and my heart beat like Koda drums.

He grinned. "You don't remember me, do you?"

"Remember you?" The drums stopped beating and the Rolodex started spinning as I reached into the banks of my foggy memory for a clue.

"Um, oh God you do look familiar."

His laugh filled the trailer, deep and sugary. "We met a few years ago on that Alex Harvey picture. I was his stand-in. I mighta' looked different. Y'know, buzz cut and all."

My mouth dropped open. "Barney?"

"It's Brett now. Brett Haney. I took your advice and changed it. I hope you like it better."

"Uh-huh." I needed a cigarette. I started to fish one out of my purse when I remembered he didn't like smoking. I pulled out some mints instead. "Um...Altoid?" I proffered.

"Thanks. I have some." He patted his pants pocket. "I always keep 'em on hand when there's a love scene to do," he said, raising his eyebrows and grinning. He got up from the chair and stretched. Waves of muscles rippled down his back. I staggered back.

"By the way Jackie, I have my own trailer now. If you care to drop by, it's the *really* big one, right next to yours."

DISSOLVE TO:

INT. HOSPITAL ICU
EVENING
DAY 46

It is hollow and cold behind the waterfall. Wavy shapes slide past, whispering. A plastic and steel wet nurse pumps life into my lungs. I am drowning in air; compressed and earthbound. I long to go back to heaven or wherever the hell that was. My body feels bound, mummified as if I'm buried in sand, struggling to break loose before the tide comes in to claim me.

A figure looms up and passes his hand over the ventilator as if casting a spell. "Jackie!" Brett calls but the sound is muffled. He twists and hurls his body out of the room.

Daddy bursts into my cubicle and pushes past the waterfall. I want to warn him about the slippery rocks, but I am too late. He collapses. Nurses rush in but Daddy pushes them back with one arm while fumbling to pull the sheets from my body. The nurses guide, push, pull him away from my bed. The tide washes over me. I am floating down at the ocean's base. Above, my father swims past a shimmering kelp bed of helping hands and out the door.

A hot Santa Ana blows the door open bringing Anna in a pink warm-up suit with an alligator emblem. A nurse stands guard at each padded shoulder for support. Her body looks compressed as if the space between her bones and organs has been sucked out.

Anna motions the nurses to leave her. She comes to my bedside and bends over, arms extending like the branches of a desert willow. My body cools in her shade. From somewhere a bell sounds, and nurses scurry down the hall. Anna loosens my sheets, reaches under, and presses something cold into my palm. Her gold cross floods my senses, and I am looking up into those dark eyes, safe again, lying on her unmade bed in the little room over the garage. With everything in me, I will my hand to squeeze hers, to let her see I am receiving this gift, this proof of that precious time we shared. Anna entwines the chain around my fingers so that the necklace will not fall away.

"No te vayas, Jackie. Don't leave us." She kisses my forehead. "Quedarse, okay? Stick around."

PARAMOUNT STUDIOS
INT. SPACESHIP - DAY AND NIGHT
1995

Our chemistry was undeniable. Between takes, we joked and bantered. We ate our lunches together and played pranks on each other. I put gummies inside Brett's helmet and as revenge, he poured ice into my spacesuit. We talked about our families, touched on past relationships, mine with Peter, his with Kelly, a woman from his theater department at the University of Texas.

When our characters kissed for the first time, the cameras saw my skin flush and perspiration spring up on Brett's neck and chest. What was happening between us was real. Dressed in our Mylar space suits (due to our PG rating there was no nudity), we acted out our love scenes authentically, discovering one another's bodies. During the weightless scenes, we tumbled around together, gripping each other's arms and legs, inhaling one another's scent as we performed step-by-step, move-by-move, the choreography we'd rehearsed. No matter that a dozen crewmembers were looking on. The experience was intense, and I was left trembling long after Vilmar cut the scene.

Naturally, everyone assumed we were sleeping together. Our publicists advised us neither to confirm nor deny the rumors—the suspense over our personal relationship was great for the film. The studio was ecstatic. The tabloids were already running stories. Admittedly, I hoped the rumors would find their way to Peter Haskell, who still slaved away on *Circle of Life*. He had left the show briefly to do a film that turned out to be a giant flop. Now he was back on Daytime TV, and it wasn't my imagination that he was getting pudgy.

But despite the rumors, the press releases, and tabloids, the truth was that Brett and I hadn't gotten past first base.

"Use it, Jackie. Put it into the scene," he said earnestly.

We were in his Winnebago, running lines. I had once again managed to inch my body almost on top of his, hoping to seduce him.

"Why?" There was a sour, needy tinge to my voice. I tried to disguise it with a joke. "You're not secretly doing my stand-in, are you, Barney?" I ran my fingers up the slick fabric of his spacesuit.

Brett grinned, shook his head, and moved over to the captain's chair opposite me.

"We don't want to dissipate our chemistry."

"Let's just make out," I offered sensibly.

"I'll tell you what. When the movie is over, Jackie, I'll take you away for a romantic weekend."

"Swear it?"

I had been with a lot of different men, but this guy was a different breed. Brett was even-tempered, Texas-born, and Mormon-raised. To a girl who'd grown up in show business where everyone acted out and expressed every little feeling, all that repression was a turn-on.

Waiting was excruciating, but Brett promised we'd go away right after the movie ended, and with that big ol' Texas-sized carrot dangled in front of me (his thin Mylar space suit left nothing to the imagination), I concentrated my energy on making myself irresistible. I bought enough lingerie to outfit a fleet of prostitutes and waxed, scrubbed, and sloughed my body so when the time came for my unveiling, Brett would not be disappointed.

At exactly 8:35 p.m. on our final day of filming, Vilmar called out, "That's a wrap, folks!" A half-hour later, strapped into five-inch heels and squeezed into a tight, black mini-dress, I returned to the sound stage, now magically transformed with paper lanterns and space-theme decorations. A band was tuning up, and the festivities were already in full swing. We planned to spend the required time at the wrap party and then drive up the coast to the Biltmore Hotel in Santa Barbara, where Brett had booked our suite.

Despite my excitement about the weekend, my stomach was upset, and I felt anxious. I was desperate for a drink or at least a joint, but it was out of the question. For twelve weeks, I hadn't had any alcohol or even smoked a cigarette. It had been hard but worth the sacrifice. Brett was a gentleman, polite and decent to all he encountered, and I resolved to be the kind of woman he deserved. I thought I might be in love. I had no idea where Brett stood. For all I knew, we would go to Santa Barbara, have wild sex and that would be it.

Popping a couple of Tums, I took a deep breath and headed into the throng, weaving through the crowd to where Brett stood with several crewmembers and Vilmar. I waved but he continued nodding and laughing at something Vilmar had said. I pressed myself into him to let him know I was there and then laughed along as if I'd heard whatever they were saying. I reached for his hand, but he pulled it away to shake hands with the lighting director.

"Hey." I tapped him gently on the shoulder, and he held up his forefinger in an impatient "one-minute" gesture. My ego stung from the dismissal. I stood paralyzed, arms locked against my sides as Brett reached past me, again and again, to shake hands with several mucky mucks from the studio. I felt heartsick. My world was grinding to a stop like an old movie projector choking on a strip of film.

"Great work, fella," one said.

"Oh, well, I had Jackie for inspiration." Brett circled his arm around my waist and pulled me close. He flashed his million-dollar smile at me. His blue eyes were warm and sparkling. Blood rushed back into my veins. Air pumped into my lungs. I sprang to life. Lights, sound, action!

"Thank you, darling," I said easily, as though I had not just experienced the collapse of my whole world.

Everything was fine. I was fortified, fixed! I could thank the crew, schmooze with Vilmar, and the studio schmucks. I turned my face into Brett's shoulder, snorting him, smoking him, drinking him in.

Around midnight, Brett and I trickled our way out of the party, tossing compliments like confetti, making promises to people we would never see again that we would see them again soon. Then, at last, we were seated in Brett's red Mustang, driving out the Paramount gates.

Cruising down the Coast Highway, Brett's hands locked on the steering wheel, his eyes fixed on the road. I'd started the ride chatty and upbeat but since leaving the party, Brett had barely spoken a word. Instead, he hummed along to some godawful country twang on the radio leaving me once again nervous and unsure of his feelings for me. I picked up the car phone Brett had recently installed and fiddled with the buttons.

"No reception here," Brett grunted.

"Oh, I wasn't calling anyone, I was just… Is that Garth Brooks?" I asked, hoping to engage him.

"Clint Black."

"Oh." I had exhausted my knowledge of country musicians, so we lapsed back into silence.

We approached Oxnard when Brett leaned over me, pushed in the car lighter, opened the glove compartment, and took out a pack of Marlboros.

I watched stupefied as he lit up and inhaled. All this time I'd been acting like good girl Laura on *Little House on the Prairie* and he was a closet smoker? I decided to stay in character until I figured out what was going on.

"Why, Barney Macahaney! When on earth did you pick up that filthy habit?" I chided.

"I hope you're not disappointed in me, Jackie. I've been under a tremendous amount of pressure." He rolled down his window and exhaled the smoke outside. Then to my utter astonishment, he reached under his seat and pulled out a pint of whiskey.

Was there a hidden camera? Was I being pranked? Brett had told me he was a Mormon-raised teetotaler who neither smoked nor drank. He had not had even a sip of champagne at the wrap party. What was happening? And who was this other guy? More importantly, why the hell had I turned myself inside out to make him think I was squeaky-clean if I could have been dancing on the bar all along!

With one hand Brett broke the seal and slugged from the bottle. Then he settled the pint between his legs.

"I figured tonight being the end of the movie and all. I hope you're okay with this?"

"Mmm-hmm." I nodded.

Hell yeah, I was ready to party. Only I would have to figure out a way to cast off my prairie bonnet without looking as if I'd been a complete phony all along. I turned down the radio. Brett shot me a look.

"Um, sweetie?" I eyed the pint of Jack Daniels nestled in his crotch. I wanted it almost as badly as I wanted him. "Is there anything you want to tell me?"

He took a drag of his cigarette and shook his head.

"Do you still want to spend this weekend together? Because if you don't, it's okay with me."

Fat stinking lie, but I with Brett's atypical behavior, I was fishing for reassurance.

He took another gulp of whiskey. I could taste it going down.

"I'm sorry." He stubbed his cigarette in the ashtray. "I have a lot on my mind. I absolutely want to spend the weekend together." He reached over, took my hand, and gently squeezed. Restraining myself, I squeezed back, just the right measured amount. Inside, I fainted with relief. Brett held up the pint.

"Care to join me?" he asked.

"Gee. Well, sure, I guess."

I wanted to suck on that bottle so hard my lips puckered. I forbade my hands to grab the whiskey, forcing them to stay folded in my lap until Brett handed it to me. I took the pint, raised it slowly to my mouth, and when Brett wasn't looking, guzzled down as much as I could in one swallow.

"Wow, this stuff burns," I said, innocently.

By the time we drove up to the hotel, I had the pint between my legs, a cigarette in one hand, and Brett's penis in the other.

Brett opened the door to our suite, and we stumbled inside, falling together on the bed. We kissed furiously. This was what I'd been waiting for! I climbed on top of him, pulled his T-shirt over his head, and ripped open the bodice of my dress. In my fantasy, it was supposed to be Brett who ripped my dress, but Brett didn't seem to be picking up the cue, so I ran the show for us both. Finally, we were naked, our bodies grinding, entwined. I worked my way on top of him, opened myself, and took that hard, big, Texas-sized penis inside me. Brett groaned with pleasure, I thought, but simultaneously he shrank. I swiveled my hips, bounced a little, kissed him, sucked on his earlobe, but he continued to melt inside me. In a desperate attempt to salvage the situation, I bit one of his nipples.

"Ow!" he cried out and slipped out at the same time.

"Sorry. I was just trying to, y'know..." I felt exposed, afraid I had revealed too much of my lustful nature and turned him off.

Brett lay on his side not looking at me. Then, after a few moments of silence, he reached for the remote control and turned on the TV.

"Hey, there's a Jacuzzi in the bathroom, want to test it out?" I raised my brows suggestively.

Brett remained silent.

"Oh, great," I said. "Am I supposed to just go to sleep now and pretend that none of this has happened? Hey!" I softly smacked him on the ass, and he turned over and looked at me. His face was screwed up and red. "Honey, what is it?" I softened my tone and faced him sideways on the bed.

"It's... I'm feeling insecure," he whispered. He jutted out his quivering chin.

"About us?" I shifted around and cradled his head in my arms. "Oh, sweetie."

He hid his face in my bosom, his lashes fluttered against my breasts. "About work." His voice was muffled.

"Work?" The word plopped out like a stone. "You mean acting?"

"What if they hate me? What if I never work again?"

Brett covered his handsome face with his hands and burrowed deeper. I fought an enormous urge to shake him, hard. Instead, I stroked his head. "Look, honey, I know how you feel. We all feel this way after a movie. But I don't think you, we, should let it get in the way of our vacation."

Brett nodded miserably and kissed me on the cheek. "I'm sorry," he said, pinching his eyes. "I'm such a jackbutt! If my pop ever saw me like this... Let's just say he'd whup the man into me."

I kissed his forehead. Part of me was pleased and touched that Brett was so open and vulnerable. But the other part wanted to climb back in the saddle and whup the man into him myself.

Brett ran his hands through his thick hair. "Sorry. Didn't mean to spoil things."

"You didn't spoil anything," I lied. "Feel better?"

"Yeah." He nodded. "Yeah, I do. Thanks, Jackie. I've been holding it in all night. I didn't want to ruin our time. Anyway, I just want to say that I've never met anyone like you. I feel like I can be myself with you, and in this town that is saying a lot."

"Well, you can and you're welcome." I made my tone extra easy-going so as not to betray my frustration.

We gazed into each other's eyes. I waited for him to make a move, get us going again. All I needed was a little jump-start.

"Mmmmm, Brett," I sighed. I tickled behind his ear and he smiled, but his eyes had shifted focus. I followed his gaze, landing on the sports news. Suddenly self-conscious about my nakedness, I pulled my torn dress back over my head.

"Hey, um, I'm just gonna check out that tub," I said, hoping Brett would ask to join me.

"Hurry back," he said, still looking at the television.

When I returned, Brett was under the covers, asleep. A feeling of hysteria rose in my throat. He must not have been attracted to me. I must have done something wrong. I wanted to wake him up and make him talk to me, but I couldn't let myself tumble over that cliff. I didn't want to scare Brett away. I tiptoed over to the mini bar, took out a few mini vodkas and an assortment of chocolate and dry roasted nuts, and piled them on the nightstand. Then I settled back against the pillows, opened a chocolate bar, and put on the Playboy Channel.

The next morning, the sun pried my eyes open. I turned to the clock. Eleven a.m. Groggy and hungover, I groped around for Brett, worming myself over to his side of the bed. It was empty. I sat up. My head hurt. My swollen eyes itched. I needed coffee. Maybe Brett was in the restaurant. I would look for him there.

I rolled over to the side of the bed and swung my legs down onto the floor.

"Whoa, there!"

"Aaah!" I yelled.

Brett lay on the carpet in his underwear, doing sit-ups. "Good morning, Jackie Gold." He gave me a big smile. "I'm almost finished. One ninety-seven. One ninety-eight. One ninety-nine… Done."

"Good morning, yourself," I answered, testing the waters. Was he happy? Did he still like me?

Brett jumped up and opened the curtains, flooding the room with light.

"Whoa," I moaned, covering my eyes with one hand and scooching back under the blankets.

Inside my suitcase, tempering the arsenal of sexy lingerie, was a demure robe I had planned to wear only for greeting room service. "Umm, can you please hand me that bag?" I pointed. I wasn't ready for him to see me naked in the light of day, especially not after last night's coitus interruptus.

My mouth tasted terrible. My head ached. I needed Tylenol or Alka Seltzer. Or better, a Campari and soda. Brett, on the other hand, appeared as if he'd emerged from a health spa.

He strutted over to where our bags still lay in the entryway. I tried not to ogle him as he approached in his tighty-whities.

"Here you go, ma'am." He hoisted my suitcase on the bed.

Ma'am? I bristled, taken aback, then reminded myself he was from a part of the country where that was considered polite. "Thanks."

I extracted my cosmetics case and retrieved the robe. "Would you mind closing the curtains a bit?"

"Okay, but it's a gorgeous day! We gotta get outside into that sunshine." His voice was about a hundred decibels too loud. As he walked toward the window, I scurried into the bathroom.

A shower and four Tylenol later, I emerged in the robe, a towel wrapped around my head, feeling not quite refreshed but at least passable.

Brett lay on the bed still in his underwear, a light film of sweat on his skin. Did he have to be so goddamn gorgeous? It wasn't fair. I averted my eyes. I didn't want him to see how much I wanted him. I couldn't handle more rejection.

"Jackie?" His voice was husky.

"Yup?"

"Come over here."

I walked over and sat on the edge of the bed. I wasn't getting my hopes up. He stretched over and pulled the towel from my head, then slowly tugged the robe off my shoulders. Pulling me down until I was facing him, he kissed me lightly. I kissed him lightly back. He stroked my arms. I stroked his arms. Then he took me into his embrace and slowly we began making love. He was gentle, I was gentle. No ripped clothing, no hair pulling, and no crotchless panties.

"Well, that was nice," Brett sighed when it was over. He kissed me on the forehead, rolled off me, went into the bathroom, and shut the door.

A moment later the shower turned on. Unsure what to do, I slipped into my robe, lit a cigarette, lay back on the pillows, and reflected on our lovemaking. The sex hadn't been as long or wild or as passionate as I had pictured, but it *had* happened, and he had clearly wanted me. Still, something wasn't sitting right. Our coupling had been successful if you measured success by us both achieving orgasm. And Brett had been a perfect gentleman, making sure I came first. "Nice," Brett had said. And it was nice. So why did I feel discontent? Maybe there was something wrong with me. Maybe those contraptions and contortions with Palucci had ruined me for nice, normal sex. I was crazy about Brett. Possibly in love. Maybe *nice* was how sex was supposed to be when you met the right person.

For the rest of the weekend, I kept myself in check, consciously slowing my racing libido to match Brett's. We played tennis, brunched in Montecito, and took long walks on the beach. In the afternoons we made love, but I discovered that when I took any initiative Brett's penis wilted. So, I completely surrendered the lead, matching his rhythms like an obedient high school band member. A cheerleader, but not a head cheerleader. The kind of girl I imagined Brett would have been attracted to in his hometown.

On Sunday after our lovemaking, Brett brushed his teeth while I rinsed off in the shower. Checkout was in an hour and soon we would drive home to L.A. I watched through the steamy glass while he packed his toiletry kit, razor, and toothbrush into separate plastic cases, toothpaste neatly rolled halfway with a metal key. I stifled the desire to grab him from behind, bite his neck, and lick away the beads of sweat that dripped down the fuzzy gully between his back and his ass. I turned off the water and reached for a towel.

"Hey, Jackie Gold."

"Hey yourself."

"I sure do like you, Jackie."

"I sure do like you too, Brett."

I more than liked him. A lot more. His sweetness, his good manners, his goofy Texas way of speaking. Even his acting insecurities didn't bother me. I could relate, though his were even worse than mine.

I forced myself to walk past without mauling him, out of the bathroom, over to where my suitcase sat packed and ready by the door. All my sexy lingerie, tags still on, stuffed in, strapped down, zipped up, and hidden away.

CLOSE UP: BRETT HANEY'S FACE
FX: MAGAZINE COVERS SPINNING
1996

With the film's premiere, Brett rocketed to the top of the A list. *"Space Story* is this generation's *Star Wars,"* said *Variety.* The *Hollywood Reporter* called him "the next Tom Cruise." Film offers showered him. *Vanity Fair, Rolling Stone, Swanky*, and *GQ* all booked shoots for their covers. Everybody wanted Brett Haney. Especially me. I wanted him all the time and with the attention he was receiving, I had him less and less. Not that I was faring badly; my reviews were good, if not spectacular. Penny was pouring over scripts, looking for the right "vehicle," determined I wait for a "serious" role.

Brett and I went on a press tour of eighteen cities, making love in only four of them despite my pleading. And though it wasn't the sexcapade I'd hoped for, I managed to be a good sport and refrain from the kinds of drunk-and-disorderly behaviors that plagued my previous junkets.

When we landed back in Los Angeles, Brett asked me to live with him.

"Yes," I said. "Yes!"

I couldn't wait. It would be different than with Peter. We'd be starting fresh, choosing our home together. It felt old-timey and innocent. Like sweethearts from a small town, quietly taking the next step.

A parade of media vans and two helicopters followed us as Brett drove our U-Haul through the streets of Bel-Air to our new home. The announcement set off shock waves.

"Are you engaged?" Regis asked in the morning.

"When's the big day?" Jay asked that night.

"Why the rush?" Larry asked by satellite.

"Christ, Jackie! Are you pregnant?" Daddy yelled on the phone.

"Of course not!"

"I read about this in the goddamn trades!"

"The press got wind of it so fast I—"

"Anna's upset."

"Anna? Why?"

"One of her friends said you rented in her neighborhood and Anna didn't know anything about it. It was very embarrassing for her."

Entertainment Tonight devoted segments to speculating about when and where Brett and I would marry. Astrologers were consulted on our compatibility. Psychics were questioned about our futures. Every method but police dogs were used to sniff out our intentions. And of course, the paparazzi followed us everywhere.

"Brett, Jackie, over here." Click.

"Dollface." Click.

"Gotcha!" Click, click, click, click, click, click.

We were photographed going to the market, the gym, the hairdresser. Every time we stepped out of our door, someone was there to record our every move.

People ran a cover of Brett and me walking on the boardwalk in Santa Monica holding hands. The picture had been taken by a paparazzo with a telephoto lens. No one seeing that cover photo, displayed at every check stand in America, could have guessed what was going on in our minds that day as we strolled along the beach path, skaters whizzing by, the sun setting over the calm sea. I was thinking up ways to improve our sex life while Brett was walking off a particularly gassy meal.

INT. ICU
LATE AFTERNOON
DAY 47

"The pneumonia produced a mass of empyema," Dr. Foreman told Daddy and Anna as they stood next to my intubated body. Dani hovered by the door, pretending not to eavesdrop.

"Empa…" Daddy began.

"Empyema is a thick fluid, pus that develops from chest trauma or pneumonia. We performed a thoracotomy to drain the fluid but I'm sorry to say the severity has caused a partial shutdown of Jackie's respiratory functions." He put a hand on my father's shoulder. "She'll have to stay on a ventilator. Jackie can no longer breathe on her own."

My father swayed, and Anna reached out to steady him.

Dr. Foreman continued. "She's a strong young woman. Depending on her fortitude, she could stay like this for months, even years. That is if you choose to continue to keep her on life support."

"Is there any chance at all she could recover?" Anna asked.

Dr. Foreman shook his head. "Not in my experience, but one can always hope," he said somberly. "I wish I had better news."

"Oh my God," Daddy moaned.

"I'll call Brett," Anna said softly, reaching into her purse. "We need to talk this through with him."

"Oh um, cell phones aren't permitted here," Dani said, coming up behind her. "If you give me his number, I can dial him for you at the nurse's station."

Anna raised an eyebrow. "No thank you, Dani. We will call from the car."

SLOW DISSOLVE TO:

INT. SPAGO RESTAURANT
HOLLYWOOD
NIGHT

We dropped by Spago after a publicity party for the foreign press; a boring affair where I'd managed to consume only one glass of wine. I was practicing my restraint and control, professionally and in the bedroom.

"Hey there, Donny," Brett greeted the maître d' who ushered us over to one of Spago's select tables. In the old days, Nicole would have to make a phone call just to get us in the door.

I'd given up trying to find her. The private detective I hired had come up empty-handed. I'd even contacted our high school reunion committee, but the only address they had was our old apartment in Hollywood.

"Go ahead and order," I said to Brett. "I'm going to pee."

He wagged his finger.

"Okay sorry, geez, powder my freaking nose." I kissed his cheek and left him to order our usual goat cheese and sun-dried tomato pizza.

I was pulling down my underwear when the bathroom door slammed open. I peeked through the crack of the stall to discover a man in an oversized raincoat with two cameras wrapped around his thick neck. How the hell had he snuck past Donny?

I sighed. "Give me a break, mister."

"Just one shot of you and Brett," he begged. "Don't be selfish."

Paparazzi suffer the illusion that they are responsible for our success and that we celebrities should be more appreciative.

"Go away!" I yanked up my panties.

He aimed his camera "Come on out then," he demanded.

"You'd better go before I scream," I yelled. "One, two—"

"Ungrateful bitch!" He tore out the door.

"Thought you drowned," Brett said when I stomped back to the table. The pizza had arrived, and he was happily chewing, oblivious to my frazzled state. "Wolfgang came over to say good-bye." He motioned to our waiter, for refills on his Diet Coke.

"And a double Stoli," I called.

"Please," Brett called to the waiter and gave me a look of admonishment.

"I thought I said please," I grumbled.

"What's wrong, puddin' pie?"

"Paparazzi." I gnawed on a discarded crust while recounting the episode. "I don't see the little rat around now. Either he's hiding in the men's room, or he's camped outside."

Brett chuckled. "You know what they say, 'All publicity is good publicity.'"

"That's crapola, Brett," I retorted. "A dumbass saying invented by publicists to seem indispensable."

"For Chris'sake." I twisted around. "Where's my drink?"

"Easy darling. Everyone's gotta make a living," Brett drawled.

"They're bottom feeders, not factory workers," I snapped.

"Well, just don't let it ruin our evening." He reached over and squeezed my hand.

"Uggh," I grunted and squirreled my annoyance away. It pissed me off that Brett wasn't upset. I mean, the guy had followed me into the *bathroom*. But it wasn't worth pursuing. Whenever we argued, Brett went stony.

When our waiter arrived, I snatched the vodka from his tray.

"Finally," I said under my breath.

"A drink for you, Mr. Haney?"

"No thanks, Sammy. Just the little lady. I'm working tomorrow."

Brett knew everybody's name. That was another thing that irked me. Did he have to be so goddamn friendly?

He pushed away half the pizza and took a swallow of his diet coke. "That's enough calories for me." He was starting rehearsal for *Kill Shot*, an action-adventure about mercenaries which, fortunately, shot close to home in the Santa Monica mountains.

"Kind of dead tonight," Brett said, dabbing sauce from the corners of his mouth.

"Henry's here." I motioned to where the director, Henry Jaglom, sat at his usual table by the window. He was famous for making independent films, starring whoever he was dating. Naturally, every actress in town wanted his number.

"Yeah. He never remembers my name." Brett laughed. "Guys like that hate me."

"What are you talking about?"

"The arty-types and the old-timers, you know. Like your dad."

"My dad? Since when does my dad hate you?" True, Daddy wasn't overly fond of Brett. He was often befuddled by my boyfriend's attempts to engage him with his down-home sayings and folksy manner. But Daddy didn't hate Brett. No one could hate Brett. That was another thing that bugged me.

"All right, if you must know…" He leaned in so as not to be overheard. "If you must know, there was a movie Penny suggested to me for, but your dad shot it down."

"Which one?"

"The Howard picture. Well, it was the Howard picture but now it's Reitman's."

"Why didn't you say something? I would have talked to Daddy."

"Right, Jackie. I'm gonna let my lady beg her pop for my paycheck. You know me better than that." Brett shoved his plate aside and leaned back in his chair. "Let's get the check."

"Um, Henry's waving at us to come over."

"He's waving at you. I'm just a stupid redneck." He sighed. "No one takes me seriously. Maybe I should become Jewish, I've almost got the schnoz for it," he joked.

I leaned over and kissed his nose. "You'd never pass."

"If I was Jewish, I'd be in the club," he sulked.

"Where you come from, *darlin'*," I drawled, "the clubs keep us out."

"Not in this town, princess." He picked up a spoon and checked his teeth in the reflection.

I finished my vodka and waved at Henry. Fortunately, Brett never made an issue of my drinking, though he'd returned to abstaining. He worked out a minimum of two hours a day and like most leading men, was obsessed with every aspect of his body.

That made two of us.

After stopping for a short schmooze with Henry and Victoria, his latest muse, Brett paid the check, and we went out to the parking lot. The cool breeze brushed my bare shoulders and the promise of rain hung in the air. I peered into the darkness. It was surprisingly quiet. There was usually a gaggle of paparazzi. No sign of the guy from the bathroom. Perhaps the impending weather had sent them home early.

"Where the heck did that valet get to?" Brett yawned and checked his watch.

Seconds later, lights appeared around the corner of the driveway. An engine revved and tires squealed as Brett's Mercedes coupe roared to a stop in front of us. A short dark-haired attendant jumped out and ran around to the passenger side.

"Ridin' those brakes mighty hard there, fella," Brett chided as he slid into the driver's seat.

"Sorry, sir." The man opened the door for me and smiled. "Hi, Jackie."

I was tired and didn't feel up to chatting with a fan. "Hi," I responded, curtly.

"Remember me?"

I narrowed my eyes at his features, and with a shock, I recognized him. It was Alphonse. Al from the Beverly Hills hotel. Al of the purple van and the shiny sheets. Older now but same grin, same silky black hair flopped over one eye. I felt shaken. "Hi," I stammered. "I didn't know you worked here."

"Just started." He beamed.

Brett held out a five-dollar bill, but Al waved it away. "Nah, I'm just happy to see Jackie."

"You know each other?" Brett cocked an eyebrow.

Al turned to me expectantly. I had never told Brett the sordid tale of how I'd lost my virginity. It was too far a cry from the image I'd crafted; the way I wanted him to see me.

"Sure, we do right, Jackie?" Al prodded.

What did he think I'd say? "Brett honey, shake hands with the asshole who popped my cherry when I was fourteen and barely spoke to me again?" I couldn't think about that night without feeling sick.

"Um, Al worked at a hotel we once stayed at."

"I've seen all your movies, Jackie. Every single one. I watched you on *Circle of Life* too."

What if he sold me out? Someone would pay a lot of money for his story. Then I remembered Al had been at least twenty when I was fourteen. Statutory rape by any standards. No, he'd keep his mouth shut. Even so, I couldn't handle seeing him at my regular hangout. Tomorrow, I would make a call.

I got in the car and shut the door. "Let's go," I stated brusquely.

"Sorry fella, she's just tired," Brett apologized.

"Go!" I commanded looking straight ahead.

That night in bed, I made a decision. It was time we had a heart-to-heart about our pasts. I couldn't take the chance of Brett finding out stuff about me from other people. Everywhere we went in this town, a skeleton could be waiting to jump out of the closet. Well, to be honest, it was only my closet. My great, big, walk-in closet. Brett probably had a small cupboard back in Texas filled with white cotton panties. Plus, there was so much gossip

264 · DINAH MANOFF

and rumormongering in our business. It was better if I gave it to him straight. There should be no secrets between us.

The heart-to-heart went like this:

"Brett, there's some stuff I think I should tell you."

"I don't want to know."

"But—"

"I said I don't want to know."

"But—"

"Trust me, Jackie, there are things people should just keep to themselves."

INT. JACKIE AND BRETT'S HOUSE
BEVERLY HILLS
DAY

After wrapping the mercenary film, Brett immediately went into pre-production on another picture. I hung around the house trying to fill my days, while Penny sought "the perfect vehicle to showcase my talents"—talents I wasn't at all sure I had. In my gigs thus far, not much had been demanded of me, and truthfully, I would have been content to keep it that way, but it was in Penny's nature (possible owing to her childhood as a competitive gymnast), to keep raising the bar.

In the evenings at our publicist's urging, Brett and I dutifully displayed ourselves on the red carpets of one or another premiere, smiling and posing under hot blinding Klieg lights, trying not to sweat on borrowed designer gowns and suits our stylists had procured. Afterward, we returned to our still unfurnished, six-thousand-square-foot home, a space destined to remain barren as long as Brett deemed decorators "frivolous" and I feared to might awaken my mother's design curse.

Later in bed (a king mattress lacking a headboard), Brett would disappear into his script while I fidgeted and watched Letterman. Brett didn't get Letterman's humor any more than I got country-western music. Our upbringings, our beliefs, even our political views were different. My family were Dems, his were Republicans, though Brett insisted he was an *Independent* like Arnold Schwarzenegger or Bruce Willis, which in Hollywood meant Republican without the stigma.

Regardless of our differences I was exhaustingly attracted and in love with Brett, my existence a perpetual state of puppy lust, panting and pawing for a scrap of his attention. It wasn't so much the competition of leading ladies that fed my insecurity, nor the thousands of fangirls whose provocative snapshots spilled from his mail. Brett never flirted with women in front of me or gave me reasons to be jealous. What really had me flailing on the hook was his sexual indifference and his unwillingness to discuss it. When we did have sex, every week or so, Brett was ever the gentleman making sure I orgasmed before him. But then his batteries went dead. Kaput. Sex for Brett was like a big heavy Italian meal. For me, it was Chinese food.

Inevitably, I would collapse back into my need for reassurance.

"Are you happy with me?"

"Mmm-hmm."

"Are you sure?"

"About what?"

"You know, is there something you want in bed that I'm not doing?"

"No."

"I feel like you're holding something back."

"I'm not."

"Why don't you want oral sex?"

"It's just not my thing."

"I could just do it to you, you don't have to do it back."

"For Lord's sake, Jackie. Quit harping about things."

"Is something wrong with me?"

"No, Jackie. Stop it! You're perfect."

Then fuck me, you withholding prick! I wanted to scream but instead, I'd smile sweetly. "Okay then," I'd say while putting on my PJs, "just thought I'd check in." Then I'd wait until he fell asleep before once again taking out my trusty vibrator. I'd always been insecure, not thinking myself pretty enough or tall or thin enough, but never had I doubted my proficiency. Sex was my ace in the hole.

Naturally, I toyed with the idea that Brett was gay. I had heard gossip to that effect, but rumors like that dogged every leading man in Hollywood, and my assistant Scotty, who had faultless intuition, had diagnosed Brett as "pure hetero." I knew I should be grateful. Here I was, living with the nicest, most handsome, and considerate guy in the world. Wasn't that enough?

The hardest part was keeping my fears and frustrations locked inside. Since Nicole, I hadn't had a single close friend. How could I trust anyone? You never knew who might sell you out to the tabloids. Katie, my makeup person was cool, but after a couple of drinks, she tended to gossip. I could confide some things to Penny, she knew us best having smartly signed Brett before *Space Story*, but Penny lived with three cats and was the last person to advise about relationships.

I had to stop fixating on Brett and get on with my life. But whenever I pestered Penny about wanting to work, she'd become exasperated and remind me I had to be patient and wait for a "serious" role. The last time she'd said, "Quit kvetching and get a hobby." Then, she'd hung up on me.

INT. JACKIE AND BRETT'S KITCHEN
NIGHT

"Penny thinks I should get a hobby."

Brett raised his hand. "I second that motion."

We'd come from the *Striptease* premiere where I'd had little to eat but a lot to drink. Now we were in the kitchen, shoes kicked off but still in our black-tie evening wear, having a "campout" of microwave hotdogs and marshmallows.

"I wonder who her trainer is." Brett undid his cummerbund and let out a burp.

"Who, Penny's?"

"Demi's! Sheesh." He chuckled.

"If you want Demi's body so bad, call her for Chris'sake. I hear she and Bruce are on the rocks." I was out of sorts. My feet hurt and I was sick of women throwing themselves at my boyfriend when I was standing right next to him holding his hand.

Brett finished his hotdog and crumpled his paper plate. "I want her *trainer*, Jackie, good Lord. "And the only body I want is yours."

I went up on my toes and licked a spot of mustard off his chin. "Swear?"

Brett put his arms around me. "Boy scouts honor."

"Prove it," I whispered in his ear.

His body stiffened but not in the place I was aiming for. "It's late sweetheart." He unwound from my arms and began cleaning up. I followed behind as he sponged crumbs from the counters.

"What should I do? I've never had a hobby."

"How 'bout aerobics?"

"You saying I'm fat?"

"No! You're perfect. You were just complaining about—"

"Complaining?"

"Okay, I can see there's no winning here." He tossed the sponge in the sink and swung his tuxedo jacket over his shoulder.

"I'm headin' to bed, puddin' pie. Don't forget to turn off the lights."

"Wait, Brett wanna' take a Jacuzzi?"

"Sorry sweetie, I'm whupped."

"Wanna go out for breakfast tomorrow?"

"Can't. I'm meeting Josh at the gym."

"How 'bout lunch?"

"Rehearsal, Jackie." Brett kissed my cheek and walked out of the kitchen.

"I could come to the set?" I called after him.

"Why don't you buy us some furniture?" he called back as he vanished up the stairs.

"Fuck." I grabbed a few Tums from an otherwise empty cabinet, poured a club soda, and walked into the empty living room.

My footsteps echoed off the bare floors. There were holes in the hollows of the two-story ceiling where light fixtures had yet to be hung. Across the room, I met my reflection in one of the three wide windows. We needed curtains, couches, carpets; the prospect filled me with fear. This was a massive undertaking for an experienced designer let alone for someone with my decorating DNA. I sat on the floor and took a sip of soda. I could start small, say a guest room or den. I needed to find a pastime other than Brett before I drove us both crazy. It wouldn't be a hobby like knitting or collecting Fiesta-ware, but something to keep me busy. And sooner or later, a job would come along and give me an excuse to quit. Until then, I had nothing better to do.

With the zeal of a cub reporter on my first assignment, I threw myself into my hobby. I pored over magazines and spent a fortune on decorating and design books, examining photographs of interiors where stripes, plaids, and flowers all magically coexisted. It was so random. I drove downtown to the fabric district, returning with hundreds of swatches, laying them side by side until I thought I had found the right combination. But each time I resolved to pick a motif, I would flashback to the home I grew up in with the mismatched colors and patterns. I would remember the look of determination on my mother's face, and our embarrassment at her results.

And that orange and yellow modular couch.

Brett was halfway through shooting, our house was still empty, and I was pulling my hair out, literally strand by strand, leaving a dime-sized bald spot on one side of my head. My hobby was keeping me busy all right, but now I was on the verge of a nervous breakdown. I decided to lower my sights and start shopping for small items like lamps, area rugs, or bathroom accessories. Still, whenever I went to make a purchase, I became paralyzed and left empty-handed.

Late one hot and smoggy afternoon after another fruitless day, I found myself sodden and weary, standing on Robertson Boulevard in front of yet another furniture showroom. I was exhausted and hungry. I needed to pee. The nearest public restroom was in the Ralph's, a good ten blocks away. I prayed the salesperson would recognize me and let me use the bathroom.

Inside, I was met by an officious woman in her forties.

"Restroom?" I asked meekly.

"Certainly, Ms. Gold. Right this way."

I'd made up my mind. When Brett came home from the studio tonight, I would tender my resignation. He could either relent and hire a decorator or continue living in a frat house.

I returned from the bathroom, gingerly walking on blistered feet, and found the same saleswoman in a corner of the showroom.

"Thank you," I said, handing her the restroom key.

"My pleasure."

She bent over, straightening the pillows on a large white sofa; part of an all-white living room display, with two matching chairs and a loveseat.

"What is your name?" I asked.

"Viveca."

I knew I looked a wreck, sweaty, and frayed. In contrast, Viveca was like the display; calm, collected, all restraint. Her black, sleek hair was pulled back like a ballerina's, the bun tucked like a nest in the hollow of her long neck.

"Viveca?" I pointed at the couch. "Do you mind if I...?"

She nodded. "Of course, Miss Gold." A measured shading of sympathy laced her voice. She guided my elbow as if I were infirm.

"Ohhh." It was like sinking into a cloud. And white. So basic. So relaxing. No colors to coordinate, no confusing patterns. "L-Lovely..." I sighed.

"The finest goose down," she said.

"And the fabric...?"

"Silk velvet." She kneeled before me. "May I?" she asked, slipping off one of my shoes, then the other. "Rest and enjoy."

I laid back and Viveca tucked a pillow under my knees.

I was nodding off when my purse rang. It was Brett.

"Hey, we just broke for lunch. Where are you?"

"Heaven." I dug into my wallet and signaled to Viveca waving my American Express. "The whole set, please."

She nodded serenely and walked to the cash register, just the slightest quickening in her step.

The furniture fit perfectly. The curse had been lifted. It was a miracle! My miracle. Once it was all assembled, I ran around and around, patting the cushions and pillows like I was playing duck-duck-goose. I hugged the moving guys and gave them each a hundred-dollar tip.

Emboldened I called Viveca and tackled the rest of our downstairs, measuring, ordering, buying everything in white. White carpeting, white tables, white chairs. I had found the magic key. White, white, white! In the coming months, I covered the empty walls hanging large black and white photographs by Ansel Adams, Herb Ritts, Helmut Newton, and Cindy Sherman. Color was way too risky. Who knew what could happen if a purple and a red ended up side-by-side? It was like organizing a dinner party. Why take a chance on seating strangers together when they might not get along?

And when *Architectural Digest* showed up to shoot Brett and me in our "Historic Hollywood Estate," they complimented my "fresh, minimalist styling."

"Jackie, can I ask you a question?" Brett asked.

We were lying in our new white upholstered bed after a long overdue session of lovemaking.

"Hmmm?" I nuzzled his chest. I yearned for another orgasm. I wrapped my legs around his thigh and squeezed hard.

"Hey, quit it. That hurts." He propped himself up against the white headboard.

"Sorreee." I rolled onto my stomach, took his hand, and put it between my legs. He didn't pull away, which I took as a hopeful sign.

"Jackie, do you think my torso is out of proportion to the rest of my body?"

Brett's vanity was the one thing that put the freeze on my lust. I got out of bed and grabbed my robe. "Of course not," I called on my way to the bathroom. "I think you're very proportional."

This was the downside to falling for an actor. Brett spent twice as much time fretting over his looks as I did.

I splashed water on my face and looked in the mirror. Three chin hairs had sprouted, seemingly overnight. My brows were getting bushy and the Goldstein mustache was threatening to reveal itself. Without being on camera, I was becoming feral.

I plucked out the nasty hairs then took out the Jolene.

"By the way, the house is shaping up, honey," Brett called from the other room. "But don't you think it's time to add a little color here and there?"

I peeked my head out, covering my mouth with my hand so Brett wouldn't see the paste on my mustache. "Don't push it."

Bleaching, plucking, peeing, pooping—these were things my boyfriend was averse to witnessing. If we ever had a baby, he'd be one of those old-fashioned dads handing out cigars in the waiting room rather than witnessing the miracle of his baby's head crowning in a bloody vagina.

"You could be an interior designer for a living," Brett said twenty minutes later when I emerged clean-faced. He picked up a script from the nightstand and began highlighting his lines for the next day's work.

"I might have to be if Penny doesn't find me a job."

"See, I told you so."

"You told me what?"

"You didn't need to hire one of those fruity designers. You probably saved us a fortune."

"Fruity? God, Brett, please don't use that word." What was the expression? You could take the boy out of Texas...

I went to the closet and pulled on a pair of jeans and a sweater.

"Where are you going?" Brett asked.

I didn't know. I was feeling restless and rebellious; too much domestication, not enough fornication. And really, I couldn't be expected to behave like a good little girl. It wasn't as if I had kids or even a job. I needed to go dancing, get drunk, get felt up in a coat room, snort coke off someone's lap! I would call Scotty. Or Katie!

I started looking for my phone book when I remembered it was a Sunday night. Scotty'd gotten hired as an agent's assistant at William Morris and Katie was on a mini-series. Everyone had a reason to get up in the morning. Except me.

I put my robe back on. "I'm going downstairs." I'd make myself a drink. Maybe watch a movie.

"Don't forget to alarm the house," Brett reminded me as I shut the bedroom door.

DISSOLVE TO:

INT ICU
EVENING
DAY 48

The room is quiet, Anna's jacket is unzipped, sleeves pushed up to her elbows. She washes my face with a warm cloth. "And after that, we were afraid even to go outside to school. That's how bad my village was."

Her almond skin glows in the monitor's light. She folds the steamy washcloth in half and presses it to my forehead as if treating nothing more serious than a headache.

"I always tell you I came here by airplane but really, my very first airplane ride was to my honeymoon with Sidney. First-class!" She chuckles softly and washes where the grime of childhood once collected behind my ears.

"I came with fifteen other people through Mexico, through the tunnels. Other men met us in Mexicali and took us in a bus. I watch a girl get raped in that bus. No one said a word. We were so afraid." She crosses the room and retrieves another cloth. "Before you met me, I was already working two years in a sweat-shop. Fourteen-hour days for a few dollars an hour. Hah! Stupid me, I thought that was a lot of money. I sent most home to my mother, paid twenty-five dollars a week to the cousins where I am living, sharing a small bed with one of the old aunties who would fart all night."

She wrings the warm cloth and flaps it to cool before pressing it to my chest. "I ate food from 7-Eleven. One meal a day—I was so skinny. I should write a diet book of that!"

Sweat beads at her temples, a narrow path of silver outlines her widow's peak, feathering into the strands of her black hair. When did she stop dying her roots? No. When did she start?

"The sweatshop was raided and shut down. I had maybe twenty dollars and was thinking my life is over. It's funny what you think is a tragedy and don't know is the miracle you waiting for.

"Then, a lady tells me about an agency for maids. I think no one will hire me, but they tell me there is maybe a job for live-in. But far away.

"Oh, that long bus ride to Malibu! I was already riding for an hour and still another forty-five minutes to go! But when we get to Pacific Coast Highway, I see the ocean. Maybe you can't believe this, but in the two years I am in Los Angeles, this was my first time to see the beach. The air, fresh. No buildings. I could breathe!

"It was late afternoon and your mom still in her nightgown and there was some Heinz on the front and her breasts are leaking, making two round stains that got bigger and bigger as we speak. I am thinking she must have ten children. Even my mother never look like that! She take me into the house and I am thinking, well now, I am going to meet all these screaming little monsters. But there you were, lying asleep in a bassinet. Two weeks! Just born! Little baby, and you are sleeping peaceful. I ask your mom 'where are the rest of the children?' and she tell me, 'This is it. You're looking at her.' And then she burst into tears.

"Your poor mommy. I am thinking now she must have been having postpartum. She sit me down on that ugly orange and yellow sofa, you remember? And she is supposed to be interviewing me, but instead, she is begging me to stay. 'When can you start, Anna? —How much can we pay you? —What days off?' Never even a look at my agency paper even though I held it out to her.

"Now, I should say I took the job because your poor mama needed me and because I fell in love with you. I did, but that came later.

"Your mom took me to the maid's quarters over the garage. The wallpaper was peeling and the carpets moldy, but in the bedroom, there is the window where when you lean to the side you see a bit of the ocean. Remember? The ocean, that's what did it for me. From that room, I saw the waves."

Anna finishes washing my chest, lays the cloth in the plastic bowl on my bed, stands, reties my hospital gown, and gently places my head back on the pillow. She pulls the covers up to my neck and tucks them at my sides. Removing her jacket, she folds it on the chair, unlaces her tennis shoes, and slides them under the bed. Then she climbs up and lies down with her head next to mine. Anna traces the line around my ventilator with one finger. Inhale. Exhale. We breathe together.

"From the first day, I see they are unhappy. The, what you call, tense-ness between them? Terrible. Your mother, when she drink, she say terrible things. Not just to your dad." She strokes my hair. I inhale the musky scent of her—never perfumed. The one part she hasn't changed.

"In my country, mothers leave their children to work in America to send money home, but I never know in my life a mother like yours who leaves for nothing. Selfish! At first, I am angry and hate her for you. But now I see it differently. I see that maybe she thinks you are better not with her." Anna stops stroking my hair, props herself up on one elbow, and looks at me with sharp eyes. "But now, you felt that I too abandoned you, yes Jackie? You think I stopped loving you? Never. Yes, I didn't give you all my attention anymore. That was very hard for you. And you were not nice to me and that was hard too. You think I changed? My clothes, my jewelry, friends? Where I grew up, I wanted only to survive. So maybe I became like a teenager. Maybe I wanted to be like a popular girl in school. I didn't do it perfect, that is true. But I loved you, Jackie. Not as a nanny. Not a love with a salary. No, you are my one and only child. But I am not your one and only mother."

A nurse peeks in the door, but Anna waves her away. Then she lies back down and brings her lips to my ear. "Jackie, my daughter, my sweet love," she whispers, "I've gone against your father's wishes and called your mother. She'll be here soon. Hang on."

INT. HOSPITAL ROOM
DAWN
DAY 49

I am trying my hardest to die before my mother arrives.

Nurse Dani enters, slowly pushing a metal cart. Various instruments of torture rattle as she approaches. No skip in her step now with Brett on location. I know just how that feels.

They've moved me back to my old room with its Pier One furniture and shopping center view to live out the rest of my days. There is nothing more to be done. "The die is cast," as they say. So many phrases about dying become relevant when one is actually at the end. For instance, seeing my mother is "A fate worse than death." I hope I "bite the dust" before she comes.

Dani wheels around the wicker settee and yanks open the blinds, flooding the room with light. A semi-circle of sun sits humpty-dumpty atop the roof-top parking of the Beverly Center.

She plugs the needle into a syringe and prepares to do battle with my exhausted veins. Twice a day they take my blood—pointless though it seems. Nurse Dani taps sharply on the inside of my junkie-bruised arm before finally pinching up something suitable for poking.

"Gotcha," she mutters, sticking me.

My blood flows slowly, thickly into first one then another of Dani's collection tubes. She caps them off, pulls the needle from my arm, and pastes a Band-Aid on the spot, heaving a resigned sigh like a young mother who wishes she had put off having children.

As she labels the vials and readies to leave, Emme comes through the door, edging her sizable body past the cart.

"Good morning," Emme says politely.

She wears a too-tight, yellow-embroidered cardigan over her uniform. I am embarrassed by the way I know Dani sees her. If only I could protect her from Dani's superior figure and condescending gaze.

"Oh hey, what's your name again?" Dani asks.

"Emme."

"Right, like Emmy Lou Harris. Do you know if Mr. Haney has returned yet? I, uh, have some reading materials he requested."

"Nope, I haven't heard."

Dani turns the cart and rattles toward the door. "Wonder if he knows the princess is back in the princess suite," she says.

"I wonder," Emme replies.

Emme shuts the door and lowers the blinds, turning my room a dusky violet. She takes Vaseline from the nightstand and swabs my chapped lips, concentrating on the corners of my mouth that stretch around the ventilator, then removes a tube of lotion from her pocket. I smell ginger and gardenia, the scent of Hawaii, of a lei once placed around my neck. It's the scent of regret; not a shard, but a big, fat slab of regret. I had planned one day to find Mirabelle, one day, when I was older, settled, perhaps when I had children of my own. Now, it was too late.

I'd thought I would have more time.

Emme places a chair by my bed, pulls up the bottom of my sheet, and massages the cool lotion into my calves. I want to drift off, but I'm overcome with guilt and remorse and the dark dread of my mother soon to arrive at the side of my adjustable deathbed.

Of course, she might not show. There's always that chance. Good ol' dependable Merilee.

Emme works down my legs, massaging the soles of my feet and in between my toes. Once they were ticklish, but now I feel nothing but awareness of her ministrations. *Coma-toes,* I think, and Emme nickers softly as if she's thought the same thing.

She re-tucks the sheets and moves up the bed, placing a hand under my pillow to steady my head while she gently massages my scalp line and temples. Emme's hands are soft like an animal's paws, claws retracted, drawn up inside puffy fur; the opposite of Anna's, her bony, strong fingers, and long, painted nails.

My muscles start to relax. Finally, I drift, floating, dozing as Emme continues kneading her soft paws into my neck, and shoulders, arms, hands...

As I sail to sleep, I barely hear the click of the door closing softly behind her.

Blast of light. Stench of perfume.

Lipstick and dark glasses, unreadable.

Unrecognizable.

But chic!

Gucci boots, Armani trench.

Cruella Deville from Beverly Hills.

Beware all you stim-puppies.

I'd like to grab her streaked mane, knock that head against the bed rails, and wrap my IV tubes around her neck.

The heart monitor beeps faster and faster. Holy Mother of Joe. If this doesn't wake me up nothing will. Talk about your coma-stim!

Pierre rushes in, bumping Nicole out of the way. "Step out now," he commands.

He moves to my side, glances at my blood pressure and checks my I.V.s to make sure they are flowing. As my heart monitor continues its rapid beeping, he lifts my limp wrist and takes my pulse, his eyes focused intently on the wall clock. With Nicole out of the room, my heart rate gradually drops back to normal, and after several more minutes, Pierre sighs, gently places my arm back on the bed, and makes a note on my chart.

"Weird," he mutters. Pierre opens the door to look for my visitor, but she's gone.

SLOW DISSOLVE TO:

INT. JACKIE AND BRETT'S HOUSE
DAY

I was upstairs making room in the new gym when I heard the intercom buzz.

"Arzelda, it's the dumbbells, let them in!" I shouted to our housekeeper. "And for Chris'sake, tell them to take off their shoes!"

I had ordered custom workout equipment from Switzerland as a birthday surprise for Brett. I didn't know what exactly made them special, but the complete package cost almost as much as the steam room I'd installed. In the last year, my "hobby" had become my passion. Our six-car garage overflowed with furniture and art. And with Penny still looking for my "break out role," decorating had become my raison d'etre. Unfortunately, I was running out of rooms, and with Brett on location in Arizona, I still had an abundance of time to fill.

He'd been offered the lead in *Double Barreled* when Richard Gere dropped out at the last moment.

"I can't create a character that quickly," Brett had protested when Penny called with the news.

"What do you need to know? He walks tall and carries a gun," Penny retorted.

"That's just it, it's a bunch of guys riding around, shooting people."

"It's six million."

"It's plot-driven. I want to do something more substantial than action films."

"Wake up, sweetie," Penny chortled. "That's where the longevity is for men."

"Too bad we can't swap careers," I said later that night while I rubbed his shoulders. I was sick of waiting around to be offered something "substantial." I was dying to do a nice, shallow action picture with weapons and cool costumes.

"Okay." He was lying on his stomach with his nose buried in the script. "But I'm going to find a way to make this character meaningful."

"How?" I moved my hands down his back.

"I don't know, maybe use a limp. Or a facial tic."

"Oh, yeah, the studio will love that." I laughed. "Their sexy leading man shows up as Ratso Rizzo." I massaged down his back until my hands slipped under his briefs.

"Hey, not now, I'm concentrating."

"Sorry." I tried to keep the rejection out of my voice and sat up. "So, when do we leave?"

"We?" Brett sat up. "No, Jackie, you can't come with me."

"But—"

"I need to focus, honey. And the schedule is going to be grueling. Most days we'll be out riding."

"I'll wait at the hotel."

"Honey, this is not Paris. It's Yuma. They're putting us up in a *motel*. There isn't even room service."

"I'll go sightseeing," I whined.

"There is nothing to see. You'll be bored out of your mind."

"I don't care." Tears filled my eyes. I hated being alone. I also drank way less when Brett was around. Left to my own devices, I might revert to old behaviors. Naturally, I couldn't tell him this. Brett made a religion out of self-control.

"I'll be home every weekend," he reassured me.

"I'll miss you," I fought back emotion.

"I'll miss you more," Brett said. "But I'll see you bright 'n early every Saturday morning." He kissed my forehead and went back to his script.

Another thing I loved about Brett; he was a man of his word. He didn't promise to be somewhere and then run off to Vegas with the boys. Most days, he was up at seven and asleep by midnight, and though that could get boring, I appreciated his stability.

The back doorbell was still ringing.

"Arzelda! Tell them to take the dumbbells out of the boxes before they bring them upstairs!"

Quickly, I cleared the space in the corner where the racks were to go. Making a gym for Brett was a purely selfish act. Brett loved to work out and I loved having him home. I'd done a ton of research. After all, I was in competition with every private gym in the city. If I gave Brett the best equipment, then he wouldn't go outside our home to do his pumping.

"Arzelda! What's taking so long?" I yelled.

Arzelda appeared at the door, slightly out of breath. "Sorry, missus. Is a lady, say she know you."

"A lady?"

She nodded.

"Who?" I asked impatiently. I was disappointed that the equipment hadn't arrived; Brett would be home in a few days, and I wanted everything ready.

Arzelda shook her head. "She not say."

"Shit. Okay, I'll be right down." I wiped my hands on a rag, pulled the scrunchy out of my hair, and shook out my ponytail. I hated surprises. Especially surprise visitors. I ran downstairs and came upon the last person in the world I expected to see.

"Oh my God." The blood rushed to my head.

"Hi Jax, I would have called but—"

"Nicole. I can't believe this." She had lost a lot of weight. Hair chopped short; dull and stringy. She had on an oversized sweater with frayed edges. A pair of dark glasses hid her eyes.

My heart raced. "Well, for Chris'sake, come in!"

She followed me into the living room, her sandals leaving dirt prints on the white carpeting. I motioned her to the couch,

"Yow." She glanced around. "Nice digs."

"Thanks," I said, waving off the room as if it were nothing special, as if my entire existence hadn't revolved around its creation. Nicole was here, *in my home*. I didn't want to scare her away with my success. I sat beside her and tried to keep my hands from shaking as I took a cigarette from the white lacquered box I kept on the coffee table.

"Want one?" I asked.

She shook her head and removed her sunglasses. Her eyes were red and puffy. I put down the unlit cigarette and took a deep breath. I could see she was fighting tears.

"Are you okay?"

She shook her head again and covered her face with her hands.

"Nicky?"

"Oh, Jackie!" She burst out crying.

"Let me just get you... Hang on." I ran to the powder room.

When I returned, she was hunched, wiping her nose with her sleeve. I handed her the tissues.

"I'm getting evicted," she cried. "I have no fucking money. I can't find a decent job. My life is falling apart. I'm sorry, I should go. This is humiliating." She started to rise but I put my hand on her shoulder.

"No, wait. How..." I wasn't sure what to say but I didn't want her to leave. "Just tell me what happened."

"I fucked everything up. Especially us." She turned her face into the pillows, her shoulders heaving. I had never seen Nicole vulnerable. Never. Even as a kid when she was upset or hurt, she would get tough or turn mean or take revenge. Whatever resentments I might have held gave way then, like in that fairy tale where the ice chip lodged inside the queen's heart melts. I was awash in love for Nicole and longing for our friendship.

"Nic. Nicky, come here." I pulled her into my arms. "I've missed you so much." Now, I too was crying.

"I've missed you too," she sobbed. "Oh God, I've gotten mascara on your pillow, I'll pay to have them cleaned."

"Stop it," I commanded. "It doesn't matter."

If it were anyone else, I'd have yanked that three-hundred-dollar white silk pillow out from under their heads. But this was my oldest, dearest best friend.

"Nicky you were right about Peter, about everything," I cried.

"No, I was awful, I was such a bitch," Nicole sobbed.

"We were both pretty awful," I conceded.

"I'll never be that way again."

"Me, neither."

We held each other tightly. Two girls in candy necklaces joined for life by a rusted Carter for President pin. The timing could not have been better. Now, I had someone with whom I could share confidences, not to mention movies, coffee, bikini waxes!

I unknotted the strands of Nicole's matted hair with my fingers, wiped the tears from her wet brown eyes, and smoothed the furrow between her brows. They needed waxing. I would make her an appointment.

It felt good to talk!

We stayed in our pajamas, eating, drinking, smoking, catching up on each other's lives. It was no wonder I couldn't find her; she'd been living in Atlanta of all places with Steffi's sister and had gotten involved with a musician who had neglected to inform her he had a wife and kids in another state until they all showed up at his house one morning.

"Oh, honey, that's awful."

"I think my picker is broken, Jackie. I mean, I'm a magnet for these guys."

"So, where's your mom?"

"Steffi's living on a boat in Florida with some old guy she met last summer. And Merilee? Have you seen her at all?"

"Merilee who?" I snorted.

288 · DINAH MANOFF

I filled Nicole in on Daddy's endeavors at the studio and Anna's social life. Then I backtracked to Peter and my being fired from *Circle*.

"Wow, I had no idea."

"Well, you must have read about it."

"Well, yeah, of course. But, I mean, after all you did for them. What they put you through!"

Here was the sympathy I'd longed for, the understanding and appreciation. I wanted to throw my arms around her and never let go.

Saturday morning, Brett's limo pulled into the driveway. He'd called on the way to say he wasn't feeling well. I ran up to greet him with a glass of fresh orange juice and a smile that for once held no punishment for his having been away.

He waved me off and staggered past me into the house. "I'm freezing," he croaked, getting into bed. "Do I have a fever?"

I felt his forehead. "You're a little warm," I said cheerfully, tucking him in.

"I feel like I'm going to die." He pulled the comforter up around his neck and shivered.

"I'll make you some soup," I said, starting for the door.

"Ohhhh," he whimpered. "Wait, Jackie. Can you hand me my script?" Brett waved one arm above the bedsheets. "I can't reach it."

Normally this would have annoyed me. Today, Brett's groaning rolled right off my ducky back.

I smiled. "Anything else?"

"No, thank you." He nestled further under the covers. "You're sure in a good mood."

"Yep." I went downstairs, opened a can of Campbell's, and plopped the contents in a pot. While I waited for the soup to boil, I picked up the phone and dialed Nicole at the Belair Hotel where despite her protestations I was paying her expenses.

"Hello?"

"Hey, it's me," I whispered.

"Hi! How's the Cowboy?"

"He's really sick. I haven't brought anything up yet."

"Jackie, are you sure about this?"

"Absolutely. I'll call you later, maybe we can meet for drinks."

Back upstairs, Brett sat up looking over his script. Around his shoulders was an old pink and white afghan his Meemaw had crocheted. I could swear as soon as he saw me, he purposely started shivering.

I placed the bed tray over his knees and sat beside him. "It's hot, be careful."

"You know what I miss?" Brett crumbled some Saltines into his soup.

"Me?" I asked, snuggling up to him.

He flashed a look of annoyance. "Well, of course, but..." He raised himself and brought the tray closer. "I was going to say oyster crackers. Do they make those anymore?"

"I don't know. I guess."

"Whoa, this *is* hot." He darted his tongue, poodle-like, at the steaming soup. Then began lapping it up.

I laughed.

"What?" he asked.

"Nothing."

Whenever Brett did something gross or disgusting it was a relief, a respite from my relentless attraction. I took a deep breath. "Um, Brett?" A piece of carrot clung to his chin. I handed him a napkin and motioned for him to wipe it away.

"Hmmm?"

"Guess who dropped by."

"Do you think Dr. Koblin would make a house call?" Brett sniffled. "They've got that insurance doctor on the picture, but the guy's a quack."

"Honey, listen, Nicole was here."

"Who?"

"Nicole. The girl who used to be my best friend. She um…stayed with me this last week."

That got his attention. "She stayed here? You never mentioned anything."

"Well, because you had so much going on and I didn't want to burden you. She had no place else to go."

"Is she in some kind of trouble?"

"No. Well, not like with the law or anything. She's just, y'know, having a hard time. I want her to stay with us for a while until she gets back on her feet."

"Geez, Jackie." Brett shook his head slowly back and forth, like a heavy church bell.

"Honey, listen, the house is so big we can't possibly get in each other's way. You'll never even know she's here. Please, Brett. She needs me."

He tilted the bowl into his mouth and slurped down the rest of the soup. "How long would she stay?"

"Not that long. Probably a few weeks, maybe? You're on location for another month anyway, and you know how lonely I get."

Brett handed me his empty bowl, curled up in the afghan, and nestled his head on my lap. I stroked his hair and fought against the stirrings in my pelvic region.

"Think you could order us some?" he mumbled into my crotch.

"Hmm? What are you talking about?"

"Oyster crackers."

"Please, Brett, this is important."

He sat up with a groan and leaned back against the pillows. "Okay but, what about privacy?" He coughed several times then hacked into a tissue. "What if she hears or sees something and sells it to the tabloids?"

"Oh my God, Brett, how could you think…" I forced myself to remain calm. It was important that this didn't turn into a fight.

"Look, I realize that she is a stranger to you, but Nicole would never. She's like a sister to me."

"You're sure you can trust her?"

"I would stake my life on it."

Brett put the back of his hand to his forehead for a moment, then shook his wrist as if he were shaking down a thermometer. "Can you bring me some Tylenol?"

I stalked off to the bathroom, returning with Tylenol, cough syrup, a handful of other medications, and a glass of water.

"Anything else?" I tried to sound patient, but Brett's baby act was wearing thin.

He swallowed the pills, took both my hands in his, and kissed them. "Thank you for being the world's best girlfriend," he said.

"You're welcome, but—"

"Look, Jackie, if you think it's okay, then it's okay."

"Really?"

"Yes. Just keep her out of my new gym."

"Hey! How did you know?" I slapped his butt playfully.

"They put a hold on my credit card after you charged twenty thousand dollars for exercise equipment. I knew it wasn't for you."

The reappearance of my best friend was a gift from above. Just as I was running out of rooms to decorate, here was Nicole, all run down and ready for renovation.

Penny's receptionist gave me a form for a job résumé.

"I'm pathetic," Nicole said. "I'm twenty-eight years old and I have no skills."

We sat by the pool in our pajamas having breakfast. Brett had flown back to Arizona and Nicole was all moved into our downstairs guest room.

"You're not pathetic," I chided, stirring my Bloody Mary with an oversized stalk of celery. "You sure you don't want a drink?"

"It's a little early, Jax, even by my standards."

"Make stuff up. Everyone lies on their résumé. Mine says I can horseback ride and speak Spanish. We could say that you've been my assistant. That's not entirely untrue, you know."

"Yeah, then someone's going to want me to use a computer."

"Well, maybe you *should* go back to school."

Nicole groaned.

"What about journalism? Remember when you worked on the school paper?"

Nicole took the résumé from my hands and crumpled it up. Her mood grew heavy.

I quickly changed the subject. "Hey, remember I told you about that guy Pallucci I used to date?"

"Yeah."

"He had a Pilates machine in the *bedroom*." I raised my eyebrows.

"You're kidding."

"Seriously. It was the only time in my life I worked out."

Nicole managed a laugh. "They should put *that* on an infomercial."

"Too bad Brett…" I caught myself. "Hey, I'm gonna make another drink." I rose from the chair and slipped on my flip-flops. "Last one, I swear," I said, crossing my heart.

Nicole followed me into the kitchen. "What?"

"Huh?" I took a fresh can of tomato juice from the fridge, poured the juice into my glass, and added a generous amount of vodka.

"You were about to say something."

"Um…" I skirted dangerous territory. "I was going to say that I ought to get one for our gym, but…" I was out at sea with no way back to shore. The alcohol had loosened me up and with all the intimate conversation Nicole and I had lately, I was like a shaken soda can about to explode. "Brett's not the adventurous type."

"Meaning?"

"He's kind of old-fashioned."

"You mean lousy in bed?"

"Nicole! No. Not at all. He just likes things that are…normal, you know, just nothing fancy or—"

"Kinky."

"Right."

"But you do have sex?"

"Of course," I said defensively, "but…"

"But?" Nicole raised her eyebrows.

"Well, it's not as—"

"Creative?"

"Or as often as it could be." I let out a huge sigh as a thousand pounds dropped off my shoulders from the confession to Nicole.

Nicole rinsed out her bowl and put it in the dishwasher. She laughed and shook her head.

"What?"

"Nothing," she said. "It's just that, you know, by looking at him you would think—"

"I know," I said. "Nicole?"

"What?"

"Please, whatever you do, do not repeat this conversation. Seriously, Nic. If that got out it would kill him. Even if it were just a rumor—"

"Jackie, stop it. Who would I tell? You're the only friend I have."

I began to tremble.

"Jax, are you okay?"

I shook my head and wobbled over to the kitchen stool, sat down hard, and burst into tears.

"Sorry," I cried, "I'm really fine."

Nicole pulled me into her arms.

"I'm okay," I said sobbing into her armpits. I cried so hard I felt like my guts would come loose. I'd only wailed like this twice before in my lifetime—the break-up with Peter and the afternoon my mother left. But now I cried because Nicole was my only friend too—the only person who really knew me. From the day we met by the shore huddled under that beach towel, we had always only had each other.

Finally, my tears subsided, and Nicole gently released me. She wet a paper towel under the faucet and wiped under my eyes.

"Thanks," I sniffled.

"Jackie, I had no idea you were unhappy."

"No, Nic, that's not it—" I started to protest, but Nicole looked at me with such love and sympathy. The darkness was out of her eyes. My breakdown had brought her out of her misery.

"Feeling better?" she asked.

I shrugged.

"Me too," she said.

INT. JACKIE AND BRETT'S KITCHEN
MORNING

"Pardon me for askin', but isn't it about time she found her own place?" Brett muttered. He'd strapped on a pair of yellow rubber gloves and was doing the dishes. He was a far better housekeeper than I could ever be. Arzelda always chortled how neatly he made the bed. The guy was a nut for hospital corners; he folded the sheets around the edges like crafting origami.

"Good lord, it's been a month, darlin', and she just lies around all day."

"Shhh!" I whispered, clearing the empty gallon of milk from the table. "You want her to hear you?"

"When is she going to get a job?"

"She'll find something soon," I whispered.

I wasn't backing down. Having Nicole stay with us was the only thing (other than sex) I had ever asked for. But Brett had been back now for several weeks, and the tension was mounting.

"It's like living with a teenager," Brett mumbled.

"I'm going to pay for her to go to therapy."

"What?" Brett exclaimed loudly. A dish slipped out from his soapy hands and landed back in the sink.

"Shhh!"

"And I'm GODDAMN SICK OF WHISPERING IN MY OWN HOUSE!" Brett stripped off the gloves and threw them on the counter. He stopped as if surprised by the sound of his own raised voice, then, he stomped out of the room and up the stairs throwing a last punishing look my way.

I knew he expected me to run after him. Instead, I shoved the milk in the trash and slammed the lid.

For the first time in our relationship, the shoe was on the other foot. With my best friend around, I was no longer trailing him around the house, and he was jealous. A trait seemingly as new to Brett as to me.

"What's all the yelling about?" Nicole asked sleepily.

I hadn't heard her come in. She wore one of my nightgowns, so short on her tall frame that the hem came to her knees and the elastic cuffs hung below her elbows. Socks scrunched down around her ankles like a lost child, and my heart broke for her all over again.

I smiled at her. "It's nothing, honey." The last thing I wanted was for Nicole to think we were arguing about her. "Don't worry about it. Brett's just in a mood."

"Are you okay?"

"Couldn't be better. Want some coffee?"

"Maybe later. I'm going to go back to bed." She started back down the hall, her floppy socks mopping the floor as she walked.

"I can't ask her to leave now," I insisted, a month later. Brett and I were having another one of our squabbles. Frankly, I found our fights refreshing; something to talk about other than Brett's latest film project. Feigning interest while my boyfriend went over each facet of his character was like trying to enjoy someone else's high school reunion. Anyway, Nicole was *my* project, and I was determined to do my best work.

And she did seem to be getting better. Maybe it was the spring weather or because she'd been seeing Dr. Wexler twice a week, but she *had* begun rising earlier and spending less time alone in her room. It was I who was changing the most. No longer obsessed with Brett's whereabouts, I begged off accompanying him to premieres or parties, preferring to stay home with Nicole.

"Take your publicist," I would suggest to Brett when the invitations came.

"I can't take a guy to a premiere, Jackie."

"Take Penny or one of the assistants. They would die to go with you."

Spring lapsed into summer. Brett started *Patches and Pistols,* another Western which took him on location to Texas, conveniently pushing the issue of Nicole's living arrangements to the back burner.

The shoot was difficult. Six days a week, Brett filmed most of his scenes on horseback out where I presumed the deer and the antelope played. We spoke by phone every few days.

"Sorry I didn't call last night, babe," Brett said. "I've been busier than a blind man at a strip show."

"You've been *what?*"

He'd fallen back into the jargon of his Texan childhood. Or maybe it was the character he was working on.

"Today was hotter than a goat's butt in a patch of peppers." Brett let out a few grunts.

"What are you doing?"

"Pulling off my boots, they're tighter than a—"

"So, hey," I interrupted. "When are you finishing this turkey?"

The shoot had been extended twice due to dust storms.

"Looks like another week at least. Hey! Why don't you stay for a week with my mom in Dime Box? The two of you can get to know each other better and my sisters'll bring their kids around. You'll have company."

The (no star) Giddings Hotel where Brett was staying happened to be only fifteen bumpy miles from Dime Box (pop. 1024) where he'd been raised.

"No thanks, I have company."

"Heavens to Betsy, is she still there? You said—"

"Just a while longer. Hey, have I bugged you once about being away?"

The phone beeped signaling a call waiting.

"Can you hold on?"

"Go ahead and take the call. Mom and Sissy are bringin' vittles. Love you, puddin'."

"Love you too." I pressed the button. "Hello?"

"You are going back to work, my friend."

"Penny?"

"I found the script, Jackie. It starts shooting on October sixth."

"October?" I started sweating. That was six weeks away. I would have to lose fifteen pounds. Stop drinking. Get in shape. "Uh, great. What's it about?" I tried to sound enthusiastic.

"Courtroom drama. Robert Verona is starring. You play a woman on trial for a murder she committed in self-defense. It's a supporting role but we can showcase your talent. No nude scenes, no special effects. I have a firm offer. They're sending over the script. Call me as soon as you've read it."

I hung up the phone and turned to Nicole, who was drinking coffee at the kitchen counter and writing in the journal her therapist had told her to keep.

"I got a job."

"Uh-huh."

"Nicky! Did you hear me?" I asked loudly.

"Yes! That's great, Jax," she said, matching my tone. She put down her pen and faced me. "Dr. Baxter thinks I should try this Prozac stuff everyone is raving about."

"I hear you can't have orgasms on it," I said, annoyed.

"I could care less about sex."

"You and Brett would make a great match. Anyway, they're sending the script over. I don't have to do it."

Nicole snorted, "Don't be ridiculous."

"What? It's not even a starring role."

Nicole stared at me. I stared back. For the first time since she'd returned, I felt the old tension. Then she shook her head and chuckled. "I love you, Jackie, but you are such an idiot sometimes."

INT. JACKIE AND BRETT'S HOUSE
DAY
1997

Jackie Gold Picked for Plum Spot in First Degree read the headline in the *Hollywood Reporter*. *Jackie Gold Tapped for Upcoming Verona Pic* ran on the front page of *Variety*.

Swanky Magazine wanted me for a photo spread to be shot by Jean-Marc Ricard, the famous French photographer. He'd photographed everyone from Jackie O to Meryl Streep. It was a great honor to be counted among his subjects.

With my publicist on maternity leave, the agency was sending her assistant. I vaguely remembered Edward, a harmless sycophant; balding, with a pudgy body and a shiny waxed face. He rushed into my house late, just as Jean-Marc, his translator Evette, and several other of the *Swanky* crew finished setting up in my living room.

"Edward, is that you behind those Foster Grants?" I joked. He wore wraparound shades and a silk Hawaiian shirt that hung considerably shorter in front of his egg-shaped frame. I took his hands in greeting. They felt like empty socks. We air-kissed.

"I'm ever so sorry. I got waylaid at Faaarrah's," Edward sighed. His breath smelled rancid like fruity wine. "I'm stressing! Pleeease tell me there are no problems?" He surveyed the room. Camera equipment was splayed over tarp-covered rugs. A red vinyl backdrop had been erected in one corner.

"Um, well," I pulled Edward to the side and lowered my voice. "Jean-Marc is set on my wearing this teensy silver lamé number, and I think it's wrong for the image I'm projecting."

"Why don't you slip it on and let us have a look."

"I'd rather not."

"Sweetums, no one is going to make you do anything you don't want to do. But you don't want them to think you're difficult, do you?"

He had struck at my professional jugular. "No, of course not."

"Have you a bar in this palace?"

I pointed to the corner of the living room.

"Love the white on white, by the way. Very Old Hollywood. Oh hello, *bonjour,* everyone!" Edward mingled his way to the bar while I ducked behind the shoji screen the stylist had placed by the piano. I stepped into the skimpy silver dress, aided by Gwen, a young, prodigiously competent wardrobe assistant.

"Aggh, it's too tight," I complained, as she struggled with the zipper. I'd been juice fasting for three days with no visible results except an increasingly bad temper.

"We have a girdle," Gwen said, dumping a steaming heap of Miracle Grow on my already massive insecurities.

"A-a girdle?" I sputtered. "I don't *need* a fucking girdle."

Through the shoji panels, the shadows of Jean-Marc and Edward parried back and forth in intense conversation. If only Brett was here to charm everyone. He'd left that morning for Burbank Studios to do voice-overs for *Patches and Pistols*. "Sugar catches more flies than vinegar," Brett always said. In my hands, the situation was fermenting.

Gwen gave another pull at the zipper.

"Ow! You're pinching me," I snapped.

"Soreee." Gwen flinched, her cheeks flushing.

I sucked in my stomach, held my breath, and squirmed, wriggling back and forth as Gwen tugged the zipper over my hips. At last, she yanked the bottom of the micro-mini down until it rested at the top of my thighs.

"There!" Gwen exclaimed, victorious. She placed a pair of five-inch silver stilettos by my feet. I stepped into them and turned to the mirror. I resembled a magician's assistant.

Jean-Marc, Edward, and the *Swanky* team swiveled as I hobbled out into the living room.

"Do a twirl," Edward said with a slurp on his scotch. He motioned a circle with his index finger.

I twirled. "Ghastly, right? No offense, Jean-Marc."

"And no offense to you, dear one," Edward said, "but I think you look *deee*-vine."

"C'est bon," said Evette, the translator.

"*Voila!*" Jean-Marc said, clapping his hands.

The makeup and hair team descended on me, powdering, combing, pinning.

"Whoa, whoa, hold it, everybody, please, let's all just stop!" Who the fuck was Edward to go against my opinion? I had to convince Jean-Marc and the *Swanky* people to see things my way without offending anyone.

"Everyone, please, let's sit down for a moment," I said in my chummiest voice. I herded them onto the couches and chairs. "Everyone comfy? Can I get anyone a drink?"

Jean-Marc perched his long body on the sofa arm wearing a phony patient smile under his thin mustache as if watching a three-year-old about to recite a poem. He pointed to his watch.

"We are running out of time," Evette interpreted.

"Yes, I understand," I snapped, then checked myself. "Okay everyone, first let me say thank you, Jean-Marc, for your indulgence."

As I spoke, Evette translated my words, expressionless. Jean-Marc rolled his eyes.

"Here's the thing. Um, in this film, I am trying to show that I am a…" (the words "serious actress" rose in my mouth, but I couldn't say them) "a human being, not a-a stupid sex toy."

"Une jouet de sex stupide!" Evette translated.

Titters erupted from the crew.

"Not a sex toy, that came out wrong." I turned to Evette helplessly.

She spoke several words to Jean-Marc.

"Vous pense que cette robe, elle est stupid?" Jean-Marc peered at me over his rimless glasses.

Evette translated. "You think our dress, she is stupid?"

"No, I think I look stupid in her…it," I retorted.

Jean-Marc let loose a long sentence with his hands fluttering in all directions.

"What? What's he saying?" I asked.

Evette cleared her throat. "He is telling you this is a photograph, Mademoiselle Gold. It is a work of art unto itself."

"Oui!" Jean-Marc agreed.

"Oui, oui, oui," the *Swanky* group agreed, nodding their heads.

"Okay, friends, *mes amis*," Edward interrupted. He rose and swaggered to the bar, boozy. "We are all on the same side. Am I correct, Jackie?"

I nodded vigorously despite how I felt about being on any team with Edward.

"Jean-Marc," he said, refilling his glass. "Don't you have another teensy *petite* dress?" Edward showed *petite* with his thumb and forefinger.

"No, *non, non*." With each "*non*," Jean-Marc slapped his thigh with an open palm like a stern governess.

I took a deep breath, as deep as I could without splitting seams. As soon as this was over, I would kill Edward.

"Okay, I have a solution." I forced a calm tone to my voice. "Could someone unzip me? I'll go to my room and pull out a hundred other choices for you to look at."

Jean-Marc spoke, and Evette translated. "But then it won't be the *Swanky* concept."

I turned to Edward, now reclining on the divan, his Hawaiian shirt flapped open exposing a swath of pale pink skin, the color of a hamster's belly. "Look, Edward, I'm out of options here."

"Dear, I'm on your side, but honestly," his words were cottony and slurred, "I think the dress is fucking cute."

"I'm not wearing the dress, Edward," I retorted, yanking at the stuck zipper. "Aggh!"

I heard the sound of the front door closing. Brett was home. Good. He'd handle this.

"Honey?" I called out. "Can you join us *please*?"

Edward got up ungracefully and put a hand on my shoulder for balance. He bent into my ear. "You're being difficult sweetums."

Nicole entered. She wore dark glasses and her lips had that swollen, post-therapy look they got when she'd been crying.

"Oh hi," I said, disappointed. "I thought you were Brett."

"Sorry to interrupt." She started back down the hall.

"No, no, wait!" I pulled her back into the room. "What do you think of this dress? Be honest."

She took a few steps back, pushed her glasses up for an instant, then lowered them.

"Dreadful."

I spun to face the group. "See?"

"*Allez!*" Jean-Marc announced.

"We are packing up!" Evette commanded, leading the group out the door.

"Fine," I shot back. I was done being friendly. I'd had enough of Jean-Marc and his snotty attitude.

"Nice job, Jackie," Edward spat. "Do you know how hard it was to get you that shoot?"

"Fuck off, Edward," I yelled as he headed out the door.

Nicole turned to me. "What the hell's going on?"

"Not a thing," I said sarcastically, "except I blew the shoot and I'm fat and no one will ever hire me again." I opened my arms. "Look." The dress had split all the way down the side.

"Oh, Jax."

"What? You're not going to start in on me, are you?"

Nicole grabbed my hand and pulled me outside.

"What? What are you doing?"

In the driveway, Jean-Marc and his crew had finished loading and were getting into their van.

"Hey, arrêtez! Wait!" Nicole called out. "Attendez s'il vous plait!"

Jean-Marc leaned out the passenger window and regarded us coldly. "Oui?"

Nicole took a deep breath. "Jackie a dit…a dit qu'elle est très *très*…sorry…um…désolée pour tout qui a passé."

"When the hell did you learn French?" I whispered.

"High school, duh," she whispered back.

Jean-Marc pursed his lips. "Non je ne sais pas…"

"What is he saying? I'm not wearing that dress!" I hissed to Nicole.

"Cool your jets and smile." Nicole turned back to Jean-Marc. "Ce n'était pas sa faute c'était la faute d' Edward."

That part I understood. "Oui!" I nodded. "It's Edward's fault!"

Jean-Marc blew air out through pursed lips. "Elle est une prima donna."

Nicole leaned closer. "Oui c'est vrai." They both looked at me shaking their heads.

"Mais elle aime votre art beaucoup et elle vous respecte."

"Nicole?" I asked. "What did you say?"

"I said you are a huge fan of his work."

"Oui! Oui!" I smiled and nodded.

Jean-Marc shrugged his shoulders and raised an eyebrow.

"Dinner for you and your friends at Spago?" Nicole asked.

Jean-Marc's eyes lit up. "Spago? Wolfgang Puck?"

"Oui, Compliments de Jackie. Tomorrow I'll call *Swanky* and we set up another shoot. Avec d'autres vêtements." Nicole pointed to the ripped dress.

Jean-Marc laughed, then reached through the window, took Nicole's hand, and kissed it. "Vous êtes une bonne amie."

"Yes, I am" Nicole agreed.

"*Au revoir.*" I waved as he drove away. I turned to Nicole, "What's French for 'you're hired?'"

CLOSE UP: JACKIE'S HAND HOLDING A LETTER

Dear Jacqueline,

I hope you get this letter. I know it's been a long time since we talked, and I just wanted to say a few things. Sorry I didn't see your last movie, the space one that everyone is talking about. I saw you in People magazine and I thought you were real cute. Almost as cute as your boyfriend (ha-ha).

Here is what I need to say, and I hope you don't mind. I wonder if you could spare some money. I wouldn't be asking if I wasn't desperate. I don't know whether you know this or not, but your father's checks to me finished last spring as per our agreement, and Elliot hasn't paid support since Mirabelle moved in with him. You are the only person I can turn to. I am trying to get a job, but jobs are scarce and even the waitress jobs are hard to come by or they go to younger girls. Oh, and by the way, I'm not with Bea anymore. Also, I don't sell you know what anymore. Now you're caught up.

Please write back soon about the money. I hope you are not too mad at me for asking. I hope I never have to ask you again.

Love,
Your Mom

P.S. Mirabelle still wears your leather jacket whenever it gets cold enough. It fits her now.

INT. MEDICAL OFFICE
BEVERLY HILLS
DAY

Dr. Koblin examined the welts on my chest and arms. The hives ran along the sides of my face and into my scalp. I started *First Degree* in a week, and there was no way I could shoot in this condition.

"What should I take?" I asked, panicked.

"Have you tried Calamine lotion?"

"I don't think that's gonna help here, Doc," I said a bit patronizingly. I stifled an impulse to tousle his gray hair. "I need something a bit stronger, y'know. For stress."

"Hmmm. Anything unusual happen recently that you can recall?"

"Well, as I said, I'm starting a picture."

"Anything else?"

"Not really."

"Not really?"

"I mean, no."

I hadn't told anyone about the letter, not even Nicole. I was ashamed. Ashamed that I had a mother who was such a mess, ashamed that it bothered me. Most of all I was ashamed because I was filthy, dirty rich, and I had no intention of sending her a penny. Let her suffer. She left me when I was eight years old, why should I take responsibility for her now? Let her find another lover to pay her rent. *I am not her daughter anymore. I am a motherless child. It's right to deny her. Karmic justice*, some would say. Mirabelle living with her father was not a surprise. Good news, though it pricked my guilt about not contacting her.

"I see." He took out his prescription pad and scribbled furiously. I must be getting an arsenal. I smiled to myself. Well, great. I could use a little time off before filming got underway, a nice period of bedrest enhanced by tranquilizers sounded lovely to me. I would emerge refreshed. He finished writing and handed me the paper.

The smile dropped off my face. "What the hell is this?"

"It's the name of a psychiatrist. He's excellent. Happens to be my brother-in-law."

A shrink? No way. Therapy might be working for Nicole, but I didn't have time to go into my whole life with some stranger. Maybe one day but…

"Not now," I told Dr. Koblin.

"Fine," he said. "Bathe in Aveeno. The hives eventually go away on their own." He headed for the door.

"Don't I get a prescription or something?" I raised my voice a trifle hysterically. He kept walking.

DISSOLVE TO:

INT: HOSPITAL ROOM
DAY 50

She's back.

Nicole closes the door and steps toward me, casting her shadow, blocking the sunlight, robbing me of my vitamin D. She wears a gray Armani suit and an apricot silk blouse tightly tucked into a pencil skirt. "Dressed to Kill" as they say. I can't help but admire the presentation. Once I would have picked it out and bought it for her. Now I'd like to throw her out on her Jimmy Choo's. I bet she was a hit with the paparazzi, swooping through the hospital doors, veiled behind her Gucci sunglasses, here for the Grand Goodbye.

I'm just *dying* to hear her apology.

She clears her throat. "I was thinking about our weekends at the Beverly Hills Hotel."

But first, ladies and gentlemen, one last trip down memory lane.

"Remember that time you got so drunk I put you in the shower and forgot to turn the water off and everything flooded, and we told your Dad and Anna the maids did it?"

Cue the shared laughter. Weren't we just too much?

"Remember when you called me from that payphone in Hawaii and told me about your sister? I told you she didn't count because your mom had just fucked some guy and she wasn't part of your life like I was."

Clever! Trying to soften me up by flashing the old blood sister card. Sorry, not valid. Long expired.

She takes a Kleenex from her Chanel tote, dabs her eyes then walks to the window. There is a run in her stocking behind the knee. For some reason, this cheers me.

She waves at the fans and their murmurs rise to a chant.

"Jackie, Jackie!"

Nicole slips off her jacket and tosses it onto the wicker chair. Dark circles the color of rotten peaches ring her armpits. She sits on my bed, digs under the sheets, snags my hand and clutches it in her sweaty palm.

"Jackie, sweetheart, your boyfriend was killing your career, you had no films coming out, all you had was this one golden opportunity. I was just doing my job. Keeping your name in the papers." Her eyes fill, as she fiddles with my fingers, bending and straightening each one. "So when you told me Brett was about to propose, I called the press. But Jackie, honey, I did it for you!" She exclaims. "I mean, why else would you have told me? And when I showed up and you were both dressed like for a photoshoot, I assumed yes, that's what you were thinking too. I mean even when you jumped it was so staged looking."

She regards me intensely, runs her index finger around my face, tracing my features as if preserving my memory.

"The press are calling it suicide, but I know it's not true. You'd never ever kill yourself, not in a million years, but…"

But it lets them off the hook. And you.

Her eyes narrow and she sits up straighter. "Anyway, it wasn't my fault! It wasn't! I had it all planned out. I thought nothing could go wrong, but it did. It did. It went horribly, horribly wrong. Oh God, Jackie, forgive me. Forgive me, Jackie. Please, please, forgive me."

She throws herself, sobbing, over my body. Her hands run themselves up and down my arms. "You know I would never hurt you. Not ever. I love you! More than anyone in my life, I love you."

She loves me. I let her words sink in. She did it for me. She was doing her job. It wasn't her fault.

Her tears fall, congealed with mascara. They plop like bird shit onto my face and chest. She smells of sweat, rancid with fear with the underlying scent of the Jean Nate deodorant she's worn since she was a teenager. How I loved her then.

She kisses my forehead, nervous kisses, thin and tense. There is an eggy breakfast on her breath.

"Forgive me," she weeps.

Forgive her.

"God, Jax, you were beautiful." She encircles my slack body and rocks me from side to side. After a few minutes, she lets go, sighs, and lays her cheek on my pillow like a spent lover.

"Excuse me, time's up now." Emme peeks her head in, her sweet voice a dulcimer, a dove. She shuts the door, but her shadow remains in the porthole. The promise of comfort and a warm blanket. It can't come soon enough.

Nicole pushes herself off my bed, takes several deep breaths and shakes out her hands, flicking her fingers as if casting off bad energy. I still feel the weight of her while she appears lighter, unburdened.

Fishing a ribbon of mashed tissues from her bag, she wipes around her eyes and nose, takes out lipstick and mirror, and re-applies her makeup. She walks to the window. "Your fans are out there, Jackie, at least two hundred. Press, too. Not just the paparazzi. I made sure of that." She says as if proving her worth even now.

I think back to that day she arrived at my door, tattered and homeless, lost and alone. But I was far more lost and lonely. Her misfortune was my manna from heaven. *My* golden opportunity so I wouldn't be alone. I moved her in. I made her over. I sent her to therapy and made her my publicist. Not only for her, but for me. So she would always need me.

It wasn't the monster what done the crime, it was Doctor Frankenstein.

Emme enters quietly and lightly taps Nicole's shoulder. "It's time."

Nicole nods somberly, tucks in her blouse, retrieves her jacket then bends down and whispers in my ear. "Goodbye, Jackie. I love you forever."

Till death do us part.

Can I forgive her?

Can I forgive me?

Emme closes the door. In her arms are a pile of fresh linens and a gown still warm from the dryer. Clucking her tongue, my angel takes the plastic basin from my bed table, fills it with water, and goes about the task of disinfecting me, removing all traces of Nicole's lipstick and black tears.

SLOW DISSOLVE TO:

INT. SPAGO RESTAURANT
LUNCHTIME

Penny got a tip. *Star* magazine was breaking a big story with "never before seen photographs" of me. Nicole had managed to procure an edition one day before it hit the stands. The three of us scheduled an emergency lunch at Spago.

I'd been shooting nights on *First Degree* and with little sleep, I was fragile and exhausted. The atmosphere on the set had been tense and the studio's business affairs department called an emergency meeting with the producers, fueling rumors that we were already over budget. I'd yet to shoot my big courtroom scene with Verona.

The lunchtime crowd hadn't arrived yet. As Penny, Nicole, and I waited for our smoked salmon pizza, we huddled over the copy of the *Star*.

I squinted at a photo in the top corner of the front page. "Hey look. Nicky, isn't that Andy Webb from high school? I heard he's starring on a new cop show."

"Probably not for long," she smirked.

"What do you mean?"

Nicole took the paper and opened it up to a fuzzy full-page photo of Andy and another man locked in a romantic embrace.

"Holy shit," I exhaled.

"Quite the career killer." She chuckled. "Wonder who tipped them off?"

"Jesus." I eyed her suspiciously.

She turned the page. "Here's the spread on you."

There were several photos from *Circle* and one picture of me as a baby in my mother's arms with Anna standing off to the side. An arrow pointed to her with a caption that read, "The new Mrs. Goldstein."

"Tacky," I said, "but no big deal."

Penny turned the page. "Uh-oh."

We hadn't seen the worst of it. Standing in front of a banana tree looking bloated and haggard was Merilee. She had on my old leather jacket over a purple-flowered muumuu. In quotes over her head were the words "I'M BROKE!"

"Oh dear," Penny sighed.

On the opposite page were photos of me at sixteen with Merilee, Bea, and Mirabelle—pictures from my trip to Hawaii captioned, *JACKIE'S SECRET FAMILY.*

My mother had sold me out.

I caught myself as the table spun from under me.

"Are you okay?" Penny asked as Nicole put an arm around me.

I shook my head, signaling our waiter as a group of well-dressed ladies carrying shopping bags settled in at the table next to us. "It's Jackie Gold!" one of them whispered.

"May I bring you something else?" the waiter offered.

"Stoli rocks," I managed to rasp.

Penny and Nicole exchanged glances. "Jackie, it's early, honey," Penny chided gently.

"They'll stick with their Diet Cokes," I said to the waiter, ignoring their looks. "Boy, what a stinky steaming turd!" I said, holding up the pictures. "You gotta figure she got at least fifteen grand. Too bad I hadn't been topless, right? A picture of my teenaged boobs? Wow. That could have bought her a house!"

"Jackie, shhh. Take it easy." Nicole moved her chair closer to mine and put her arm around my shoulder.

"She even used Mirabelle!"

"Who is Mirabelle?" Penny whispered.

"Jackie's half-sister," Nicole whispered back.

I didn't need to turn around to know the women next to us were hanging on my every word. The waiter returned with my drink. I held onto his sleeve while I downed it, then handed back the empty glass and told him to bring me another. I could feel

314 · DINAH MANOFF

myself starting to lose it. I hid my face and prayed those ladies weren't packing cameras.

"God, Nicole. How could she?" I whispered from behind my napkin.

"What do you want to do?" Penny whispered to me.

"What *can* I do?" I whispered back.

Nicole and Penny exchanged looks over my head.

"Send her money," Nicole stated resolutely.

"No fucking way."

"Jackie, the woman will obviously say or do anything. She could make a lot of trouble for you."

The lump in my throat made it impossible for me to speak without breaking down completely. I needed a cigarette. What happened to the days when a girl could light up in a restaurant?

As the waiter returned with my second drink and set down our pizza, a familiar voice rang out.

"Abigail, daaarling!"

Anna sailed through the restaurant and sat with the women at the next table. Kisses flew around in a circle. "Guess who is behind you?" the woman called Abigail said.

"Who?"

She pointed at me.

"Jackie?" Anna said.

I turned around.

I tried to smile. "It's me, all right."

"Honey!" Anna exclaimed. She could tell I was not okay. "Excuse me," she said to Abigail and the others and pulled her chair over to mine. "What happened?"

I handed her the magazine. Anna scanned the photo spread, releasing a long whistle, a trait acquired from my father. "Your mother must have been desperate," she said sadly.

"What are you all looking at over there?" Abigail called out.

I sighed. "Go on, show it to them. Everyone is going to see it anyway." I took the paper out of Anna's hands, tossed it on the table in front of Abigail, and walked out.

UNIVERSAL STUDIOS
INT. SOUNDSTAGE
DAY
1998

It was the day of my big scene and I was a wreck. The film was not only over budget but two weeks behind schedule, and with rumors circulating, the trades were pointing their inky fingers at me. A couple of hitmen sent by the studio lurked behind the camera, while over at the craft service table, Nicole and Penny stood poised to do damage control. There was talk of letting the director go. Fortunately, they couldn't let *me* go because most of my scenes were in the can. Still, if the numbers didn't add up, they could pull the plug and shut down the picture.

The day before we started rehearsal, I begged Penny to get me out of my contract.

"You'll be great," Penny crooned.

"What if I stink?"

"You can't stink. We won't let you stink. Right, Nicole?"

"Right, Penny."

"Why can't I just do another action flick? Why, all of a sudden, does everyone want me to act?"

They laughed and took my hands in theirs as if we were characters out of *Little Women*. "Listen to me, Jackie Gold," Penny said with so much warmth in her voice I smelled butter melting on Marmie's biscuits. "You can do this. I know you can."

I leaned my head on her shoulder, overcome by the aroma of her faith in me.

"And wait'll you hear this," she continued, her old tone edging back. "I got you photo approval and merchandising!"

Now I was facing eight pages of dramatic dialogue during which I was to break down sobbing on the witness stand and proclaim my innocence. It was *the* pivotal moment of the picture, and though Robert Verona was the star, the scene hinged on my performance.

I was petrified. On *Circle of Life*, when I had to cry, they'd stop the camera before my close-up, and Katie would rush over and puff menthol in my eyes. It wasn't as though I'd had to conjure up any real feeling. For this film, I'd spent the last month working on the script with Casey Adams, a method acting coach. Brett had used Casey on his last film and swore by her. But he'd played a sheriff who hadn't had to cry. Casey had instructed me to focus on my character's "inner life" and how she'd *feel* being accused of a crime she didn't commit; to be a woman abused and berated by men. "The tears will come," she solemnly promised me.

"How are you feeling, Jackie?" Devon Carr, the director appeared at my side. Pale, freckled, not yet thirty, he had a disturbing habit of checking his neck pulse.

"Me? Couldn't be better," I lied. Devon couldn't save me. This was only his second film. His first had been a low-budget buddy picture with a kid and a German shepherd.

"Oh, uh, great, great." His eyes trailed off me, following something I couldn't see. "Andre!" he called sharply to the D.P. "Too yellow! Too bright!"

He dashed away in the direction of the camera crew. Our working relationship was cordial, but I'd a hunch Devon was behind the rumors about me. Not that the accusations were entirely unwarranted. I *had* held up the production on several occasions, having overslept my call time twice. I was plagued with insomnia and anxiety. I'd spent one morning hyperventilating, locked in my trailer. My hives had cleared but I was still *seething* over the tabloids and that letter from my mother. Every night I lay awake composing my reply. I hadn't sent it because each night I came up with something meaner to say. Let her rot in her own gin-soaked skin.

Robert Verona, instantly recognizable with his imposing figure and iconic craggy face, walked onto the set, parting the sea of crew, cast, and extras. In his seventies, having won two Oscars, he was still a major star. We'd already shot two of our smaller scenes and it would be an understatement to say I'd found him intimidating.

The A.D. called for final touches. I climbed into the witness box trading places with my stand-in. I searched for Nicole and Penny and saw them behind the camera chatting up the studio thugs. I was nauseous. Why had I let them talk me into doing a part that required all this acting?

I forced myself to sit while Katie chased my face with a powder puff. My hands and feet felt numb. I couldn't get a deep breath. I had to keep my shit together. I couldn't afford a panic attack like in the mock plane on *Circle*. These were much higher stakes.

Steve Connigan, a rumpled fifty-year-old veteran screenwriter, paced back and forth trying to overhear everything Devon was saying to the D.P. He kept glancing over at me, and I knew he was itching to tell me how he wanted the scene played. It was no secret that he had begged the studio to let him direct.

The wardrobe woman ran forward and tugged at my blouse while the D.P. waved the light meter in front of my face. "Bring in a number four," he commanded.

A filter was inserted, and the light adjusted. Devon settled in his chair and gave the A.D. the all-clear.

"Camera ready," The D.P. called out.

Robert Verona strode to the stand and took his mark directly in front of me. The key light reflecting in his legendary, steel-blue eyes.

My heart pounded. I gulped in air. Casey's voice came into my head. *Use what you're feeling as part of your inner life.* I felt like I was going to die.

The courtroom showdown was the climax of the movie. With the production hanging in the balance, each person, down to the last grip and gaffer, knew that the success of the film depended on this scene.

"Quiet on the set!"

"Rolling."

"Speed."

"Scene 56, take one."

"Aaaaand…action!"

Shit. Okay, concentrate on my inner life. Okay, my character, Junie would be feeling nervous too…heart pounding.

"Ms. Sommer," Robert Verona spoke confidently.

"Call me Junie."

First line in the can. No. Can't think that, concentrate on inner…

"Okay, Junie, why were you following the victim?"

"He had asked me to go to his room." *Okay, the camera is moving to my right should I turn? No! Don't think about that. How am I feeling?*

"Did you go?"

"Well yes, I was suspicious." *What am I feeling?*

"Of what?"

"Of him." *I'm feeling…an itch. On my nose.*

"Why were you suspicious?"

What am I feeling?

"Because he had cheated on me and…" *I'm feeling…*

"Do you need a break?" asked the actor playing the judge.

I turned to the bench. "Sorry, what? Do you mean me? Or my character?"

"Shit!" Robert Verona spat and walked over to his chair.

Fuck. I'd blown the take.

"Cut!" Devon sprung over to the bench with a huge smile pasted on his face. His pink polo shirt stuck to his skinny chest like a soggy washcloth and his hair had somehow molded into one wet spike on his head. He resembled the host of a kiddie show.

"Sorry, Devon," I said. "I thought he was asking me if I needed a break."

"It's a line in the scene…"

"Yes, yes, I know, but I forgot for a moment."

The studio goons came up behind him; they too wore big fake smiles.

"*Do* you need a break?"

"No, Devon, no I'm just…"

"Great, Jackie. Well, let's just take it again from the top, call that a rehearsal on camera. Great. You were great." He was fingering his neck pulse.

"Sorry, Bobby! Back to the top, everyone," Devon announced, leaping off the set. A moment later, his spike popped up in the light from behind the monitor. I squinted into the darkness. Where were Penny and Nicole? Katie rushed forward and blotted the sweat from my forehead. I searched for signs of hope in her face, the way a passenger looks to a flight attendant during heavy turbulence.

"Sorry, Bob," I said to Verona as he once again moved to his mark.

"Ready here," Katie called, stepping away.

"Quiet everyone," the A.D. bellowed. "And we are *row-ling*!"

"Speed!"

"Scene fifty-six take two!"

"Aaaand…action!"

"Ms. Sommer…" Verona approached the stand.

The room was hot, the lights blazing. Someone was whispering. I shaded my eyes.

"Ms. Sommer?" Robert Verona glared at me.

"Huh?"

"Ms. Sommer?" he repeated.

"Yes? Oh, shit sorry, sorry, Bob. Line?"

"Call me Junie," the script supervisor called out.

"Call me Junie," I said.

"Okay, Junie, why were you following the victim?"

"He had asked me to go to his room."

"Did you go?"

There was scuffling over by the camera.

"No, I mean. Goddamnit! Is someone talking out there?" I yelled.

"Sorry," Devon called.

"Are you going to cut?" I asked.

"No," Devon replied.

"Line?"

"Well yes…" the script supervisor called out.

"Well yes, I was suspicious."

More scuffling and whispers. *What is going on?*

"Why were you suspicious?" Verona asked.

"Because… For Chris'sake, shut up out there!" I slammed my hand down on the railing.

"Sorry, Jackie," Devon called out.

"Devon, may we please cut and start over?"

Silence.

"Devon? Hello?"

"I'm here."

"Well, shit, cut the scene!"

"Um, no can do."

"What the hell, Devon?"

"Christ, just say your lines, young lady!" Verona barked.

"Say the lines please, Jackie," Steve Connigan pleaded.

"What is going on?" I demanded.

Silence.

"Devon?"

Silence.

Where the hell were Nicole and Penny? I squinted past the lights at Verona and the other actors' frozen faces, at Katie, and the makeup crew, the grips—everyone was staring at me. I felt like a bug frying under a magnifying glass.

"That's enough!" I yelled at the darkness. "I am done with this!" I got up from the witness stand and was about to storm off the set when out of the corner of my eye I saw Devon give a thumbs up to the producers. A thumbs up? What? Then it hit me. They *wanted* me to walk. They were driving me to quit! They had lost faith in the picture and wanted to shut it down. If I walked off the film, I'd be to blame, and insurance would have to cover the loss…they'd be off the hook.

And I'd be playing dinner theater in Wichita.

Shaking and furious, I turned around, climbed back up on the witness seat, and sat down.

"I want my line!" I yelled at the dark stage.

Verona and the actor playing the judge toggled their eyes between me and Devon, confused.

"Forget it, guys, I'm not fucking quitting. What is my next line?"

"Because he had cheated on me," Steve Connigan called out.

"Steven!" Devon warned.

"Goddamnit Devon, let her finish the scene."

Devon and the mucky schmucks whispered frantically. The crew was still, presumably awaiting orders. Finally, the A.D. called out, "We are still rolling!"

Now the actors raced back into their places. The extras playing the jurors rushed into the stands. Katie ran up to me, but I held up my hand, motioned her away, and blotted my forehead with my sleeve.

"Where from?" the script woman asked.

"From the top," I said. I took a deep breath and banished Devon, the crew, and the studio from my mind as I pivoted my look around the courtroom. I took in the judge, the jury, and then I rested my gaze on Robert Verona.

His steely blue eyes had softened. He nodded for me to begin.

"Call me Junie."

"Okay, Junie, why were you following the victim?" he urged.

"He had asked me to go to his room."

"Did you go?"

"Well yes, I was suspicious."

"Of what?"

"Because he had cheated on me!"

I was shaking, my voice quivering, the words tumbled out, my rage at Devon, and the suits propelling me. "So, I followed him. But I didn't go there to kill him. Yes, I was angry, I even hated him, but I wanted him. I wanted him to love me."

"Who had he cheated on you with?"

"I…I can't say."

"May I remind you, Miss Sommer, you are on trial for your life."

"I didn't do it!" Tears sprang to my eyes.

"Who cheated?"

"My…my sister."

The jurors let out a gasp.

"Yes, my sister. I found them together. She betrayed me."

"When?"

I turned to the judge, tears pouring from my eyes. *Holy shit, it was working!*

"Do I have to answer this sir?"

He nodded gravely.

"It was last May, just…before…"

Robert Verona walked toward me, slowly. "Before what, Ms. Sommer?"

"Oh God, before Ronnie died!" I cried out, collapsing, sobbing convulsively.

Ten minutes later when Devon finally yelled "cut," I was so lost in the emotion I didn't hear him. I had played out the entire eight-page monologue in one take.

Robert Verona helped me down from the stand. "Guess we still have a job," he grinned. Taking my arm, he escorted me to our chairs.

Devon and the studio guys sucked into a huddle. Katie, Nicole, and Penny rushed over.

"Amazing, Jackie!" Penny said. "See? What'd I tell you?"

Nicole poked me in the side. "Hey! When did you learn to act?"

Katie swabbed the mascara out from under my eyes.

"Where the fuck were you two?" I snarled.

"They threw us off the set. Honestly!" Penny crossed her heart. "They said you wanted it closed."

"We snuck back in, though, just in time," Nicole said.

I shook my head. "They were fucking with me. Devon and the producers tried to make me quit."

"*What?*" Penny and Nicole both yelled.

I motioned for them to be quiet. Steve Connigan walked toward us. "Jackie, Bob, that was great." He turned to me, "but I want you to do something different on the next take."

"Different? I nailed it, Steve. Is this another trick?"

"No, I swear to you. Just, this time instead of anger, be soft and sweet. Trust me. Then we'll have it two different ways."

I threw a look at my new pal Verona.

"What do you say, Bob?"

He shrugged. "Up to you, Jackie girl."

Devon ran over and tapped Steve on the shoulder. "She nailed it, let's move on. Good work, Jackie."

"Fuck you, Devon," I said. "Let's do one more."

Steve gave me a big hug and kiss. "Sweet and innocent," he whispered. "That's all you need to do."

DISSOLVE TO:

INT. HOSPITAL ROOM
NIGHT
DAY 50

Right before the graveyard shift, the day and night nurses exchange places and for a minute or so, the hubbub subsides. The hospital pauses to catch its breath, the loudspeaker's crackle goes quiet, the carts cease their rattling, parked in empty halls until new freshly scrubbed or gloved hands come to push them along.

In the parking lot, most of the fans and paparazzi have clocked out, gone home to apartments or houses and families. A few of the diehards will remain here overnight, camped out on the slimmest hope of a late appearance by Brett.

Mercifully, I've had no more visitors today since Nicole. I'm drained by her excuses and pleas for absolution and frustrated by my inability to respond. No penance to pay at a coma-confessional. Nary a "Hail Mary."

I too am between shifts. With my robot lungs I wake and sleep and wake again to the rhythm of the respirator: *Inhale, exhale*; each breath the same; same depth, same speed. Tempo Lento. The beat of a dirge.

How to describe this Bardo of waiting, for the turn of the final page? I search the dark unknown for clues like a tracker in the wilderness but find nothing I can identify, no footprints I recognize, no breadcrumbs to follow. I long to anchor in the familiar, the everyday sounds of garbage trucks, their brakes groaning. Traffic noise, Horns honking. Seagulls squawking and the sandpipers' patter as they scuttle away from rolling rushing crashing waves. So much I took for granted. Tasting, touching smelling; Grass, gasoline, *coffee*. Hail coffee! God, I miss coffee! The aroma of the brew before it yellows on a nurse's tongue. And smog. I miss smog. The burn in my lungs on a red-alert day. Hail smog. Hail irony. Hail belly laughs. Sarcasm. Boredom. Body odor. Farts!

Hail toast. I miss toast. If I'd known I was going to die I would have eaten more buttered toast.

I don't miss television or magazines or fashion or makeup or hairstyles or agents or contracts or Screen Actors Guild or screenings or scripts or anything to do with show business. I don't even miss acting.

I miss applause.

Hail applause.

I loved the applause.

SLOW DISSOLVE TO:

EXT. DOROTHY CHANDLER PAVILION
AFTERNOON
1999

"Jackie, Brett! Jackieeeeee!"

We paraded down the red carpet, flashbulbs exploding like cherry bombs, hundreds of fans screaming our names. TV reporters from every state, every country, analyzing our gowns, hairstyles, everything from the size of our behinds down to the size of our pores.

With our publicists mapping the way, Brett and I swiveled left and right, accommodating the photographers and interviewers. Nicole dragged me over to Joan Rivers, who despite my protestations, insisted I was named after Jackie Kennedy and wouldn't let go of my arm until I agreed with her.

Brett dutifully fulfilled his role of escort, shuttling in and out of my photo opportunities, smiling his dazzling smile as he was asked over and over and over again how it felt to be with *me* on "this, the most important day of *my* life."

"I am so proud of Jackie," he said as the cameras clicked wildly. "I am just so happy for Jackie," he said as the fans screamed around us. "I am so proud and happy."

He was lying. Since my nomination, Brett had been miserable. Though he wouldn't admit it, I knew it stuck in his craw that I— who had done little to hone my talent, who had stumbled blindly into every acting job I'd had, including (and most especially) this last picture—had somehow managed to accidentally and for all the wrong reasons give a performance worthy of being nominated for an Academy Award.

The money was on Dame Maggie Finch, who deserved to win just for breathing. Just to be in the same category as her was an honor. Still, in the Supporting Actress category, surprises happened, and the truth was, I had managed to give a good performance. Well, two halves of a good performance. With

Steve Connigan's foresight, two vastly different takes of my testimony were spliced together in the editing room, creating the performance for which I'd been nominated.

With my newfound popularity and status, I was learning that Brett's rigid ideas about manhood were not only confined to the bedroom. He might never leave me for another woman, but he might very well leave me if his ego was at stake.

We had not had sex since the morning they'd announced the nominations. He barely kissed me good night. And it didn't help that he was between pictures and had taken to lying in bed all day drinking tomato juice mixed with a thimbleful of vodka, acting out a G-rated version of *A Star Is Born*.

"You make ten times the money I do," I reminded him. "You can be a leading man until you're seventy-five!"

"You couldn't possibly understand," Brett said wistfully one evening after his vodka gobbets had finally added up to a few drinks' worth. "You were born into royalty."

He'd forgotten about Queen Marva and Princess Merilee.

"See, Jackie, no one in my family ever amounted to anything."

For the tenth time that week, I sat through the history of his no-good father, Barney Senior, and what a failure he'd been.

"It would bring light into my mama's heart if I won one of those golden guys," he said wistfully. "Why, my whole town would come out for a parade."

"Seventy-six trombones," I mumbled.

"Thanks a lot." He stalked down the hall to the gym. Several minutes later I heard his weights clanking along to Clint Black.

"Jackie." Nicole poked my arm bringing me back to the moment.

In her white, satin Armani suit, blonde hair cut, highlighted and blown out to perfection, Nicole was a far cry from the person who had landed on my doorstep two years earlier. She displayed confidence and elegance in her tuxedo jacket and beaded bustier, as she shuffled Brett and me into our seats. I couldn't help qvelling like a proud parent.

I whistled in admiration. "Don't you look fabulous!"

"You're the fourth and fifth seat in," she replied, all business.

Everyone in our section was either nominated or presenting; all of us pretending to be casual and relaxed in our heavy beaded gowns and borrowed Harry Winstons as if this were (yawn) just another day. I wondered if my mother was watching. Despite Penny and Nicole's advice, I hadn't sent money. She could publish all the pictures she wanted; she'd get nothing from me. Christ, Mirabelle had to be at least eighteen by now, she could probably loan Mom a few bucks. Mirabelle. Would she be watching?

I shook off the thought and looked around at the famous faces. Meryl, Jack, Holly, Shirley. It was exciting to see this many of my idols in one place. I remembered an autograph book I'd had as a child, a peach vinyl one that read "Autographs" in embossed script letters. Nicole had the same book in lime green. On weekends, we'd chase down the famous on their way in or out of the Colony gates, competing to see who could collect the most autographs. I suddenly felt overwhelmed with emotion. Nicole and I had come so far together. It was incredible to have a best friend with whom I shared so much history. I searched for her. She stood at the end of our row shaking hands with that weasel Devon Carr.

"Excuse me," I said to Brett, stepping over him and nudging past Ed Harris and Kathy Bates. "Nicole!"

"Hey, Jax, I'm leaving for the Green Room. You'd better take your seat." She turned to go.

"Wait." I gripped her hand. "Nicky, remember our autograph books?" I put my arms around her gingerly, careful of hair and makeup.

"Yeah, honey."

"But Nic, really. Can you believe we're here?"

She ducked out from the circle of my embrace as if she had been overcome by too much perfume. "Save it for your acceptance speech," she chortled. Then she patted my shoulder and ran down the aisle.

"Good luck, Jackie," Devon called from across the aisle where he stood schmoozing with Steve Connigan. Steve had been nominated for best screenplay. Devon had been left out of the best director category. The power had shifted.

I avoided stepping on all the famous toes as I made my way back to where Brett slumped in his seat. I sensed the auditorium of eyes zoom in on us. "Sit up," I whispered.

"Nobody here takes me seriously," he whispered back as the lights dimmed and the orchestra began to play.

"Oh God, please!" The spotlights flew past us. "You're only thirty-one. With the money your films make, you'll be knighted by the time you're thirty-five. Sir Barney."

"Ha-ha, Jackie."

"Brett, can't you just be happy for me for one second?"

He slumped lower. "Can't you be happy for yourself? Why do we both have to be happy for you to be happy?"

Gwynneth Paltrow sat in front of Brett. I hoped she hadn't overheard.

"Besides, I am happy for you," Brett mumbled. "Do I have to be jumping up and down twenty-four hours a day for you to think I'm happy for you?"

The supporting actress category came right after the opening number and the host's monologue. I couldn't concentrate. I applauded and pretended to laugh at the jokes, but inside I was festering, obsessing over how I could get Brett to see what an asshole he was being. I wished I could slip out to the ladies' room, and slug at the pint of vodka in my satin and pearl Prada evening bag.

And I was worried about Daddy. He and Anna had dropped by the house earlier to wish me luck. The *Entertainment Tonight* crew was filming me as I got dressed and made-up. Daddy never went to awards ceremonies. Even when his films were nominated, he and Anna watched at home and then went to Swifty Lazar's after-party.

"Jackie, please listen!"

Anna held the sleeve of my robe as I scurried around my bedroom followed by the makeup and camera crew. She ducked every time the lens turned her way.

"You need to talk to your daddy about seeing a doctor," she whispered. "His pee looks funny to me. Dark. You know? Talk to him."

"PULL THE PLUG! PULL THE GODDAMN PLUG! GO TO THE SET AND TAKE FABRINI OUT BY THE SHORT HAIRS!" My father was in the hallway screaming into the phone. A Bible epic shooting in Rome had gone over budget. I shut the door.

"Evie, lose the barrette, please," I said to the hair woman. "Listen, Anna, I will, I promise, it's just that now is not a great time. I'll talk to him soon, okay?"

"When do we see you?"

"Me? You're the one who travels half the year." I turned back to Evie. "It clashes with the earrings."

"Fine. If he dies—"

I pulled her away from the cameraman and the microphone hanging overhead. "Anna, I will call him tomorrow. Okay?"

"Okay, I just hope it's not too late."

"Jackie!" Brett hissed bringing me back to the auditorium. My face filled the giant monitors as they started the clip from the courtroom scene in *First Degree*. When it was over, the audience burst into applause. Suddenly, I wanted to win. I wanted my name to be in the envelope. I wanted to be the special one up at the podium crying and thanking everyone. I reached for Brett's hand.

"And the Oscar goes to…"

DISSOLVE TO:

INT. HOSPITAL ROOM
NOON
DAY 51

I measure my time in seconds. Each tick of the clock like a drip of water striking the bottom of the bucket I'm soon to kick.

Nurse Pierre is extra careful with me now; dimming lights, tenderly tucking the sheets around my feet. His soulful green eyes fill with tears whenever he looks at me. He no longer bends the rules or allows unscheduled nurse visits, not even from his friend Amanda. I send a telepathic request to Daddy and Anna. *Please do something for Nurse Pierre after I'm gone.* Dying has made me nicer. In the old days, I wouldn't have remembered his name.

Pierre hangs and adjusts a new I.V. bag, and I wonder why bother? Why hydrate? It seems pointless to give sustenance to a body chugging down the assembly line to *God only knows.* This matter consumes my thinking. I'm desperate for logistics now that my number is up. What awaits me? Will there be others? Will I look like I do now, or will I revert to my original boobs and nose? Will I even have a body?

Is there *anything* after?

I enjoyed meeting Jesus Joe, but let's face it, he was probably a hallucination, a reaction to pain meds. Anyway, he didn't provide hard evidence.

Hopefully there's *someplace* not painful or awful. I'm not asking for the Ritz. I'd be happy with an afterlife at the Embassy Suites.

Pierre turns on the radio, skips through the dial to *The Dr. Dave Show.* Together we listen while he goes on about his duties, emptying my waste, adjusting my feeding tube.

"What I'm telling you, friend is this: Success isn't measured by the work you've accomplished or the money you've made. Can you imagine lying on your deathbed, wishing you had spent more time on the job?" Dr. Dave asks the caller.

I can answer that one. Definitely not.

334 · DINAH MANOFF

"See, friend, at the end of the day, who cares whether you were the top guy at the firm? It won't amount to a hill of beans if you're not coming from love."

"Ain't that the truth," Pierre murmurs as he wipes down my bed rails with disinfectant.

"Your life is a success," Dr. Dave continues, "if at the end you can answer yes to two questions: Number one, did I love well? And Number two, have I forgiven my enemies?"

Um…what?

"Yes, friends, that and a dollar in the salvation army bucket will get you past the pearly gates." Dr. Dave chuckles. And we'll be right back with another caller after a message from Friskies, maker of Meow mix and other…"

Question: Did I love well?

Answer: I have loved so-so.

Question: Can I forgive my enemies?

Answer: A few. Maybe.

Where does that leave me?

I can *pretend* to forgive my enemies. I'm an actress after all. I can dress the part and fake my way into heaven. Or will God see right through me? Is my whole life a failure because I ran out of time before I could fix my mistakes? Hey Dr. Dave, how about a waiver for a girl with a boulder-sized chip on her shoulder? And *is* there a God? Because God might be nothing but a pimply-faced adolescent who tortures cats and throws guppies against the rocks to watch their guts explode. Should we forgive Hitler and rapists? How about the paparazzi or the mother who abandons her child?

Did God make me fall, or is God keeping me alive? Is God the chicken or the egg? Or both?

What comes next?

Where am I going?

What am I feeling?

"And we are back with Jean from Ohio, You're on with Dr. Dave…"

Pierre turns off the radio and adjusts my pillows. He doesn't look worried about where he's going. He's loved well and probably forgiven all the bullies who made fun of him for being gay. He sniffles as he makes a note on my chart, then loads up his supply cart, and with one last woeful glance my way rolls out the door.

SLOW DISSOLVE TO:

INT. DOROTHY CHANDLER PAVILION NIGHT

The Oscar went to…Maggie Finch!

From that moment, Brett was like a man dancing out of a wheelchair at a tent revival. Not only was he no longer depressed, he turned into a love machine. For the first time, he couldn't get enough of me. Breakfast in bed, make love. Candlelight dinner, make love. Again on the floor in front of the fireplace. And the sex was better. Not perfect, but often and spontaneous. Finally, my dreams were coming true, though unfortunately, not all at once. It seemed to be an either-or situation.

For a while before the Oscars, I'd been intercepting mail delivery at the gate so he wouldn't see the scripts I was sent. Now, I was extra guarded. I didn't want anything to affect our latent romance, especially with Brett between pictures. If there were even a hint of my success, he would almost certainly crawl out of our conjugal bed and back into his hole. Brett felt sorry for me now that I'd lost and fucking me was his way of cheering me up, therefore I would stay in need of cheering. I hid scripts in the trunk of my car and called Penny from my cell phone to discuss them. I pled with her to find Brett a vehicle that would showcase him as she had done for me. He knew I was receiving scripts, but when he asked if I'd read anything interesting, I would shake my head and lament the lack of good roles for women. And it was true that I hadn't read anything spectacular yet, but a few offers had come my way that I would have accepted if it hadn't meant sacrificing my love life.

One Monday morning, a messenger slipped past the gate and came to the front door.

"Who's the script from?" Brett asked after I sent the kid on his way.

"Penny."

"I know *that*. I'm not an idiot."

"Well, lemme see." I tore open the manila envelope and scanned the cover letter.

"Oh!" I tried to keep the excitement out of my voice. "It's an offer for the new Reiner film."

I loved Reiner and was dying to work with him. Penny knew this and must have sent the messenger herself which explained how he know the gate code.

"Well, then, you ought to do it." Brett's jaw tightened. I didn't need a weather report to see the dark clouds gathering. He went to the couch. His thick, black brows knit together.

"Reiner's overrated," Brett said, turning his face into the pillows. Thunder, lightning, downpour.

"Well, he did make that awful picture with Bruce Willis," I said finally.

Brett looked up from the pillows. The clouds parted. He chuckled, then he took me in his arms and the sun streamed down.

I knew the parameters. One move too far in any direction and I'd be back out in the rain.

We melted into each other and as Brett undid the zipper on my skirt. I let the Reiner script fall to the floor.

DISSOLVE TO:

INT. HOSPITAL ROOM
NIGHT
DAY 52

"Jackie darlin'. Oh honey, are you there? Can you hear me? I flew right in when they called. The nurses told me I shouldn't stay too long, they say you need to rest. How can they know that?" Brett takes off his cap and twists it in his hands. "I don't know if you can hear me Jackie, and well, in a way I hope that you won't. No, that's not what I mean. I wish you could hear me, honey, you know I am praying for you with every bone in my body. Mama and the girls put you on every prayer list in the world."

He crosses the room, rubbing his temples, then puts his hands on his knees and breathes in and out several times. "I guess I'm trying to say, Jackie…if you do hear me, I hope…"

He walks quickly to my bed and takes my hand. He wiggles my fingers, then lays my hand back on the covers and takes a deep breath.

"Okay. You know how I told you I was going to see a shrink. Well, I've been talking to him almost every day now. He's Reiner's guy in New York but he says we can do phone sessions while I'm here. Oh, and not that it matters, but he's Jewish and I don't know but it does seem the Jews have a talent for psychology. And comedy. Reiner, man that guy… Rob, he said to tell you he's pulling for you, baby. Everyone on the set signed a card." He fumbles around in his jacket pocket and pulls out a crumpled envelope.

"See?" He waves it in front of my face. "I'll just, well, I'll hold it for you 'til you…um…" He stuffs it back in his pocket.

"Anyway, Dr. Markowitz, Lenny, he thinks it would be help-ful for my therapy if I told you a few things that, have, uh…" Brett goes to my door, opens it, and peeks up and down the hall, then shuts it and pulls the chair up to my bedside.

"Okay, so," he says in a low voice, "when you and I first got together, I mentioned I had been seeing someone in Texas. Kelly. Okay, here's the thing. Kelly was older, was married. With two children. The family went to our church and all. No one found out, but, well, it went on for almost two years. We…we met in places far out of town. I moved to California to break it off. Clean. I was not going to wreck his family and if anyone ever found out… I'm trying to say…" He leans in close to my ear. "Kelly was a man," he whispers. "Is a man."

Brett leaps to his feet. "Whooh, whooh, whooh," he exhales, springing up and down on his toes like a boxer. He cracks his neck left then right. He whips off his jacket and throws it on the couch. Then, resuming his position at my bedside, he takes both my hands in his.

"I swear to you, baby, if I were gay that would be it, case closed," he whispers, "but the thing with Kelly, see he was my drama teacher, and you know how vulnerable you get when you're acting. That's how it began, anyway. And I swear to you, this is the God's honest truth, I never felt good with the sex part. It was just oral and always him wanting to do that to me. That's why I always felt kind of funny about that particular thing with us or about all that kinky stuff you like; it's all kind of tangled up in my mind with Kelly. That *surfaced* in my last session. Lenny, Dr. Markowitz, says what I wanted was to be physically touched lovingly by a male because my pop never not *once* in my G.D. life gave me hugs or told me he loved me."

Brett stands and begins pacing. "He hit that rusty nail right on the head cause sweetheart when he said that, I just broke down and cried. Jackie. Do you know, twice when I was just a little squirt, my daddy hit my mom right in front of me and there was nothing I could do about it. Nothing! Oh, baby, I have all this anger I didn't even know about. Been smoking a pack a day. I'd like to wring my daddy's fat, red neck. I've been going to the gym nights after work just to get all this anger O-U-T. Too bad I'm doing a comedy, huh?"

He places both hands on the foot of my bed and leans down. "And baby, I was wrong about Reiner. I was a jealous ass and, God honey, I don't know how you put up with me. I am so sorry. If I could go back, I would tell you to take the picture, Jackie Gold! You would have been amazing. Way better than the gal they hired."

Brett comes back to the chair and sits. "Anyway, one thing for sure," he drops his voice, "I can't be in love with a man. I'm just not wired that way. I had a whole buncha' girlfriends before Kelly and one or two after, but then I met you, and I never felt for any of them what I felt for you. What I *feel*. Not ever." He grasps my hand, slides to his knees on the floor, and rests his chin on the bed. "I love you, honey," he sobs. "I love you. Jackie? Can you hear me, honey? Are you there?"

Am I here? If a tree falls in the forest? If a comatose woman doesn't wake when her fiancé confesses his two-year affair with a gay lover does that mean she is really gone?

Maybe if I'd known in the beginning. We could have started from there, worked through the issue, or not. At least it would have been the truth.

Maybe if I had been *myself* from the beginning, he would have told me the truth.

Which comes first?

How am I feeling?

Where am I going?

Brett goes to the couch, lies down, and puts his cap over his eyes. Tears stream down the sides of his face. He covers himself with his jacket and rocks back and forth. I never knew Brett was capable of expressing such deep feelings. I long to put my arms around him and tell him that I love him. And that I am proud of him for being so brave.

One thing was for sure though: Brett wouldn't have told me if he thought I could hear him.

There is a tap tap on the door and Nurse Dani pops her coppery head in. "Hey, you. Welcome back!" she says, equal parts cheer and sympathy.

Brett does not sit up. He does not invite her in. Instead, he puts up a hand and waves her out of the room.

SLOW DISSOLVE TO:

INT. BEL AIR MANSION
ANNA AND SIDNEY'S BEDROOM
NIGHT
SFX: PHONE RINGING

"Jackie, it's me."

"Who is this?"

"Anna!" she whispered, "I need to talk."

"Anna, what's wrong?"

"I can't say anymore, he's coming."

Something was very wrong. I sped around the curves of Coldwater Canyon until I arrived at the Mausoleum gates. I pressed the special security code and let myself in. No sooner had I shut the front door than I saw my father descend the staircase in his trademark silk robe.

"So, you heard," he said gravely.

"What is it, Daddy?"

"It's cancer. I'm dying," he said simply.

I reached out for something to hold onto, but with nothing there, I sat on the marble floor. Anna rushed in and saw me, my legs splayed out in front of me like a child playing a game of roll the ball.

"You told her?" she said to my father. "Just like that!"

"Well, *you* called her in the middle of the night!" Their voices came in waves. I hadn't quite fainted, but I wasn't quite all there either.

"Did you tell her everything?"

"Mostly," he said.

What else could there be? He was dying.

"Did you tell her the good part?"

"The good part?" I asked weakly.

"Yeah. Well," my father said, "the good part is that even though it's stage-two prostate, the doctor says I should have a full recovery."

"What?" I shook my head in disbelief. "How could you do that to me?"

"Do what?" My father looked at Anna, pulling his robe around himself protectively.

"You told me you were dying!" I yelled at my father.

"No, I didn't."

"No, he didn't," Anna chimed in behind him.

I was going crazy but decided not to fight it. "Okay, fine. You didn't." I got up from the floor and stamped the tingling away from my feet and legs.

"Remember the pee I was telling you about the night you were busy?" Anna said pointedly.

"I wasn't *busy*, I was going to the Oscars."

Anna waved my explanation away as if it were smoke in her eyes. "I got your father to the doctor to have the pee-pee checked. The pee was fine. Dark from vitamins your father was taking. But when the doctor had him there, they did a physical, and thank God from the bottom of my heart because they found a little tumor in your daddy's behind."

"Anna, please." My father pulled his robe tighter and headed in the direction of his study. Daddy couldn't bear conversation of this sort.

"What happens now?" I asked.

Her face became somber. "Now, your father begins radiation."

I could see the fear in her eyes. And that made me afraid too.

I put my arms around her. She wrapped me in a hug, then held me away from her and combed my hair from my face. Suddenly, I was exhausted, much too tired to drive home.

"Anna? Can I spend the night?"

Anna looked surprised but happy. "Of course," she said. "You can stay in your room."

"I'm not sure I remember how to find it," I teased. I hadn't stayed overnight in the Mausoleum since I was seventeen. Anna rang the elevator, and we ascended to her bed chambers. I trailed after to her sweet-smelling, cedar-lined dressing room, the size of the apartment Nicole and I had once shared.

"How are things going with Brett?" Anna asked as she rummaged through a drawer.

"Great actually."

She held out an array of different nighties to pick from. I chose a striped flannel Lanz.

"When are you going back to work?"

"I don't know. I'm in no hurry."

"You want to have a baby?" She cocked an eyebrow.

"Oh my God, no. I mean, yeah sure, but not for like ten years." I took off my shirt and jeans, pulled the nightgown over my head.

"Brett doesn't want you to work."

"Of course he wants me to work. I just haven't found a good script."

Anna looked at me, her eyes narrowing. "What about the Reiner film?"

"How did you know about that?"

"Penny called me."

"Oh great, so much for client confidentiality."

"She's an agent, not a lawyer. Penny says they won't wait forever."

"Well, I'm turning it down."

"Why?" she exclaimed.

"Because it's just not…the timing is…the script isn't that great and I don't want to be on location that long."

Anna picked up my clothes, folded my jeans and T-shirt, and laid them on the tufted ottoman then she turned to me. "Take the movie, Jackie. It's important for you."

"Anna, no offense," I chuckled, "but I don't think you're in a position to be giving professional advice."

"Is that so?" Anna spun to the dressing room door, slammed it shut, and turned. "Tu piensas que no valgo nada? Tu piensas que todo lo que hago es jugar golf con tu Papa?"

"Anna, I don't…"

"Ju tink all I do ees play golf with your daddy?" she spat. "Ju don't think that what I do is valuable? Do ju know how much money I raised for ceeestik feebrrrosis dees year? Or dee Seeherra Club, or dee Amerrrican Cancerr Societeee?" Her cheeks were flushed, eyes flashing. I'd never seen Anna angry in my whole life. It was shocking and unexpected like a tornado ripping through a sleeping neighborhood.

"No, Anna, please don't be upset. I think what you do is important. I don't know what I'm saying. Okay? I'm sorry."

Anna took a few deep breaths. She put her hands on her hips and bent over.

"Anna?"

She nodded and held up a hand.

"Hey, I know you're worried about Dad. I didn't mean to upset you more."

From her bent position Anna reached for my discarded shoes and socks and placed them at the foot of the ottoman. For years she had swept my mess; picked up my clothes, removed plates, tidied homework papers into order. Had I ever so much as said thank you?

"Thank you," I said weakly. "I'm sorry, really."

She brushed away my apology and stood. "Yes, I am worried about your daddy, Jackie. But I am also very worried about you."

"I'm fine, Anna."

She took my face in both her hands. "Take the goddamn picture, Jackie."

My father's words coming from Anna's lips made me smile. "I'll think about it, okay? I promise."

DISSOLVE TO:

INT. HOSPITAL ROOM
DAWN
DAY 53

Merilee is here. Right here in my room. White-knuckled, gripping the back of the chair, swaying slightly. I'm guessing she had a few stiff ones before coming.

From her expression, I look worse than she expected. She, however, looks better than I expected. She's lost weight since the *Star Magazine* photos; her hair now short and light gray. She is dressed in tan slacks and a flowery cotton blouse. She could be someone's nice aunt, even someone's mother.

It was Emme who brought her. "Don't leave us," I wanted to cry out as the door shut. "Pull the plug!"

Tentatively she sits and places her white, vinyl purse in her lap. It shines a warning. I brace myself for…what? The onslaught of apologies for all the terrible things she's done. The "I was a lousy mother and now it's too late" speech. Is that what she's prepared for our deathbed reunion? Or the opposite. Maybe she will tell me of the hurt I caused her, the unanswered phone messages, the appeal for letters, for news, and then finally the desperate plea for money. No check, Jacqueline? You were rich and I had nothing! You left your mother and your sister with nothing!

It is all true.

Did I love well?

Can I forgive my enemies?

My mother bends down, removes her shoe, and scratches at a place on the inside of her foot. Then she rises, crosses unsteadily to the window. She leans on the sill and looks out at the sky, the stars fading in the morning light, hoping as I am, to be rescued.

SLOW DISSOLVE TO:

INT. JACKIE AND BRETT'S HOUSE
BEVERLY HILLS
DAY
1999

Brett continued showering me with love, attention, and sex, after which I'd lie awake running pros and cons, trying to come up with an equation that would let me take the Reiner picture and hang on to my boyfriend. I'd witnessed many show-business marriages break up where egos were involved. I was pretty sure our relationship was no exception.

Just as the offer was set to expire, Brett received a call from Manuel Vargas, the director who had won the Palme D'or at Cannes. *Eighth Dimension* wasn't a brilliant script, but the character of "Pablo, a conflicted priest" was the kind of role into which Brett could finally sink his perfect teeth. And best of all, it shot in Zagreb for twelve weeks, freeing me up for Reiner.

I called Penny. "I'll take the picture. Just keep it under wraps for a few days."

"Great, I can get your dad off my back."

Suddenly I had a sense that maybe the timing had been too convenient. "Penny, did you and Daddy have something to do with Brett getting that film in Zagreb?"

"Gotta go, sweetie. Call coming in." Click.

Patches and Pistols was scheduled to open and as the date approached, the tabloids began grinding out story after story about our relationship. We were breaking up, we were secretly engaged, Brett was having an affair, I was pregnant with twins; stories engineered by the studio's publicity department to gin up attention for the film.

It was a Thursday afternoon and we had finished making love. I was planning to tell Brett my big news about the Reiner picture over the weekend.

He loped up behind me as I was getting into the shower. "Let's go away this weekend."

"Are you kidding? I'd love to!"

"Leave tomorrow?" he asked, following me into the shower. He shut the door and wrapped his arms around me from behind. I wriggled against him, turning the shower on as hot as I could stand it.

"Oh, shit, I have something on Saturday."

Nicole had managed to wrangle a cover of *Esquire* and I had reluctantly agreed. Ever since that *Swanky* debacle, I loathed photoshoots. But Nicole had made such an issue out of it I had given in.

"It's going to be a very special occasion," Brett said. "I have a big surprise for you."

"What is it?" I demanded. "You know I hate surprises."

"Trust me." Brett reached over me and turned up the cold faucet. Brett's idea of a hot shower always gave me goosebumps. I jumped a little and he kissed me on the mouth. "I love you, Jackie," he said, looking deeply into my eyes.

That's when it struck me: Brett was taking me away to propose. There was no other possible explanation. He'd been on the phone to his mother at least three times this week. When I'd asked him why, he mumbled something about her wanting some real estate advice. I would have to feign shock and surprise when he popped the question. My big news about Reiner could wait until after we were engaged. Engaged! No way was I rocking this boat.

Brett finished showering and toweled off. He drew a heart in the steamy mirror with our initials and blew me a kiss before going back into the bedroom. Suddenly, I felt tired and heavy. I made the water hot, squeezed shampoo into my palms, and lathered my hair. Why was I feeling so low? Brett was going to ask me to *marry* him, for Chris'sake. I should be elated!

I rinsed my hair, then toweled off and dialed Nicole from the bathroom phone. I knew she'd be irate about canceling the shoot. She was constantly hounding me to do publicity and I was sick and tired of her lectures about how I was hurting my career. She picked up on the fourth ring.

"Guess what?" I infused my voice with excitement I was still waiting to feel.

"Who is this?" Nicole asked, froggy with sleep.

"Me, you idiot. Wake up, it's three o'clock!"

"What do you want?" I heard the click of a cigarette lighter, followed by a deep inhale.

"Well, Mary Sunshine, since you're being so friendly, I've decided not to tell you," I said, knowing I would tell her anyway.

Nicole let out a laugh, which morphed into a wet cough.

"Pretty," I said. "You gotta quit smoking."

"You gotta quit drinking. What are you calling about? Please tell me you've got a job."

"Hold on." I turned on the fan to cover the sound of my voice. "Brett's going to propose," I whispered.

Silence.

"Nicole, can you hear me?"

"Yeah, I heard you. Well, that's great, Jax, congratulations."

"You don't sound very happy for me."

"Hey, I'm happy if you're happy."

"Well, I'm fucking happy," I said defensively.

"Then I'm fucking happy too," Nicole snapped back.

This was not how I had envisioned the conversation. Why weren't the people closest to me ever thrilled for my success? Maybe I expected too much. I put down the toilet lid and sat.

"Nic, what's going on? You've been in bed since the stupid Oscars."

"We were robbed."

"Jesus, Nicole," I said. "I lost to Maggie Finch."

"I didn't do enough for you, Jackie."

"Honey, if you'd had Dame Maggie murdered…"

"Believe me, I thought about it."

I laughed, "Well she still would have won." I waited for her comeback but only heard the sound of her dragging on her cigarette. "Anyway, you have to reschedule the *Esquire* shoot."

"What? No, Jackie, I can't do that. We're already at the edge of their lead time!"

"Okay, then cancel."

"You are fucking up your life."

"I called to tell you I'm getting engaged." I was steamed but had to keep my voice down or Brett would hear me.

"Did you tell Brett about Reiner?"

"Shhh! What? How did you know about—"

"There are no secrets in this town, Jax. You need this picture."

Ugh, Penny. I was going to kill her.

"I'm planning to soon, I just—"

"You want to sacrifice your career for this guy?"

"This *guy* is going to be my husband," I hissed.

"You're losing your heat, Jax."

"My *heat?*"

"It's been a year since *First Degree,* and you have nothing in the can."

"The can?" I mocked her. "Wow, all of a sudden you're Miss Show Business."

"You know what, Jackie? Fuck you. I could represent a hundred other actresses."

"So, go," I said, "represent. It'll give you something to do while you're sleeping away my paycheck."

There was a click, then silence on the other end of the line.

I traded my towel for a robe and stomped back to the bedroom. The Lakers were playing their final game against the Knicks. Brett watched, propped up on pillows, his script lazy in his hand. I got in next to him and waited for a break in the action.

"So, where are we going Friday?"

"What about the *Esquire* shoot?"

"They'll postpone. Where are we going?"

"Can't tell you. It's part of the surprise."

A small voice inside me said this was the moment to tell Brett about the Reiner picture. I needed to be honest with my boyfriend, my future husband, regardless of the results. I took a deep breath and gathered all my reserves, then I told the voice to shut up. I'd handle this in my own fucked up way.

DISSOLVE TO:

INT. HOSPITAL ROOM
MORNING

My mother is back, pacing in circles like a caged animal. I know what she's working up to—the final chapter, the long goodbye. She wants to say her piece. Then she can escape back to Hawaii and drink herself to death.

Outside, more fans have gathered. We are in the final act. Chants of "Jackie, Jackie," rise from the parking lot. I worry they'll disturb the other patients.

"Go home!" I want to scream at them. "Go home!" But it's too late. They'll never go home; I'm under contract. Fame is a gift that keeps on giving long after your blood runs dry. Ask the Jimmys. Morrison Hendrix and Dean. Ask Princess Di.

Merilee's shoulders jump at the sound of the door opening. It is Emme. She asks my mother if she is okay and if she needs anything. I'm irritated by Emme's interest in my mother. I want to report her, turn her in, tell Emme my side of the story, extol the horrors of Merilee. I want a warm blanket. My feet rubbed. Emme pours Merilee a glass of water from the pitcher next to my bed. "That's mine!" I want to yell. "I'll decide who gets water here." Emme touches her on the shoulder and goes back out the heavy door. I console myself that she's just doing her job. Nurses can't pick and choose who they are nice to. Besides, she has no way of knowing what I feel. If she did, she would take my side, back me up, and throw that paper cup of water in Merilee's face.

No. She wouldn't. Not my Emme.

Emme is a real nurse. It is her calling to tend to wounds. And like it or not, when it comes to being wounded, my mother, with her shaking, sweaty hands kneading her pocketbook and breath coming in little hiccups, gives me a run for my money.

Merilee takes a few short sips of water, makes her way over, and sits on the wicker chair. She rests for a moment, then undoes the top button of her blouse, takes a Kleenex from under the cuff, and dips it in the cup. She wrings out the soggy tissue and presses it to her chest, moving the tissue up around the back of her neck. Gradually, her breathing steadies.

She tosses the clump of Kleenex in a wastebasket across the room, then pops open the clasp on her pocketbook and pulls forth a pint of gin. She glances at the door, hunches down where she can't be seen and swallows long and deeply. She screws the top back on, returns the bottle to her purse, leans back in the chair, and closes her eyes. She is waiting—I know—for the click, the magic moment when the drink hits its mark, making the sharp edges of reality cottony and bearable. Together we wait, but the click doesn't come. She takes out the bottle, finishes it, and returns the empty to her purse.

She weaves her way to the door and puts her hand on the knob. I am hoping she'll leave forever and spare us both this embarrassment, this awkward and hideous farewell. Instead, she turns and places her feet wide as in a fighter's stance. Her hands ball into fists, her mouth opens wide. The sound, when it comes, is horrible, guttural, primal. It trumpets beyond the walls of my room like a mother elephant crying out for her devoured calf. Shadows move outside my door—bodies darken the window.

Merilee kicks off her shoes and squats. She wails and moans and wails, her arms wrapped around herself, rocking back and forth, the pocketbook dangling from her wrist.

Emme comes in. Silently, she lowers the shades and places a glass of water on the floor next to my keening mother. When she leaves, my mother curls up in a ball on the floor, puts her pocketbook under her head, and falls asleep.

INT. HOSPITAL ROOM
NIGHT

My mother is gone. Flo B. sits in the chair next to my bed devouring the latest issue of the *Enquirer*. The cover photo is the one old Flo herself took; blurry and grainy but undeniably me lying there, eyes open mouth slack. *JACKIE'S LAST DAYS*. The Australian's photos must have sold to the International Tabloids. That's where the big bucks lie. *LES DERNIER JOURS DE JACKIE! LOS ULTIMOS DIAS DE JACKIE GOLD!*

Of course, more reputable news outlets are also raking in the cash. Programs from *Nightline* to *Hard Copy* dug up footage of that former star of coma-controversy, Karen Ann Quinlan. Op-Ed pieces in the *Times*, debate the religious and moral ramifications of my plug-pulling. Will I be taken off life support? *Enquiring* minds want to know.

Here's my vote: Pull the plug. Pull the *goddamn plug*! But they are afraid to seal the deal. "God forbid…" they whisper. "What if? What if…?"

What if I am that one in ten million who manages to pull through? No one wants the responsibility of signing off on me.

In the weeks after my mother left us, Daddy came home every night with a present for me. Sometimes it was a doll, a Barbie or Skipper, sometimes a coloring book or a puzzle. One night, he walked into the house carrying a cage with two hamsters. I threw my arms around my father's neck, my heart bursting with joy. Daddy was allergic to cats and dogs, so these were my first ever pets! I stayed awake all night watching them burrow under their bedding and spin the wheel. I named the fat one Ed and the skinny one Johnny, for the Carson show, Daddy's favorite. A week after their arrival, Fat Ed gave birth.

It was a wondrous thing, witnessing the tiny hamster pups, bald and vitreous as they tumbled out, Ed maneuvering around the cage to keep her new babies from being crushed under her body. One after another they emerged while Johnny watched from atop his wheel, a baker's dozen in full until Ed was as empty and skinny as her mate. I huddled with Anna until after midnight when the last baby was born. The next morning, I jumped out of bed and rushed to see them. The babies were dead, every one of them murdered while Ed and Johnny huddled in a corner of the cage.

Anna held me in her lap while I sobbed. "Why?" I wailed long and hard while Daddy covered the cage with a tablecloth and rushed it out of the room.

"Because the babies must have been sick or diseased, and the mother killed them because she loved her babies. She did not want them to suffer."

"That is the stupidest thing I have ever heard," I screamed.

The next day, my father bought me a pink Barbie convertible. Ed and Johnny were banished.

Who will decide to end my suffering? Not my mother; Merilee couldn't find the plug much less pull it. Not Brett. He could put a lame horse down in the movies but killing me would kill him. Daddy? No, Anna?

Definitely Anna. I pray she it does soon.

Flo is snoring now, a cluster of spit bubbles in the corners of her open mouth. If I could reach the call button, someone would come in and catch her red-handed, *Enquirer* on her lap, sleeping on the job.

But maybe the money she made from my photo will help in ways I can't imagine. Maybe she has kids in college. Or a husband with cancer.

Can I forgive Florence? Sure. Too easy. Ask me another.

SLOW DISSOLVE TO:

INT. MALIBU SHORES INN
AFTERNOON
JANUARY 14, 1999

It took only basic sleuthing to find out Brett's plans—one call to the credit card company. Still, when we drove up to the Malibu Shores, I feigned shock and surprise. To our knowledge, the paparazzi hadn't followed us, but just in case, Brett checked in under an assumed name while I took the back stairs up to our third-floor room.

The hotel sat on the same stretch of beach as the Colony. In the years since I'd lived here, much of the sand had eroded. Houses that once had a comfortable apron of beachfront now suffered the battering of surf and rocks against their exposed wooden and cement pilings.

Brett laid our suitcases on the sofa. I pulled several bills out of my purse and handed them to him. "Thanks, Barney."

"Will that be all, ma'am?" he played along.

"Uh, not quite," I teased, pulling him to me. He yanked his T-shirt off, and I began undoing his belt buckle.

The phone by the bed rang. We stopped and stared at it.

"Who is that?" I asked.

"I don't know. Did you tell anybody we were coming here?"

"Of course not. You surprised me, remember?" I wasn't lying, exactly. I had left a message for Nicole outlining our plans, but only because I wanted to make up for having been so shitty.

"Don't pick it up," I cautioned on the fourth ring. If it *was* Nicole, I was going to kill her.

"Hello?" Brett picked up the phone. "Yeah? Yeah? Okay, fine." He hung up and frowned at me.

"What?"

"It seems they're gonna bring the paper in the morning." Brett laughed and wrestled me onto my back.

"I love you, Jackie Gold," he said tenderly.

Winter sunsets in Malibu are normally spectacular displays of reds and orange, but on that day, the sun wouldn't break through the clouds. It hung passively, like a flashlight shining through the back of a sheet.

I lit a cigarette on the balcony and peered over the railing. Three floors below, the sea swirled in and around giant rocks exposed by the stormy pull of the tide, their crevices filled with driftwood and sea treasures, their jagged edges coated with slippery green moss. Under the sea foam, something white caught my eye and as the tide receded, I saw a seagull floating dead, its foot caught in the ring of a plastic six-pack holder. I watched as over and over the waves roared in, the seagull carcass crashing upon the rocks, only to be pulled back under when the ocean water swirled away.

Brett came up behind me wearing a hotel robe that on his muscular frame was several sizes too small. He took the cigarette out of my fingers and put it to his lips, then followed my gaze to where the shackled seagull tossed in the tidewater.

"Jackie?"

"Huh?"

"I have a very important question to ask you."

Oh my God, was it happening now? I wasn't ready. Brett took my chin in his hands. My heart raced.

"You hungry?" he asked.

"Huh?"

"I made reservations for six-thirty. Should I make them later?"

"That's your question?"

"Well yes. Why? What did you think I was going to say?"

"Nothing. Yes. I'm starving. Let's go."

DISSOLVE TO:

INT. HOSPITAL ROOM
MORNING
DAY 54

It Emme wheels in a cart piled with warm towels. Her movements are buffered, noiseless as she switches off the overhead fluorescents left on by Florence, and raises the blinds sending dust particles in the sunlight around her soft frame. She fills the shallow basin and washes the area around my feeding tube tenderly as if it were the stump of an infant's umbilical cord. Lately, she comes at odd hours and spends a long time bathing me, washing my hair, and massaging my limbs; I wonder how she can devote so much of her shift just to my care. Maybe Daddy or Anna made arrangements with the hospital or are paying her directly. Whatever the situation, I am grateful.

It's been twenty-four hours since my mother's visit. Likely she's passed out in her hotel room., or maybe flown back to Hawaii. Regardless, her absence is a mercy.

Emme hums as she begins rubbing her sweet-scented cream into my hands and feet; soft melodies, lullabies. *"The north wind doth blow, and we shall have snow… and what will the robin do then? Poor thing…"* Bobby pins hold back the bangs that normally frame her face. A new sprinkling of freckles suggests an afternoon spent in the sun, perhaps gardening. *"He'll sleep in the barn and keep himself warm and hide his head under his wing poor thing…"*

If I could do my life over, I would pick Emme for my best friend. We would spend our evenings watching *I Love Lucy* reruns and eating Chinese takeout. And I wouldn't be in show business. No, I would be something dear and decent like Emme; a nurse or a kindergarten teacher. Okay, maybe that's pushing it. I don't know what I'd be, but I would have my old nose and boobs. And I would be nicer to waiters and remember their names. And I would have children. And I would raise them someplace in nature with lakes and with seasons so that they could know about snow and spring and cycles; that birth and death and coming and going are not necessarily personal. And my children and I would visit Anna and Daddy on the holidays and send cards and photos to all our relatives. And I would find it in my heart—my new heart, bigger like my old nose—I would find it in my big new plus-size open heart to forgive.

SLOW DISSOLVE TO:

INT. MALIBU SHORES INN
MORNING
JANUARY 15, 1999

I woke with a start. I'd had a dream about my mother and sister.
There was a tidal wave. Mirabelle wore my old leather jacket and
my mother was pulling at the sleeve. I tried to capture details, but
they slipped away. I felt shaky and sad as if something terrible
had happened like maybe they had died. It had been a decade
since I had spoken to them. Now, I'd be getting married. There
was no way to tone down the exclusion, my engagement would
scream from the headlines. For my mother, that was karmic
justice, but for my sister... I felt sorry for her. She couldn't help
being born into the system.

Brett was still sound asleep. I slid out, past the blackout
curtains, and onto the balcony. The sun was blinding, the sky,
clear blue, the sea calm. The rough waters had receded in the low
tide, exposing the rocks below and a wide strip of sand. People
were already out strolling and walking their dogs.

A hotel worker kneeled on the rocks below, sawing away at
the plastic ring now wedged in a cranny and cuffed around the
leg of the dead gull. When it was loosed, he put the mangled bird
in a sack, flung the bag over his shoulder, and climbed down to
the sand and past guests enjoying their free continental breakfast
on the patio.

I walked back inside the dark room where Brett slept, his face
slack and peaceful. He had thrown the covers off during the night
and his body was crunched together in a child's pose, clutching a
pillow with his knees drawn up to his chest. He snorted and
pulled the pillow closer. Brett hardly ever slept past seven. I
considered crawling back in bed, but I was restless and off-kilter.
The dream or nerves, I didn't know.

I was having doubts. Big ones. I was sure Brett loved me, but
could I sustain a future with someone whose happiness and well-

being depended on being more successful than me? This thought had kept me up half the night.

I needed coffee. I needed to clear my mind and focus on the day ahead. *The* day.

And then, even though I was still pissed at her, I needed to talk to the one person who knew me best.

"Hello?" Nicole answered the phone on the first ring. "Hello?"

I'd taken the back stairs down to Brett's car where he'd left our phone. It was difficult to get cell reception in Malibu, but I had managed to find a weak signal by driving to the other side of the parking lot and standing on the hood.

"Nic, it's me." Out of nowhere, I burst into tears.

"Jackie?"

"Yes."

"I can't hear you very well. You're breaking up."

"Sorry. I'm outside."

"What's going on? Did he ask you yet?"

"No," I shouted into the phone. "He's got this brunch planned today."

"Brunch?"

"Yes, in our room, and I'm pretty sure it's going to happen then but—"

"Are you okay? You sound terrible."

"I'm fine, I just… I guess I'm having second thoughts."

"What?"

"I don't know what to do about—"

"Jackie? I can't hear you!"

The line had gone static. I went around to the other side of the car. The traffic on Pacific Coast Highway made it hard to hear. I plugged one ear. "Nicole!" I yelled. "Can you hear me, Nicole?"

DISSOLVE TO:

INT. HOSPITAL ROOM
MORNING
DAY 55

My mother enters carefully as if stepping over invisible obstacles, waving her hands in front of her face like she's clearing spider webs. She goes to the window and paces, her breathing shallow. A moment later, Anna and Daddy enter, hand in hand. They nod to my mother who manages a nod in return. I have not seen these three people in a room together since I was eight years old. It's time. They're letting me go. There isn't another scenario that would bring my parents together.

The voices from the parking lot are getting louder. My mother stares out the window, oblivious to the crowd. My father stares at the floor. Anna's eyes are on me, but I know she is thinking of my father, planning what she will say to soothe him when I am gone.

Emme opens the door and Brett rushes in behind her, mumbling an apology. He goes to my father and shakes his hand, hugs Anna, and starts toward my mother, who holds up a hand either in greeting or to avoid the introduction. For a time, everyone is silent, then slowly, awkwardly, like adolescents at their first dance, they join together at the foot of my bed. Anna reaches for my mother, who reaches for Brett, who completes the circle by taking hold of my father's hand, which is trembling, his other hand in Anna's firm grip: Daddy, Anna, Merilee, Brett.

They bow their heads.

Anna prays in English and Spanish, Brett follows, tossing in "Amens." Daddy murmurs his own prayer, fragments of child-hood Hebrew; a Kaddish prayer half remembered. Behind his fogged lenses, his eyes are squeezed shut. Tears seep from the corners. Merilee sways along, humming to herself.

Emme stands by the door, silent, watchful. Her presence is my only true comfort in this cacophony of grief; this hokey pokey of unresolved feelings; this final family portrait.

Outside, the fan's chants grow, fevered.

Anna throws her head back and her black hair tumbles loose over her shoulders. The pitch of her voice rises as she pleads not for my life but my comfort, for my safety on the journey ahead.

My mother's pocketbook swings from her arm. Her head is bowed low, chin touching her chest. I know how badly she wants to get that pocketbook open and the gin to her gut.

"It's time." Emme taps Anna gently on the shoulder. Anna responds with a nod and winds up her prayer with a whisper and a crossing of her chest. The others follow suit, their words trailing off as they drop hands, wipe tears, and blow noses.

I belong to this family. I belong to them all.

Anna comes first, holds my face, kisses my cheeks. "Goodbye, my darling. Goodbye, my love."

Daddy stumbles over, grasps my hands, and kisses my forehead. "I love you, baby. Oh God, baby. I love you. I love you so much, baby."

Brett strokes my cheek and kisses where my mouth is stretched around the ventilator. "Goodbye, my angel. I'll love you, forever."

Merilee stands to the side. Anna gestures her over and Daddy offers up my other hand. My mother sobs into my fingers and kisses them one by one, as if discovering them for the first time. "I'm sorry baby. I'm sorry. I love you, Jacqueline…Jackie. I love you."

Anna strokes my forehead. "It's okay, Jackie. It's okay to go now."

Time to go.

Let go, let go, let go…

Goodbye, I call to each of them. *I love you. I love you. I love you. I love you.*

I breathe in the sachet in my mother's nightgown drawer, the scent of my father's shoe polish, the gin on my mother's breath, Anna's chocolate breath, Daddy's Listerine breath, and the mildew in our pillows from the damp ocean air.

But now they are in each other's embrace, dancing around the orange and yellow sofa, and I am transported back to the beach, the ocean.

Anna covers me with sunscreen. Daddy builds me a sandcastle.

Mommy sings me a lullaby.

"The north wind doth blow, and we shall have snow, and what will the Robin do then? Poor thing…"

The waves roll in, one after another. Big and powerful, right through our door, up the stairs into my bedroom where I sleep. No one can stop a wave from breaking. Not Brett, not Daddy not Anna, not me.

"Are you ready, Sidney?" Anna whispers to my father. He nods, kisses my forehead, his face soaked with tears. Anna takes his arm and guides him out the door.

Brett kisses the back of my hand. "Sleep, my princess." I breathe in his scent.

I love you I love you I love you.

Brett closes the door softly behind him.

Emme holds my weeping mother and pushes the damp hairs off her forehead.

"I'm sorry," my mother says to Emme.

"Don't be," Emme says to my mother. "That's what I'm here for."

"I'm ashamed," my mother says to Emme.

"You're doing fine," Emme says to my mother.

"You're a good girl," my mother says to Emme.

"Go sit with the others. I'll wait for the respiratory team," Emme says.

My mother starts to say something else but squeezes Emme's shoulder and goes out the door. Emme walks to my bedside and takes my hand in her own.

SLOW DISSOLVE TO:

EXT. MALIBU SHORES INN
11:35 A.M.

Brett and I sat on the balcony eating the last of brunch. Or I should say Brett ate brunch. I was too nervous. I pushed around my eggs Benedict and poured another cup of coffee. I had kept up a steady stream of one-sided conversation all morning while Brett seemed more engrossed in carving out grapefruit sections and reading his script than in anything I was saying. Finally, I shut my mouth and focused on the waves.

My forehead was damp with sweat. I gulped down some ice water and closed my eyes. I was about to be engaged! Why was I feeling this way? Shouldn't I be feeling excitement and happy anticipation instead of terror and tumult? A pain knifed in my stomach. Christ! This was no time for a flare-up. There were Tums in the car with my cigarettes. On the room service cart was a chilled, pre-opened bottle of champagne. I knew I should wait until after the proposal before I drank it, but this was an emergency.

"I'm a little thirsty, do you mind?"

"Huh?" Brett was mouthing his Pablo lines, lecturing an invisible nun. He bowed his head and made the sign of a cross.

I poured myself a glass and drank it straight down, swallowed a bite of croissant to soak up the alcohol, and poured another. I returned the bottle to the ice bucket and suppressed a burp. That was better. I mean, what was the big deal? Okay, I wasn't a hundred percent sure I wanted to spend my life with Brett but was anyone a hundred percent sure about anything? I was *pretty* sure I wanted to marry Brett and I knew for certain that I wanted *him* to want to marry *me*. I was definitely telling Brett about the Reiner film once we were engaged. If he wanted to break it off fine, but I'd be on stronger footing with a ring on my finger. Besides, he was so immersed in this Spanish priest role that maybe he wouldn't care.

The pain in my stomach hit again, stronger this time and longer. I would have to tough it out. I considered polishing off the bottle but that would be rude, perhaps alcoholic, and certainly not beneficial to the dewy-eyed moment I was waiting to experience.

Why couldn't he just hurry up and pop the question, for Chris'sake? Did he have to study his lines and finish every last dried-out piece of grapefruit? I was desperate for the Tums but going to the car meant getting dressed and I would no longer be in the sexy white silk robe I had purposely donned for the proposal. Brett slurped his last shred of grapefruit and started scraping away at the inside of his eggshell. He turned to another page in his script and began making notes.

I could set the mood. Put on music. The TV had one of those built-in radios; I would find something romantic. "Be right back."

"Uh-huh."

I went inside and fiddled around on the dial but found mostly static or news. Why, in an area with more rich people per capita than anyplace else in the world, could they not manage to come up with decent reception? Only the talk radio station came in clearly. *The Dr. Dave Show* was on.

"…way I could find out was by checking his emails."

"Well, how honest have you been with him about your actions and…"

I switched off the radio. In the bathroom, I splashed water on my face, re-brushed my teeth, re-applied my lip gloss, and went back onto the deck, picked up my coffee, and opened the complimentary copy of the *Times*. If I did normal things, I would begin to feel normal. I read the same paragraph over and over as I tried to regulate my heart rate.

Brett stretched his legs.

"Gotta use the little boys' room." He rose, pushed aside the service cart, and disappeared through the curtains. A flock of sea-gulls in symmetric formation swooped past the balcony like dive-bombers. I covered the basket of rolls to protect it. They were awful scavengers. Once a seagull had plucked a hot dog right from my hand.

Ten minutes passed and Brett had not emerged. What could be taking him so long?

Suddenly it occurred to me; I had been mistaken. Brett had no intention of proposing. This had all been my imagination. Wishful thinking. Here I was trying to keep my composure while Brett was sitting on the toilet reading a magazine cover to cover, performing his morning evacuation. What an idiot I had been! The realization that he would not ask me to marry him came as such a relief that I laughed out loud.

"What's so funny?"

I looked up.

Brett stood over me, dressed in a white tuxedo, freshly shaved, and hair slicked back. His blue eyes—bluer than the perfect sky above—were moist and shining. He pulled me to my feet, took out a black velvet box from the pocket of his jacket, and placed it in my hands.

Then he knelt in front of me.

It was happening.

"Oh my God," I said.

I was no match for this moment. All my doubts, fears, all obstacles evaporated. I would have given my life to remain the focus of those eyes.

"Jackie?" his voice was sure and strong. His thick black lashes glistened with unshed tears.

I couldn't have scripted it more perfectly: Brett in a tailored tux, I in a white robe, demure yet revealing and fluttering in the wind, my hair draped just so around my shoulders.

"Y-Yes Brett?" I quavered.

"Will you marry me?"

I opened my perfectly glossed lips to answer, head tilted back just the right amount, breath still fresh from toothpaste, and in that second, in that pause, I heard the helicopter.

DISSOLVE TO:

INT. HOSPITAL ROOM
MORNING
9:14 A.M.

Emme, my best friend and now my hero, sits next to me, and together we wait.

The ventilator is off, the tubing removed. My face has been washed clean of adhesive and my bed linens freshly changed.

The therapist has cautioned that my respiratory reflexes will continue to function for, at most, ten or fifteen minutes before shutting down. For now, I am breathing my own unsteadying rhythm.

How my family has convinced Emme to oversee this ultimate act of mercy is beyond me. Could Daddy have slipped her a couple grand? No, my Emme could not have been bought. Perhaps it was the despair in Brett's eyes, or the timbre of my mother's cry, or the stoop in my father's back. Whatever prompted her, I am grateful.

Emme bends her head down to mine. A strand of hair falls against my cheek, soft and feathery. She smells of goodness and coconut cream rinse. She extracts a small amber bottle from her pocket and puts several drops on my hand. The scent is musky, tropical, like under the cool, shaded canopy of a rainforest.

Let go.

"It's okay now, Jackie, I'm right here with you."

I release my body and tumble over the falls, cleansed by Emme's words and anointed with oil. Life ebbs, the end credits roll, and Emme's sweet voice will be the last thing I know. She rubs her potion up my arms into my shoulders and neck. Wisps of hair brush against my eyes. Butterfly kisses.

"Jackie?" she whispers.

"Jackie." Her voice finds me behind the waterfall.

I swim out to meet her and we float on the surface, making ripples in the water. She swims around me, sure strokes, and picks up my other hand. Together we drift.

"I read a poem once about death by the poet Emily Dickenson: 'Because I could not stop for death, he kindly stopped for me. The carriage held but just ourselves, and immortality.' I remembered it this morning when I was coming here. I wanted to say it to you because I do believe that something is waiting for us when we die."

Her sweet words wash over me; warm, pure, like a tropical rain as we lie on our backs treading water.

"Emme is my nickname, by the way. I gave it to myself in high school. I hated my name. Just like you hated yours. Em. Me. Get it? I used to write it in my notebook. Emme Donner.

Emme. Emme Donner and I drift closer to the waterfall where soon it will gently take me under.

Emme looks at the clock, frowns, and wipes her brow with the back of her arm. "Once, when I was about sixteen, I tried tracking you down."

Emme's words grow fainter, swallowed by the roar of the falls.

"I called your agent but they probably never gave you the message. My dad sent me here to the mainland for nursing school. You met him once. He always talks about it. Makes it seem as if you and he got to be best friends. I bet that happens to you a lot. Anyway, I finished school and worked in a convalescent hospital in the Valley, and then I got hired here.

"And I want you to know, I never went around telling people we were sisters."

Sisters.

"I didn't think you would like it if I did, and besides, the way I look, who would have believed me?"

My sister's eyes, dark green, like wet grass.

"I didn't say it before, I was afraid to disturb your rest. I thought you would wake up and that's when I would tell you. But I can't just say goodbye to you and have you think I'm just some stranger or a fan, or just doing this because it's my job. And if I'd known back in Hawaii that you were going away forever and that

I would never see you again, I would have hidden in your suitcase. But I can't do that now."

Tears spill over the curve of her cheeks down the sides of her neck.

"And one more thing. It wasn't Mom who sold those pictures to the magazines. It was me. I'm sorry, but I had to. Mom had been evicted. She didn't have any money for food. She was desperate. It was all I could think of to do."

Mirabelle.

"Mirabelle, is it time?" my mother cries from behind the door.

Emme continues to cry as she takes my pulse and holds two fingers in front of my nose. She wipes her eyes with the back of her hand and clears her throat.

"Not yet," she calls back. "Soon very soon." She takes my hands in her own.

My sister and I holding hands, walking to a school bus, dancing to the radio, and trying on each other's clothes; pictures in a make-believe album; memories that never happened, so sweet in their imagining. My sister and I holding hands, waiting for my breath to stop. Down the hall my family sitting, standing, pacing in a room with other people's families, praying, weeping, waiting…waiting.

The credits are over, but the film keeps rolling.

Emme and I breathe in rhythm as I flow weightlessly in and out of the room.

This is the spot where X is marked, here where Emme touches my heart.

I beg my heart to pump my blood to the spot where we are connected. To tell her before I leave her this time, with just one tiny throb, that she hasn't been forgotten, that I love her too. That she will always be with me in the great wherever. I launch my missive from my heart, up the veins of my neck, down the passages of my arteries, through the vessels in my arm and into my fingers.

"Oh," she says. "Oh, my God."

She squeezes my hand. I squeeze back.

"Oh!" Again, she turns my hand over and takes my pulse, resting her fingertips on my veins.

We do this together a few more times, and then Emme lets go of my hands.

"Don't move. I mean… I'll be right back."

She runs to the door, flings it open, and dashes out into the hall.

FADE TO BLACK

FADE IN:
HANALEI BAY, HAWAII
JANUARY 15
2006
JACKIE GOLD VOICE OVER:

Today is my thirty-seventh birthday. I was born on the same day Liliuokalani was crowned Queen of the Hawaiian Islands almost two hundred years ago. In my honor, all the towns on the North Shore of the island are coming together, preparing for a giant luau replete with roast pig and hula dancers. Actually, the whole fuss is for Lili, but I like to pretend it's for me.

People on Kauai don't limo to premieres or even watch much television. We drive rusty cars corroded by the salty air. The Hurricane of '94 blew down the only movie theater on this side of the island, so most of the locals here don't know or care who I am. Children sometimes point me out to their parents and giggle, but that's because I walk funny, not because I'm a movie star.

Recovering from a brain injury is a slow process; in some ways like being reborn. I am discovering who I am, and more importantly, who I am not.

Here is what I've learned so far:

1. I don't like large groups of people. I get overwhelmed. I am lousy at small talk even without my speech impediments.

2. I don't like poetry or Shakespeare. It's way too confusing, especially with my brain wires in a kerfuffle. I love action movies. Simple plot lines, lots of excitement.

3. Oddly, I do like exercise, something I always avoided. I can hike if the path is not too steep and I use two walking sticks. Swimming in the ocean is the best! My arms and legs feel normal in water.

4. I don't miss acting.

5. I do miss being a movie star.

Every morning Emme and I walk the three miles up and down Hanalei Bay as part of my rehabilitation. Then, after physical therapy, I work on my blog. Blogging is a perfect creative outlet for me. I am a one-handed typing wizard. I can translate my thoughts far faster by hand than converting them to speech. For now, I blog anonymously under the pseudonym *Goldytalks* writing movie reviews and commentary, but someday I'll write under my name. I want to tell my story. Especially what it's been like to recover from brain trauma.

"Waking up" is a major shock to a body pre-approved for takeoff to the great hereafter. And coming out of a coma takes way longer than what you see in the movies. In the beginning, I was alert only minutes at a time. Even as the physical therapists began to work my legs and arms or changed my positions to sitting or even standing, my mind slept. It's hard to explain but I felt more "conscious" in the coma than in the early stages of being "awake."

When I was able to remain alert for longer periods they moved me into another part of the hospital to begin recovery. Then, after six months when my reflexes were restored and I could sit up without assistance and swallow food and water, I was pronounced "fully conscious."

"Jackie Gold," Dr. Foreman said, while shining his trusty penlight into my truly open eyes, "you have either blown science completely out of the picture or have given it new meaning." He looked pleased though, and not as if I had destroyed the fabric of his whole existence.

I'd heard enough of my prognosis to know that even with significant progress, I would never again be "normal." The brain damage had left me initially without any speech and paralyzed on my right side. For nine months, I relied on animal sounds to communicate: barking, yipping, whimpering, yowling.

I sank into a deep depression; not uncommon for someone with brain trauma. When my dad or Anna or Brett visited, I rallied to the best of my abilities, showing as much joy and enthusiasm the left side of my face could muster. After all, they were celebrating my miraculous return to life. But later, I would lie in bed thinking we'd all have been better off if I'd died.

Then one day in December, on an afternoon when I was feeling particularly sorry for myself, Nurse Dani waltzed into my room dressed in holly and ivy-patterned Christmas scrubs, carrying a poinsettia wrapped in green foil and tied up with the telltale pink ribbon from the gift shop florist.

"I bet you don't know who I am," Dani said in singsong.

I knew her, all right. And while I appreciated that she'd likely saved my life back when my spleen ruptured, I still boiled from the weeks of pent-up frustration of being unable to even lift my middle finger while she schemed to steal my oblivious boyfriend from under my almost-dead body.

Figures that a woman in a coma could see what a fully conscious man could not.

Dani placed the poinsettia on my nightstand. "My name is Da-ni," she said, pointing to her nametag, and enunciating slowly as if I were mentally challenged instead of just brain damaged. "How-are-you-feeling-today?"

With my good arm, I swept my dinner tray off the bed stand. Mashed potatoes and peas splattered her Stride Rites.

"Oh!" She jumped back.

Empowered, I barked several times and threw the remote control. It smacked her on the forehead.

"Ow!" She backed up quickly as I continued to throw whatever was in my reach: books, a juice box…

"Quit it!" She ducked inside my bathroom and slammed the door. I happily pelted it with more objects; hairbrush, pudding, a Perrier bottle.

Hearing the noise, Emme rushed in. "What's going on?" She looked toward the bathroom. The door was spattered with food. Broken glass was everywhere.

"Help!" called Dani.

"Woof, woof-woof," I explained cheerfully.

Emme went to the bathroom and opened the door. "Oh, it's you," she said. "Well, no wonder."

It may have been the medication they prescribed after that episode to control my "outbursts," but after my visit from Dani, I began to feel better.

Brett visited faithfully during recovery. He brought scripts or the trades to read, often falling asleep next to me. After several months when I was able to get around in a wheelchair, Dr. Foreman moved me to a facility where I could begin speech therapy and more intensive physical rehabilitation.

I made slow but steady progress, learning to maneuver in and out of the wheelchair, and to write simple words. I was still unable to speak or read anything but the most basic texts. Ironically though, alliterated headlines like "Reiner's Romp Receives Raves," from *The Hollywood Reporter* made perfect sense to my jumbled brain.

I never acknowledged Brett's big confession. Several times he tested the waters, mentioning Kelly's name, and when I didn't react, I knew he was relieved his secret had gone to the grave even if I hadn't.

On my thirty-first birthday, a year and a week after the accident, Brett arrived with chilled sparkling cider, Spago pizza, and an offer to perform oral sex, a startling new development and I suspect a cognitive exercise suggested by his shrink, Dr. Markowitz. We had attempted intercourse several times, but between my physical constraints and Brett's anxiety about hurting me, we'd thrown in the towel.

I wolfed down the pizza and declined the sex, and though Brett tried to look disappointed, I knew he was relieved. If I'd had the verbal means I would have reassured Brett that eating pussy is neither proof of love nor one's manhood, it's just one of those things you either love to do or hate to do. But I appreciated the offer and how hard Brett was working in therapy.

When we finished our pizza, Brett took my hands in his. "Honey, you'll be ready to come back home soon. I want you to know that you won't have to worry about anything. I've installed a ramp and next week I'm going to have the entire house made handicap accessible."

Then Brett opened a small velvet box. Nestled inside was the platinum ring, purchased over a year ago now, sparkling with five perfect carats. This was the first time I'd really looked at it. It was stunning; exactly the ring I would have chosen.

He slid off the bed and got down on one knee. "You know you never gave me your answer."

Here we were again, only this time I had none of the fear or the doubt I'd been racked with when he had proposed on the balcony of our hotel. I felt calm—serene. I looked into his beautiful blue eyes and saw his concern for me. I saw the pain, the worry, and the despair he had felt this last year. I saw his strength and his courage and his commitment to being there for me in sickness and in health. There were many reasons to say "Yes." Brett accepted and loved me with my disabilities.

"Will you marry me, Jackie Gold?"

But twelve weeks in a coma had rewired my brain, and now Brett's disabilities were no longer acceptable to me. I was done living under my own surveillance, taming and shushing my inner shrew. How much of myself had I buried out of fear of disapproval? I wasn't just speaking sexually either. I couldn't say when I would be ready for another relationship, but I knew that when the time came, I wanted a partner who would not just love my weaknesses but welcome my successes and relish the healthiest and best parts of me.

My speech was still not sufficient for the task. Barking and whining were not suitable for the occasion. I had a dry-erase board that I was learning to rely on for my missives. First, I stroked Brett's face gently, to set a loving tone, and then I wrote that I was sorry to hurt him but that I was breaking off our relationship, only it came out:

"I no breakfast off you. Can no more. Sorry."

"I don't get it." He shrugged, not understanding.

I handed him the ring and shook my head.

"No," I said.

It was my first spoken word.

That was six years ago. Brett is married to a fellow Texan, Becky. I always call her Becky Thatcher because she looks just like the illustrations in Tom Sawyer with her blue eyes, straw-colored hair, and freckles everywhere. She is adorable and funny and perfect for Brett. I met her for the first time when they came to Kauai on their honeymoon. They've since had two kids and bought a sheep ranch near Austin where they plan to raise their family. It's incredible where we all eventually plop down and with whom we find ourselves plopping.

I keep a steady e-mail correspondence with friends and family. Dr. Foreman and I chat once a week and play Scrabble online. I know he plays easy on me. I'm guessing that monitoring my Scrabble abilities is his way of tracking my brain's progress without having to constantly ask medical questions.

Recently Daddy and Anna sold the Mausoleum and moved into a smaller home in the flats of Beverly Hills. Daddy still reports to the studio every day, but I know from Anna that he functions more as a consultant. After my father's bypass surgery last year, Anna insisted they get more exercise. When they visited this summer, we went swimming in the bay every morning; Daddy clutching a kickboard and me belted into my floaty vest. Anna swam right beside us, her long strokes sure and strong in the calm warm sea. When the sun was at its hottest in the afternoons, the three of us strolled to the village for Shave Ice, Daddy and Anna in matching sun visors laughing like teenagers as they slurped from their mango pineapple coconut flavored cones. They are already planning to come back in the spring.

I saw Nicole once more before I moved to Kauai. She stopped by the apartment Emme and I had moved into near the hospital. She went on and on nervously about her career and her many clients. I could tell it was hard for her to hear my fragmented speech and watch me struggle with my canes. I know deep down she feels guilty about her part in my accident. Truthfully, I still haven't forgiven her. Maybe one day, Dr. Dave. I've still got time.

And even though I have officially retired from show business, show business has not retired me. There was a television movie transparently based on my story several years ago, titled *The Rise and Fall of Markie Silver.* Seriously. The actress playing "Markie" was a former swimsuit model with huge boobs and a foot taller than me. That wasn't the worst part. Peter Hamlet played the role based on himself. Only fifty pounds heavier. Unbelievable.

I continue to pop up here and there on *Entertainment Tonight* or *Inside Hollywood.* Especially now around my birthday. I am thankful that during the peak of my career, there weren't these cellphone cameras and all this Internet stuff. I pity the young actors and actresses today whose every misstep is recorded. I thought it was bad enough with the *Enquirer,* but now there's TMZ and this Perez Hilton guy who has revamped the whole game. I've got a whole rant about him in my blog.

Even though I'm retired, part of me will always be drawn to show business. I confess to reading *People* magazine and one can never underestimate how tempting an offer can be to a recovering movie star. Like pouring a drink under the nose of an alcoholic.

Just this morning I got a surprise IM from Penny.

PENPAL: Happy Birthday.
JAKS: Thanks. How did you know?
PENPAL: Entertainment Tonight, CNN, the papers.

JAKS: Oh them. How's the hood?

PENPAL: Dangerous. I'm at CAA now. How's paradise?

JAKS: Great. But my hula skirt gives me a rash.

PENPAL: Seriously?

JAKS: No.

PENPAL: I have an offer for you to do a television show.

JAKS: Are you kidding?

PENPAL: A reality show. They want to film you at home.

JAKS: Yeah…

PENPAL: Jackie?

JAKS: Film here? On Kauai?

PENPAL: Yes.

PENPAL: It's a lot of money.

PENPAL: Eight episodes guaranteed two hundred thousand per.

PENPAL: Jackie?

PENPAL: Are you there?

JAKS: Yes.

PENPAL: I've got lunch at the Ivy.

JAKS: Okay. I'll get back to you.

I took a swig of my Kona coffee and leaned back in the ergonomically correct chair Daddy had sent for my birthday.

A reality show. I've watched a few of them, *Survivor* of course, and that one with the cute couple and eight babies. Oh, and the *Osbournes*. It would be fun to be part of a production again. I wouldn't have to learn lines. And a couple million dollars would buy a lot of taro chips.

If I had my own show, I could share my story. The real true story. Not the tabloid stuff. How having a brain injury isn't the end of the world, in fact just the opposite. I have never been happier. I have learned to keep things simple. I am sober. I have my family, my sister Emme, a community, and Tommy, my love of the last two years, a talented woodworker and carpenter whose

Koa bowls and paddles are displayed throughout the islands and whose ten-year-old son, Jessie, stays with us every other week. We both volunteer at a food bank and twice a week at the nature preserve. Wouldn't that bring people hope? Isn't that an important message to share?

But a reality show would mean opening our home and exposing our private lives. Tommy might consent, but we wouldn't want his son involved. And what of sweet Emme? The network would perceive her quiet nature as boring. They'd want to exaggerate her personality. Make her uber-nice in contrast to my sarcasm and edge. The fat to my skinny. Stable to my wacky. And they would want to film Merilee. That would present all kinds of problems. She might stay dry for a day or two, but eventually, she would be on camera slurring her words or passed out on the couch. It would be hard to find an entertaining or humorous angle for that. She'd just be humiliated. Merilee is no Ozzie Osbourne.

There is also the practical matter of the time it takes me to do simple things; put on a sweater or walk from the living room to the kitchen. I still struggle to form the words I need to express myself coherently. Yes, I have found love and contentment, but can anyone stand still long enough for me to tell them? The network would take one look at the footage and edit my stutters and slow way of speaking into soundbites and quick-cuts that would condense and repackage my wonderful life into a fucking freak show.

Not to mention the paparazzi.

Our neighbors would be hounded by television crews, our peaceful paradise forever invaded…

I got up in a cold sweat, went back to my computer, and emailed Penny.

"Please do not let me know of any more offers. Ever. I am no longer available for work."

But I sent and unsent the message five times before I let it go through.

My mother lives nearby, in a condominium high on the bluff in Princeville, close to where I visited her years ago. Emme and I chose it for its tall ceilings and 360-degree views. On one side, the mountains where Merilee once grew her illegal crops sweep across the windows of the living room. On the other, Hanalei Bay winds down to the Napali Coast and Bali Hai. The rooms are expansive, open, and breezy, with light, plank floors of pinewood the color of dry sand; the furniture is rattan with Hawaiian print cushions and curtains to match.

On the day escrow closed, we told Merilee we were picking her up and taking her to a lunch party at the home of a friend. Lunch was a safe time—Merilee didn't start drinking until the afternoon. She lived in a rented room and rarely went out, only to get groceries or on the occasions when Emme and I persuaded her to come on our walks.

We had invited a small group, a dozen or so co-workers and friends of Emme's, and a few checkers from the Big Five where Merilee had been employed on and off over the years. Everyone had been sworn to secrecy.

The gathering was already in full swing when we arrived. My mother tried to scramble into a corner, but Emme and I pulled her along with us, making sure she spoke a few words to everyone until gradually she started to relax.

"Which one is the hostess?" Merilee asked me. "I want to tell her how beautiful her home is."

I nodded at Emme.

"You're the hostess, Mom," she said.

"Welcome home, Mom," I said, and handed her a set of keys.

She looked confused for a moment and then buried her face in her hands and started to cry. I put my good arm around her shoulders and the guests all gathered around and applauded. Then we sang, "For She's a Jolly Good Fellow."

Last year, Emme and I convinced Merilee to go to Betty Ford. She stayed there for three months. She went to all the twelve-step meetings and therapies but could not bring herself to open up and communicate in ways so unfamiliar to her nature and upbringing. Dried out and miserable, she came home feeling like a failure and wanting to die. She went back to drinking and we never tried to sober her up again.

My mother still drinks, but she drinks sitting comfortably in her rattan swivel chair, looking at views of the waterfalls pouring from the green mountains above Hanalei and the glorious sunsets over the blue Pacific and Bali Hai.

FREEZE FRAME: ROLL CREDITS

THE END

ABOUT THE *Author*

Dinah Manoff is an award-winning actor and director. She has written for both stage and television and had several short stories presented at the prestigious writer's forum *Spoken Interludes* and recorded for KCRW.

She has had numerous roles on stage and in film, among them, *Grease, Ordinary People,* and *Child's Play.* Dinah has starred in the television series, *Soap, Empty Nest,* and *State of Grace.*

She received a Tony award for her role in Neil Simon's play, *I Ought to Be in Pictures,* and won the prestigious L.A. Theater award for her stage adaptation and direction of her father's novel, *A Telegram for Heaven.*

Dinah is the daughter of actress/director Lee Grant and the late writer Arnold Manoff; she resides with her husband and sons in the Seattle area.

The Real True Hollywood Story of Jackie Gold is her first novel.

Acknowledgements

There are so many people who have nudged and coaxed and nurtured this book along. From the beginning: Thank you John Rechy, fabulous writer and teacher, for everything I learned at sitting around your dining table. Gratitude for my darling talented Phyllis Spiva, for your guidance and wisdom and for believing this novel would be published, even when I'd given up hope. To Rhonda Hayter, my beloved friend, brilliant editor, and writer who has helped me through more drafts than I can count. Ditto the incomparable Mary Guterson for her insightful critiques and unwavering support. Thank you always and forever, Valerie Landsburg, for holding my hand through the last round of queries, and for holding my hand through everything.

To my publisher and editor Myra Fiacco, thank you and bless you! For taking a chance on Jackie, for "getting it" for your sharp eye and excellent sentence structure, and for always pushing me farther and deeper. I have loved every single minute of our collaboration. Huge hugs coming your way post-pandemic.

I would also like to thank my fellow writers Lynn Brunelle, Warren Read, Carole Glickfeld, Danielle Durkin, and Olivia Hall for their notes and encouragement.

To the Sunday night women, the Thursday morning women, and the Saturday morning women, thank you for my sanity and serenity and for seeing me through it all.

Thank you to Lee, Joey, Belinda, Zia Phyllis, Eva, Tommy, and the rest of my warm, funny, loving, complicated, crazy, creative, impossible family of origin. For always encouraging my endeavors and for being an inspiration. This book isn't about you so don't worry.

To Honoré Kotler R.N. and Lisa Rose R.N., thank you for sharing your expertise with me. You are warrior women!

Thank you to anyone I've forgotten to thank, I'm sure it will keep me up nights and I will write you a guilt-filled email.

Thank you to my boys Desi, Oliver, Dashiell, and Tyler because being a mom is the only thing better than getting this book published!

And to my darling husband Arthur, thank you for your wisdom, your love and support; your patience; your silly dances when I take myself too seriously, and for always bringing me my morning coffee.

CATCH UP WITH

Dinah Manoff

and other stars at

WelcometoStarAlley.com

STAR ALLEY

CPSIA information can be obtained
at www.ICGtesting.com
Printed in the USA
BVHW081136060721
611236BV00006B/74